CHELSEA WIVES

Anna-Lou Weatherley was born in Hampshire and grew up in London where she still lives with her partner and two children. An award-winning journalist and women's lifestyle writer for over fifteen years, she is the former editor and acting editor of *J-17* and *Smash Hits* respectively and has written for all the major glossies including, *Grazia*, *More*, *Company*, and *Marie Claire* among others.

She is the author of two teen titles, *Ibiza Summer* and *The Wrong Boy* (Piccadilly Press). *Chelsea Wives* is her first adult novel.

ANNA-LOU WEATHERLEY

Chelsea Wives

AVON

This novel is entirely a work of fiction.
The names, characters and incidents portrayed in it are the work of the author's imagination. Any resemblance to actual persons, living or dead, events or localities is entirely coincidental.

AVON
A division of HarperCollins*Publishers*
1 London Bridge Street
London SE1 9GF

www.harpercollins.co.uk

A Paperback Original 2012

First published in Great Britain by
HarperCollins*Publishers* 2012

Anna-Lou Weatherley asserts the moral right to be identified as the author of this work

A catalogue record for this book is available from the British Library

ISBN-13: 978-1-84756-330-9

I have so many people to thank from the bottom of my heart that I'm not sure where to start. So, in no particular order, here goes; my amazing agent, Madeleine Buston and all the team at the wonderful Darley Anderson Agency. Maddie, I can never thank you enough for taking a chance on me and for all your editorial suggestions throughout that have helped make this a better read. I am so proud to be part of the Darley Anderson team and your constant support, faith and advice got me through the tough times. I will never forget the day I received the e-mail from you saying you were interested in *Chelsea Wives*. Alongside giving birth, it really was one of the best moments of my life!

My wonderful editor and fantastic lunch companion, Sammia Rafique and all the lovely Avon team for their amazing enthusiasm and belief in *Chelsea Wives* – and for the immensely helpful notes that helped make the end product so polished. I'm honoured to be part of the team and I can't thank you enough for all your help and support.

To Lee Kynaston for giving me my first real break into journalism and to Marina Gask, Steve Beale, Jane Bruton and Marianne Jones at *Grazia* magazine. Averyl Oates for some insightful fashion knowledge and to the women of Chelsea who let me in on some insider secrets – you know who you are!

Thanks to Claire Wright and all the amazing girls (and boys) at Polesecrets (PS Group) for helping me to keep a healthy body and mind! Pole really is good for the soul and I've made some amazing friends through it.

My lovely Mum; thanks for the good genes and for all your help, support and advice, and for the brilliant conversations we always have about life, love and the universe – you are an inspiration to me. And of course to my dearest pops; again for his support and always being there for me – you are a true friend. I'm lucky to have such loving, supportive parents. I know if you weren't who you were, then I wouldn't be who I am either! Thanks to my sisters, Lisa and Hannah, and to my not so little brother, Marc. You always put a smile on my boat-race, kiddo!

As well as an amazing family, I have been blessed with the most wonderful friends. Susie Ember, my dearest rabbit, for all the advice, support, and above all, the laughs. I don't know what I would do without you. Ditto the wonderful Laura Millar (LM!), who has been a huge support, a true friend and always an inspiration. To my dearest Michelle Langan, fellow writer and Aquarian, for all of your words of support and positivity when I've needed it most – your turn now, love. Also to Andie, Maya, Nyree and Karen Thorn. And to Sarah, whose domestic help I cannot live without! Thanks also to the Dawbers, Pat, Jade, Lee, Lisa and the gang.

I would like to say a huge heartfelt thank you to my two best boys, Louie and Felix, who probably think everyone's mummy is joined at the hip to their laptop. You are my pride and joy and I love you both more than anything. And lastly, but by no means least, to Alan. It's been a rollercoaster of a ride, but I know I could never have done this without you. Thank you for all the help, support and personal sacrifices you have made to enable me to realise my dreams, even when you had your own to chase. Words will never be enough to express how grateful I am. And so, darling, this is for you.

For Alan

PROLOGUE

Detective Inspector Mitch McLaren glanced around the magnificent library, casually perusing the literature that was neatly stacked inside the antique wooden bookcases. The fact that he had been kept waiting seemed to irk him more than usual, so much so that he had helped himself to a cheeky nip of cognac from a decanter on the sideboard. Something told him he was going to need it.

You could tell a lot about a person by the books they owned, he thought, as he threw back the cognac in one hit. Somehow he hadn't had Sebastian Forbes down as a Jane Austen man. Must be his wife's, he thought, smiling as he came across Milan Kundera's *The Unbearable Lightness of Being*. Exhaling softly as he pulled it from the shelf, it immediately evoked a strong memory of her; her long, dark hair, shyly falling over her face like a silk curtain as she pretended not to notice him looking at her . . .

'Detective Inspector McLaren?' Sebastian Forbes's clipped tones sliced through Mitch's thoughts with all the subtlety of an axe as he stormed into the library, his face a crimson colour, veins protruding in his neck in what looked like protest.

'Pleased to meet you, Mr Forbes,' Mitch said, his hand outstretched in greeting.

Sebastian did not take it.

'The Commissioner said you're the best he's got,' Sebastian said, matter of fact, casting the Inspector a rather disdainful glance. 'Well, I hope for your sake he's right because I want this case solved pronto, do you understand me, Inspector? I said *pronto*.' Sebastian poured himself an extra large champagne cognac and threw it back without offering Mitch one.

'It's a fucking disaster, that's what this is,' he growled, pulling his lips over his teeth as the alcohol hit the back of his throat. 'That diamond is worth more than the national debt, and somehow those bastards knew exactly how to get inside my bank and get their thieving hands on it.' Sebastian was incandescent, his hands shaking with rage. 'I want them *found*, Inspector. I want you to find the scum that did this and I want you to throw the bloody book at them, do you hear me?'

Mitch watched Forbes carefully. It was immediately obvious that the man was a tyrant. It was written right through him like a stick of Blackpool rock. He hadn't even asked about the unfortunate security guard, currently fighting for his life in hospital.

'Mr Forbes, I need to ask you a few questions if that's OK.' Mitch cleared his throat. 'Questions you might find impertinent, but are necessary nonetheless.'

Sebastian didn't care much for the DI's abruptness but given the circumstances had little choice but to comply.

'You say you were the only one who knew the codes to the security system, that is right isn't it?'

'Yes,' Sebastian snapped back, the irritation in his voice tangible. 'I changed the codes myself, a few hours before leaving to catch the plane. Look,' he said tightly, 'that system is infallible, Inspector; it's one of a kind, pioneering technology from America which *I* helped create.' He thumped his chest, indignant. 'Only *I* knew the codes to gain access to the vault and only *I* have access to the room where the diamond was kept. The Interlocking System has an in-built scanner that relies on facial recognition. *My* face, Inspector, is the key that unlocks it.'

'Is there somewhere I can play this?' Mitch asked, producing a CD from his inside pocket. 'I think it might be of some interest to you,' he said as Sebastian nodded towards the flat-screen on the wall. 'It's CCTV footage taken from last night. I want you to look carefully at it, Mr Forbes,' Mitch instructed him. 'Tell me if you recognise any of the men.'

Sebastian downed another cognac, squinting at the images as they came into view.

'Good . . . good God . . .' he said after a moment, taking a step back in alarm, pointing at the screen in shock and confusion. 'That man . . . it's . . . it's me! But . . . it isn't *me* . . . that's impossible. I told you, I was on a plane to Rio last night. I was on a goddamn plane!' Sebastian's voice was high-pitched in protest. 'Surely you're not stupid enough to think this really *is* me? A hundred or more people can vouch for me!'

Mitch nodded. 'We will have to check all your alibis, of course,' he said with an even smile.

'Jesus fucking Christ!' Sebastian slammed his glass down onto the antique desk with such force that it was testament to the quality of the crystal that it didn't break.

'I'm going to need to speak to your wife, Mr Forbes,' Mitch said after a moment's pause. 'Ask her a few questions, if that's OK.'

Sebastian looked up.

'My wife?'

'It's merely a formality,' he reassured him.

Sebastian sighed heavily, his temper dissolving into self-pity.

'As you wish. Though I can't imagine she'll be of much help.' He picked up the internal line. 'Jalena, ask Mrs Forbes to come down to the library immediately will you? What? I don't care if she's still sleeping, goddamn it, this is important!' he bellowed, slamming the telephone down.

Muttering under his breath, Sebastian reached for the cognac decanter once more, this time having the decency to pour the Inspector one.

Accepting it, Mitch turned away from him and wandered towards the bay window, looking out onto the pristine terrace at the pruned topiary and expensive Lloyd Loom furniture.

He was still looking out of the window, cognac in hand, as he heard the door to the library open. It was only as he slowly turned round that he felt the glass suddenly slip from his fingers and his heart stop dead.

CHAPTER 1

Imogen Forbes looked at her Cartier watch: 3:03 p.m. Shit, she was late. No doubt the photographer would be cursing her blue by now. Pressing her foot on the accelerator of her brand-new Bentley Continental, she revved the engine impatiently, absentmindedly checking her reflection in the interior mirror. Tired eyes hidden underneath lashings of Touche Éclat blinked back at her as she wearily inspected a new rash of fine lines that had seemingly appeared overnight. She turned the air con up to maximum and sighed deeply. It was a warm Friday afternoon in June and the King's Road was thick with rush hour traffic. Summer stretched out before her, full of promise and potential, giving her a fleeting feeling of hope and excitement.

Leaning over, she began rifling through the glossy store bags that were piled high in a heap on the passenger seat, souvenirs of that morning's trip to Harvey Nichols, via a little breeze along Sloane Street: Seb's dry cleaning from Jeeves of Belgravia, Lime, Basil and Mandarin candles from Jo Malone, a gorgeous silk dress from Stella McCartney – perfect for between seasons – and a divine pair of knotted platform pumps from Christian Louboutin. She wondered whether the shoes might be a little overstated with the rest of her outfit for today's photo shoot or if the stylist already had something in mind for her.

Momentarily forgetting any sense of urgency as tissue paper rustled satisfactorily between her fingers, Imogen looked past the traffic and out onto the bustling high street. People were out in their droves, dropping cash in the spring sales faster than they could earn it. Designer bags swung on the crooks of lithe, suntanned arms and the clips of Bugaboo prams. Tourists stood on street corners, maps in hand, pointing at the sugared almond-colour mews houses that were tucked away from the throbbing masses. Glamorous yummy mummies dressed in Diane von Fürstenberg wrap dresses and young, fashion-forward teenagers sat crossed-legged outside the myriad cafés, sipping their skinny soya macchiatos, people-watching from behind their oversized designer shades, hoping they might be noticed.

The King's Road still had that buzz, that style and vibrancy that had made it famous in the 60s, Imogen thought. Regardless of how commercial it had now become, it was by far her favourite London high street.

Her phone rang, dragging her from her thoughts.

'Where the bloody hell are you?' Calvary snapped, irritation thick in her voice. 'Sophie Montgomery-Smith has already let me down so now there's just going to be the three of us and the photographer is having a hissy fit. You're holding everything up.'

'I'm sorry, Cal,' she apologised. 'The traffic . . .'

Calvary sighed impatiently. 'You're beginning to look like a terrible diva, Ims. Put your foot down, will you? Anyway,' she said, her voice dropping to a whisper, 'I'm dying to see what you'll make of the journalist. Can't make my mind up about her . . .'

Having been the fashion editor of the once highly successful, but now defunct, pretentious fashion tome that was *Dernier Cri* magazine, Calvary Rothschild knew all about hidden agendas of the press and the need to make a name for oneself.

'Seems a little big for her shooboots. Mui Mui by the way. This season,' she added.

'And the stylist?' Imogen inquired hopefully. 'I suppose everything decent has been snatched up already.'

'Well, if you *will* be so bloody late . . .' she shot back, defensively. 'But I've saved you a purple Alberta Ferretti shift and a Lanvin necklace,' she added begrudgingly.

'Oh Cal, thanks.' Imogen was touched by her friend's rare display of fashion altruism.

'I'll be there as quick as I can.'

Imogen threw her phone into her open Zagliani python bag in the well of the passenger seat. It was bad form to be late, especially since Calvary had been good enough to ask her to take part in the shoot in the first place.

'Chelsea Wives,' she had squealed with excitement down the phone to Imogen just a few days earlier, eschewing her usual cool composure. '*ESL* magazine want to do an insightful lifestyle piece on women who live in Chelsea. Fabulous women, darling, like us! Say you'll do it.'

Imogen hadn't needed asking twice. Even after all these years she still missed the buzz of being in front of the lens. Her phone rang again and she snatched it up.

'What now?' She rolled her eyes.

'Now that's no way to talk to an old friend, is it?' The gravelly female voice sounded familiar but she couldn't immediately place it.

'Who is this?' Imogen asked tentatively.

'Oh darling, it hasn't been *that* long . . . surely you remember?' the voice said, full of mock offence. There was a pause. 'The bench at Hersham station? You were wearing the most ghastly stone wash denim jacket I'd ever seen in my life and you had a home perm, but even then I could see you had something special.'

Imogen gasped.

'*Cressida*? Good God, Cressie Lucas. Is that you?'

'The very same, darls. The very same,' she said, snorting with laughter.

Cressida Lucas, MD and scout for *Models à la Mode* and one-time queen of the London party scene, was a small, fierce redhead with killer dress sense and an unrivalled sixth sense when it came to spotting the Next Big Thing in modelling.

The day Imogen had been 'spotted' by the infamous fashionista would be imprinted on her mind forever. It had been the final week of what had been an uneventful summer holiday and a then sixteen-year-old Imogen had been on her way to visit a friend. She had been quite oblivious to the short, voluptuous woman, glamorously dressed in a bright canary yellow power suit, blowing cigarette smoke into the air above her. Suddenly she was next to her, her neon manicured hand outstretched in greeting.

'The name's Lucas. Cressida Lucas, and I run a modelling agency in London called *Models à la Mode*. Have you heard of it?' She did not give Imogen time to answer. 'I see you like fashion?' she nodded approvingly at the well-thumbed copy of *Just Seventeen* Imogen had been reading.

'Yeah, I s'pose,' Imogen had replied a little shyly, catching the intoxicating scent of the stranger's perfume, which she would later come to recognise as Calvin Klein's 'Obsession'. Even to this day she could not smell it without thinking of her.

'I would absolutely love to see what the camera would make of you,' Cressida had said, tucking Imogen's hair behind her ear and inspecting her as if she were a rare piece of art. 'Tell me, what are you doing now?'

*

As Cressida's unfailing eye had predicted, Imogen was sensational in front of the camera and within a year her name became the new buzzword on every UK fashion editor's lips. Elbows sharpened as designers scrambled to book the doe-eyed, quirky-cool brunette for their latest campaigns. A breath of fresh air from the highly polished glamazonians who had dominated the early 80s, her waif-like, unconventional beauty meant she would be a perfect figurehead for the rising grunge movement. Cressida could smell change in the air. Yuppie culture and Thatcherism was dying. Ever ahead of the zeitgeist, she had sensed it was time for something new.

By the time Imogen had reached her eighteenth birthday she had become the youngest UK *Vogue* cover girl and had walked for most of the major designers of the day, including Lacroix, Armani, Katherine Hamnett, Pam Hogg and Vivienne Westwood. She had flown first class to shoots in Rio, Paris, New York, the Bahamas . . . partied on millionaire's yachts with fellow supermodels, A-list celebrities, even royalty. Imogen 'Immie' Lennard was the new face of British fashion and on the verge of global success. Cressida Lucas had hit the jackpot and Imogen was happier than she'd ever been; she was young, beautiful and successful. But above all, she was in love . . .

'It's been ages, Cress,' Imogen said, suddenly feeling a flash of guilt that she had not kept in touch with a woman to whom she had once owed so much. 'How have you been?'

'Gorgeous, sweets. Bloody marvellous. Had a facelift last year. Taken ten bloody years off me, I swear. Wish I'd done it five years ago. Bagged myself a little toy boy too, darling. Twenty-six. Hung like a horse. Not a bad cook either. But enough about me. How the fuck are *you*?'

Imogen smiled. By the sounds of things, her old friend hadn't changed a bit.

'Well, I . . . '

'No, don't tell me now,' Cressida interrupted. 'I want to hear *everything* over lunch. Daphne's. Monday. 1:00 p.m. It's all booked,' she said in her matter-of-fact manner which Imogen had always found equally endearing and annoying. 'Try and make it, poppet. It's terribly important I see you.'

Imogen felt a flutter of concern and intrigue.

'Has something happened?' she asked.

'It could be about to,' Cressida replied cryptically. '1:00 p.m. Don't be late, darling. I have a meeting with Kate Moss at 2:30 sharp and don't want to keep the old love waiting.'

Call waiting angrily flashed up on Imogen's phone. It was Calvary. Shit.

'Sorry, hang on, Cress. I just need to take this . . .' She switched calls. 'Cal, I am five minutes away . . . promise, promise . . . OK, bye.' She pressed call retrieve. 'Sorry about that, Cress. Where were we . . . Cressida . . . Cress?' But she had gone. Shit. Imogen checked 'calls received' but the number came up as 'unknown'. Shit. Shit. Shit. She threw her iPhone down into her bag in annoyance. What could possibly warrant a call from Cressida Lucas after all this time?

CHAPTER 2

'Ah, so you've finally decided to grace us with your presence then I see,' Calvary Rothschild remarked sarcastically as she ushered Imogen through the vast front door of her stucco-fronted Chelsea town house.

'I'm so sorry,' Imogen apologised, the tip of her nose lightly brushing her friend's cheek as she went in for an air kiss. 'Traffic was horrendous and then, well, you're never going to guess . . .'

'Later, darling,' Calvary said dismissively as she made off down the hallway. Imogen trotted after her apologetically, the clack-clack sound of her new Louboutin Roger Vivier pumps amplified by the antique polished wooden floors.

Calvary had certainly accrued some rather impressive new pieces since her last visit, Imogen thought, glancing up at an imposing 12-light, rococo style chandelier that hung like a vast jewel from the ornate ceiling rose.

'Antique French cut-glass crystal, darling,' Calvary smiled without turning round. 'Cost an absolute bloody fortune from Sotheby's. And before you ask, yes, it was a present from Douglas,' she added dryly.

'Someone must've been a *very* bad boy this time,' Imogen remarked.

'Ha!' Calvary snorted derisively. 'You don't want to know.'

Calvary couldn't bear to discuss her husband's latest infidelity; it was just too sordid even by Douglas's standards. Returning home from a perfectly lovely lunch at Langan's, she had heard strange noises coming from her bedroom and had gone to investigate, worried that Beluga or Cashmere had somehow managed to creep undetected into her walk-in closet and were busy chewing through her priceless Manolo Blahnik collection. Throwing open the bedroom door with purpose, the scene before her had caused her to stumble back through the doorway as if she had been winded by a heavy object.

Over the years Calvary Rothschild had become adept at coping with the humiliation of her husband's indiscretions. She had taught herself how to forget if not to forgive. Learning how to brush it all under the expensive Persian carpet, it was all par for the course as far as her marriage was concerned. This time however, she was not to be the only casualty in Douglas's latest mess. Others would be hurt too. Others she loved. This time, she could not forget.

'Cal?' Imogen lightly touched her friend's arm in concern. This small act of kindness was enough to undo Calvary and she turned away from her, fighting back tears.

'Don't tell me he's got another little floosie on the side again?'

Calvary drew audible breath.

'Like I said, darling, you don't want to know.' She ran her hands lightly over her red Issa dress as if such filthy memories had left a residue, and, composing herself, opened the door to the drawing room.

'About bloody time,' the photographer remarked, making a point of looking at his Rolex. He was setting up his equipment in a corner of Calvary's impressive regency themed dining room. 'This is perfect,' he gushed to no one in particular. 'We'll shoot them on the chaise longue underneath the Monet. With the reflection in the glass coffee table, it'll be like they're actually, you know, *inside* the painting.'

'Everyone, this is my very good friend, Imogen Forbes,' Calvary announced.

'Great to meet you,' Imogen said, shaking the slim, manicured hand of a stunning platinum blonde whose breasts were spilling out of her tiny dress. Calvary flashed Imogen a secret smile. Finally Imogen could put a face to the person who had been such a source of gossip over the past weeks.

'Nice to meet you too,' Lady Belmont-Jones said with a firm shake.

'Help yourself to champagne and canapés, ladies, won't you,' Calvary smiled, topping up the half-full Tiffany flutes in front of her.

'They look delicious,' Imogen remarked, popping a quail's egg crostini between her lips.

'Don't they? Beluga and Cashmere became positively demented by the cooking smells earlier.'

'Beluga and Cashmere?' Yasmin queried. 'Your children?'

Calvary threw her head back and let out a roar of laughter.

'Of a sort! They're dogs, darling, my dogs. Two black Labradors. Love them to bits. One of the housekeepers has taken them out from under our feet for the afternoon. They have a tendency to get overexcited when guests are present.'

Like their owner, Yasmin thought sardonically.

'Come on then, dig in to the canapés. I don't want to be the only one pounding the treadmill come Monday morning and we certainly don't want that journalist getting her grubby hands on them, do we? We all know how the press love a freebie.' The three women simultaneously glanced over in the direction of Sammie, the young, attractive journalist who was busy in conversation with the photographer. Sensing three pairs of eyes on her, she momentarily looked up only to flash a small smile and look away again. Knowing that her usual H&M attire would probably not cut it among such well-dressed, affluent women, Sammie had borrowed an outfit from the accommodating stylist for today's shoot, ensuring she looked the part. It was her first big piece for *ESL* magazine and she was keen to make a good impression. If she got this right and produced a great feature, it might just be enough to get her name noticed among the bigwigs at the magazine; something she was desperate for.

'Bloody parasites, the lot of them,' Calvary whispered under her breath.

'Steady on,' Yasmin said. 'She's a fashion writer for *ESL* magazine not a snout for the *Daily Mail*.'

'Don't be fooled, darling,' Calvary scoffed. 'They're all the same; sell their firstborn for a front-page scoop.'

'Didn't *you* used to work for a fashion magazine yourself at one time?' Yasmin enquired with a sideways glance.

Calvary was beginning to wonder if she had not made a mistake in inviting Lady Belmont on today's photo shoot. She sensed those rumours of a less than salubrious upbringing weren't quite as unfounded as they sounded and could tell the girl was desperate to hog the limelight today, preening and flirting as she was in front of the camera. Still, she had been more than intrigued after having met her at a prominent charity event some months ago.

Dubbed by the style press as the epitome of 'Chav Sloane', Yasmin Jones was a little too tanned and platinum, her jewellery too gaudy and her skirts too short for her to have originated from true aristo stock; in fact, she was sailing dangerously close to footballer's wife territory. However, her main London residence, a vast, stucco-fronted, five-storey town house on Cheyne Walk and the title of Lady alone more than qualified her place in *ESL*'s feature. Besides, with a property portfolio the world over, which included impressive piles in Mustique, Monaco, The Hamptons and Portofino, Calvary figured a few choice lunches and the occasional dinner party *chez* Rothschild would practically guarantee her visitation rights. It was shameless social climbing and she knew it but there had been something else about the new Lady Belmont, a certain vulnerability underneath all the brassiness which had instantly elicited Calvary's nurturing instincts.

'Yes, the fashion editor's an old friend of mine,' Calvary replied, tartly. 'Which is why I couldn't say no when he asked. Anyway, do excuse me, ladies,' she said. 'We need more champagne.' She flounced off leaving a waft of Coco Chanel and an awkward silence behind her.

Yasmin eventually broke it.

'I'm getting used to all this magazine lark,' she sighed, glancing at Imogen, 'what with the *Hello!* shoot and everything.' It was a crass attempt at bringing the subject round to her recent and vastly extravagant nuptials, which had commanded no less than eight pages in the weekly glossy.

'Yes, I think I saw that,' Imogen smiled, sipping her champagne. 'A castle in Capri, wasn't it?'

'That's right,' Yasmin said, not realising quite how smug she sounded.

The union of one Lord Jeremy Belmont and Miss Yasmin Jones had been dubbed the wedding of the season among the society press. It hadn't been difficult to see why: thanks to his shady playboy past, royal connections (which he never failed to exploit at any given opportunity), two highly publicised failed marriages and a penchant for courting conjecture, the Eton-educated lord was a society journo's wet dream. And Yasmin was the ultimate trophy wife.

'Anyway, I'm thrilled Calvary invited me along today,' Yasmin said, changing tack and smiling forcibly at Imogen. Much as she hated socialising with all these stuck-up, rich bitches, it was a necessary evil if she was to be Lady Belmont-Jones. Ha! The absurdity of it made her want to laugh out loud. Her! With a title! Yasmin straightened her thoughts. She mustn't let her guard slip. Not now that she was so close to achieving her ultimate goal.

'It's such a beautiful house,' Yasmin gushed, her eyes wandering around the room. 'Pierre Yves Rochon, of course,' she added, with a knowing smile. 'I brought him in to do a complete redesign when I moved in with my husband.' Imogen smiled and raised an eyebrow. 'Had to really, the place looked like something out of *Grey Gardens*,' Yasmin cackled.

'Will you excuse me?' she said suddenly. She was growing a little bored of the conversation and wanted to scrape a final line from the reserve wrap of coke she had stashed in the secret compartment of her Fendi bag for a quick livener. 'I need the little girl's room.' As she turned to leave she knew what Imogen was thinking: the same as everyone else in the room was thinking. That she was nothing but a gold-digger, a disingenuous nobody who had married that old soak Belmont for his money and title.

And they were half right.

Calvary returned from the kitchen and sidled up to Imogen.

'So, what do you think?'

'About what?' Imogen's mind had been elsewhere since her earlier unexpected call from Cressida. Just hearing the woman's voice after all this time had stirred up so many memories for her. Memories of him . . .

'About my new friend, Lady Belmont-Jones, silly. Rumour has it she is doing her damnedest to make a dent in Jeremy's inheritance fund,' Calvary remarked from the side of her mouth, placing a tray of canapés down onto the vast oak sideboard and taking one for herself.

'Some might say it serves him right,' Imogen retorted,

her thoughts returning to the present.

'I'd heard she'd ripped up all the original antique flooring in the house and replaced it with Versace carpet. Can you imagine! Versace!' Calvary looked appalled.

'I'm not sure what to make of her,' Imogen shrugged.

'Do you think she knows about the scandal? Moreover, do you think she cares?' Calvary raised an eyebrow.

'Who knows?' Imogen sighed. 'Though it's hardly a secret. Anyway, perhaps it's genuine and they really *do* love each other,' she remarked, flashing her friend a playful smile.

'Hmm,' Calvary mused. 'So, Miss Jones, what first attracted you to the *multi-millionaire* property tycoon *Lord* Belmont, then?' They both giggled into their champagne flutes conspiratorially.

'Have you seen him lately?' Calvary shuddered. 'Overweight with a comb-over that makes Donald Trump look positively hirsute. You've got to hand it to her: she must have the stomach of an ox getting into bed with *that* every night.'

Imogen pulled a face. 'You're putting me off the canapés.'

'Well, darling, if you ask me,' Calvary stooped to whisper, 'there's more to Lady Belmont than meets the eye . . .'

'Ready when you are!' The make-up artist popped her head around the door and gave Imogen a friendly smile.

'Much more,' Calvary surmised, watching as Yasmin's D&G clad behind swished provocatively from the room.

CHAPTER 3

Standing in front of the well-lit mirror in the ladies' room at Daphne's, Cressida Lucas saw the reflection of a woman for whom youth was now a distant memory. Though her recent appointment with the surgeon's knife had undeniably worked miracles it was safe to say that, physically speaking, her best days were behind her.

How beauty is wasted on the young, she thought, eyeing the two attractive twenty-somethings who were fixing their lip gloss in the mirror and spritzing themselves with Coco Mademoiselle. Before they know it, they'll wake up to fifty with their tits round their waists wondering what the hell had happened to their lives, she thought bitterly.

Cressida slunk into a cubicle, pulled out a snuff box filled with cocaine from her quilted Chanel handbag and heaped some of the fine white powder onto the tiny silver spoon that was inside. Once she was convinced she was alone, she took a deep sniff, waiting a few seconds to allow the familiar warm rush to hit her bloodstream.

Despite her full and varied life, not having had enough sex in her twenties was one of the things Cressida regretted most. Back then, when she'd been beautiful and smooth-skinned with no cellulite and thread veins to think of, she'd been too bloody preoccupied with proving herself in a man's world to waste time on sex – far too distracting. Besides, she didn't need to suck some executive's dick to claw her way to the top. Now however, Cressida was beginning to wonder just how much more fun it would have been if she had.

Leaning back against the cubicle wall, she let out a small sigh and, impervious to the blatant 'NO SMOKING' sign, lit a pink Sobranie cocktail cigarette and inhaled deeply. Hers had been a life of such extremes; incredible highs and soul-destroying lows. She had achieved more in her fifty years on the planet than ten women her age had put together. But lately, Cressida had caught herself wondering what life might've been like if she'd never possessed such single-minded ambition and drive; what it would've been like to have a family, to be a wife and mother. And these were not the only thoughts keeping her awake at night. With her divorce settlement funds dwindling, the equity on her various properties ploughed into her ailing business, not to mention a wildly extravagant lifestyle to support, Cressida found herself in dire financial straits and once again needed a miracle (or a rich man) to get her out of it.

Spooning a little more powder up her left nostril, she knew she would have to play this one very carefully indeed if she was to get the result she needed. It would require delicacy and tact; there could be no room for error. With her momentary lapse of confidence masked by the cocaine rush, she exited the cubicle, smoothed down her Chanel pencil skirt, and took a deep breath. It was show time.

*

'Darling . . .' Cressida stood up from the table with her arms outstretched. She hugged Imogen tightly, air-kissing both cheeks. 'Let me look at you,' she gushed, grasping both her hands and standing back to survey her. 'You're just as beautiful as I remember.'

Imogen gave her old friend a warm smile. 'You look wonderful too, Cress,' she said, getting a waft of Cressida's signature scent as she released herself from her grip. She had certainly not lost any of her inimitable presence, even if she had maintained a distinct 80s whiff about her.

'So, what have you been doing in the last fifteen or so years?' Imogen said with a friendly dose of irony as she pulled the shabby chic rattan chair from the table and slipped into it.

'Love the Zagliani, darls,' Cressida gasped, eyeing the oversized purple python bag Imogen was carrying with approval.

'Thanks,' Imogen smiled, giving it a little squeeze. 'It's been treated with Botox, can you believe it?'

'Who hasn't, darling?' Cressida threw her head back and let out her familiar throaty laugh.

She took a sip of her San Pellegrino, watching Imogen from over the rim of her glass. She had hardly changed in fifteen years, she thought. Her complexion remained untarnished by age, her hair still thick and lustrous, though much longer than the short, androgynous elfin crop that had made all the fashion editors quiver back in the day. Her lips were still full and fleshy, her smile dazzling and infectious. Of course, she had aged a little in that indefinable way people do, but at thirty-six years old she had maintained an air of youth about her that most women would sell a kidney for.

A waiter approached the table.

'Give us five, Marcello, there's a poppet,' Cressida cooed, watching his tight arse as it wiggled off to the next table. She turned her attentions back to Imogen.

'So, darling, I want to know everything. Work, life,

love . . . the whole shebang.' She was disappointed to note that the plain platinum wedding band was still very much on Imogen's finger. 'How's Sebastian?' she asked tightly.

Sebastian Forbes the man who had killed her protégée's career stone dead with his controlling demands and ultimatums, forcing Imogen to choose between motherhood and marriage and modelling, cutting short her meteoric rise to stardom and taking her biggest cash cow with him.

If only Imogen and Sebastian had never met, thought Cressida bitterly. She could have been the most successful, fabulous model that had ever lived; forget your Twiggys and your Shrimptons, your Campbells and your Mosses, Imogen Lennard (as she was then) could've cleaned up, and moreover, so could she.

'Seb's . . . well, Seb's still Seb,' Imogen shrugged almost apologetically. Cressida had never made her dislike for her husband a secret. 'Bryony is thirteen now,' she said, deliberately changing the subject. 'She's so grown up, Cress, you wouldn't recognise her.'

Bryony Forbes attended the highly respected Mont-Fleuri Swiss boarding school in Montreux and it had been eight weeks, though it felt like eight months, since Imogen had last seen her daughter, something that caused a lump as hard as granite to form in her throat whenever she thought of it. She hated being apart from her beautiful, sweetly shy Bryony who was so much like she had been at that age; gangly and awkward, yet to grow into her own skin, but Seb had insisted she must receive the best education money could buy, even if that education happened to be hundreds of miles away from her family.

'If she's inherited your looks darling, I'll get her signed on the spot,' Cressida said in all seriousness.

'As if Seb would ever allow it! Anyway, she's far too busy trying to save the planet and the plight of the African elephant at the moment.'

'Ah, beauty with a conscience, a devastating combination,' Cressida smiled. 'Listen, darling,' she began, feeling the sudden need to get to the point, 'the reason I've asked you here . . . well, it was for business reasons as well as pleasure.'

Imogen clutched her chest, mock wounded.

'And there I was thinking you just missed me after all this time.'

Cressida smiled. She was glad to see that being married to such a controlling dullard all these years hadn't completely robbed Imogen of her sense of humour.

'It's L'Orelie,' she said, suddenly leaning in closer. 'They're looking for someone to become the face of their fab new make-up range for the forty-plus market. It's top secret though, poppet – you know what a competitive business the beauty industry is. It's an absolutely fucking *huge* contract. We're talking national and international campaigns, billboards, TV ads, the whole goddamn enchilada.'

Imogen placed her starchy white napkin over her lap and tried not to look as excited as she suddenly felt.

'I'm not entirely sure how your name was thrown into the ring,' Cressida tore up a bread roll and continued, 'but out of the blue I get a call from Lorraine Harlech, the CEO, asking if I still had contact with you and if you'd be interested in testing for the campaign. Apparently she was flicking through an old copy of *Vogue*, saw you and wondered what had happened to such a beautiful rising star after all these years. She asked me to track you down and sound you out. That's about the size of it, really,' Cressida concluded. 'Oh, that and you stand to make yourself a very rich woman in your own right, if you agree that is,' she added poignantly. 'So, darling,' she drew breath and looked at Imogen expectantly, 'tell Mummy what you're thinking.'

Stunned, Imogen took a swig of water, wishing she had ordered something stronger.

'Well, I, me . . . modelling again. I don't know, Cress. I'm thirty-six now and . . .'

'Thirties are the new twenties!' Cressida interjected, sensing her reticence. 'Everyone wants the thirty-somethings nowadays. It's the market with the most cash to spend.'

Imogen shook her head.

'I'm not even sure I've got what it takes anymore.' She felt her heart pounding loudly inside her chest and hoped that Cressida could not hear it.

'Nonsense,' Cressida snapped dismissively. 'Darling, listen to me. You were the best back in the day, a born natural in front of the camera. You *owned* it. I know as well as you do that you weren't ready to leave the modelling world when you did and this is your chance at another shot. Oh, come on, Ims, offers like this hardly come by every day as well you know. What do you say?' She cocked her head to one side and held her breath.

Imogen looked up from the table.

'Oh, I don't know, Cress,' she eventually said. 'I'm different now. I'm not that girl you found at the train station. My life's changed. *I've* changed.'

Cressida felt the first flutters of panic settle on her intestines. She knew that if she could just get Imogen to test she would win the job hands down, just like she always used to, and then all her problems would be solved. She *had* to get her to agree.

'If this is about Seb . . .'

'No, no,' Imogen shook her head. 'It's not Seb.'

But it *was* Seb, partly at least. Imogen knew he would unequivocally hate the idea, that he would forbid her to do it and she was not sure she had the strength for another war between them.

'Then what is it?' Cressida asked, the softness in her voice masking desperation. 'This is a golden opportunity, darling, the sort the likes of Cindy Crawford would cut her mole off for.'

'I can't even begin to tell you how flattered I am to be asked but I just don't think I can do it. I'm not a model anymore. Those days are gone, Cress. I'm sorry.'

Cressida placed her glass down carefully. It was not something she had wanted to do but backed into a corner like this, she was left with little choice. It was time to revert to Plan B.

'It's OK, darling, I understand.' Cressida slid her hand across the table and placed it on Imogen's. 'I'm disappointed, naturally. After all, you were my first big star. I had hoped you might be my last and that I might go out on a high note.'

'Go out on a high note? Don't tell me you're planning to retire?'

Cressida lowered her eyes dramatically.

'Something like that.'

Now it was Imogen's turn to feel a flutter of panic.

'Listen, darling,' Cressida said, fixing her with an earnest stare. 'What I'm about to say, well, I don't want any fuss or tears, promise me now.' Imogen's mouth suddenly felt dry.

'You're scaring me,' Imogen said, taking a sip of her San Pellegrino.

Cressida met her eyes with a doleful expression.

'Well, it's my doctor,' she began, her voice a crackling whisper. 'Gorgeous thing he is, young Asian chap with lovely teeth,' she said, twisting her napkin nervously. 'He says I've got the big C . . .'

Imogen felt her heart miss a beat.

'The big C?'

'Yes, darling, you know, *cancer*. Apparently, I'm riddled with the damn stuff. I'm afraid there's nothing they can do.'

Imogen gasped. They may have been estranged for some years, but this made the news no less shocking.

'Please don't cry, darling, you'll set me off,' Cressida said, reaching her hand across the table and welling up herself. It was easy to cry. All she need do was think about the imminent repossession of her Mayfair pied-à-terre.

'Oh God, cancer.' Imogen fought back tears. 'How long have you known?'

'About two months,' Cressida said gently. 'Since then I've been trying to live life to the full, darling. You know the usual clichés, travel a bit, see a few sights, achieve some goals before it's a wrap and I head to the giant Prada store in the sky.' Cressida let out a bitter laugh.

'Don't joke,' Imogen said, shaking her head. She couldn't bear it.

Cressida sighed deeply.

'The fact is, my name's down on heaven's guest list and I'm going in. That's all there is to it.'

Cressida watched as a lone grey tear ran the length of her former protégée's beautiful face and thought how she would burn on a pyre for this one.

'How long?' Imogen asked, her voice cracking like glass.

'They can't say exactly,' Cressida replied, dabbing at Imogen's tears with her napkin in motherly concern. 'A few months maybe . . . who knows?'

Imogen almost knocked her bread plate from the table.

'Oh no, Cressie, no!' She began to sob into the white linen napkin. 'But treatment . . . there must be something . . . *anything* they can do!'

'Come on now, darling, it's OK, it's OK,' Cressida soothed. 'Look, I'm so sorry to have sprung it on you like this, but when the call from L'Orelie came I thought, well, this is it, one last chance for us to work our magic together.' She paused for effect. 'But I appreciate your life has moved on. They say it's never a good idea to go backwards anyway, darling. Who needs a reminder of their past when they have a future? If they're lucky enough to have a future, that is.' Cressida added, wondering if she was beginning to lay it on a little too thick.

She glanced at Imogen who looked to be in thought from across the table.

'I'll do it,' she said after a moment's pause. 'I'll test for the L'Orelie campaign. You've been like a second mother to me in the past and, well, it's the least I can do.'

Cressida felt her batteries recharging.

'I prefer sister,' Cressida bristled good-humouredly. 'But what about Seb?' she enquired, careful to mask her sense of relief.

Imogen shrugged. 'Screw Seb. Seb can deal with it. I owe you, Cress.'

'Really, darling, you'll do it for me?' Caught up in the drama of it all, Cressida found herself welling up for real. She squeezed Imogen's hand tightly and let out a little squeal. 'It'll be just like the old days again, darling,' she said, eyes shining victoriously. 'You really don't know how much this means to me. Let's order a bottle of fizz to celebrate.' Cressida waved her hand in the air. 'Marcello darling, a bottle of vintage Krug please . . . nice and chilled. We're celebrating.'

'Very good, Ms Lucas,' he nodded obligingly.

'I'm sorry, Cress,' Imogen explained, 'I can't stay for champagne. I've got to be somewhere this afternoon and I'm driving.' It felt somehow wrong to celebrate after what she'd just been told.

Cressida pouted.

'Ah well, not to worry, poppet. The test shoot takes place next week in LA. Can you get away?'

Imogen nodded. 'Leave it with me.'

'I'll call you with all the itinerary, flights, hotels etcetera . . .'

Imogen stood to leave.

'I hope you don't mind if I head off. The sooner I get back, the sooner I can square it all with Seb. I promise I'll celebrate with you properly in LA. We'll stay at the Chateaux Marmont, get trashed on cocktails, like we used to . . .' her voice trailed off, sadly.

Cressida nodded, understanding.

'You've saved my life by agreeing to this shoot. That's more than enough for me.' She looked up at Imogen's dark, soulful eyes and her full lips, which were fixed in a pensive half smile and felt a hideous flash of guilt at deceiving her.

'If only it were that easy,' Imogen said, leaning in and wrapping her arms tightly around her old friend. 'I'm here for you,' she choked, inhaling her familiar scent deeply. 'Till the end.'

'I'll call you,' Cressida said as she watched Imogen leave the restaurant, her silky chestnut hair glimmering in the sunlight. She still had the fabulous strut, she thought as she watched her walk towards the door.

CHAPTER 4

Yasmin Belmont-Jones stretched a long, toned leg high up into the air, sighed and signalled for a crew member to come and refill her empty champagne flute.

A young, attractive deckhand duly made his way over and tried not to stare at her bronzed, firm breasts, which were proudly on display. She adjusted the ties of her Missoni bikini and tightened her matching headscarf, aware of his chaste attempts not to stare, deliberately teasing him. *Go on, I dare you,* she thought as she twisted her body slightly towards him affording him a better view, *get a load of these babies.* She watched him intently as he poured the champagne into a fresh, ice-cold crystal flute and did his best to refrain from making eye contact. He could tell this one had trouble written all over her.

Yasmin peered over her giant dark Dior sunglasses and surveyed the surrounding view with a deep sense of satisfaction. *The Magus* really was the most stunning boat she could have ever imagined; four polished-wood decks of luxurious, elegant living all on one state of the art 170 foot-long motor yacht. The impressive vessel boasted its own seaplane, a crew of seventeen, a heated top deck Jacuzzi, a freshwater swimming pool, twelve beautifully appointed guest suites and an exotic master suite apartment filled with antiques, embroidered silk fabrics and plush overstuffed furniture. Though he owned a rather impressive (albeit more modest) boat himself, *The Magus* did not belong to Lord Jeremy Belmont, rather he had won a week's possession from his billionaire Greek shipping magnate friend, Demiris, in an exceptionally well-executed game of poker, and Yasmin Jones was determined to enjoy *everything* the boat had to offer.

'Is there anything else, my lady?' the blonde, blue-eyed deckhand asked.

'Yes,' she said, taking a long sip of the cool, dry liquid. 'As a matter of fact, there is.'

He looked at her for the first time, careful to keep his eyes firmly on her neck.

'I need you to rub some oil into my back. My husband's taking a nap, you see, and I don't want to burn.'

He hesitated.

'Is there a problem?' she asked, peering at him from over the top of her shades, enjoying his sense of unease.

He swallowed dryly. There was nothing he would like more than to get his hands all over her naked flesh; after all she was a total fox and clearly gagging for it. But what about the husband? He could come lumbering up the stairs at any minute and catch them. It would almost certainly cost him his job, a job he enjoyed almost as much as he needed. He sensed, however, that the 'Lady' stretched out in front of him was not about to take no for an answer.

'No problem, Lady Belmont,' he said, thinking how they were all the same, these gold-diggers who married rich men. In time, they all grew bored of spending their husband's money and instead searched for their thrills elsewhere.

She looked up at him, her glossy lips glimmering and he imagined them around his cock.

'Forget it,' she said dismissively, her tone suddenly

switching from flirtatious to cold in an instant. 'That's all, thank you.' He hesitated for a moment, confused by her sudden turnaround. Cock-teasing bitch, he thought as he walked away, his hard-on rapidly diminishing. If he ever did get the chance to fuck her he'd make sure the pleasure would be all his.

Yasmin took another generous sip of champagne and exhaled. She stared out towards the cobalt blue Aegean Sea stretched out in front of her, mesmerised by the sunlight dancing on the ocean's surface.

It seemed incredible to think that less than eighteen months ago Yasmin Belmont-Jones had been plain old Stacey Jones, a nobody struggling to pay the rent on her poky one bedroom flat in Croydon, South London. What's more, when she thought about it, getting there had been far easier than she could ever have imagined.

Though Yasmin's rise from rags to riches appeared meteoric on the surface, every detail had to be meticulously researched to ensure success. Such patience and dedication had ultimately paid off though because so far, Stacey Jones had fooled everyone.

A small, slow smile crept across her lips as she sucked deeply on her thin Vogue cigarette. A waiter appeared.

'Lunch will be served shortly, Lady Belmont,' he said. 'Lord Belmont has requested that you join him on the lower deck in half an hour.'

Yasmin smiled, acknowledging his message without making eye contact.

She knew what the crew were thinking the moment she had set a French pedicured foot on board *The Magus*; there could only be one reason why a young, attractive woman like her could possibly be with a man like Belmont. It suited Yasmin for them to think she was little more than a gold-digging opportunist. That she could handle.

Yasmin padded barefoot across the polished deck to the

edge of the boat and looked out onto the crystal blue water. The sea was as still as a pond and its tranquillity instilled a momentary calmness within her. But it was short-lived and soon replaced by a more familiar feeling of self-doubt. Since the wedding, the press had begun to show an inordinate amount of interest in her personal life. They wouldn't have to dig too deep to uncover her true provenance.

'Give me strength, Chloe,' she said in soft prayer. 'I'm doing this for you. Stay with me . . . stay with me.'

'Ah, there you are, my darling.' Lord Belmont lumbered up the last few steps to the top deck, panting and wheezing like an old boiler on its last knockings.

Yasmin spun round, startled, her thoughts interrupted.

'Darling,' she said. 'I thought you were sleeping.'

'Mmm,' he nuzzled his face into the back of her neck. 'I managed an hour or so. But then I missed you.' He pressed his bulk against her, willing her to feel his semi-erection. He had woken with the most impressive hard-on he'd had in years and was desperate to make good use of it.

Jeremy let his plump fingers wander up towards his wife's new breasts. She did not resist. From experience, she knew it was best to let him get on with it. Besides, it would all be over in a matter of minutes.

He untied the sides of her Missoni bikini and let them slip to the floor, wasting no time as he thrust himself into her, his hands gripping and squeezing at her breasts. Yasmin continued to stare out onto the horizon. Her face expressionless, her mind detached from her body as he pumped away at her from behind.

'Yes, that's it,' he wheezed into Yasmin's ear, panting heavily. 'That's what you want, isn't it, you little minx. Let daddy show you . . .' His voice began to crack, signalling that he was on the edge of orgasm. Jesus, it could've only been 60 seconds or so, a record even for him.

Yasmin knew what to do to finish the job.

'Ah yes, yes, oooh, daddy, yes . . . show me, daddy, show me what a filthy little bitch I am . . .' She smiled wryly, her eyes glazed and focused on the horizon as he groaned and coughed into climax.

'Jesus!' Yasmin screamed, suddenly pulling away from her husband. She ran to the edge of the boat, still naked save for a pair of ridiculously high Louboutin sandals.

'What is it, darling?' Belmont said, concerned, his pathetic erection withering to nothing almost instantly.

'I saw flashes,' Yasmin said, pointing towards the rocks. 'Camera flashes over there.'

'Jesus bloody Christ,' Belmont said, alarmed. 'The press, they must have followed us here.'

'Oh Jeremy.' Yasmin bit her lip, her voice thick with panic. 'What if they've seen us?'

'Put some clothes on,' Belmont barked. 'I'm going to get the binoculars and a bloody great shotgun!' As he disappeared below deck, Yasmin reached for her phone inside her Gucci raffia beach tote.

'Did you get them?' she hissed.

'Yes. I got them,' the gruff voice replied. 'And might I say you are one fit looking lady.'

'Save it,' Yasmin remarked. 'Now stay where you are. He's gone to get a gun. But don't worry,' she smiled cruelly, 'I won't let him kill you. Just do and say what we agreed and you'll get your reward, OK?'

'Whatever you say, my *lady*,' the man said sarcastically.

Yasmin smiled triumphantly to herself as she threw her phone back into her bag. She did so love it when a plan came together.

CHAPTER 5

Imogen swung the steering wheel of her Bentley Continental CTG sharply to the right, the tyres making a satisfactory sound as they met with gravel, and pulled into the underground garage of her impressive 7-bedroom house on Chelsea Square. Switching the engine off, she took out the folded A4 piece of fax paper from her Fendi tote and read it over again.

'L'ORELIE PHOTOSHOOT – LA CALL SHEET'

Her eyes scanned the photographer's details in bold type: Mylo: 001 213 5570581.

He was obviously way too cool and important to need a surname she thought, allowing herself to feel the first flutters of excitement.

Imogen had put off talking to Seb about the shoot for long enough, telling herself she needed to get her own head around the whole business before braving the inevitable showdown with her husband. She was due to fly to LA next week.

She checked her Cartier watch. It was coming up for 5:00 p.m. She would catch Seb just before the Lamberts arrived. That way the conversation would have to be kept short, tactically avoiding a full-blown argument. The thought did nothing to help disperse the knot of dread in the pit of her stomach though.

'Let the fun commence!' she said under her breath as she opened the car door.

*

Sebastian Forbes, Imogen's husband of some thirteen years, was sitting at the island breakfast bar of the couple's bespoke Clive Christian kitchen sipping espresso from a small white cup, his head buried in a copy of *The Financial Times*. Her car keys made a startlingly loud clatter as she dropped them into the Lalique glass bowl positioned on top of the highly polished granite work surface. He did not look up.

She noticed Seb was dressed in his Lacoste tennis whites instead of his usual suited work attire. He'd obviously been on the courts, unusual for him this time of the day, she thought.

'Afternoon, Seb,' she said breezily.

'Imogen,' he acknowledged her with disinterest, continuing to read.

She slung her Fendi tote onto the breakfast bar and kicked off her Tod's driving shoes, padding across the marble floor towards the stainless steel American fridge.

Her heart was knocking against her ribs as she opened the double doors, wondering briefly if a gin and tonic might help steady her nerves, deciding it probably wouldn't and opening a bottle of chilled Evian instead.

'Good day?' she asked.

'Yes,' he answered evenly, continuing to speed read. 'I thrashed Damien on the courts. Had him darting all over the place. Thought the old bastard was going to have a heart attack at one point.'

'The Lamberts are here already?' She was surprised.

Sebastian finally looked up at her.

'Oh, for Chrissakes Imogen, don't tell me you'd forgotten they were coming for the weekend?' he said crossly.

The weekend? She knew about dinner but *the weekend*?

'Of course I hadn't forgotten,' she lied. Her husband was obviously in a caustic mood and she felt her earlier confidence diminish.

'I've had Jalena prepare the master guest suite – everything's in order. Look, I told you all this last week,' he snapped irritably.

Imogen frantically tried to recall. She felt sure he hadn't mentioned that the Lamberts were coming to stay.

'I . . . well, I've had a lot on my mind . . .'

Sebastian drained his cup and snorted derisively.

'Well, yes,' he sneered. 'It must be *terribly* taxing deciding what to wear for lunch every day.'

Imogen felt her hackles rise. He had no idea.

'This weekend is important to me, *Imogen*,' he snapped. 'I don't want it messed up, OK?'

She hated it when he made a point of using her name, like a father chiding a child. And why was he so bothered about the Lamberts all of a sudden? He usually did his level best to put off their annual visit, let alone have them stay for the whole weekend. She was suspicious.

'Are they here now, the Lamberts?' she enquired. She knew she would lose her nerve if she had to wait out the entire weekend before telling him about the shoot. *It was now or never.*

'They'll be back here at 7:00 p.m. They've gone to see a musical in the West End,' he said, pulling a face. Sebastian detested musicals. 'The chef's coming at 6:00 p.m. to prepare.'

'Chef?' Imogen recoiled in shock. For the Lamberts? He usually reserved such extravagant gestures for VIPs only – a category of which the Lamberts most certainly did not fall into, at least not as far as he was concerned.

'Yes, darling, you know, they cook food and shout a lot – a chef. I told you.' He looked at his wife crossly and wondered what the hell went on in that beautiful, empty head of hers.

Now he came to think of it though, perhaps he had forgotten to mention that part to her. The chef idea had been somewhat of an inspired afterthought, the *pièce de résistance* in his grand plan to seduce the Lamberts. Sebastian knew it would impress his epicurean friend – it had bloody well better, it was costing him a small fortune.

She watched as he began to fold his paper up into a neat square.

'I'm taking a shower then I need to make a few calls.' He made to stand, signalling the end of the conversation. 'I'll be in my office. I've told Jalena and the rest of the staff to prepare the orangery for dinner and give the chef free run of the kitchen.' He turned to leave.

'Aren't you going to ask me how my week has been?' Imogen said quickly in a clumsy attempt to stall him.

Sebastian rolled his eyes facetiously. 'Oh darling, do forgive me. Did someone have a handbag party to end all handbag parties?'

Imogen smirked. She would enjoy this.

'Guess who I saw for lunch the other day?' she chirped casually.

'Do tell?' he sighed impatiently.

'Cressida Lucas,' she said slowly.'You remember her, don't you?'

The room fell silent and she heard the buzzing of electricity as it pulsed through the giant impressive silver William V chandelier above them. She felt a brief rush of satisfaction as she caught a flicker of panic on his face.

Sebastian swallowed dryly. He remembered Cressida Lucas alright. That odious, gauche little woman who had tried her damnedest to come between them all those years ago, filling Imogen's head with crazy ideas of modelling and fame and all that nonsense; she had damn near succeeded too.

Sebastian looked at his wife with barely concealed bitterness. She was just so beautiful, too beautiful really. From the moment he had seen her sublime face in a glossy fashion magazine, he had decided that she had to be his. And what Sebastian Forbes wanted, he invariably got. Whatever the cost.

It had not been an easy seduction; Imogen had been grieving for a previous relationship with some no-mark and he had whisked her off to Necker Island – his friend Richard's luxury Caribbean retreat – at the first opportunity in a bid to help her forget her heartbreak and fall in love with him. His plan had worked, partly at least. Three months later they were married and Imogen was carrying their child.

Though he steadfastly refused to admit it, deep down, Sebastian knew that Imogen did not truly love him. Not in the way he had wanted her to. Not in the same way she had loved that nobody she'd been dating before. But love or not, Sebastian Forbes had won the big prize in the end. He always did.

'What could *she* possibly want after all these years?' he asked cautiously. He had hoped never to hear that wretched woman's name ever again.

Imogen took a deep breath and another gulp of Evian.

'She's got cancer,' she said gravely. It felt unreal to say it out loud.

A small smirk crept across his face and he made no pains to hide it.

'So there is a God after all,' he murmured.

Imogen glowered at her husband in disbelief, her eyes filling with hatred.

'Jesus, Seb! How can you say that? The woman's *dying*, for fuck's sake!'

He raised an eyebrow, amused. Imogen rarely swore.

'She's asked me to test for a new cosmetics campaign, for L'Orelie,' she continued, her voice stoic. 'I'm flying out to LA next week. And before you say anything, it's not up for discussion. She's my oldest friend and I'm granting her dying wish. You won't stop me.' She visibly stood back letting the words hang heavy in the air above them.

Sebastian stared at his wife's defiant face and thought how appealing she looked when she was angry and upset, her dark hair a little dishevelled, her eyes glassy with tears.

She was so uptight; perhaps now that she'd had this little outburst, got it out of her system, she might loosen up a bit, maybe even offer him a place back in her bed again. It wasn't too much to ask, was it? After all, he had given her everything she could ever want over the years. Thanks to him she had escaped her distinctly aspiring middle-class roots and the transient, empty life of a model. Those super-models, they might look great on the covers of all those magazines but you took away all that airbrushing and you saw what they had become after years in the business; ravaged old whores, the lot of them.

Sebastian thought for a moment. He had to play his hand carefully. The last thing he needed tonight was a frosty atmosphere, not when there was so much riding on it. He'd play ball. For now, at least.

'Good for you, darling,' he said, careful not to inject any sarcasm in his voice. 'It all sounds terribly . . . exciting. And Imogen,' he added, earnestly, 'really, I *am* sorry to hear about Cressida. We may not always have seen eye to eye over the years but I wouldn't wish that upon her, upon anyone.'

Imogen was floored. This was not the reaction she had anticipated and it had taken her clean off guard.'Oh . . . well, then,' she stammered, 'so you're OK with it?'

'Listen, darling,' Sebastian's tone was uncharacteristically sweet. 'If it makes you happy to grant the woman's dying wish then so be it. After all, what are friends for?'

She eyed him cautiously.

'Right. Well. Thank you,' she said, the sharp edge of her voice softening a touch. 'I appreciate it, Seb. It means a lot to me.'

'I can see that,' he said, moving closer towards her, lightly touching her arm and stooping in for a kiss. His dry lips met with hers and she did her best to respond.

'I'll dress for dinner,' she said, gently pulling away from him.

'Right you are,' he said, feeling her discomfort and resisting the urge to pull her roughly back towards him. 'Oh, and Imogen,' he added as he watched her pick up her tote and walk from the room. 'Wear something fabulous tonight, yes? Sexy but not slutty, OK?'

She forced a smile. Since when had she ever done slutty?

Once he was sure she had left the room, Sebastian picked up the call sheet his wife had left on the granite work surface, briefly scanned it, then folded it up neatly into a square and placed it inside the pocket of his tennis shorts. Catching his reflection in the shiny worktop, Sebastian gave a small sneer exposing his perfect set of Hollywood veneers. If that ungrateful bitch of a wife of his thought she was starting with all that modelling lark again then she was sorely mistaken.

CHAPTER 6

'Good God, man, you've done us proud,' Damien Lambert said, eyeing the table of gastronomical delights in front of him greedily. 'It's a bloody feast!'

'This is just for starters, Lambers, my old friend, just for starters,' Sebastian slapped Damien's back good-naturedly and gestured for him and his wife, Celeste, to sit.

'You really should not have gone to all this trouble,' Celeste said, turning to Imogen who was smiling warmly at her guests. 'A light supper would have been plenty.' She surveyed the regency table which was brimming with a variety of steaming *fruits de mer* including a spectacular array of fresh lobsters, piled high into a giant crustacean pyramid, aromatic butter seductively sliding down their glossy pink shells.

Imogen stole a glance at Sebastian from across the table and inwardly sighed. Seb had always thought that giving her everything would make her happy, make her love him. He bought people; it was what he did, the only way he knew how to operate. But the adage was true: money couldn't buy love, and everything she owned, the houses, the cars, the jewellery, she would've swapped it all in a heartbeat for what she really wanted. For what she'd once had with *him*. She thought of him then. Truth was, since Cressida's initial phone call she had thought of little else. How his hair fell in front of his eyes when he spoke and the way he flicked it away with his hand . . . that day in the library, the day they had first met, the feeling of something taking place between them, some invisible connection, like a magnet drawing them together . . . she could almost smell the musty scent of the old books as they glanced furtively at each other, the intensity between them almost tangible.

Momentarily lost in reverie, Imogen took a large swig of vintage 1995 Dom Perignon and stared at her husband as if he were a stranger. Though she felt they would both be happier apart, she knew Seb would rather see her dead than divorce him. Perhaps she would let him into her bed tonight, show him that she was grateful to him for not making a fuss about the shoot at least. Perhaps it would not be so bad . . .

'That was something else, Forbsie.' Damien Lambert patted his large protruding stomach satisfactorily. 'I'll not eat again for a month.'

Sebastian smiled, eyeing his friend with expertly concealed disdain.

Damien loosened his bow tie as if it might somehow help with his gastric discomfort.

'Take it off, man,' Seb implored. He knew that Damien wore his Eton tie as some kind of ridiculous sentimental gesture and he detested him for it.

Lambert had always been a follower, a cling-on who had looked up to him at school with a perpetual wide expectant grin on his chubby face. But for the first time in his life, Damien Lambert had something Sebastian Forbes needed. Or at least the means to help him get it.

'The shares are up, I see. Caught it in *The FT*, yes . . . bloody marvellous stuff, Lambers, you must be like a dog with two dicks.' Sebastian raised his eyes and took a large sip of scotch.

'Aye, the good ol' North Sea; she's given about all she can but it's not done too bad all told. And when she stops giving, I'm moving into the energy business. I'm talking really bloody big. Got the Arabs on board and everything.' Damien slapped himself across the chest triumphantly. 'Not bad for a Trustafarian eh, Forbsie?'

Imogen strained to listen from across the table as she chatted superficially with Celeste Lambert. Sebastian was being suspiciously and uncharacteristically amenable and this aroused her suspicion.

'Yes, I did hear something that you're mixing with royalty. Arabian royalty no less.'

Sebastian smiled, the expression on his face like one of a snake about to strike. 'That Prince Saud al-Khahoutam, isn't it?'

'Aye,' Damien belched a little, tasting scotch and *soubaise* with a hint of vanilla. 'A real likeable chap he is too – for an Ab-dab. Met him at an oil convention in Dubai. His father owns the Montpelier Hotel group. Got enough money to buy up heaven with change left over. He's coming over to the UK in a couple of weeks' time. We've invited him up to the castle. Celeste's getting sheets shipped in from Egypt, fretting about it already!' Damien roared again displaying port-stained teeth and a thick yellow coating on his tongue. 'He's made up to be staying in a real Scottish castle, mind, cannot wait. Good job really. You'd need a bloody castle to put up his entourage. He travels with his own private army, you know.'

Imogen watched her husband carefully as he lifted his leg over his knee in a forced nonchalant gesture.

'Why so much security? Is he under threat of assassination or something?'

It was a question he already knew the answer to.

Damien leaned in towards his friend conspiratorially, the buttons on his shirt straining open, exposing a little white flesh and wiry hair.

'I shouldn't be telling you this,' Damien hissed.

'Another?' Sebastian said, filling his friend's half full tumbler with more scotch.

Lambert took a generous slug and curled his lips over his teeth.

'He's bringing in a diamond.'

Sebastian feigned shock.

'A diamond?' His eyes were glowing now, as if lit by the very jewels themselves. Imogen watched Seb carefully.

'Yes. The Bluebird. It's a rare brilliant blue. Completely and utterly flawless, all 798.67 carats of it. It's insured for over £500 million,' Damien explained, 'though that's supposed to be a fraction of what it's really worth. He's scouting for suitable places to house it while he goes off on a round the world cruise or something. It's far too much of a security risk to take it with him.'

Sebastian settled back in his chair and raised an eyebrow.

'£500 million? That's some stone, old boy.'

'Indeed it is. He's got the hots for this British actress totty, wants to impress her with it while he's here.'

Sebastian nodded in understanding.

'That'll need some looking after,' he said, his eyes widening.

'The rock or the woman?' Damien let out yet another booming roar and Sebastian surreptitiously rolled his eyes. The man was insufferable.

'You say he'll be here in a couple of weeks? That's around the same time as the ball, isn't it? I trust you and the lovely Mrs Lambert will be attending as a matter of tradition?'

'Wild horses wouldn't keep us away.' Damien clapped his old friend's arm. 'I say wild horses . . .'

Forbes's Annual Summer Ball was a lavish,

no-expense-spared affair that had been running for decades. A date firmly imprinted on high society's social calendar, it boasted a roll call that read like something from *The Times Rich List*.

'Now you mention it, yes, it will be around the same time. '

A light suddenly switched on inside Damien Lambert's alcohol-addled brain.

'Why don't I bring him along to the ball!' he bellowed, a little scotch sloshing over the edge of his tumbler with the momentum. 'We'll show those Ab-dabs how it's really done, eh? He'll bloody love it, rubbing shoulders with all the aristos. Maybe you can invite that actress sort he's gone giddy over . . . Charlotte somebody. You'll be doing me a favour, Forbsie.'

Damien Lambert patted his nose with his forefinger and winked. 'Might even help with a wee bit o' business.'

Imogen saw the look of satisfaction on her husband's face.

'Super idea, Lambers,' he said, already picturing himself inside the Arab's private jet, sipping champagne in the Jacuzzi and chewing the fat with his new Middle Eastern friend. 'Bring the man along. I'll get my PA to sort out an invitation right away.'

'Thanks Forbsie, you're a pal.'

'Not at all, Lambers,' Seb said, clinking his glass. 'After all, what are friends for?'

CHAPTER 7

Marshall Jackson, or Mylo to his friends, let his head flop back onto his shoulders and wondered if he was just not the luckiest dude alive right now. With his arms outstretched either side of him, resting against the pool edge, he closed his eyes and allowed the unforgiving Nevada sun to warm his face while the rest of him kept cool in the Olympic-sized rooftop swimming pool.

'You having fun, ladies?' he asked from underneath his mirrored Ray-Bans. ''Cause I'm having the time of my frickin' life.'

'Sure, Mylo,' Lindsay giggled, whipping off her small triangle bikini top and letting it float away. 'But I need more champagne.'

'Yeah, and Cheetos,' piped up Britney. 'We want champagne and Cheetos.'

Britney was already topless and Mylo surveyed her tits as they gently bobbed up and down in the water. Not bad for a chick with a couple of Rugrats, he reasoned.

'Hey, honey,' Mylo called out to a blonde pool hop who on closer inspection turned out to be Paris. She was wearing nothing but a small French Maid's apron and a pair of killer thigh-high black patent leather boots; the rounded curves of her breasts peeping out from the barely-there straps of her pinafore.

'A magnum of Krug, please.'

'And Cheetos,' Britney added. 'Don't forget the Cheetos.'

'Anything you say, Mylo, baby.' Paris flashed a megawatt smile, removing her tiny outfit to reveal her nakedness, save for the kinky boots. With a hard-on the size of Queens, Mylo found himself faced with a real dilemma: which of these chicks was he gonna give it to first?

'Hey, Lindsay,' he said, 'you wanna be first to have some fun?'

'You bet, baby,' she grinned, thrilled. He pulled her closer to him, ripples of water sliding around their naked bodies like streams of silk ribbon. But just as he was about to give her the full Mylo experience, he was distracted by the distant trill of an alarm sounding . . .

'Beep beep beep beep – beep beep beep beep.'

A car alarm? But there were no cars, man, not for miles. Mylo made to continue but it was getting louder now, the trills more shrill and urgent.

'Beep beep beep beep – da-da – da da da-da da da daaaa.'

Shit. As the distracting noise grew closer, Mylo realised it wasn't the sound of a car alarm at all; it was a ringtone. Somebody's phone was ringing.

Fuck, man; it was *his* phone.

*

Mylo opened his eyes with a start and let out an involuntary groan. The stream of light that tore through the room from a crack in the curtain told him it was morning. Early morning. He sat up, disorientated, his brain slowly registering his surroundings. He was at home, in his studio apartment, a poky affair on 86th Street in Jackson Heights, NYC. He rubbed the corners of his mouth with his thumb and forefinger; his mouth was as dry as the bottom of a budgie's cage. Feeling through the dimness, his hands clumsy, he scrabbled for his cell on the small bedside table. It wasn't there. Where the hell had he put the damn thing?

Tearing back the covers, Mylo swung his legs over the edge of the bed and only then noticed the naked girl next to him. She was lying face down, her straggly peroxide blonde hair fanning the pillow like straw. He had no idea who she was but he had a sneaky suspicion she wasn't Britney.

It must've been some little party they'd had the night before though, he surmised, surveying the damage to his bijou digs; the floor was covered with empty bottles of Jim Beam and discarded items of clothing; a black lacy bra, his Calvin Klein shorts, an empty pack of Trojans . . .

He caught sight of the time on his snide Rolex (he hoped to upgrade to the real deal one of these days); it was 5:55 a.m. Jesus man. Whoever it was, they had better be dying.

'Beep beep beep beep – beep beep beep beep.'

The blonde in the bed moaned lightly and rolled over to her left exposing Mylo's BlackBerry. Silly bitch had been lying on it.

He snatched it up.

'Yeah.' Mylo rubbed his gritty eyes with his thumb and forefinger. 'Who is this, dude? It's six o'clock in the frickin' morning.'

The voice on the other end sounded distant and unfamiliar.

'Can I speak with Mylo? I'm afraid I don't have a surname.'

The accent was clipped. British, he thought.

'Yeah, it's Mylo. It's just Mylo. No surname. You know, like Madonna and Prince and stuff. Anyway, who did you say this is?'

'I apologise for calling you so early. I do hope I didn't disturb you.'

'Nah man, it's no biggie. I was only just about to have a three-way with a trio of the hottest, most famous chicks in Hollywood.'

He could almost hear the caller smiling.

'Correct me if I'm wrong, Mylo – may I call you Mylo?'

'Whatever, man, it's my name, right?'

'Well, Mylo, correct me if I'm wrong but I've got you down as a Ferrari man, no?'

Mylo rubbed his throbbing temples. He needed hydration. Grabbing a used mug from the sink he ran it under the cold tap and gulped back the contents.

'Ferrari? What the . . . listen, is this some kind of sales pitch? 'Cause if it is, I'm hanging up right about now.'

The caller interrupted.

'Now don't tell me, you're an F430 man? A thrill-seeker, yes? You like a responsive machine with superior speed and lots of pizzazz. Or are you more of a connoisseur? In which case you'll prefer the 612 Scaglietti; elegant and sophisticated, a thoroughbred race horse of a drive. But you know what I'm thinking, Mylo?'

'Dude, I have no idea what the fuck you're talking about . . . who *is* this?'

The voice ignored him.

'I'm going out on a limb here, Mylo, but I'm thinking the Ferrari 599 is *the* car for you. A GTB Fiorano. Red. A classic 12 cyclinder configuration, iconic in its style. The ultimate performance car. Superlative, purposeful yet refined luxury. Just on the right side of flashy. Perfect for pulling the ladies and making that all important first impression. Am I right, Mylo, or am I right?'

Mylo scratched his head, bewildered. The Ferrari 599 was indeed his dream vehicle. Just thinking about what a pussy magnet a piece of machinery like that would be gave him a semi hard-on. Still, how did the dude know about his love for the big F? Mylo came back down to earth with a start.

'Listen, er, whoever you are. I know you're probably on commission or some shit, but the birds are frickin' tweeting right about now and I got just about fifty bucks to my goddamn name . . .'

'Look outside your window, Mylo,' the caller said. His clipped British voice had taken on a slightly malevolent tone to it now which prevented Mylo from immediately hanging up.

'Listen, dude, how'd you get my digits anyway?' He could not recall handing his number out to anyone who didn't own a pair of silicone breasts in months.

The caller's voice softened.

'Let's just say I'm your Fairy Godfather, Mylo. So be a good boy and look outside your window. Tell me what you see.'

Intrigued by the strange, authoritative voice, Mylo walked towards the window, tentatively pulling back a little of the curtain fabric from the window so as not to expose too much of himself; what if there was some sick fuck waiting to blow a frickin' great hole in his cranium? Perhaps it was the husband or boyfriend of some chick he'd screwed – after all, he never thought to ask any of them if they were single. Mylo was nervous. And then he looked down onto the pavement.

In place of his old 1991 Chevrolet Caprice, which he'd inherited from his mother upon leaving home some two years ago, parked on the kerb was a gleaming, glossy red Ferrari 599, sparkling like a ruby in the dust against the rest of the standard family saloons that belonged to the neighbourhood.

'What the . . . ?' Mylo shook his head in disbelief. 'I'm still frickin' dreaming, right?'

'You see it, Mylo? You see the car?'

The emotionless voice on the other end of the phone brought him spinning back to reality.

'Yeah, dude. I see it. It's the 599. It's a fucking awesome ride, man, but what's it doing parked outside my apartment?'

There was a slight pause before the caller casually announced, 'It's yours, Mylo.'

Mylo absentmindedly took another swig of water from the mug and glanced at the catatonic blonde, her peachy butt proudly on display. He still had to be dreaming, right?

'I ain't ordered no goddamn car, man. You got the wrong address or something.'

'86th Street, Jackson Heights, New York, USA – that's right isn't it? That is your address, if I am correct.'

'Yeah, dude. That's right. But like I said, I didn't order no Ferrari. Man, I can't even afford to order pizza right about now.'

The caller laughed but it had a hollow, almost sinister ring to it that caused the hairs on Mylo's arms to stand on end.

'Now listen to me, Mylo,' the voice said softly but sternly. 'Listen very carefully. That car you see parked on the kerb right outside your apartment block indeed belongs to you. At least, it *could* if you do exactly as I tell you and don't ask questions, do I make myself clear?'

Mylo nodded.

'Yeah. I hear you.'

There was a pause on the line and for a second he thought the caller might've hung up.

'I believe you've been hired to shoot the new L'Orelie commercial. Is that right?'

'Yeah, dude, that's right,' Mylo replied, wondering what the hell it had to do with anything.

The L'Orelie shoot was the gig that was about to pull his sorry ass right from the doldrums and propel him into the big time. It was just pure luck that a couple of months ago he'd been at a *W* magazine party and ended up boning some older chick who turned out to be the CEO of L'Orelie no less. She'd taken quite a fancy to him; promised him she'd help him out with his career, get him on track with some of the big players. She'd been a bit of a goer in the sack too, even teaching him a few new moves, which was no mean feat.

'You're test shooting someone by the name of Imogen Forbes, yes?'

Mylo couldn't think straight. He rubbed his forehead with his free hand.

'The British chick? She was big, like, years ago, right?'

'Yes, that's her.'

'Dark hair. Dark eyes. Pretty damn foxy. Lips like pillows. I've seen some old shots of her.'

'Yes, yes.' The voice was growing tetchy.

'What about her?'

'I want you to make sure that she is not successful on the shoot, Mylo. By that I mean she must not get the L'Orelie contract – not even a look in. Do you understand?'

There was a silence while Mylo digested this information. The line crackled.

'I'm not interested in how you might go about achieving this,' the voice continued, 'but achieve it you must. If, of course, you want the keys to that perfect piece of machinery you're no doubt still looking at right now.'

Paranoid, Mylo dropped the curtain in alarm. Was he being watched?

'The keys will be delivered to you personally by courier the very moment I get the news that she hasn't got the job. Have I made this all very clear, Mylo?'

Mylo closed his eyes and opened them again as if this somehow might give him more clarity on the situation.

'OK, dude. So you're telling me you're going to *give* me

300,000 bucks' worth of car if I take dud shots of some British broad so that she don't get this L'Orelie gig, right?'

'In a nutshell, Mylo, yes.'

'And if I don't . . . ?'

'Then the deal's off and you go back to driving your mother's old Chevvie, I suppose.'

Mylo frowned.

'Hey! How'd you know it was my mother's . . . ?'

'Do we have a deal, Mylo?' the caller repeated, impatient.

The blonde in the bed stirred suddenly, lifting her head from the pillow.

'Morning, baby,' she husked, her southern drawl breaking the intensity of the moment.

Mylo put his finger to his lips angrily and waved her away.

He lifted the curtain back from the window again and glimpsed the glossy red masterpiece on the pavement. He could almost hear it purring softly as he imagined himself turning the key in the ignition and hitting the big red START button. He thought of all that willing pussy making itself available on the buttery soft leather interior, of all the heads that would turn when he roared up in that little baby. Mylo: photographer *du jour*. He didn't stop to think why the caller might want to scupper the British chick's chances of getting the gig. Like the caller said: no questions asked.

Mylo dropped the curtain and allowed a small chuckle to escape from his lips.

'You have a deal, my friend,' he said finally. Frankly, it was a no frickin' brainer.

CHAPTER 8

'Mr Mystern will see you now, Mrs Rothschild,' the young, raven-haired receptionist said as she ushered Calvary through to the modestly grand offices in Temple where Nikolas Mystern was sitting in his perfectly worn leather chair, hand outstretched in warm acceptance.

'Calvary,' he stood, smiling. 'It's been too long. You look wonderful. Please, sit down, sit down. Luci, fetch us some coffee, will you.'

Calvary waited until the door had firmly shut behind her before grasping Nikolas's hand in both of her own.

'Nikolas, it's so good of you to see me,' she said, gratitude audible in her voice. 'I know it's terribly short notice.'

'Never too busy to see an old friend,' he replied with genuine warmth.

Nikolas Mystern QC was one of the top divorce lawyers in Britain and an old family friend. Having secured some of the heftiest alimony payouts on UK record, including £5 million for a spouse married to her cheating footballer husband for all of eighteen months, he had deservedly earned the moniker, 'Nik the Great' and certain others he would rather not have mentioned.

Somewhat of a dandy in his *de rigueur* braces, perfectly

styled hair and Gucci brogues, he looked younger than his sixty-eight years, his soft, rather jovial features belying his fearsome reputation; he was not nearly as frightening in the flesh as he could be in the courts.

'Tell me. How are you keeping?' Nikolas asked brightly, detecting her lachrymose mood. He imagined she wasn't here to catch up on old times. 'And the boys? Though I say boys . . . I heard on the grapevine that your eldest is getting hitched no less. Good Lord, I remember that boy in his Moses basket!' He shook his head. 'Where *do* the years go?'

'I'm fine, Nikolas,' Calvary said, though both of them knew this to be to the contrary. 'Tom is all set for Oxford and Hen, well, yes, Henry is planning to tie the knot with his fiancée, *Tamara*.' She hissed the girl's name as though it were blasphemous. 'Actually, Hen's the reason I'm here, in a manner of sorts.'

'Oh?'

There was a brief knock at the door before the beaming receptionist walked in with a tray of refreshments.

'Thank you, Luci,' he smiled, pouring them both coffee in a Wedgwood china cup as the young girl withdrew from the room once more.

'I need your help, Nikolas,' Calvary said, shocked by the sound of her own desperation.

'I need a divorce.'

Nikolas sighed. He had heard the divorce word a thousand times over during his career and yet still it continued to provoke a genuine sadness in him.

'I'm sorry to hear that, Calvary,' he said softly. 'Have you thought about counselling?'

Calvary snorted derisively.

'Douglas at Relate? I hardly think so!'

Mystern linked his fingers together and let them rest on top of his polished desk.

'I can recommend a terribly good woman . . .'

Calvary let out a hollow laugh.

'Knowing Douglas he'd probably be screwing her within the week,' she remarked dryly.

Over the years, Calvary had fought so hard to prevent her marriage from becoming the ridiculous charade that it was. She had tolerated Douglas's need to find his jollies elsewhere for nigh on two decades, turning a blind eye to the hastily scribbled numbers on the back of napkins, the scent of another woman on his shirt, little gifts she had found that she would never receive . . .

Calvary considered it to be her lot in life; most society wives had to turn the other cheek at one time or another throughout their marriage. It was par for the course if you wanted to keep the status and the trappings. *Trappings* being the operative word. Up until now though, Douglas had stuck to the unspoken rules between them regarding his 'dalliances'. Discretion was key; as long as he didn't flaunt it, Calvary could look the other way and console herself with extravagant purchases and luxury holidays. But not this time; this time Douglas had gone too far.

Calvary took a deep breath. What she was about to say was not going to be easy for her but she knew it was necessary if Nikolas was going to secure her the payout of the century. Even a cheating, immoral son-of-a-bitch like Douglas would want this particular indiscretion kept quiet.

'He's been screwing our son's fiancée.' Calvary fought to banish the image inside her mind of a naked Tamara on top of her husband, her glossy chestnut head thrown back in ecstasy as she rode him furiously, Douglas's hand grabbing at her pert young breasts as they bounced in slow-motion. She glanced up at Nikolas. If he was shocked by such a revelation he certainly didn't show it. Perhaps he had seen and heard it all. The thought made Calvary feel deeply depressed.

'I am sorry, Calvary,' Mystern said finally, his tone one of fatherly concern and causing a lump as hard as granite to form in her throat. 'That must've been a dreadful shock.'

Calvary nodded, unable to speak for fear of unravelling like a ball of wool. 'Are you sure I can't offer you a drink? A real drink, perhaps?' Nikolas stood, straightened his braces and made his way over to a huge antique globe that stood proudly by the large sash window like a prop from a James Bond film set. It was a little early to start on the hard stuff but today he felt like making an exception.

'Care to join me? A G&T perhaps?'

'What the hell,' Calvary sniffed.

'That's a girl,' Nikolas said, pouring her an exceptionally large measure.

Calvary gulped back half the contents of her glass and hoped it wouldn't be long before she would feel the warming effects of the alcohol.

'I want half of everything,' she announced, her change of tone causing Nikolas to look up from his glass. 'All of it. The houses, the cars, even his beloved bloody jet! I want to keep the jewellery and, of course, the dogs – definitely the dogs . . .' Calvary was animated now, almost up out of her chair, years of hurt and anger emanating from her like radiation. 'I want to nail that bastard so hard to the wall he really will think he's bloody Jesus Christ!' she spat. 'I deserve to be handsomely rewarded for the years I've put up with him sniffing after anything in a skirt, Nikolas. Humiliating me, robbing me of my self-esteem and dignity. But above all, above everything, I want him to pay for betraying our son; his own *son*, for God's sake!' Tears were stinging her eyes now and she sniffed them back.

Nikolas Mystern drained his glass. He was up on his feet now too, pacing behind his desk, his brow furrowed in thought.

'Did you tell Douglas you were coming to see me today?' he enquired earnestly.

'Of course not!' Calvary laughed incredulously. 'I'll be the first to admit that I have been foolish over the years, allowing that bastard of a husband of mine to continue to make a mockery of our marriage, but even I'm not that stupid!' The look on Nikolas Mystern's face was beginning to trouble her. 'Why do you ask?'

'It's odd,' Nikolas said, continuing to pace the room, 'but it seems as though Douglas may have pre-empted your moves.'

'What do you mean, pre-empted my moves?' Calvary felt the first flutters of fear inside her stomach.

'Well,' Mystern began, 'I figured when you called a few days ago and said you wanted to see me that it might be prudent, if a little premature of me, to start looking into Douglas's affairs – financial affairs you understand,' he felt the need to clarify.

'Go on,' Calvary encouraged him, her heart beating a song in her chest.

'Taking into account the businesses and his portfolio of properties, Douglas must be worth in excess of £200 million, would you agree?'

Calvary nodded.

'Tell me, why do you ask?' she repeated shakily.

Nikolas took an audible breath, sat back down into his chair and fixed Calvary with a watery-eyed stare. In the most part he enjoyed his job, always had done, but there were times, like this, when he wished he was retired and enjoying his twilight years out on his yacht somewhere on the French Riviera.

'Well, according to my well-placed sources, Douglas Rothschild is worth a big fat sum of nothing.'

Calvary met his gaze. The room suddenly felt hot and airless.

'That's ridiculous,' she snorted dismissively after a long moment. 'Douglas is the walking epitome of "filthy rich".' She laughed then, a hollow, bitter sound.

'That may be,' Mystern said solemnly. 'But according to my sources whatever fortune he may have amassed over the years, it's gone.'

'Gone? *Gone*?' Calvary repeated the word as though it were foreign. Her first flutters of fear had now rapidly escalated into full blown panic. 'But I . . . I don't understand,' she said. The room had begun to spin and she placed a hand on the walnut desk in a bid to steady herself.

'It's very odd,' Mystern continued, picking up his Mont Blanc ink pen and stabbing a fresh clean sheet of notebook paper. 'But the day after you called to make an appointment here, large sums of money were withdrawn from various bank accounts belonging to your husband and an application was made to liquidate his business. It's as if he somehow knew, or suspected that you were coming to see me.'

Calvary's jaw loosened and she began to feel a little faint.

'But . . . but that's impossible . . .' she stammered.

'Calvary, are you alright? Here, have some water,' Mystern said, pouring her a glass.

Douglas Rothschild was a hugely successful property tycoon and was what was known as a 'fixer' to the wealthy. If someone needed a house, Douglas would get them a house. If they needed a nice car, he'd get them a car. His main business was peddling expensive properties though, which he largely sold to Russian oligarchs and European billionaires.

'My guess is that somehow he's got wind of our meeting,' Mystern said. 'He suspects you're looking into divorcing him and he's squirrelled all his cash away somewhere. Somewhere you can't get your hands on it.'

Calvary's mind was racing in time with her heart. Douglas

would never suspect her of seeking a divorce from him, such was the extent of his inflated ego. He'd betrayed her a million times before now and she had never so much as threatened him with the 'D' word, not once. So how had he got wind of her intentions?

'You'll have to find the money!' Calvary shrieked, standing now, the full force of what she had learned piercing her mind with vicious clarity. 'It has to be somewhere! He can't . . . oh God, that bastard! He can't do this to me!'

She finally started to cry then. Big fat sorrowful tears streaking her carefully made-up face.After everything he had done to her, Douglas would have the last laugh; he would cut her off financially, see her penniless on the street!

'I assure you, Calvary,' Nikolas Mystern said, his tone low and reassuring, 'that I will find what has happened to your husband's money and, assuming you wish to appoint me and follow the divorce route, ensure you receive what you're entitled to.' In fact, Nikolas Mystern would rather look forward to it. 'In the meantime,' he said authoritatively, 'I urge you not to panic. I will get my people onto this straight away.'

Calvary nodded, glad of his reassurances. It was what she needed; someone to take control, tell her it would all be alright. The fact was, she would rather be dead than have to scrimp and scrape by after everything she had put up with over the years.

'I'll have more to tell you soon, I promise,' Nikolas said, his voice settling into the kindly fatherly tones of earlier. 'In the meantime I suggest you mull everything over. Maybe even talk to Douglas. You don't have to tell him any of what we've discussed here today. In my experience a holiday together sometimes helps put things on the right track. You're welcome to take a trip out to my place in Mustique. It might do you both the power of good.'

Calvary smiled at Nikolas but it was an empty gesture and he knew it.

'You really don't have to follow the divorce route, Calvary,' he added in a last ditch attempt to dissuade her. 'It can get awfully messy – and very expensive.'

'Thank you, Nikolas,' she replied, her tears dried and her demeanour back to businesslike. 'I really do appreciate it.' Calvary stood to leave. It had been a draining conversation and she needed time to get her head around it. In short, she realised that dissolving her marriage meant risking her status as a prominent Chelsea wife and everything she owned.

After saying her goodbyes, Calvary walked soberly through the plush reception area of Mystern's office. The smiling, raven-haired receptionist was sitting behind a large ornate desk, admiring a huge, impressive bouquet of the most beautiful blood red roses, Calvary's favourites and she couldn't help but give a small smile as she passed.

'They're beautiful,' she commented, suddenly wishing she too was young again and in the first flushes of love. Oh, how she would do it all so differently, given the chance.

'Aren't they just?' the girl said, looking terribly pleased with herself.

'Whoever he is, he obviously thinks the world of you,' Calvary remarked.

The receptionist smiled.

'You really think so?'

'Oh yes,' Calvary replied before stepping into the lift. 'A man who sends you flowers as beautiful as that shouldn't be kept waiting too long. Mark my words!'

As the lift doors closed behind Calvary the receptionist inhaled the scent of one of the roses and sighed as she read the accompanying card; 'To Luci, thanks for everything. Dinner tonight? Douglas. X'

She smiled smugly as she picked up the phone and began to dial.

CHAPTER 9

Yasmin observed herself with pleasure in the ornate full-length mirror and poured herself a glass of pink champagne from the well-chilled complimentary bottle. The skin-tight grey boned cashmere Bottega Veneta dress she was wearing caressed her neat curves perfectly, displaying her breasts to their pneumatic best. She ran her hands along her minuscule waist and down to her thighs satisfactorily. Hmm, not bad, she thought approvingly. But not quite right for the ball. Not fancy enough, she mused, unzipping herself and allowing the dress to slide provocatively to the floor.

'I want people to gasp out loud when I enter the room,' she called out to the assistant loudly without taking her eyes from the mirror. 'It has to be a complete show stopper.' The harried-looking sales assistant nodded emphatically from behind her.

'Ah, now that's more like it,' Yasmin said, spying an Oscar de la Renta strapless feather embellished number and snatching it up from the assistant's arm.

'Help me into it, will you?'

'Certainly, madam,' she said with as much enthusiasm as she could muster. She had been helping Lady Belmont-Jones try on dresses solidly for the past two hours, watching as she stalked up and down the plush carpeted dressing room, casting admiring glances at herself in the mirror only to discard each and every one, tossing thousands of pounds' worth of designer gowns onto the floor in a heap like they were cheap tat from Primark. 'This special something you're looking for, Lady Belmont, is it for Forbes' annual ball?' she asked, feigning interest.

'It is for the ball, as a matter of fact,' Yasmin said, her ears pricking up. 'I have to look better than divine because we're on *the* table with Mr & Mrs Forbes this year. You know, all eyes on us.'

'It's always the same this time of year,' the assistant said, barely able to hide her weariness as she fastened the zip of Yasmin's dress. 'Everyone coming in for a last minute fitting. I must say though, Lady Belmont, none of them have your amazing figure.'

Yasmin smirked. She knew she had a figure to die for and was not afraid to use it to her advantage.

All the women in the Jones family had been blessed with killer bodies. Her mother, who had ended up using her own to feed her crippling addiction, had said it was more of a curse than a blessing. Yasmin, however, was determined that in her case it would be the latter.

Catching sight of herself in the mirror once more, she wondered what her mother might think if she could see her now; standing in Harvey Nichols, a glass of Perrier-Jouet vintage rose champagne in her hand and a pile of designer dresses being handed to her by an obliging assistant who would break into song if she was asked to. Would she be proud? Envious perhaps? The truth was she probably wouldn't have given a toss. Junkies cared about nothing save for their next fix. A fact Yasmin knew only too well.

When their mother's miserable life was eventually claimed by a heroin overdose, Chloe, at just seventeen years old, had given up her ambition to go to beauty college and became a mother to her seven-year-old sister. Social services had wanted to take them both into care but somehow Chloe had managed to convince them that she was responsible enough for the both of them, and, when she had turned eighteen just three months later, with their errant father nowhere to be found, Chloe had been awarded custody of her baby sister, Stacey. They had even got to keep their poky little council flat. A right result.

Though money was tight, they scraped by – and they were never short of what counted most: love. If only Chloe had never met that wretched old slag, June Larkin. That woman had been trouble from the very moment she had set a cheap stiletto-clad foot through their front door. Even at her tender age, Stacey Jones had sensed a bad vibe about June. The very air around her seemed somehow thick with discord.

June Larkin was a local brass who had lived on their estate; she was a looker right enough, but a brass nonetheless. At thirty-one, she was a good few years older than Chloe, wore nice clothes and drove a flash motor and therefore had a bit of sway on the estate. For all her loose morals however, June Larkin had been an astute woman with a nose for business. She had a little number going whereby she supplied 'hostesses' to rich men who liked to party with good-looking girls to make themselves feel more attractive than they really were. At least that's how she had sold it to Chloe anyway.

'It's not prostitution, love,' she had said to her sister, her cheap jewellery rattling in earnest. 'They just want to hire you for the night to sit there and look pretty. I promise ya, there ain't no funny business. You get paid a few quid just to wear a pretty dress.'

It had sounded like easy money. Money they had desperately needed.

Chloe had been a striking girl; prettier than most with

long naturally blonde bouncy hair and huge, kind brown eyes that were unusual for her colouring. She looked older than her years and her long legs and full bosom were already beginning to draw admiring glances from men and envious ones from women wherever she went.

Yasmin thought of June Larkin then, all teeth and tits and yellow blonde hair and felt a sudden rush of hatred for her. Her sister had trusted her, thought of her as a friend. As it was, not even June Larkin herself could've known just what part she would eventually play in the Jones sisters' destiny.

As far as Yasmin was concerned, there were three people responsible, in their own way, for what had happened to her beloved sister. Fate had taken care of the first two; with her mother already dead, some years later June Larkin would eventually take her own miserable life, citing her guilt of what had happened to Chloe as one in a long list of reasons. Now it was up to her to deal with the third.

Up until the day June Larkin had done the decent thing and topped herself, Stacey had always believed that her beloved sister had died in a tragic car accident.

'You were too young to know the truth,' June had written in a final swan-song letter to a fifteen-year-old Stacey. 'But you're old enough now to know what really happened.'

She had enclosed a large file of newspaper cuttings in with the note that had taken Stacey a whole evening to read, the print blurred from the tears she cried, her heart burning with hatred as she digested every word.

The contents of that letter were to change the course of Stacey Jones's life forever. That day she had made a promise to herself and to Chloe; she would avenge her sister's death if it was the very last thing she did on earth.

*

Yasmin stared at her reflection in the mirror and saw her sister's beautiful, kind face staring back at her. Chloe had sacrificed everything to ensure that she be spared a life in care and she felt a sharp stab of sadness in her guts that for all her sister's valiant efforts, that's exactly where she had ended up.

Following Chloe's death, the next eight years of Stacey's life had been a living nightmare of relentless abuse and neglect – no one wanted to foster the older ones, not cute enough, not malleable enough, so she had been shunted from one 'care' home to another, though why they ever called them that was anyone's guess. No one 'cared' about you in a home. You were just another little bastard to feed; a drain on society; and, in the case of the nonces, another orifice to fill. She had finally broken free at just sixteen years old, entering the world with knowledge a girl her age should never have had; street-wise and tough. And alone.

Yasmin took a large swig of her champagne in a bid to try and wash away her toxic thoughts. Deep down, however, she was almost grateful for such hatred; it was her fuel, the power behind all the deception and tissue of lies she had created around herself and her past. A past that would surely give that contemptuous piece of shit she was married to a fucking great coronary if he were to discover the truth.

Jeremy Belmont hadn't the first clue of his wife's true provenance. To his knowledge, Yasmin Jones was the well-bred daughter of a wealthy Welsh farmer and had been schooled at various acclaimed establishments across Europe. At least, that's what she'd had him believe.

They had met a little over a year ago at the Cartier International Polo at the Guards Polo Club in Windsor. According to Yasmin, both her parents were dead (as a result of a tragic farming accident), and that the poor lamb had promptly blown her inheritance and was coming to live in London ('Chelsea, of all places!'), aged just twenty-six, to 'grieve and find my path in life' as she had breathlessly put it, her chest rising and falling between heavy sighs. Belmont had no reason to doubt her; she spoke with a clipped home counties accent, carried herself well and was a social delight, charming everyone she came into contact with. Above all, she was utterly stunning; long platinum blonde hair, enormous sapphire blue eyes and fleshy pink lips and *that* body – Good Lord, it was something else. Clapping eyes on it for the first time Belmont had felt almost weak with desire. The fact that she seemed to reciprocate his feelings did not strike the bloated, ageing lord as in the least bit odd, such was his inflated ego. As it was, it had taken Stacey Jones years of meticulous preparation and careful plotting to ensure their paths would cross, and that when they eventually did, she would be ready to strike with a charm offensive of epic proportions.

Yasmin surveyed herself in the mirror once more. The Oscar de la Renta did nothing for her and she dumped it onto the ever-increasing pile of discarded gowns.

She checked her Chopard diamond-encrusted watch, an eternity gift from Jeremy on their six month anniversary. It was 5:45 p.m. Ricardo would be on a plane back to Athens by now. She thought of him sipping a Peroni, all pleased with himself, marvelling at how clever he was and a sly smile crept across her perfectly made-up face. She wished she could be there to see the look on that smug mug of his when he discovered the little surprise she had sprung on him.

Their joint enterprise, stinging Jeremy out of half a million pounds, had gone without a glitch. At her instruction, Ricardo had taken the shots of Yasmin and her husband having sex on the yacht and had sent the photos, plus a ransom note, to their Chelsea home.

Jeremy had paid up of course, especially once she had

turned the water works on. Half a million was a drop in the ocean to him, and if it meant keeping pictures of his naked wife out of the press then it was a no brainer.

Earlier that day, Yasmin had held her hand out as she sat in the greasy spoon café on the Old Kent Road – a venue where no one would ever think of finding her.

'I believe you owe me £250,000,' she had smiled at Ricardo who grinned back lasciviously, displaying his small white teeth that showed too much gum.

'You drive a hard bargain, *Lady* Belmont,' Ricardo had smirked, flicking back his black greasy hair from his pock-marked face. 'But then again, with a body like that . . .' He raised an eyebrow.

'Hand it over, Ricardo,' she said, lowering her playful tone. 'Fifty-fifty, that's what we agreed.'

Truth was, Yasmin couldn't have cared less about the money. For the first time in her life she was rich beyond her comprehension and wanted for nothing. It was doing her husband out of half a million that was the ultimate buzz.

Ricardo surreptitiously slid one of the two black holdalls that he had brought with him across the floor. Yasmin stopped it with her Louboutin-clad foot, unzipped it a little, peered at the contents and nodded in satisfaction.

'And the negs,' she said.

Ricardo sighed and pushed a small brown envelope across the Formica table.

'I could've made double that selling those shots,' he sniffed, taking a noisy slurp of his tea.

'Greed is one of the seven deadly sins you know,' she replied dryly.

Ricardo let out a hollow laugh.

'And I suppose blackmailing your own husband isn't?'

Yasmin sighed, a little exasperated.

'No one would believe a snivelling little weasel like you

anyway, Ricardo, but how about another ten thousand to keep you quiet,' she suggested, sweetly.

The corners of Ricardo's mouth turned outwards and he shrugged.

'It's a more than generous offer,' she said, her voice hardening.

Ricardo placed the mug down on to the table precariously. He leaned forward affording her a waft of his fetid breath.

'I tell you what. How about I take that extra ten grand and you throw in a couple of hours of your time, if you catch my drift.' He raised his eyebrows in a gesture so loaded with sexual connotation that it could've been classed as an indecent act in itself. 'Then we'll call it quits. What do you say?'

Yasmin laughed coldly at the paparazzo in front of her, her stomach lurching. Her plan was taking better shape than she could've imagined. What fools these men were, she thought to herself. Led by their dicks, all of them.

'Well then,' she stood to leave, 'lead the way.'

Ricardo smiled, displaying those small white teeth and too much gum.

'Ladies first,' he said, his lazy hard-on already twitching in anticipation.

*

Yasmin could still detect the remnants of Ricardo's alcoholic breath and cheap aftershave on her skin as she stepped out of yet another gown and reached into her handbag, spritzing herself generously with a large bottle of Chanel Beige perfume in a bid to mask the offensive stench.

Ricardo had thought he'd got one up on her with his thinly veiled attempt at blackmailing her into sleeping with him, but, brainless scumbag that he was, had instead wandered blindly into the trap she had laid for him without a second thought. She'd always had every intention of sleeping with him.

It had been an unpleasant experience, a drunk Ricardo throwing her down onto the filthy mattress and plunging himself deep into her. As usual, Yasmin closed her mind to what was happening, a trick she had mastered from far too young an age.

Afterwards, just as she had anticipated, Ricardo had promptly dozed off in a post-coital slumber, his heavy alcoholic snores resounding against the thin, sodden walls. Yasmin had quickly dressed herself in the tiny bathroom and, searching through his scruffy possessions, found the original negatives from the film inside the pocket of his dirty jeans.

'Bingo!' she had whispered to herself triumphantly as she replaced Ricardo's black holdall with one of her own, filling it with a pile of old newspapers and magazines she had found in a cupboard under the stairs. Leaving it next to the bed, she had picked up the original holdall alongside her own, collected the small envelope of negatives and dragged them both out onto the street where she had hailed a cab to Mayfair.

'Ciao for now, Ricardo, you sick piece of shit,' she had said as she blew him an air kiss from the back of the taxi. She imagined the look of horror on his swarthy face when he finally discovered that in fact, it was *she* who had fucked *him* in the end. Fucked him good and proper. The thought had cheered her up no end.

*

'I've found this,' the sales assistant called out to Yasmin from behind the curtain. 'It's Alexander McQueen couture. J-Lo once wore something similar to the VMAs, but I thought of you the moment I saw it on the rail.'

Yasmin tore back the curtain and poked her head out. It was *the* dress. She knew it instantly as she observed it in all its inky black floor length, sequinned embellished, one-shoulder glory.

'I'll take it,' Yasmin said nonchalantly.

The assistant stared at her, incredulous. 'Wouldn't you like to see if it fits first, Lady Belmont? I would advise it.'

'No. That's the dress. Just have them all wrapped for me, yes,' Yasmin spoke hurriedly.

'All?' The assistant was perplexed.

Yasmin shot her an impatient look.

'Yes. *All* of them,' she snapped, pointing to the enormous pile of couture on the floor. 'I want them all wrapped and charged to my husband's account, please.'

The sales assistant closed her mouth. She was accustomed to observing obscene amounts of cash change hands but she had never seen anything like this.

'Ye . . . yes, Lady Belmont,' she stammered. 'I'll get it done right away. Would you like them sent on to your Chelsea residence? And can I get you a car? I see you already have some luggage.'

'If you don't mind,' Yasmin said, pulling on her spray-on DVB black jeans and Rick Owens tank and hurriedly throwing her Balmain leather biker jacket over the top.

'Not at all,' the sales assistant said, instantly buoyed by the realisation that she would meet her sales target this week and then some.

'Oh, and I've left a tip for you in the dressing room, for all your help,' Yasmin smiled kindly at the assistant as she breathlessly made her way past her. 'Don't spend it all at once, will you? Got to dash,' she said, checking the time on her watch. 'Mustn't keep hubby waiting – bye for now!'

'Yes, er, goodbye, Lady Belmont. See you again soon?'

She watched incredulously as Yasmin Belmont strutted

from the room carrying a black holdall, her long platinum hair swishing behind her. Oh, to be that young and have so much money, she thought enviously as she stepped into the curtained changing room to clear up the mass of padded hangers and empty champagne bottle. It was then she noticed a large black holdall on the chair and called out, 'Lady Belmont, your bag! You've forgotten your bag!' But Yasmin was long gone.

Sighing as she picked it up it was awfully heavy she noticed an envelope on the top: 'To the helpful assistant. It's *all* yours – Treat yourself and your family! Love, Lady B XX.'

Opening it, the assistant put her hand to her mouth to prevent herself from screaming. The holdall was full to bursting with fifty pound notes. She stared, dumbstruck, at the cash, her breath coming in short, sharp bursts. The Queen's face smiled wryly back up at her as she stood rooted to the spot. Looking around her, convinced it had to be some kind of prank, she picked up the note and re-read it.

' – it's *all* yours . . .'

Gripped by a potent combination of shock and elation, with her heart thumping so hard in her chest that it almost hurt, the assistant began to empty out the contents of the bag, turning it upside down, watching as a seemingly never-ending flurry of notes fluttered to the floor in a makeshift money-snowstorm. And then she started to laugh, great belly laughs until tears fell from her eyes.

CHAPTER 10

Bibendum was exceptionally busy, even for a Friday lunchtime.

'I thought perhaps we might go for a little meander around Knightsbridge after lunch,' Calvary announced as she cast a critical eye over Yasmin's choice of lunch outfit – a colourful Julien Macdonald dress that displayed far too much leg *and* cleavage – a major fashion *faux pas*. 'Browse for something to wear for the ball perhaps.' She was determined to push her protégée in a more demure sartorial direction if it killed her.

Yasmin bristled, affronted. What exactly was she trying to say? Anyway, she already had her outfit sorted, and just wait until Calvary got a load of it! If she thought her usual attire was a little on the risqué side then the woman's eyes would fall out of her head once she saw the sheer, split-to-the-crotch McQueen she was planning to unveil!

Yasmin was wise enough to hold her tongue, however. She had learned quickly that it was best to indulge Calvary Rothschild. Interfering and bossy though the woman was, Yasmin was not naive enough to think that she couldn't learn anything from her. She hoped Calvary's knowledge of society might prove useful when it came to gleaning information she needed. Information about the night her sister died.

Reluctantly, Yasmin knew she should be grateful to Calvary for taking her under her wing, especially since she had been largely ostracised by the other women on the society circuit. In an odd way, they both needed each other; Yasmin wanted information and to fit in, and Calvary needed a distraction from her ever increasing marital problems. Their fledgling friendship suited them both.

'Fine with me,' Yasmin shrugged. If it meant blowing yet more of her husband's cash then she was more than game.

'And I suppose you'll want to pick up a few last minute bits for LA, won't you, darling?' Calvary turned to Imogen. 'You're flying out the day after tomorrow, aren't you?'

'What? Hmm . . .' Imogen replied, her mind clearly elsewhere. 'Oh, yes,' she said, jerking her thoughts back to reality. 'LA.'

'You must be excited,' Yasmin remarked, shovelling a forkful of walnut salad in between her shimmery lips. She was off the coke today and as usual her appetite had returned with an insatiable vengeance. 'Getting back in front of the camera again. Calvary told me you were, like, as big as Kate Moss back in the day.'

Calvary shot Imogen an apologetic look.

'Back in the day,' Imogen repeated, her mind drifting towards him once more.

Ever since meeting with Cressida again, it was as if the door to her past had been flung wide open and, struggle as she might, she could not seem to close it again.

Her head throbbed with thoughts of *him* so much that it hurt. Images of the two of them together constantly flicked like still frames through her mind; she saw his sparsely furnished apartment in Camden where they had first made love . . . the rickety old boat they had taken out on the canals during a weekend trip to Amsterdam, laughing until their sides hurt. Try as she did to stop herself from going there, she saw the stunning white beach house in Ibiza, the sound of the waves in the distance as they made love on the sand one last time. And Aimee . . . she could not forget Aimee . . .

'So, what made you give it all up in the first place, the modelling, I mean?' Yasmin asked, genuinely intrigued.

'More like *who* made her give it up,' Calvary explained, throwing one leg dramatically over the other as she smoothed down the front of her Alberta Ferretti shift dress.

Imogen sighed. She hated answering this question. It always made her feel so weak and pathetic.

'Seb wanted me to concentrate on motherhood rather than my career,' she explained quietly, fiddling nervously with her small silver necklace, the necklace *he* had placed around her neck all those years ago and that had remained there ever since. 'He didn't think I could do both.'

Yasmin pulled her chin into her neck, outrage written all over her young, heavily made-up face.

'Jesus, what a dinosaur,' she shook her head ruefully. 'Well, no man could ever make *me* do anything I didn't want to do, uh-uh,' she announced defiantly, though secretly she knew this had not always been the case. On the contrary, Yasmin had spent most of her young life doing *exactly* what men wanted her to do. It was partly why she felt such a fierce loathing for them all.

'You haven't met Sebastian Forbes,' Calvary deadpanned. 'Actually, I'm surprised he's been OK about this LA trip. I must say, Ims, I thought he would've thrown his toys out of the pram at the very mention of it.'

'That makes two of us,' Imogen replied, still unable to quite believe her husband's easy-going attitude. 'Though I made it clear that I'm doing this for Cressida and he couldn't stop me even if he tried. This time I stood up to him,' she said, enjoying a small rush of pleasure as she remembered the scene in the kitchen.

'Sounds to me like you were fifteen years too late,' Yasmin retorted, unable to help herself from wondering how someone as beautiful and seemingly smart as Imogen had ended up with a man like Sebastian Forbes who, by all accounts, sounded like a misogynistic bully.

'Better late than never, I suppose,' Imogen smiled unconvincingly, dipping her spoon into her celeriac soup.

'Relationships, darling,' Calvary interjected, sighing and trying hard not to think too much about the mess her own was in. 'I've always thought that love makes people do the silliest things.' She shot Yasmin a humorous look. 'Like marrying a man old enough to be her grandfather.'

Imogen bit her lip and cast her friend a look that told her she was a wicked woman.

'Oh yes, bravo, very funny,' Yasmin retorted, slowly clapping her hands. 'You may mock, Calvary Rothschild, but I'll have you know that Jeremy is the love of my life.' This statement sounded almost as ridiculous as it was unconvincing. 'I knew as soon as I saw him,' she added, the natural drama queen within her unable to stop herself from overegging the pudding.

'Love at first sight, was it?' Calvary raised a sceptical eyebrow, adding dryly, 'if such a thing even exists.'

Suddenly it was the summer of 1995 and Imogen was in the British Library. He had been taking a sly look at her from behind the dusty bookshelves as she casually thumbed the pages of an old copy of *The Unbearable Lightness of Being*, pretending not to have noticed him.

She had been instinctively aware of someone watching her, longing eyes leaving imprints on her skin. When she had eventually looked up and met his gaze, it had felt as if a bomb had gone off inside her. He had immediately looked down at the book he was reading as if furious with himself at having been caught staring, and the memory of it still made her smile, even now.

He had asked to buy her coffee and then screwed his eyes tightly shut as if embarrassed by the suggestion, and they had both laughed with an ease that she had never experienced with a man.

He had been a day or so off clean shaven and his soft sandy-coloured hair had hung in his eyes with a nonchalance that was almost contrived. He was tall, and well built, and his eyes were the most unusual teal green colour, protected by thick, dark lashes that were so glossy they looked almost wet, as if he had just stepped from the deepest lagoon. Uncharacteristically, she had found herself wondering what it would be like to make love with him. Later, that afternoon, she got to find out. Subconsciously, she had already made the decision to do so before her cappuccino had arrived. Afterwards, when he had confessed that he had a girlfriend called Aimee, who he no longer loved 'in that way', she had believed him.

Somehow she had known this man would be her destiny.

*

'So it wasn't instant with you and Douglas then? More of a grower, was he?' Yasmin enquired. She had noticed that Calvary rarely spoke of her husband and that whenever she did, her expression seemed to cloud over. Jeremy had told her all about Douglas Rothschild's infamous incapability of keeping his cock in his trousers.

'Rothschild would shag a hole in the wall,' Jeremy had crudely guffawed, as if it were something to be proud of.

'Ha! Me and Douglas?' Calvary snorted derisively. 'Oh yes, darling, it was love at first sight alright! Only trouble is, it's also love at first sight with every other bloody woman he meets!' She threw her head back and laughed, though it sounded so desperate and hollow that Yasmin had to stop herself from placing her hand on her arm in empathy. It wouldn't do to start getting emotionally attached. She had a job to do and emotions would only complicate things. They always did.

'Well, I believe in love at first sight,' Imogen confessed, the champagne making her feel unusually candid.

Calvary raised her eyebrows.

'Oh darling, next you'll be telling us that you've met the tooth fairy!' she retorted with a heavy dose of good-humoured sarcasm.

'No, really,' Imogen insisted, suddenly gripped by an urge to talk about *him*. The truth was, she had never spoken about that time in her life before. Not even to Calvary, her oldest and dearest friend.

Imogen had always believed it was better that way. By staying silent, it was almost as if she could convince herself that part of her life had never existed. Only it *had* existed, and now it was as if those memories, confined to the deepest part of her mind all those years ago, had suddenly glimpsed daylight again and now wanted out.

'There was this man, once . . .'

Yasmin's eyes lit up in anticipation.

'A man!' Calvary spluttered, clearly thrilled and surprised. 'Oh Ims, you dark horse! Do tell.'

Imogen's eyes began to glaze over as the image of his face flashed before her with such clarity that she felt the imprint of it on her heart.

'Yes,' she said quietly. 'His name was Michael. But to me he was always Mickey . . .'

CHAPTER 11

Mylo was having a problem. One helluva frickin' problem. No matter what he did, what angle he shot from, the chick in front of him just wouldn't look anything other than fierce.

'That's it, baby, to the left a little. Give me a grimace. Yeah, like that. Grrr. Like you're an animal. I bet you're an animal, right? A proper little tigress in the sack, huh?'

Imogen inwardly winced. This photographer was a total arsehole. What were L'Orelie thinking employing such a sleazebag? From the moment they had started shooting he had bombarded her with a torrent of schoolboy sexual innuendo and loaded remarks about her 'tits and ass'. It was unprofessional, not to mention disrespectful. Moreover it was putting her off. She'd half a mind to complain but had quickly decided against it. At least until Cressida got here. She'd sort him out in a second with the sharp end of her tongue. If she ever bothered to show, that is.

Imogen glanced at the wall clock; Cress, who was due in on the next flight after hers, was a little over an hour late turning up for the shoot. Quite unlike her, she thought. Cressida was always an absolute stickler for timekeeping.

Standing with her back to the camera, Imogen flicked

her head round and flashed her devastating smile. Sleazy though the photographer was, she was still loving every minute of being back in front of the lens and was upset Cress was missing it all.

'Let's take five, huh, pussy cat?' Mylo winked, letting his camera drop down to his side. It was all part of his plan, the sleazy photographer bit – not that he'd had to dig too deep to appear convincing.

In truth, Mylo kind of resented having to make out to this woman that he was a total douchebag. It bothered him that she might think him cheap and tacky – a first for him. Mylo's insouciance was his trademark; usually, he couldn't have given a toss what any chick thought at the end of the day – just so long as she said 'yes.'

He was nervous too; Imogen Forbes was a complete fox. Mylo could see that without some serious intervention, this chick would walk it. The gig was hers the moment she had strutted through the double doors, dressed in regular JBrand Jeans and a plain white t-shirt; her dark glossy hair scraped back from her sun-kissed face, looking a million frickin' bucks, even before hair and make-up.

Imogen smiled at Mylo, nodded and walked off set towards the make-up artist, Rhianna, who stood, brush poised in hand, waiting for her.

Glancing around the studio at all the terribly cool people milling around, attempting to look integral to the day's events, Imogen noticed a young girl, little more than a teenager really, with bleached yellow hair, too much make-up and not enough skirt, sitting on a bean bag. The girl was watching Mylo's every move. Her eyes filled with longing as he stood in front of a laptop uploading images and talking animatedly to his assistant, Josh. Imogen strained a little in an attempt to hear their conversation but the sound of Beyonce's voice on the stereo in the background drowned out their voices.

Imogen's iPhone beeped and she picked it up, assuming it was Cressida with an explanation. She wanted this stay in LA to be memorable for Cress, as well as herself. It was her chance to say her final goodbyes to her friend and she had hoped to build lasting memories, ones she would be able to look back on with fondness.

But the message wasn't from Cressida, it was from her daughter, Bryony.

Imogen felt her heart lift. Bryony was such a thoughtful girl; she had remembered her mother would be shooting today and had wanted to send her best. Imogen felt a small pang of guilt as she read the message. It seemed wrong somehow, her beautiful girl a million miles away from her, texting her best wishes while she was attempting to resurrect her career in LA.

'My daughter,' she held the phone up to Rhianna. 'Wishing me luck.'

'Your daughter, huh? I bet she's a little knockout, right? Just like her momma.'

'She is,' Imogen beamed and began to text her daughter back.

'We're having cocktails after the shoot today. Y'all should join us you know, honey. It'd be nice to have some female company. Help me hold my own against Dumb and Dumber over there.' Rhianna nodded in the direction of Mylo and his assistant.

Imogen stifled a giggle.

'So what's the deal with the photographer anyway?' she asked, intrigued.

Rhianna pulled a face and snorted.

'Y'see that little lady over there?' She pointed her comb in the direction of the bored looking young blonde. 'The one with the short skirt and over made-up face?'

Imogen nodded.

'Well, that's Candy. My little sister. She's completely

ga-ga about Mylo. Reckons he's the one, ya know?'

Rhianna sighed ruefully. 'Poor baby. He said he'd help her. Get her doing some shots and all – she's like, *so* desperate to be a model. But I told her, "honey, the only person that guy is gonna help is himself".' Rhianna leaned in closer, her tanned, powdered face almost touching Imogen's. 'I heard a rumour that he's more than a lil' friendly with the number one at L'Orelie. Y'all know what I'm saying?'

Imogen raised an eyebrow and looked over at Candy, desperate to be noticed. She felt sorry for the young girl. Mylo had 'user' written all over him.

'When Cressida gets here, I'll ask her to have a chat with her. She can put her in contact with some people who might be able to help her – Cress knows everyone.'

'Y'all would do that? Oh my, honey, that's so kind of you. Candy will love you forever.'

Imogen smiled, glad to be of assistance. But inside she was beginning to worry. Where *was* Cressida?

*

'*Fuck, man*!' Mylo cursed under his breath. The images staring back at him were some of the best he'd ever taken. If only he could bottle what this broad had and sell it on to the constant stream of wannabe models he encountered on a daily basis; he'd be the richest dude on earth. Mylo thought hard for a moment, so hard you could almost hear the cogs turning inside his brain.

'Listen, Josh.' He turned to his young, enthusiastic assistant. 'I want you to fiddle around with these shots on the computer.'

Josh nodded emphatically as if he'd been asked to undertake the most important mission of his entire life. 'Make her face a little rounder, her nose a little flatter. Lighten her eyes a bit and mess around with the symmetry. Know what I'm saying?'

Josh looked puzzled. He might be a novice but even he knew the idea was to try and *improve* a shot.

'But these pictures, boss,' he shrugged, perplexed, 'they're pretty damn perfect as they are. You know, like, if it ain't broke, don't fix it n' shit.'

Mylo smirked as he put his arm around his shoulder in a mock friendly gesture.

'You like working as my assistant, Josh?' he asked.

'Sure,' Josh nodded. 'It's way cool, man.'

'Good,' Mylo hissed, his soft tone taking on a subtle sharp edge. 'If you wanna keep it cool then do the fuck as I ask and don't ask questions, got it?'

Josh shrugged.

'Sure. You're the boss, boss.'

Mylo clapped him on the back.

'I think we're done here,' Mylo called over to Imogen and Rhianna.

'We are?' Imogen replied, a little shocked. They'd only been shooting for five minutes. She'd not even had an outfit change.

'Hey, guys,' Mylo called out to the rest of the studio. 'It's a wrap!'

Rhianna shrugged at Imogen.

Perplexed, Imogen padded over to where Mylo and Josh stood, the rest of the studio watching as she moved with supermodel grace and purpose.

'Can I see the shots?' Imogen asked, pointing at the computer. Josh nodded, standing back a little to make way for her.

Imogen cocked her head to one side and scanned the pictures of herself on screen. Despite always being her own worst critic, even she had to conclude that she looked fantastic. Her skin glowed and her smile lit up the frame.

She had that 'everyday with an edge' look about her, just the brief Cressida had told her L'Orelie wanted.

'You pleased with them?' She glanced up at Mylo tentatively.

'Sure. They're hot,' he said, refraining from making eye contact with her. He felt a little rush of guilt then, seeing the look of disappointment on her beautiful face, and had to visualise himself cruising around in that Ferrari until it passed. 'You did good.'

Imogen felt herself relax a bit, though she cursed Cressida for not being here to give her objective opinion. Cressida would've made him take more film, give the client as much choice as possible, she felt sure.

'What about the others, Mylo?' Candy suddenly piped up from her beanbag seat.

'Others?' Imogen asked, puzzled.

'The shots I saw Josh working on . . .' she offered helpfully.

'There are no others,' Mylo shot back a little too defensively, causing Imogen to look at him in alarm.

Josh nodded his agreement.

'Yeah, there were no others,' he added a little too emphatically.

'Oh, but I thought I saw . . .'

'Hey, Candy,' Mylo snapped, his tone nasty. 'Were you even invited on this shoot, huh?'

Candy stared up at Mylo, a wounded look on her young, impressionable face.

'Well, like . . . not exactly, but I just thought that seeing as though you and me . . .'

Mylo had only slept with the girl a handful of times and now he couldn't get rid of the bitch; she was like a particularly persistent case of herpes.

'*You* and *me*?' He stifled a chuckle. 'Baby, there ain't no you and me. You got that, huh, Candy?'

A crushed looking Candy nodded slowly, her head dropping down onto her voluminous chest. Imogen shot Mylo a disgusted look. This guy was a complete arsehole.

'Good,' Mylo said, abruptly snapping the lid of his laptop shut, signalling the end of their little discussion. 'Alrighty,' he said brightly, addressing the rest of the studio who were pretending not to have listened to his little outburst. 'Who's up for a Bud?'

*

Imogen stepped into the shower and let the powerful jet of water wash over her, the hotness prickling her naked skin. Soaping herself with the complimentary Aveda products, she thought of the evening's events and smiled, blowing water from her lips.

He certainly had some neck, that Mylo character, coming onto her like that.

'I'll say something for you British broads, you know how to turn it on for the camera,' he'd said as he'd moved in on her, his 'ironic' neon pink Paul Frank hoodie glowing in the low evening light as his pungent Armani aftershave filled the soft, cool air around her.

'Thanks,' she had graciously replied. 'We try our best.'

'Hmm, I'll bet you do,' he'd said, casting his wide blue eyes over her body, a half smile on his lips. 'You got plans for the rest of your stay?'

'Yes, as a matter of fact, I have,' Imogen had smiled sweetly up at him. This was all she needed, the prick-of-a-photographer making a move on her. She inwardly sighed. Some things in the industry, it seemed, never changed.

'It wasn't a question,' Mylo replied, smirking as he watched her face flush a little pink.

He'd embarrassed her. It was kinda cute.

'I have to get back to meet my agent,' Imogen stammered.

'She was supposed to be at the shoot but she must've been waylaid. She'll probably be waiting for me back at the Marmont.' Imogen cursed herself. She'd just let on where they were staying and hoped Mylo wouldn't take this accidental admission as a green light.

'Cool digs,' he smiled, slurping his bottle of Bud and placing his arm against the wall in a makeshift barrier to prevent her from escaping.

'Anyways, there's this hot new club opened downtown, The Playground. I'm on the guest list, so how about you and me . . .'

'Mylo,' Imogen interrupted him, 'let's get one thing straight,' she looked up at him earnestly and said with as much sarcasm as she could inject into her voice, 'there is *no* you and me.'

Mylo began to laugh.

'Touché, lady,' he grinned, glancing over at Candy who was hovering nearby. 'But you're way more my "cup of tea" as they say in England, or so I'm told. She don't mean nothing to me.'

He gave a nonchalant shrug.

'And that's the problem, Mylo,' Imogen raised an eyebrow. '*That's* the problem.'

*

Drying herself and wrapping a cream silk Calvin Klein robe around her, Imogen stepped out onto the 1,500 square foot private terrace and let out a little 'ooh' of pleasure as she surveyed the breathtaking panoramic views of Hollywood that surrounded her.

Hollywood, Los Angeles; the City of Angels, a place where dreams became reality. Imogen looked up at the sign, blinking in the darkness at the enormous iconic letters emblazoned into the horizon. The gentle evening breeze lifted her robe a little and she exhaled softly. Try as she might, she could not seem to shake this terrible sense of melancholy. The feeling of her past becoming her present once more.

Heading back into the penthouse, keen to distract herself from her thoughts, Imogen decided to order room service. A club sandwich perhaps. Settling onto the king-sized bed and pulling a cashmere throw up around her, she switched on the huge flat-screen TV.

Flicking through the channels she stopped at CNN, concerned voices catching her attention. She heard her iPhone beep in her Mulberry tote, momentarily distracting her. The newsreader was saying something about a plane crash. She hit the volume button.

'. . . Virgin Atlantic flight VA02367 from London Heathrow to LAX. Reports suggest a defective latching mechanism in the cargo door was to blame causing the 747 to fail in flight resulting in decompression and loss of hydraulic control. This is one of the worst aircraft accidents of the century, Barbara,' the all-American presenter said gravely, turning to his on-screen partner.

'I know, John. It's shocking stuff,' the schmaltzy blonde responded, equally full of gravitas. '329 dead, including all 15 crew members and 2 pilots . . .'

Imogen put her hand to her mouth in horror as she listened to the on-screen voices. '329 dead . . . no survivors . . .' Her phone beeped again and she scrabbled for her bag, unable to take her eyes from the screen. She had seven new messages! She placed the phone down on the bed and continued to watch the reportage on CNN.

'Jesus,' she shook her head, visibly shocked. All those poor people and their families. That was a lot of dead bodies, she thought, a mix of guilt and relief suddenly engulfing her. She could've been on that flight herself! Imogen shuddered. It didn't bear thinking about.

Shaken by the news, she felt the urge to order something alcoholic, and, picking up the room service menu she briefly scanned it. She'd get Cress something too, some Dom Perignon and a club sandwich with a side of fries perhaps. She was always so vocal about how much she loathed in-flight food and . . . *Plane journey*. London Heathrow to LAX. *No survivors*. And suddenly it hit her like a comet.

'OH MY GOD!' Imogen screamed as the room service menu slid from her grasp. 'CRESSIDA!'

CHAPTER 12

Sammie Grainger looked up from her desk.

'Hey, Sammie, the boss wants a quick word when you've got a mo,' her colleague, Lara Bradshaw poked her head around the door and raised an eyebrow. 'You been missing deadlines again, or what?'

Sammie let out a heavy sigh.

'I take it he's in one of his good moods?' she asked sarcastically, already knowing the answer. Her boss only had one mood that she knew of: surly.

Lara pulled her mouth to the side and widened her eyes.

'And there was me thinking he might be wanting to congratulate me on the *faaabulous* Chelsea Wives piece,' Sammie said theatrically, thumbing the pages of the magazine in front of her until she came to the colourful double page spread.

'Hmm.' Lara leaned over Sammie's shoulder, glanced at the spread and murmured her congratulations. 'Looks great,' she said, picking it up and beginning to read the copy aloud.

'"It's harder than it looks, maintaining oneself to such a high standard", says Calvary Rothschild, one-time Fashion Director on the now defunct *Dernier Cri* magazine, of her twice-weekly hair appointment at Jo Hansford.' Lara mimicked a posh voice, flicking her short brown bobbed hair behind her.

'Oh, the heart simply bleeds for you, darling,' she scoffed, continuing. '"We spent a little over a million pounds on our wedding in Capri," gushes Lady Belmont-Jones. "But it's not about the money at the end of the day. I would've been just as happy with a little do in a local register office".' Lara clutched her chest in mock sincerity. 'Yeah! Right! Course you would, love.'

Sammie laughed.

'Must be nice,' Lara sighed, throwing the magazine back down onto Sammie's desk, 'all that money.'

Sammie cocked her head and shrugged.

'Yeah, but you know, they didn't strike me as being, like, any happier than you or me.'

Lara let out a little whinny of disbelief.

'You sure about that, Sammie?' Lara wasn't convinced. 'I'm off now to interview Boris Johnson's missus about the merits of being married to a mayor and riding bicycles around Shoreditch. Woo-hoo!'

Smiling, Sammie shook her head and watched as Lara flounced from the office. She was a great girl; fun and engaging. Not a bad little journalist either. Even if it had been a healthy dose of nepotism that had got her to where she was now. Thanks to her well-connected media mogul father, there had been no grass route slog for Lara Bradshaw; no mountain of rejection letters or three-year underpaid apprenticeship on some old rag with a readership of one for her. Not like it had been for Sammie Grainger. She'd had to chase her dream with all the fierceness and determination of a Rottweiler going after an intruder in a steak suit.

Sammie had always played down her lowly south London, council estate origins. A privileged background still gave you the professional advantage, even today. But it wasn't just her provenance she was grappling with. Just lately Sammie had been faced with an altogether more intimate struggle: her sexuality.

'My mum is so proud of me. I know it would break her heart. She wants the whole white wedding and kids stuff, you know. I want to let her have that dream a little longer before I take it away from her,' Sammie said to her first and former girlfriend of her decision to stay in the closet. She'd not told anyone at work either, not that it would necessarily be a problem, this was the media after all, it was just that she didn't want her sexual persuasion to become an issue, a potential stumbling block – and she certainly didn't want to be lumbered with all the gay stories either. She had no desire to fly the flag for lesbians.

No, Sammie Grainger was determined that nothing was going to get in the way of her flourishing career. This job at *ESL* was a dream role and would afford her the perfect opportunity to make her name in the mainstream.

So far though, and much to her chagrin, the job wasn't quite living up to expectation. To date, her repertoire had amounted to writing a 'comedy' piece on becoming an extra in a play at The Garrick and more recently, this sycophantic homage to brainless rich cows with more plastic in their Mulberry purses than brain cells in their heads. She doubted Jeremy Paxman was quaking in his boots.

Sammie looked at the glossy spread in front of her, the poised faces of the three well-heeled women staring back up at her, and ran her fingers through her black, choppy Victoria Beckham-esque crop. Her eye was continually drawn to one of the women in particular; Yasmin Belmont-Jones. *Lady Belmont*. She was very attractive in a WAG-ish kind of way. Not really her type though, if indeed she had one, but there was definitely something about her. Something vaguely familiar, she had felt it when they had met too, this odd feeling of déjà vu.

Sammie Grainger never forgot a face, her memory was almost photographic – and as such, this lack of placement was beginning to bother her. Googling Lady Belmont had turned up nothing of note either. Prior to her engagement and subsequent marriage to Lord Jeremy Belmont it was as if she had never existed.

Sammie looked out of her office window at the grey Kensington skyline and pondered, lost in her thoughts for a moment. Her sharp, journalistic nose instinctively told her there was a story behind Yasmin Belmont-Jones, a secret lurking behind that smiling, overly-made-up, oddly familiar face. Sammie was onto something and she knew it. The thought excited her, giving her a rush of adrenalin through her system as potent as a shot of amphetamine.

Her phone buzzed. It was her boss's PA, Helena.

'The big guy wants to see you, Sam,' she said. 'He's in his office and he's getting impatient.'

'I'm walking through the door right now,' Sammie said, standing, straightening out her smart black Reiss trousers and applying a slick of clear gloss.

Taking a marker pen from her desk organiser she drew a large black circle around Lady Yasmin Belmont-Jones's face. The more she looked at her, the more she was convinced she had seen her somewhere before. But where?

CHAPTER 13

'It's just shopping, Calvary. I don't know why you're making such a fuss about it, you usually love nothing more.' Douglas Rothschild turned to face his wife who was sitting at her dressing table, nervously applying and re-applying her make-up, her actions deliberate as she struggled to contain her simmering rage.

'Just shopping! *Just* shopping! Well, that's something, even coming from you, Douglas,' she spat.

'You're being melodramatic,' he replied, dismissively. 'The girl only wants you to go with her, give her a bit of advice. Can't you at least put your own feelings aside for a few hours? It's not so much to ask really, is it?'

Incredulous, Calvary frantically began pulling a brush through her hair, the sharp bristles scratching at her scalp like a thousand fingernails.

'So you actually acknowledge I have feelings to put aside at least,' she snorted. 'That's a first for you, Douglas.'

'How long is this going to go on for?' He rolled his eyes, exasperated. 'The wedding is weeks away yet. Are you planning to keep this up until then?'

Calvary fought down the urge to throw her hairbrush at him.

'If I have my way there won't be a wedding,' she replied casually, her tone belying the anger inside that was threatening to choke her.

'Don't be ridiculous, Calvary,' Douglas whined. 'There's going to be a wedding whether you like it or not. Henry will start asking questions soon if you don't put a stop to this petulant behaviour.'

Calvary could contain herself no longer. 'And what could possibly have happened for me to make such an about-turn, hmm? Nothing to do with finding you and Tamara going at it like a shed door in a gale in this very bed!' She turned round and threw her hairbrush down onto the offending duvet, narrowly missing him. It made a soft whooshing sound as it sank into the goose Yves Dolorme eiderdown.

'Why can't you just move on?' he sighed. 'I've apologised for what happened, after all. I mean, I realise it can't have been nice for you but . . .'

'*Nice*?' Calvary growled. '*Nice*?' She shook her head in despair. 'I don't believe I am hearing this, Douglas.'

'Look,' his face softened now, giving her a glimpse of the handsome man he had once been, the one she had fallen so hopelessly, so tragically in love with all those years ago. 'Can't we just put the whole horrid business behind us and move on?' he implored. 'Our eldest son's getting married in a few months' time. The least we can do is give him the support he – and Tamara, for that matter – need right now.'

Calvary threw her head back and let out a hollow, shrill laugh, causing him to wince.

'You are something else, Douglas Rothschild, do you know that? Giving me, *me,* all the spiel about our eldest son getting married, how we must support him, be there for him like good parents.' She threw her hands up to the ceiling. 'It would be bloody laughable were it not so utterly disgusting!' She faced him now, anger emanating from her like sound waves as she stood.

'I'll give that little madam some advice alright,' Calvary continued, the veins in her neck protruding like rivers of poison. 'How about not fucking one's prospective father-in-law behind one's fiancé's back? That's a start, isn't it?'

Douglas glared back at his wife. He'd eaten more than his fair share of humble pie as far as he was concerned and now he was growing impatient with her histrionics.

'Calvary, this has to stop,' he commanded. 'I told you it was nothing. That I was sorry. It was a silly mistake. We'd had too much to drink one afternoon and got a bit carried away, that was all. As far as I'm concerned, it never happened.'

Calvary laughed in derision.

'You know, Douglas, even if that were true, *you* should have known better. But you just can't help yourself. You never could keep it zipped in your pants, could you? Even your own son's wife-to-be isn't off limits. You disgust me, Douglas Rothschild. Disgust me!' Calvary glowered at her husband with a fierceness he had never seen in her before and his heart sank. He had a horrible feeling that this time it was going to take more than an antique sideboard from Sotheby's to sort this blasted mess out.

The last thing Douglas wanted was a scandal that would invariably lead to divorce. Thank goodness that little receptionist strumpet he'd been seeing to every now and again had given him the nod, allowing him to get a head start on squirrelling away some of his assets. This thought cheered him instantly. Once that wife of his realised she'd be left without a bean she'd soon put an end to any ideas of divorce. Douglas knew her too well; she may be able to give him up, but give up the money? Never.

Why couldn't she just bloody well do the same with this one? He knew it was a bit of an ask, what with it being

Henry's fiancée and all but still, it was only the one time and hardly his fault; the girl had given him the come on, all big eyed and heavy breasted, parading herself around in front of him in barely-there outfits, sighing breathlessly as she spoke in husky, dulcet tones, licking her glossy lips at him. What was a man supposed to do? She'd been as game as he was. More so, in fact. And on top of things he was now having to contend with her as well, coming to him all teary-eyed and remorseful, terrified that Calvary would put the mockers on her much anticipated nuptials to his son. Even the greatest sex in the world wasn't worth this much aggravation.

Calvary stared at her husband contemptuously, wondering how she had ever come to marry such a complete and utter shit.

'I'm taking the dogs for a walk,' she announced, her voice cracking like the embers of a bonfire as she pulled on a Brora cashmere cardigan. She could no longer stand to be in the same room as him.

With a heavy heart, Calvary knew she would have to live with his dirty little secret. Swallow it down like a particularly bitter pill. At least for now . . .

'Listen,' Douglas made to reach out for her hand but she snatched it away. 'The Ivanovs have said we can have their house up in Lake Como for a couple of weeks – why don't you go? Get away for a while, take some friends with you. Have a spa break, or whatever it is that you women do. It'll do you good to clear your head a bit.'

As usual, he was trying to buy back some kind of equilibrium between them, though secretly Calvary was a little taken with this suggestion. Perhaps a holiday *was* just what she needed. She'd invite Imogen and maybe even Yasmin Belmont-Jones too. She had grown rather fond of her in recent weeks and was sure Imogen wouldn't mind if the girl tagged along.

Imogen Forbes was Calvary's oldest and truest friend. Having been introduced at a rather stuffy charity event by their respective husbands some twelve years ago, Calvary often joked that their meeting was one of the best things to have come out of her marriage to Douglas. Though in fact, it was no joke at all.

Hailing from similar backgrounds – the worlds of fashion and modelling – the two women had struck up an instant rapport and had spent the entire evening in deep conversation and fits of giggles. They had both left the party that evening feeling as if they had met a kindred spirit. Over the years their friendship had strengthened and deepened into something they both cherished dearly. Like sisters, they bickered occasionally, but were fiercely loyal and protective towards one another.

'You could fly out next week, after the ball,' Douglas suggested, hopefully. 'Relax, sun yourself for a few days. Just wait until you see the Ivanovs' place; it's absolutely spectacular.' He detected the slightest flicker of interest in Calvary's eyes, and felt himself relax a little.

'I'll arrange for you all to fly out on the jet,' he said in a childlike voice, attempting to lock the deal down, 'and,' he added as an extra sweetener, 'you can have free run of the Black Amex card.' He sang the last bit like a game show host enticing a contestant to gamble for the big prize.

Calvary watched as her body visibly sagged in front of the mirror. She felt utterly defeated.

'I'll take Tamara shopping tomorrow,' she said quietly with her back to him, tucking her jeans into her Tod's leather riding boots.

A small, satisfied smile crept across Douglas's face and he had to stop himself from letting out an audible sigh of relief.

'That's it, old girl,' he said, immediately buoyed. He could go and have that game of golf now without all this nasty business hanging over him, threatening to put him off his swing.

'Get yourself something fantastic for Forbes's do as well, spend what you like.'

Calvary grabbed a packet of Vogue cigarettes from the stash in her dressing table and threw them into her Smythson tote.

'Oh, don't you worry, Douglas,' she said, brushing his shoulder with her own as she flounced past him. 'I damn well intend to.'

CHAPTER 14

Yasmin Belmont-Jones hated funerals. Even more so than most people. They reminded her of her sister. And anything that reminded her of her sister hurt. It hurt like hell.

Still, she had to hand it to her, Yasmin thought as she looked around the magnificent church filled with celebrities and VIPs, whoever this Cressida Lucas woman was, she sure was one hell of a well-connected lady.

It had been at Calvary Rothschild's blithe insistence that she attend today's ceremony.

'But I'd never even met the woman when she was alive,' Yasmin had protested. 'It doesn't feel right me being there.'

'Minor details,' Calvary had replied dismissively. 'It's the perfect setting to introduce your new look to society, show the press – and your detractors – that you won't be down-beaten by their pernicious comments. Besides, it's not as if the deceased will mind, is it?' she added facetiously, casting an approving eye over the demure Victoria Beckham black shift dress that she had cajoled Yasmin into wearing for the occasion. She was determined to rid the girl of her Chav-Sloane persuasions if it killed her.

Yasmin was silently horrified. Calvary viewed today as little more than a photo opportunity! Reluctantly though, she also knew that she had a point; she had to brazen it out in front of the press, who had so far been most unforgiving about her. Hiding herself away would only serve as fuel to their ever increasing interest. The last thing she needed was them digging for dirt.

Despite her earlier misgivings, as Yasmin looked around at the church humming full of A-listers, she was almost glad she had made the decision to come after all.

'All these celebrities . . .' Yasmin whispered into Calvary's ear, trying not to sound as star struck as she actually was. 'It's like '*An Audience with . . .*'

A regal looking lady in a huge avant-garde hat with a giant lobster on top of it passed them and took a seat in an adjacent pew.

Calvary raised a critical eyebrow.

'If it blows off, dear, I wouldn't chase it,' she remarked sardonically. Yasmin stifled a snigger. Calvary could be quite amusing when she hit her stride. If she wasn't careful she might actually start liking the woman.

'Cal,' Imogen came towards them, greeting her warmly with a big hug, 'I'm so glad you're here,' she said, enjoying the reassuring warmth of her friend's embrace. Calvary brushed an imaginary tear from Imogen's face and smiled affectionately at her. She was dying to ask her friend if she'd heard any news about the campaign from L'Orelie yet but thought it an inappropriate moment, given the situation.

'How are you feeling, darling?' Calvary asked earnestly. 'Nervous about the eulogy?'

'Nervous?' Imogen spluttered. 'That's the understatement of the century. My guts are in knots, Cal. I feel sick. I'm really not sure I can do it, not in front of all these people.'

'Oh, nonsense!' Calvary said in that dismissive way of hers that stopped short of telling you to pull yourself together. 'Of course you can do it, can't she, Yasmin?' Calvary briefly turned to her for confirmation.

'Er, yes,' Yasmin nodded. 'Of course. It'll be fine,' she smiled weakly at Imogen as she remembered her own sister's eulogy all those years ago. She had cried all the way through her speech, great heart-wrenching sobs that had echoed around the rundown old church. Just thinking about it turned her mood black.

'Thank you,' Imogen smiled gratefully at Yasmin, taking the tips of her long, French manicured fingers briefly in her own. The press may have portrayed the new Lady Belmont in a less than favourable light, calling her a cold, gold-digging opportunist, but Imogen had seen flashes of a kind and generous soul on the occasions they had met, which made her think they had misjudged her. 'I realise you've only come here today to support me,' she addressed Yasmin with a grateful smile, 'and I can't tell you how much I appreciate it.'

Yasmin swallowed back a pang of guilt.

Taking a nervous seat, Imogen began going over the speech she had prepared for today's service in her mind. Only she was distracted by a conversation taking place between two women in front of her.

'You know, I heard that she was going under financially . . .' one of the women whispered a little too loudly.

'Who? Cressida Lucas? Really?' the other replied conspiratorially, shuffling in closer towards her.

'Uh-huh. Bailiffs at the door of her Mayfair apartment and *everything*. Died in debt by all accounts.'

The woman tutted and shook her head.

'How positively awful.'

'I heard she was in the red to the tune of at least five mil.'

The other woman whistled.

'Bet she's glad she's dead. I mean, who'd want to live with the shame of having their assets repossessed?'

'Quite.'

'At least this way her debt is automatically written off, isn't it?'

'Don't ask me how it all works, darling. I know nothing about money, other than how to spend it!'

They both began to laugh then, and Imogen cleared her throat loudly, causing the two women to turn round and look at her sheepishly.

Imogen was hardly surprised by what she'd overheard. Cressida had lurched from one financial crisis to another her whole life. But being the resourceful woman she was, or at least had been, she had always found a way out of it.

Imogen smoothed out the creases in her dress and sighed. She had worn a scarlet Chanel shift today in Cressida's honour, teamed with black studded leather gloves and sky-high Louboutin platform pumps. Cressida would have wanted a splash of colour. She'd always hated black.

As she stepped up to the pulpit, Imogen's legs almost buckled beneath her. Clearing her throat, she took a deep breath as she looked out at the sea of people, suddenly wishing she'd had a stiff vodka cocktail to take the edge off her nerves.

'The day I met Cressie – as she was known to me – was the day my life changed forever . . .'

As Imogen began her speech, Sammie Grainger slipped inside the church and scanned the vast congregation. She had never seen so many celebrities all in one room together before and felt a small frisson of excitement. Spotting Yasmin Belmont, she made her way over and sat down beside Calvary, who turned to look her up and down like she was something the cat had dragged in.

'What are *you* doing here?' Calvary hissed. 'I thought *Hello!* had the monopoly on today.'

'I'm here for the canapés and champagne at Claridge's afterwards,' Sammie quipped.

'Hmm, I'll bet you are!' Calvary retorted.

Out of the corner of her eye, Sammie watched Yasmin Belmont-Jones surreptitiously.

Those icy blue eyes and that distinctive upturned nose. She looked so familiar, it was like that elusive word on the tip of your tongue.

*

'That was wonderful,' a young, attractive Asian man congratulated Imogen as she stepped down from the pulpit to rapturous applause. 'Really wonderful. Cressida would've been so touched.'

'You think so? Oh, thank you,' Imogen said, exhaling loudly. She was glad it was over. It had been such an honour to be asked to speak at the service but her nerves were shot to pieces and she needed a drink.

'It's Imogen, isn't it? Imogen Forbes?'

'Yes,' she smiled, shaking the man's hand.

'Well, I thought you captured Cressida's essence perfectly,' he reassured her. 'And I know she thought the world of you. She talked about you a lot, especially recently. Said you were about to "go massive" again, or something, though I assume she meant your career and not you personally.' He laughed, inwardly cursed himself. Why did he always have to make a prick of himself in front of attractive women by putting his great big size elevens in his mouth?

Imogen smiled modestly.

'I'm sorry,' she said. 'I didn't catch your name.'

The man shook his head in consternation.

'Please forgive me,' he apologised, finally releasing her hand. 'The name's Metesh Ali. Doctor Metesh Ali.'

'Ahh,' Imogen smiled in recognition. *The handsome young doctor who had broken the bad news.*

'Cressida mentioned you.'

'She did?'

Dr Ali looked genuinely delighted at this revelation.

'Yes. When she told me about the whole horrible cancer business.' Imogen lowered her voice. 'I didn't mention it in the speech of course, I know Cressida wanted it kept a secret. She would've hated any kind of pity.'

Dr Ali blinked at Imogen, a blank expression on his face.

'Cancer business?'

'Yes,' she returned his quizzical look with one of her own. 'I don't think I could've faced watching her die of such a horrible disease. I mean, I know she only had months to go, so perhaps, thanks to some sort of twisted fate, it was better this way – quicker and more dignified at least.'

Dr Ali pulled his head into his chin.

'Months to go?' he said, brow furrowed. 'I assure you, she was in perfect health at her last full check-up just a few weeks ago. Passed her MOT – as she called it – with flying colours,' he chuckled. 'There was definitely no cancer.'

Imogen felt her heartbeat accelerate. What was he talking about?

'You must be mistaken,' the doctor said, watching the colour drain from Imogen's face, wondering if this extremely beautiful woman in front of him was all the ticket. Grief could do some truly odd things to people, he'd seen it happen.

'Yes. You're right. My mistake.' She composed herself. 'Please excuse me, Dr Ali. It was very nice chatting with you.'

He watched her as she strutted off, a vision in red, her long legs striding purposefully away from him. Beautiful, he thought. Mad as a March hare, but utterly, breathtakingly beautiful.

*

Claridge's was perfect. Just what Cressida would've wanted, Imogen thought as she watched the congregation in all its sartorial glory sipping Veuve Clicquot and nibbling on canapés as they mingled and tried not to smile too much.

As she gulped back her fourth glass of champagne, desperately trying to blot out the conversation she'd had with Dr Ali, Imogen scoured her racing mind for a justifiable reason as to why Cressida might possibly have told such an abhorrent lie. And then it had struck her like a wayward freight train, the full force of the realisation almost physically knocking her backwards onto the banquette.

When Cressida had initially asked her to test for the shoot, Imogen had been adamant that she had no desire to return to modelling. And so Cressida, presumably in desperation, had spun her a terrible lie to get her out of her financial woes. After all, how could Imogen have refused her after that bombshell?

Draining her champagne flute, she swiped another from a passing waiter and threw it back. It was all starting to make much more sense. She did not know why she was so shocked. After all, Cressida Lucas was one of life's survivors. She'd resort to anything to haul her sorry ass from the doldrums. Though she had really scraped the barrel this time. Imogen felt nauseous with a mix of anger and despair. Cressida must've really been on the bones of her backside to have lied in such a despicable way, yet still it was pretty unforgivable.

Out of the corner of her eye, Yasmin watched Imogen knock back the champagne and, noting her pained expression, willed the stab of pity she felt in her ribs to subside.

Making friends had never been part of her plan. Yet seeing the look of despair on Imogen's face had made her want to go to her and comfort her, as a friend would. Yasmin, above all people, knew all about losing someone you loved. The desperate emptiness they left behind, like a hole in your heart, and the need to blot it all out with anything that could help numb the pain.

'Get me out of here, Cal,' Imogen said as she approached them through the crowd, her eyes a bloodshot red to match her dress. 'I can't face it. I think I just need to be alone . . . all these people . . .'

'Yes, yes, of course,' Calvary discarded her glass instantly and gently led her friend away from the congregation. 'I'll arrange for my driver to take you home, darling, it'll be OK,' she comforted her. 'It's been a difficult day.'

Yasmin followed them outside and watched as Calvary poured a tipsy and emotional Imogen into an awaiting chauffeur-driven Bentley. She imagined concern would be etched on Calvary's brow, if only she could move it.

'I'm sorry, Cal.' Imogen sniffed back the tears she could no longer contain, her mascara-smudged face finally giving way to her conflicting emotions.

'Oh, darling.' Calvary crouched down and wrapped her arms tightly around her friend. 'You have nothing to be sorry about, nothing at all,' she said, kissing the top of her head like a child.

Yasmin couldn't help but be touched by the scene in front of her. A part of her even felt a pang of jealousy. She had never experienced friendship on such a deep level herself, choosing instead to keep her distance from people, cutting them off before they got too close. To let someone in meant to trust them and Yasmin trusted no one. As far as she was concerned, it was better that way.

As the Bentley pulled away, taking Imogen with it, Yasmin turned to a concerned looking Calvary.

'Will she be OK?' she found herself asking.

'Of course,' Calvary said, her face softening into a genuine smile. 'She's got her friends to help her through her grief – us,' she added.

Yasmin nodded, part elated and part horrified at being included in that statement.

'Right then,' Calvary snapped back to her usual brusque, no-nonsense manner. 'Let's go back inside and see if we can't get up a few of these ghastly people's noses, shall we?'

She took Yasmin's arm and linked it proprietarily in her own.

'Lead the way,' Yasmin said, suddenly grateful that she was there.

'No please, after you,' Calvary remarked with trademark dryness. 'After all, *ladies* first.'

CHAPTER 15

Taking her dogs for a stroll through Chelsea, Calvary pulled her Brora cardigan around her like a shield to ward off the light evening chill and bristled. Summer was proving to be one of utter discontent – her marriage was in shreds and she'd already been to one funeral and she sensed she would have to dig deeper than ever before if she was to find the strength to get through it.

'Beluga! Cashmere! Here, girls, here!' She watched with satisfaction as her beloved Labradors bounded off into the open space of Duke of York Square.

It was these simple things that made her truly happy; watching her dogs playing as she sat opposite the impressive Saachi Gallery; the strategically placed up-lighting illuminating the trees around her, the sound of foreign voices wafting through the air as people took an evening walk or grabbed a coffee outside Valerie's Gelateria.

Calvary lit a Vogue cigarette and watched as the blue smoke curled up into the air around her. Her heart was here, in Chelsea. She knew these streets like she knew her own children; the very pavement she trod felt like her own flesh and blood.

Douglas could take everything from her; her dignity, her

standing in society, her material possessions, but he could never take her beloved Chelsea – for her, Chelsea was the jewel in the city's decadent crown. Where else could you find fresh bread next to Bottega Veneta?

'Beautiful evening, huh?'

Calvary spun round, her thoughts rudely interrupted. She had not noticed the young man sitting a few seats down from her on the bench.

'Yes,' she smiled politely. She really wasn't in the mood to make small talk to strangers. To talk, full stop.

'I love it here,' he said. 'It's a great place to sit and people watch.'

Calvary nodded silently, not wanting to encourage him further.

'Or just sit quietly with your thoughts,' he added, as much to himself as to her.

'Like I was trying to do?' she retorted, pithily.

The young man stared ahead of him silently and Calvary berated herself. It was terribly rude of her to have snapped like that. After all, he was only trying to be polite. It wasn't his fault she was married to such a bastard.

Beluga began foraging around in a bin, emptying its contents with her cold, wet nose, littering the otherwise pristine square with old McDonald's drink cartons and yesterday's evening newspaper. Cashmere sauntered over, eager to join in with her sister's mischief.

'Beluga! No! Beluga . . . Cashmere! Come here!' Calvary called out hoarsely to her dogs.

'Naughty girls!' The dogs did not even look up. Sighing, Calvary rose to stand but the man next to her began making a whistling sound and within seconds the dogs had bounded over towards him, their tongues hanging out, tails wagging in excited unison behind them.

'Hey, ladies,' the young man said, stroking their eager heads as they sniffed him affectionately.

Calvary flashed him a wide-eyed look.

'That's remarkable,' she said, impressed. 'Are you an expert or something?'

The young man shrugged.

'I just like dogs . . . and they seem to like me,' he laughed as Cashmere jumped up onto him and began licking his face.

'So I see!' Calvary laughed too, a little embarrassed, as she clapped at Cashmere to leave the stranger alone.

There was a slight pause before Calvary said, 'I do apologise for being so rude just then.'

The man turned to face her. She guessed he wasn't much older than Tom. He had a distinctive face that was warm and inviting, from what she could see of it anyway, most of it was covered by a floppy-fringed hairstyle. 'That's OK,' he said graciously. 'Sometimes I don't feel like talking either.'

Calvary smiled. Though she really did not much feel up to it, talking to someone was probably exactly what she needed right now and he did have such a terribly inviting manner about him.

'Are you local?' she asked, detecting a slight accent; Australian perhaps?

'Yeah, if you call South Africa local,' he smiled again, displaying a set of neat white teeth.

'Oh!' Calvary remarked, a little surprised. 'Beautiful country. Been there many times.'

'You have?' He swivelled round a little to face her properly. 'Whereabouts?'

There was no going back now, a conversation had ignited and so she resigned herself to it.

'Oh, The Karoo, Cape Town, Johannesburg – a few places.'

'No way!' The young man stared at her wide-eyed. 'I'm from Cape Town!' He looked impressed.

Calvary gave a modest smile. 'I've shot there, on location. Beautiful place.'

'Films?' he enquired, his head slightly cocked to one side.

'Fashion shoots,' she replied, hoping this wouldn't disappoint him.

'Yes,' he nodded, casting an admiring glance in her direction. 'Of course.'

'So you're here as a student?' Calvary asked. She had noticed him staring at her intently and suddenly felt rather self-conscious.

'I make my living as a personal trainer,' he said.

'Really?' Calvary tried to conceal her surprise. He was the least-looking personal trainer she had ever encountered, though admittedly, it was getting rather dark now and she could not fully inspect his physique hidden beneath all the layers of clothing.

'But really I'm an artist,' he said, his accent more apparent now that she could place it.

'An artist,' Calvary nodded. 'Oh, how marvellous. Graphic or fine?'

'I paint people. There's more life, more emotion in a face than in anything else on earth.'

Calvary smiled at this observation.

'So, what can you see in mine?' she asked, indulging herself.

'Pain,' he shot back immediately. 'Anguish. Hurt. Shame – it's all there,' he said, matter-of-fact.

Calvary recoiled in shock. She had no idea it was so plainly obvious.

'Good Lord,' she responded, unsure whether to take offence or not. 'You can see all that just by looking at me?'

The man gave her a wry smile. 'Josia Jarvis,' he said, taking her hand and shaking it. His hand felt soft and warm in hers and Calvary felt a little frisson as he released it.

'Calvary Rothschild,' she murmured in reply, still reeling from his face-reading revelation.

'Wanna talk about it?' he asked, looking at her and smiling. He could tell she had money; it was all over her; the clothes, the jewellery, even her hair looked expensive. On the surface she was a typical looking Chelsea Sloane, of the like he trained on a daily basis, only there was something indiscernible about this particular one that was not typical of her kind.

Calvary shook her head.

'No offence, Josia,' she said, 'but I don't think it's anything you can help me with.'

'Try me, I've been told I'm a good listener,' he encouraged.

'It's personal,' Calvary explained, fidgeting uncomfortably on the bench.

'Well, of course it is,' Josia shrugged. 'Everything is personal.'

Calvary dropped her shoulders. Why was he so interested in her problems anyway?

'You don't *have* to tell me,' he said, as if reading her thoughts. 'It's just that I sense you *want* to.'

Calvary snorted with mirth.

'You certainly sense a lot for a young man, don't you?'

Josia shrugged again.

'Young, old, somewhere in between, we're animals at the end of the day – we sense everything.'

Calvary surreptitiously rolled her eyes at this cod-philosophy. He had an air of confidence about him, like he knew some big secret that she didn't.

She really wasn't sure whether she was warming to the stranger or not. Still, what did it matter? It was unlikely she would ever see him again. And perhaps he was right. Perhaps sharing her problems might help.

'It's my husband,' she said quietly. 'He's a complete and utter bastard.'

Josia looked at Calvary, his expression unchanged.

'Why's that?' he asked, his tone sitting just in the right place between concern and intrigue.

Calvary had never done anything like this in her life, opening up to a complete stranger, telling them her most intimate personal business. Suddenly she felt vulnerable and exposed.

'Aside from spending our whole married life cheating on me with other women – notably younger ones I must add – I recently walked in on him screwing our son's fiancée whom he is due to marry in a matter of months.' Calvary took an audible breath.

Josia blinked.

'Jesus that's harsh.'

'Ha!' Calvary threw her head back releasing her trademark laugh. 'If you think that's *harsh* then get this . . .' She was on a roll now, forgetting where she was and who she was talking to. 'I can't even divorce him!'

'Why?' Josia asked, watching her intently.

'Because he's embezzled all his goddamn money, that's why. Hidden it from me. He'll declare himself bankrupt and I'll get nothing!'

Josia shrugged.

'But you could still divorce him.'

Calvary laughed again. Harder this time.

'What, and lose everything? I think not!'

'Sounds as though you have nothing to lose and everything to gain.' Josia flicked his long fringe away from his dark eyes.

'No. You don't understand,' she retorted, a little irritated by such a sweeping statement. 'It's not as cut and dried as that.'

'Isn't it?' Josia looked a little puzzled.

Calvary noticed he was a day or two off clean shaven and that he was much more attractive up close. Like a young Johnny Depp. She bristled, turning to face him.

'I have given everything to this man; the best years of my bloody life. I have born him two beautiful children and have remained faithful to him throughout our marriage – not that I haven't had the opportunity to stray,' she felt compelled to add.

Josia smiled.

'He owes me big time. And now he owes our son as well. His own son. How could he do it to his own child?' Calvary's voice was shaking now and she felt the light touch of the stranger's fingers on her arm. Oddly, for someone who fiercely guarded her personal space, she did not seem to mind.

'Be not afraid of growing slowly, be afraid of standing still,' Josia spoke softly, almost in a whisper.

Calvary turned to him.

'And what the hell's that supposed to mean?'

'It's pretty self-explanatory,' he replied calmly.

'Not to me it isn't!' she interjected, suddenly feeling cross with herself. What had she been thinking? Now he was spouting some irritating New Age crap at her that made no sense at all.

'It's a Chinese proverb actually,' Josia said quietly.

'Well, thanks a million,' Calvary snapped derisively. 'Next time I need advice I'll buy a bag of fortune cookies.'

Josia blinked at her. He seemed indifferent and this only served to annoy her further.

As she stood to leave, he noticed her hands were shaking.

'Well, I'd like to say it was nice to meet you,' Calvary blathered, embarrassed and upset with herself. 'But I'm not sure that would be entirely true.'

Josia looked up at her with intense, dark eyes. Infuriatingly, his expression was still unchanged.

'Beluga! Cashmere!' she called out to her dogs who, sensing playtime was well and truly over, trotted over to their mistress.

'Forgive me,' she coughed, turning away from him, ready to leave. 'I should've known better than to pour my heart out to a complete stranger – and one so young. It was a silly idea.'

'I'm thirty-four,' he replied, a look of bemusement on his boyish face. This woman was troubled, he thought. Really troubled. 'And a stranger is simply a friend you have not yet met.'

Calvary laughed, a mocking sound that rang through the air like a bell tolling.

'You've been reading the back of too many cereal packets.' She raised her eyebrows, though she did not really know why she was mocking him, it was obvious that he was only trying to be friendly. And she was surprised by his age. She really had thought he was much younger.

'You know, I see something else in your face,' he said, hoping to stall this caustic, enchanting woman a moment longer. He did not want her to leave their encounter feeling more upset than when she had arrived.

'Don't tell me,' she deadpanned, 'Botox?'

He didn't laugh.

'Kindness, selflessness – and beauty. You really are a very beautiful woman, Calvary Rothschild.'

The fact that he had remembered her name – and then used it in such a familiar way – stopped her dead in her tracks. Unable to make eye contact with him for fear of blushing, something Calvary had not done in years, she turned on her heels.

'I'd like to paint you sometime,' he called out after her. 'I think you'd really be something on canvas.' He watched her as she stalked off, her dogs trotting haphazardly behind her. 'Really something,' he said quietly as she shrank into the distance.

CHAPTER 16

Sammie Grainger stared at the cardboard boxes in front of her. It wasn't a lot to show for twenty-four years on the planet, she decided, as she stacked the last of them, but at least she wouldn't even need to enlist the help of a friend to shift this lot. She was moving onwards and upwards at least, waving goodbye to her old student lifestyle and saying hello to independence, to her own studio crash pad in Earls Court, no less.

Sammie exhaled deeply. She had thought this day would never come, but now that it had, she was beginning to have some reservations. Would she be lonely all on her own?

The people she lived with, her housemates – two guys and a girl – had started out as perfect strangers, thrown together at random, all sharing a need to find shelter in this crazy, relentless metropolis they found themselves calling home. Now though, they had become friends, their lives forever intrinsically linked by circumstance. And she would miss them all.

As if on cue, Krista burst into Sammie's room. As usual, she didn't bother knocking.

Krista was a particularly vivacious twenty-three-year-old blonde Aussie girl with beach babe sun-kissed yellow hair and a smile as wide as the Thames. She was enviously unself-conscious and boundlessly enthusiastic about everything, even her overworked and underpaid barmaid's job in a local backpackers' bar in West Kensington. Life according to Krista was always 'awesome' and in the three years that Sammie had known her she had never once seen her in anything other than an effervescent, upbeat mood.

'So you're all packed then, hon?' Krista nodded in the direction of Sammie's meagre collection of boxes.

'Uh-huh,' Sammie sighed. 'Not much to show for my life is it?'

Krista shrugged. 'Who wants baggage? Besides, it saves on removal costs. Aw,' she cooed, picking up Sammie's old moth-eaten teddy bear from the top of an open box. 'I see you're taking Tinker with you. I was hoping you might leave him,' she said, clutching him to her chest. 'He's kinda cute.'

'Not a chance,' Sammie smiled. 'Wherever I go, Tinker goes. It's the law.'

Krista beamed her mile-wide smile and began digging around in the open box, hoping to unearth a little keepsake in memory of her favourite housemate.

'So, you'll be inviting us round to help christen the new pad, of course.'

'Of course,' Sammie nodded, fretting at the thought of the damage to her new carpet already.

'And you promise to call me and tell me all about this swanky party you're off to. Ford's thingemywotsit.'

Sammie giggled. 'Forbes's Annual Ball.'

'That's the one. Man, your job is just the coolest.'

Sammie had had to stop herself from openly whooping for joy when old Sasquatch had invited her to be his plus one at Forbes's Annual Ball.

'I like to give the younger members of my team the opportunity to come along to these events,' Pugh, her hirsute editor, had said as he eyed his latest recruit with a quietly lascivious eye. 'It's good practice, great for making contacts. I was impressed with your Chelsea Wives piece, it showed a maturity beyond your years. I think it's time for you to take the next step, Samantha,' he had said, wondering how many bottles of Chateau Margaux he would have to pour down her neck before she let him screw her.

'I don't know what to say!' Sammie had had to stop herself from leaning over her editor's desk and planting a big smacker on his swarthy old face. Perhaps he wasn't such an old bastard after all. This was the best news she had heard all year, bar actually getting the job on *ESL* itself of course, and what was even better about it was that Yasmin Belmont-Jones was undoubtedly going to be there.

'Lady Belmont-Jones' had become Sammie's secret obsession. Ever since their first meeting she had almost turned herself inside out trying to fathom just how and why this aristocratic young woman seemed so familiar to her. Not that she'd let on to old Sasquatch of course, she was going to make this *her* story – for she was absolutely convinced there was one and sensed that if she could just get to the bottom of it, it would be the making of her career.

*

Krista pulled out a wallet of old photographs and brazenly began to look through them. She had no sense of privacy.

'Oh my God!' Krista began to laugh, 'is this you as a kid?'

She held up a picture of a young teenage girl with mad curls and braces who was smiling up into the camera and giving the peace sign.

Sammie lurched forward in an attempt to snatch the offending photo from her but Krista was way too quick for her and held it high above her head.

'Give me that!' Sammie cried, mildly annoyed and embarrassed.

'Nah-ah!' Krista teased, flicking through the rest of them. 'What else have we got here?'

'Krista, give them back!' Sammie pleaded, trying to grab hold of her friend's wrist.

'Look at you in this one! Wow! You look so different, Sam, like a proper black girl with cornrows and shit.' Krista shook her head and giggled. 'Man, you know I forget when I look at you that you've got a touch of the tar brush in there.'

Sammie felt a little offended but hid it. She was used to such comments.

'Is this you with your mum?' Krista asked, holding up a picture of Sammie and another girl standing next to a pretty, well-dressed woman.

Sammie sighed. It was futile trying to prevent Krista from looking so she went along with it, standing next to her as she shuffled through the pictures.

'No, that's my friend Rachel's mum. Jesus, what was her surname? Rachel . . . Rachel . . . Adsmith, yeah, that was it. Her mum ran the local youth centre. We hung out there most nights when we were kids. There wasn't much else to do where I came from.'

'How old were you in this one?' Krista asked, giggling at a snapshot of Sammie dressed in a pair of baggy jeans with braces and DMs. 'Bit of a tomboy, weren't you?'

Sammie blushed. She hadn't seen these photographs in years, had forgotten they even existed.

'I must've been about ten there. Nine or ten perhaps.'

'God. That's like, fifteen or so years ago, dude! I swear I don't remember anything that far back.'

'That'll be all the Thai grass you smoke,' Sammie deadpanned.

Krista laughed and rolled her eyes.

'You look like a boy.'

Sammie felt herself blush again.

'It was the fashion!' she protested. 'Look!' Sammie replied defensively. 'Look at what everyone else is wearing!'

She took the bunch of photographs from Krista now and began searching through them herself.

'Look, see!' she said, finding a group shot that showed a bunch of kids all together, smiling and pulling faces at the camera.

'There's Susan Roper in the stripy jumpsuit, rocking the Andy Pandy vibe, and there's Caroline Baker – she was another estate kid, thought she was a hard nut – she's the one in the England football shirt, and . . . Oh, God!' Sammie stared open-mouthed at the picture.

'What?' Krista said, sensing real shock in her friend's voice. 'What is it?'

Clutching the photograph, Sammie's hand began to shake.

'Jesus, it can't be . . .' Her eyes were focussed on the face of a young, mousey brown-haired girl wearing a tatty pair of tight jeans and an old smiley-face t-shirt. She was standing to the far left of the shot, a little further back from the others. Her face wasn't as sharp as the others but Sammie recognised it instantly. The prominent cheekbones, the rosebud lips and those sad, yet mesmerising sapphire blue eyes. It was her, alright.

'Well, I'll be damned . . .' Sammie whispered aloud, lost in the moment, forgetting that Krista was even in the room.

'What, what will you be damned?' Krista was insistent now, desperately trying to see whatever it was that had got Sammie so unusually worked up.

'I knew that I had seen her somewhere before.'

'Seen *who*?' Krista was almost beside herself now.

'Let's just say you've helped me solve a riddle,' she said, feeling a potent rush of excitement.

'You *talk* in riddles,' Krista said, raising her eyebrows.

Sammie smiled obliviously, unable to remove her gaze from the picture.

Well, well, well, she thought to herself as she gripped the dog-eared photo. Her instincts had been correct all along.

Krista, having lost interest already, was busying herself with Sammie's CD collection now.

'Do you think you'll still remember *me* in fifteen years' time?' she pouted, as she held up an old Smiths CD.

Sammie stared up at her friend and smiled so broadly that her cheeks hurt.

'Oh, I think so,' she said, reassuring her. 'I never forget a face.'

CHAPTER 17

Imogen held her breath as the chauffeur-driven Bentley drew up towards the magnificent rose-coloured up-lit splendour of Lancaster House, its wheels making a satisfactory crunch against asphalt as it came to a halt.

'Sir, madam. We've arrived,' their driver announced.

'Jolly good, Raoul, but give it five minutes will you. I just need to gather my thoughts.' Sebastian snapped, his mood tetchy. He had been fretting the whole journey there, barking last minute orders into his phone to his numerous minions, his voice hoarse with discord. In truth, however, as much as anything else, he wanted to make sure there were as many paparazzi as possible waiting for him when he made his grand entrance.

'Those bloody flowers better have turned up,' he spat, tapping his fingers nervously against the leather seat. 'I'll have that Mark Wainwright out of business if not.'

'Stay calm, Seb. You've got Janet and a whole team of people to worry about all that sort of thing for you. Just try and concentrate on having a good evening.' Imogen did her best to placate her husband, even if a little bit of her was relishing his anxiety.

It was the same thing every year when it came to the

night of the annual ball, Sebastian working himself up into a lather of epic proportions over the tiniest detail. Only this year he seemed even more fretful than usual.

Sebastian ignored her.

'I said white and green *and* blue hydrangeas in the foyer,' he hissed, glimpsing up at the pastel coloured blooms that were just visible from inside the huge entrance. 'Bloody great faggot. You can never trust those gays. Too busy preening themselves in the mirror to know what's what.'

Imogen sighed and looked out of the car window. It had been a hellish few weeks, what with losing Cressida, and then the bombshell discovery about the terrible lie. Now, on top of everything, she had to endure the chore that was the annual ball, where false smiles and strained conversation were the order of the day. Just thinking about the evening ahead exhausted her.

'I just hope he hasn't mucked up the Dorchester,' Sebastian spat. 'I said a thousand *white* roses for the prince. I mean, what part of one thousand white roses could the man not understand? Bloody fool's one teddy bear short of a picnic.'

'Why all the flowers anyway?' Imogen queried. 'Bit over the top, isn't it?' Sebastian cursed himself for having mentioned it. He had wanted it kept quiet that it was his hospitality that Prince Saud and his entourage would be enjoying during their stay in London, lest anyone think – rightly as it happened – that he had attempted to buy his way into the prince's confidence. He had even arranged to have that little actress the prince had taken a shine to flown in from LA. He had gone to a lot of trouble. A *hell* of a lot of trouble. Still, it would all be worth it, he thought smugly, once he made his spectacular announcement tonight.

Sebastian looked out onto the 200ft white carpet that he'd had flown in from Persia that morning for his guests to walk along and waited for the onslaught of the paparazzi lenses. Secretly, he had become quite enamoured with the whole idea of becoming something of a celebrity; he could just see himself with a guest slot on one of those TV shows, something along the lines of *The Apprentice*.

The moment Sebastian had shaken hands with the prince and sealed the deal over the diamond, he had gone about making plans for his transition from prominent banker into 'celebrity businessman' and had hired the best PR firm in London to help make sure this happened as smoothly as possible.

Securing the Bluebird Diamond was a big deal for him, professionally. Having that diamond in his pocket, figuratively speaking, sent a clear message out to all his business rivals that his institution was a leader in terms of security, and that thanks to the pioneering patented Inter-Face Locking system he had help create and implement, it was unrivalled anywhere in the world.

Sebastian sensed this was only the beginning; in ten years' time he envisaged his system to be the number one security choice the world over. Not simply for banks, but for anywhere that needed to implement a measure of safety: schools and hospitals, shops and offices and casinos to name but a few. Thanks to his ingenious idea, methods like chip and pin would soon be a thing of the past. And he would be one of the richest men on the planet.

Not that Sebastian wanted Imogen to know any of this, of course – at least not yet. There could only be one celebrity in the Forbes' household as far as he was concerned. His wife's career, her own selfish quest for attention and adoration could never usurp that of his own.

Imogen raised a perfectly arched eyebrow. So Sebastian was bankrolling the prince's stay in London. Well, well, well. Suddenly it all made perfect sense to her now. He was soft soaping him for that diamond. She had known all along that there had to be a motive for Seb's unexpected interest in the Lamberts. He had needed Damien's contact to get to the prince.

Imogen decided she would play dumb like she usually did, pretend she didn't have the first clue about what her husband was up to, but she was worried. If Sebastian had managed to accrue a rock as infamous as the Bluebird Diamond then it would open doors for him – a lot of doors. It would afford him even more publicity and power than he had already. And for a ruthless megalomaniac like Seb, this was a truly terrifying prospect.

Now, more than ever, Imogen hoped that the L'Orelie contract would come off. Resurrecting her career would be the confidence boost she so desperately needed. Maybe in time, it would help her gain enough strength to do what she should have done years ago and leave him. But years of his emotional bullying, subtle put-downs and dictatorial ways had seriously corroded her once healthy self-esteem and it seemed that the stronger her husband got, the weaker she felt. Just being around him seemed to zap her of all energy and strength.

Imogen decided to keep her suspicions about Sebastian and the prince quiet. It would not do well for her to let on to him that she knew what he was up to.

'The flowers for the prince were a gesture,' Sebastian said casually. 'To welcome him and his people to London, to the UK.'

'A very *grand* gesture,' Imogen said carefully.

'Yes, well, I'm sure you won't be complaining when he invites us to his Saudi Palace or on board one of his magnificent yachts. Anyway,' he said, tactically changing the subject, 'you look magnificent tonight, darling, I must say.'

Imogen had chosen to wear a floor-length dark aubergine silk Marchesa gown with a plunging neckline that was so deep it stopped just above her belly button, displaying the swell of her small round breasts. She had teamed the gown with a vintage lace shrug and subtle, yet stunning jewellery; a single large Graff solitaire diamond – bought for her by her husband, of course – that sat perfectly in her décolletage, complete with matching diamond waterfall earrings and a dazzling bracelet. Her hair was fashioned into a smooth, silky chignon secured with an ornate diamond hair pin, loose tendrils shaping her beautiful, olive-skinned face, accentuating her high cheekbones and naturally full lips that were slicked with the palest gloss.

Imogen smiled gently as she glanced at her husband. It was typical Seb; swinging pendulously from acerbic to charming in a heartbeat.

Sebastain gave his driver the nod and Raoul opened the car door.

'Sir . . .'

'Thank you, Raoul. Imogen?' Seb said, helping her out of the car.

Imogen forced herself to smile at the awaiting photographers, the flashbulbs popping like fireworks as they went off in the night air around them.

Sebastian had no idea how much his wife had come to dread the annual ball. This year Imogen had begged him to allow Bryony to attend, to make it more bearable for her, but he had balked at the mere mention of it.

'Maybe next year,' he had said dismissively. 'Plenty of time for all that later.'

Later. It was always 'later' as far as anything to do with Bryony was concerned, Imogen thought. It was almost as though he were ashamed of her; schooling her hundreds of miles away; keeping her away from social events, a stranger from her family. It wasn't right. She was a young woman now; charming and eloquent, not to mention devastatingly beautiful. Imogen knew that their guests would find her daughter utterly enchanting and she suspected this might partly be the reason for Seb's reluctance to allow her to attend; Bryony would inevitably steal her father's limelight.

In her heart, Imogen knew that Seb was jealous of their close and loving relationship. He had never forged much of a bond with his only child, something deep down she felt responsible for.

'She's her mother's daughter,' he would often say, somewhat disparagingly.

He had never wanted to share Imogen's love and attention with anyone. Not even with his own daughter.

Sebastian watched his wife as she smiled up at the paparazzi. It was a shame really, he thought, as the camera bulbs went off, lighting up her perfectly sublime face. She looked so utterly beguiling standing there, absorbing all the attention. He knew she had some ridiculous notion, thanks in part to that dreadful, and thankfully now deceased, woman, Cressida Lucas, of resurrecting her modelling career. Well, tonight he would put paid to that idea once and for all. Imogen needed reminding who was in charge in this marriage, and smiling wryly to himself, Sebastian would make sure she would be left in no doubt after tonight.

CHAPTER 18

The spectacular Louis Roederer champagne fountain drew gasps from the steady flow of guests as they made their way through the sumptuous hallway of Lancaster House.

Accompanied by the music of famous Italian pianist, Carlos Berlotti, waiters dressed in full pinstriped city splendour, complete with bowler hats and umbrellas swinging from the crooks of their arms, greeted guests with a glass from the fountain and a selection of the most sumptuous looking canapés.

Sebastian had pulled out all the stops for this year's extravaganza. He'd even reviewed the guest list, introducing a fresh young set of movers and shakers into the Forbes' fold. It was all part of his grand plan. Sebastian knew that if he was going to get a leg up on the fame ladder then what he needed was contacts, contacts, contacts.

'Ach, here he is! The man of the moment! Sebastian Forbes!' Damien Lambert, great lumbering oaf that he was, was making his way towards them. Imogen heard her husband audibly groan.

'Looking good, old boy, looking good!' Damien held his arms out towards Sebastian in embrace. 'How's that for an old champers fountain,' he said, admiring the impressive pyramid of glasses, a river of bubbling amber fizz constantly flowing from them.

Sebastian humoured him by clapping him hard on the back.

'Lambers. How great to see you again,' he remarked disingenuously, shaking his old friend's hand as he looked past him into the sea of guests.

After tonight, Damien Lambert would be *persona non grata* as far as Sebastian Forbes was concerned. Now that this in-road with Prince Saud was firmly cemented, he could drop off the face of the earth for all he cared. The sooner, the bloody better.

Imogen, listening to her husband and Damien drone on, suppressed the urge to run from the room and keep running. She had a sense of foreboding about this evening. Something was about to happen; she could feel it.

They were turning up in their droves now, the Viscounts and the Earls, Ladies and Duchesses, Right Honourables and the Marquises, all gloriously milling around dripping in jewels and self-importance. Then you had the big players; the casino owners and property developers, the fashion heavyweights and the shipping magnates, not to mention the oligarchs and their extravagant wives sporting rocks the size of small mountains on their fingers.

It was certainly a less than subtle departure from the usual stiff upper class aristo-traditionalism crowd of previous years. Why the sudden turnaround? Her suspicions were heightened.

Imogen drained her Grey Goose cocktail. She never really felt as if she belonged in this ostentatious world; she was not a socialite at heart. Not like Calvary. Calvary played the hostess role with such ease and charm as if she were born to it; which she had been, really. Imogen, on the other hand, found the whole Good Little Society Wife role ultimately more challenging. After all, it was really just tragic circumstance that had brought her this life, a life she had never really chosen for herself.

For a moment Imogen wondered how different it all might've been had fate not dealt her the hand it had. And once more her thoughts were invaded by images of *him*. Of the two of them together; so young and happy and in love, their lives stretched out before them, full of hope and promise.

She saw him then, in her mind's eye, standing on a beach in Ibiza all those years ago. His hair a little sandy and mussed up; his skin, nut-brown and sun-kissed and those teal green eyes, shining like emeralds. She remembered how she had felt when she had looked into them; like everything was right with the world. Like somehow they knew all her secrets; her hopes and dreams.

They had made love that morning, in the sea, the sun rising behind them, casting a low orange glow on their salty skin. He had carried her out towards the waves, her legs wrapped around his waist, and they had kissed, deeply, soft tongues exploring each other with a gentle urgency that had gradually built into something more frenzied and passionate.

She had never wanted a man like she had wanted *him*. Feeling his hardness pressed against her body had caused an ache in her so deep that she had cried out, wrapping her legs tighter around him, grinding herself into him, needing him as she pulled at his swim shorts with the backs of her heels.

'Not so fast,' he had smiled, gently teasing.

'I need to get you out of those wet clothes,' she had giggled softly in his ear.

'Naughty imp,' he had replied, wrinkling his nose at her. And he had kissed her again.

Mickey. Imogen said his name over in her mind as she smiled wanly at the memories. It had never really suited him.

He was a law student with a bright future ahead of him. He was brilliant and articulate but above all, kind and funny with a subtle but intense sexiness that was highlighted all the more by the fact that he was blissfully unaware of it.

When she had asked him why he had chosen to study law, he had replied resolutely, 'because I hate any kind of injustice,' and somehow this answer had told her everything she needed to know about him.

The connection between them had been instant and powerful. The moment she had read about in books and magazines. That bolt from the blue; the kind of thing that made people want to write poetry; a feeling that took the breath from your body and consumed every fibre of your being.

Making love in his scruffy Camden apartment the same afternoon had simply confirmed it to her. Something happened when their skin touched. She had felt the pull of him so strongly that it had taken the breath from her. Somehow, as he had gently pushed himself into her body over and over again, she had instinctively known this man would be part of her destiny. Making love to him had felt like coming home. Only there was one snag; one blot on the horizon that had marred their star-crossed union. Her name was Aimee.

Aimee was a highly strung and fragile individual and Mickey was a gentle soul who had felt a responsibility towards her, something that Aimee relentlessly played on to her advantage. Consequently, he had found it difficult to turn his back on her entirely when he had fallen out of love with her. Some might've deemed his behaviour weak; to him it was simply being kind.

But then he had met Imogen Lennard and it was as if he was seeing the world in colour for the first time. Suddenly he could imagine a real future for himself. And so he had no choice but to tell Aimee it was over between them. For good this time. Only Aimee simply couldn't, *wouldn't* accept that it was the end . . .

Imogen looked out across the magnificent hall of Lancaster House at all the opulence and wealth around her and wondered if she would have been happier with a semi in suburbia with *him* by her side. Would it ever have been enough for her?

She already knew the answer to her own question. And tonight, she felt it so acutely that it burned like fire inside her.

*

'Impressive,' Yasmin Belmont-Jones remarked as she surveyed the imposing champagne fountain and pair of white panthers, linking her arm firmly inside her husband's.

'No expense spared tonight according to Forbes. Reckons it's going to be his most spectacular shindig to date,' Jeremy Belmont said, swiping glasses of Louis Roederer for himself and his wife from a passing waiter in a bowler hat. He had been looking forward to this evening for weeks. It would be the first major event he had attended as a married man with his devastatingly gorgeous and sexy new wife in tow.

Forbes's Annual Ball was the perfect showcase for them to make their society debut. As it was, the paps had gone wild with excitement the moment he and Yasmin had stepped from the car. Cameras firing off all over the place like machine guns. It was hardly a surprise. Yasmin's show-stopping, split to the crotch Alexander McQueen gown with matching embellished underwear had sent the awaiting photographers into an absolute feeding frenzy.

'Over 'ere, Lady Belmont-Jones . . . this way, this way!'

Jeremy smiled to himself. He was loving every moment of the renewed press attention in him and his young bride.

Everyone was talking about them, the new couple *du jour* – and at his age as well! The thought tickled him pink.

*

Calvary Rothschild sipped her 'Forbes' Financial Ruin' cocktail and eyed her surroundings with satisfaction. She glanced over at Douglas who was deep in conversation with Lord Belmont; they were throwing their heads back intermittently with mirth and she watched them both as their eyes followed every pretty young thing who sashayed past.

Douglas, she noted, was knocking back the Roederer like there was about to be a drought. She turned away from them in mild disgust. Douglas could be unpredictable after a few too many. As it was, they were still barely on speaking terms and she was worried that this would not go unnoticed by the watchful eyes of others. The last thing she needed was the rumour mill going into overdrive about the state of her marriage. Tonight she must exude confidence, come across as though everything in her life was perfectly fabulous. Thank God she had chosen to wear Westwood tonight; it always gave her a welcome confidence boost.

*

'Mr Forbes, my friend.' Prince Saud al-Khahoutam stood in all his Arabian regal glory, flanked by his loyal security guards, and threw his thick arms around a visibly relieved Sebastian. 'There is bad traffic in your city, no? I almost ask for a . . . how do you say, a chopper to get us here!' He boomed with laughter.

Sebastian joined in, though his laugh had a ring of hysteria to it. For a moment there he had thought that the prince might be a no-show. 'Please, your highness,' he fawned, 'shall we be seated? You've obviously had a trying journey.'

Imogen watched the two men closely as Sebastian led the way towards their prominent table. The prince was much older than she had imagined. He was in his fifties at least. Dressed in a striking white linen collarless suit and a pristine white kaffiyeh – a classic Arab headdress – with a shiny gold band, a mark of his status, holding it in place, his eyelashes were as thick as a brush and his skin smooth and waxy-looking.

'And this must be the lovely Mrs Forbes, no?' Prince Saud bowed towards Imogen as she took her seat next to Sebastian and she graciously dipped her head in return. 'I bring you a gift,' the prince announced as one of his omnipresent menacing looking security guards stepped forward to hand him a large, black velvet box. 'A token of my gratitude to you and your generous husband. It is an honour to meet you, and to be here tonight.'

Imogen accepted the box graciously, aware of the twelve sets of eyes around the table simultaneously upon her. Gasping as she opened it, she stared down at the enormous fringe diamond necklace, its fancy yellow and white cushion and radiant cut diamonds almost blinding her as they lit up her face.

'It's stunning,' Imogen breathed, unable to take her eyes from its garish opulence.

'It is nothing.' He waved his hand modestly. 'Just 400 carats. What you find in one of your Christmas crackers, no?' He laughed heartily.

Yasmin Belmont-Jones half stood to take a look but Calvary gently pulled her back into her seat and shook her head brusquely.

'Bloody show off,' Jeremy Belmont quietly muttered. 'I'll get you something much bigger and better for Christmas, darling,' he turned to Yasmin, who was still craning her neck to get a better look at the stunning piece.

'I'll have to wait *that* long?' she simpered, casting him a coquettish look and rubbing her hand the length of his meaty thigh underneath the table. Jeremy smiled lasciviously.

'Depends how much of a *bad* girl you are,' he whispered flirtatiously in her ear, returning the gesture, his stubby digits jabbing at her jewelled underwear and the soft flesh it barely covered.

Yasmin had to stop herself from smacking his hand away and grimacing. She had snorted a generous line of cocaine before arriving tonight but the effects were beginning to wear off and she decided it was time for a little more anaesthetic.

'Will you excuse me,' she announced to the rest of the table, snatching up her Swarovski crystal clutch bag, Jeremy grinning like the proverbial Cheshire cat as he watched her tight behind wiggle off in the direction of the restrooms.

*

The world-renowned, infamous chef, Raymonde Rousse, had been flown in from Lyon especially to create and prepare the finest six course gastronomic masterpiece for tonight's event and so far he had not disappointed. The Kobe beef carpaccio appetiser was drawing murmurs of approval from around the table.

'So tell me, Charlotte. How are you finding life in LA?' Calvary enquired, wondering what the whole deal was with her attendance. While there was definitely a higher celebrity turnout tonight, Charlotte Macclesfield was the real deal. A bona fide Hollywood A-lister who hung out with the likes of George Clooney and Colin Farrell. Just last week she had been pictured in *Grazia* magazine, half naked, sunning herself on Clooney's yacht with a gaggle of the usual Tinsel Towners.

'I adore LA,' she replied coolly. 'Sunshine twenty-four seven, being near the beach,' she patted her radiant skin. 'It's worked wonders for my health.'

And tits by the looks of it, Calvary thought, eyeing her newly acquired, impressive cleavage. 'And are you working on something exciting? A new script perhaps?'

Charlotte smiled sweetly, suddenly aware that the whole table was listening in. She had only agreed to come tonight because Sebastian Forbes had promised to pay her a quarter of a million in 'expenses' and fly her in via private jet. Not half bad for an evening's work, all told. He had put her up at The Dorchester too, in a suite next to the old Saudi prince, who incidentally, upon her arrival had filled her entire room – even the bidet with red roses and champagne. He had even left a gift on her pillow; a dazzling diamond bracelet that had sent her into a fit of excited giggles. Her smile had soon waned however once it dawned on her what she might have to give in return for such overwhelming generosity. Charlotte Macclesfield was young and naive but she wasn't completely void of nous.

'I'm considering my options,' she replied, noncommittal.

'How wonderful,' Calvary remarked. 'It must be like a dream come true for you, a girl from a council estate taking Hollywood by storm.'

Charlotte smirked. Bloody bitch. She could keep her back-handed compliments to herself.

'Oh, it is, it is,' she replied, all sweetness and light. 'I realise I am one lucky girl.'

'And a very beautiful one,' Prince Saud interjected. 'You look stunning, my dear. Even better in the flesh than on screen. I loved you in *Me and You, Baby*. It is my favourite film of all time.'

Yasmin cast her eye towards Calvary and Imogen and made the slightest flick of her brow.

'I'd be interested to see his DVD collection,' she muttered under her breath and Calvary hid her smiles beneath her napkin.

*

Sebastian surveyed his guests with satisfaction. He had excelled himself this year; the exquisite food, the constant flow of champagne, the opulent venue and the A-list attendance. Following dinner he had an even bigger treat in store for them all; Shirley Bassey and Michael Bublé would be providing the entertainment! He couldn't wait to see the look on his guests' faces when he announced them.

All he needed now to round off the perfect evening was for his moment behind the microphone to go without a hitch. His speeches in previous years had, on occasion, been described as a little on the 'dry' side. A criticism that had bothered him immensely. Well, not tonight, he thought. Sebastian Forbes was going to give the speech of his whole goddamn life, one they would all be talking about for weeks, months, hell, maybe even *years* later. And the thought made him smile from ear to ear.

CHAPTER 19

Yasmin Belmont-Jones felt an enormous sense of relief as she snorted the remains of the white powder from the pristine white toilet seat. She wasn't sure how much more of her lecherous husband's pawing she could take but at least this took the edge off it.

Wiping any tell-tale signs of powder from her nose, she took a deep breath and placed the small wrap of coke back into her jewelled clutch. Much as she tried not to admit it to herself, all this pretence was beginning to wear her down. She wasn't sure how much longer she could keep it up. Worst of all, she was nowhere closer to getting the answers she so desperately needed and was fast running out of ideas of where to look for them.

Yasmin had searched her husband's home from top to bottom; rifled through his office particulars with a fine tooth comb; been through every drawer and bureau, every cupboard and dresser in the whole house and had found nothing. Not so much as a newspaper clipping.

The most frustrating part of it all was that Yasmin wasn't even sure what it was she was looking for. In her suicide note, June Larkin had alluded to there being some sort of videotape from that fateful evening. 'Incriminating evidence', she had called it. Apparently, Belmont had it hidden in a secret 'underground' location, though what that meant was anyone's guess. Bloody June Larkin. As useless in death as she had been in life, Yasmin thought to herself bitterly.

She exited the cubicle distinctly more bright eyed than when she had entered it, something that had not gone unnoticed by Sammie Grainger who was standing by the wash basins, pretending to adjust her make-up in the mirror. She had been watching 'Lady Belmont' closely all evening, just waiting to seize the perfect opportunity to catch her alone.

She had no intentions of jumping in feet first and revealing her discovery, however. There was a good chance Stacey would disappear off the face of the earth and take her story with her. She couldn't risk spilling the beans. Not yet.

Oblivious to Sammie's presence, Yasmin ran her hands underneath the tap and studied her reflection in the mirror.

'Some party,' Sammie said. 'I won't need to eat for a month if I make my way through the feast out there.' She smiled brightly at Yasmin in the mirror, suddenly struck by how attractive she was up close with her flawless skin, perfectly neat curves and voluptuous fake breasts. There was a softness in her face too, a vulnerability that had been there in her young photograph, and it caused Sammie to feel a sudden stab of empathy for her.

Yasmin looked up, making eye contact with Sammie's reflection.

'Indeed,' she smiled affably. 'Though I have to say I'm not a big fan of anything that's been smoked in tea. *Bleurgh*!' She pulled a face.

Sammie laughed.

'Sammie Grainger,' she said brightly, holding her hand out.

'Yasmin Belmont-Jones.'

'Of course, Lady Belmont-Jones. We've already been introduced.'

'We have?'

'You don't remember?'

Yasmin shrugged apologetically.

'I meet a lot of people, darling,' she said, realising to her horror just how much she was beginning to sound like Calvary Rothschild.

'The Chelsea Wives feature . . . I'm the journalist who interviewed you.'

Yasmin's hackles rose. *Journalist.*

'Ah yes, now you come to mention it, your face does ring a bell.' *An alarm bell.*

'So, you're here on business tonight?'

Sammie detected a defensive tone in Yasmin's voice and told herself to go easy.

'Not exactly. Though I am here with my boss.'

Yasmin raised an eyebrow.

'People will talk,' she retorted.

'I think you might be right!' Sammie said truthfully. 'He's arranged for us to stay in the same hotel room. Something about there being a double booking apparently.'

Yasmin smirked.

'That old chestnut.'

'Afraid so. Not sure how I'm going to get myself out of this one.' She rolled her eyes.

Yasmin took in the girl's features for a moment; her lightly tanned skin and short dark hair, the look of steely determination in her hazelnut eyes.

'Not your cup of tea, then?'

'Not exactly, no,' she replied. 'Let's just say I'm not a big fan of tea either.'

Yasmin smiled. She figured they had to be around the same sort of age and that by the sound of her accent those same drawn out vowels that she herself had been at such pains to disguise she was a South London girl. Come to think of it, looking at her properly now, she wondered if in fact she *did* recognise her after all.

'Well, good luck, er, Sammie, is it? Hope it all works out with the boss. If all else fails, a swift kick to the bollocks always does the trick.' Yasmin winced as soon as the words had left her glossy mouth. This was not the language of a lady.

Sammie stifled a giggle. You could take the girl out of Croydon . . .

'Thanks for the tip,' she smiled. 'Oh, and Lady Belmont!'

Yasmin turned to face her. Her heartbeat had begun to accelerate in her chest now. The coke, probably.

'If you're interested, I'd really like to do a little follow-up piece on you. You know, a profile life after marriage, any business plans you might have, that sort of thing. Perhaps we can chat about it over lunch sometime. What do you think?' Sammie proffered her business card.

Yasmin tentatively accepted it, eyeing her cautiously.

'Yes. Why not?' she said, not wanting it to look as though she had anything to hide.

'Great!' Sammie beamed.

'But I'm afraid there's really not much to tell.'

'Oh, I'm sure there's plenty,' Sammie said brightly. *Plenty indeed.* 'Enjoy the rest of the evening.'

Yasmin watched as she closed the door behind her.

'Bloody hell,' she muttered, tearing the card in half before throwing it in the bin.

Much as she hated to admit it, Jeremy had been right about one thing; journalists: they were bloody parasites, the lot of them.

*

'My Lords, Ladies, Gentlemen, Scholars and Your Royal Highnesses.' Sebastian Forbes took to the stage to the sound of applause. 'It is with enormous pleasure that I stand before you tonight, in this most sumptuous of surroundings here at Lancaster House.' The audience duly clapped their appreciation and Sebastian felt the first potent rush of adrenalin pump through his system. 'As most of you here can lay testament to, Forbes Bank prides itself on taking the utmost care of its customers and has done for over two hundred years now. In the words of my father, my grandfather and his father before him, "In Forbes We Put Our Trust . . . Fund." There was rapturous laughter among the crowd and Sebastian felt his chest swell.

'I think it is no coincidence then, that with safety being the highest on our list of priorities, I can welcome a new and most prestigious client into the Forbes fold. My lords, ladies and gentlemen, it is with the most sincere and genuine pleasure that I introduce to you someone whom I both admire and thank unreservedly for choosing to put his faith and trust – not to mention his most precious of belongings quite literally, in our hands. Please, be upstanding for his Royal Highness, Prince Saud al-Khahoutam of Arabia!'

The room erupted.

Imogen smiled to herself as she stood. She bloody well knew it!

Calvary raised her eyebrows.

'So the rumours were true then? He's in bed with the prince?'

'Looks that way,' Imogen remarked, watching her husband's self-satisfied face as he lapped up all the applause and adoration.

'By all accounts, he might not be the only one tonight.' Calvary cast her eye to Charlotte Macclesfield and placed her tongue firmly in her cheek.

Imogen struggled to raise a smile. Her earlier sense of foreboding had reached flood alert and was now threatening to drown her. She just couldn't seem to shake off the feeling that something dreadful was about to happen.

Prince Saud took to the stage accompanied by his security staff and bowed regally.

'Thank you . . . you are most kind,' he said, relishing his moment in the spotlight. Like Sebastian, he never could resist an audience. He took an audible breath.

'Those of you who are reading the papers will know that I have come to England for two purposes. The first, if you must believe what you are reading, is being to find myself a new princess, although judging by what I see before me tonight, I am, how do you say, spoilt for choices.' There was uproar amongst the audience, as various predatory socialites blushed and giggled, sharpening their elbows at the ready.

Charlotte Macclesfield almost choked on her champagne. *Jesus fucking Christ!* She hoped he didn't think that *she* might be in the running as the next Mrs Prince Saud al-Khahoutam!

'The second reason,' continued Prince Saud, 'and the real reason I am visiting your most beautiful country, is to find a safe home for the only woman in my life who has never let me down, or indeed, left my side – the Bluebird Diamond!'

The audience gasped as one of the prince's meaty bodyguards ambled up on stage, displaying the gigantic rock for all to see. It lit up the room like a giant disco ball, sending prisms of rainbow-coloured light dancing across the open-mouthed faces of the cheering guests.

'Now that's what I call a rock,' Yasmin said to her husband, unable to take her eyes from the enormous jewel.

'It's the most exquisite example in the world by all accounts,' Jeremy said. 'Absolutely flawless. Apparently, it even has a *mind* of its own.'

'Oh, really?' Yasmin was intrigued.

'Yes. According to rumour, it can actually tell the difference between good and evil.'

'Don't be ridiculous, Jeremy,' Yasmin scoffed. 'I didn't think you went in for all that superstitious nonsense.'

Jeremy shrugged.

'I look forward to our long and prosperous relationship, Mr Forbes,' the prince announced, handing an eager Sebastian the priceless jewel, just as they had earlier rehearsed.

He turned to address the crowd.

'She is now in safe hands.'

Everyone began to cheer and, given the nod by Sebastian, the paparazzi sprung into action.

'Well, that's some coup,' Jeremy sniffed, slowly clapping his hands. 'He's a very clever man, that husband of yours, announcing their coalition tonight like that,' he said, turning to Imogen. 'That diamond will be the making of him, mark my words; they'll all come in their droves now; Saudi royalty like to keep things in the family.'

Imogen knew Belmont was right and the thought unnerved her. As the crowd settled, Sebastian took the microphone again.

'Before I round off tonight's speech and introduce our next guests – very excited about that one – I would like to just say one more thing.' Imogen looked out at her husband. He was relishing his moment in the spotlight.

'As we all know, behind every great man in business, there is always a great woman.'

She felt her stomach lurch. Oh no. Please don't say Seb was about to bring her into proceedings. 'And none come any greater than my beautiful wife. Please,' he said, holding his hand out in her direction. 'Everyone . . . Mrs Imogen Forbes!'

Imogen's nausea reached crisis point and she instinctively covered her mouth with her hand, lest she throw up there and then. Seb had not mentioned anything to her about inviting her up on stage with him. The last thing she wanted was to be wheeled out in front of an audience, forced to act out the devoted wife role. Forced to rise from her seat, she was aware of the intense glare of a thousand pairs of eyes upon her and Calvary squeezed her shaking hand reassuringly. Imogen made her way up to the stage where she briefly embraced her husband.

'What are you doing, Seb?' she hissed in his ear. Sebastian gave her a slow, small smile that was far from reassuring.

'Ladies and gentlemen, I have a story to tell,' he began, his voice smooth and practised. 'Just recently, I came very close to losing my wife in a plane crash.' He paused for effect, adding to the drama. It seemed to work as the room fell hushed.

'For those of you who can remember, my wife was once a very famous model, and at the request of a rather well-known cosmetics company, recently flew out to LA to test shoot for a potentially life-changing campaign that she hoped was going to put her back on the map, so to speak.'

Imogen stared out towards a sea of faces who seemed to be hanging on to his every word, her stomach lurching like a porpoise. Where was Seb going with all this?

'Sadly,' Seb continued, 'the day she arrived, a terrible tragedy occurred; one of the most devastating plane crashes in UK history in which over 300 people lost their lives, including that of my wife's dear, dear friend, Cressida Lucas.'

Various members of the audience murmured their sympathies.

'For the first time in my life I came this close,' he held his thumb and forefinger together, 'to losing someone I love with all my heart and, my dear friends and associates, it brought it home to me. This most tragic of accidents showed me just how much I owe my brilliant, beautiful wife. I realise now that without her by my side, I am nothing at all.'

People began to clap and a collective 'ahhhh,' emanated from the crowd.

'Which is why I want to take this opportunity to tell her. Imogen . . .' he took her shaking hand and faced her, 'I love you so much.' He kissed her then, his dry lips smothering hers.

The crowd erupted in a cacophony of cheers and whoops.

Imogen drew on her acting skills as hard as she could, smiling at Seb coquettishly, appearing to be touched by such a tender ode.

'And to finish my tale,' Seb shouted out over the din, 'can you believe that after all that, she did not even get the job!' Imogen froze. 'They turned my wife down saying that they had found someone younger, someone better suited to their campaign!' The cheering abruptly subsided, leaving a low silence. The room suddenly felt hot and airless. 'They must be mad!'

Imogen picked out her friend's faces among the crowd. Yasmin's eyes were wide with shock and Calvary had her hand over her mouth.

'But their loss is ultimately my gain,' Sebastian continued, sincerity thick in his voice. Imogen lightly tugged at his tuxedo in a bid to prevent him from continuing but he ignored her protests.

'They might think she is "past her best" as they so insultingly put it, a "has-been", but I for one think my amazing, stunning wife simply continues to grow more and more beautiful by the day. As I'm sure you'll all agree.'

Guests began turning to one another, their eyebrows raised, not sure how they should react. Some started clapping and Imogen thought she heard the odd, 'here, here.' But the mood in the room had distinctly shifted.

'The bastard,' Calvary whispered under her breath, incredulous, her eyes fixated on the stage.

'Bloody hell,' Yasmin said, her eyes wide with the excitement of all the drama. 'Did she tell you she hadn't got the contract?'

'No.'

'Do you think she knew about it?'

Calvary shrugged, dumbfounded. Her heart went out to her friend as she saw the pained expression behind her eyes.

'Bloody hell,' Yasmin repeated herself. 'In front of all these people as well.'

Imogen felt the icy grip of panic wrap itself around her throat, threatening to choke her. The room had begun to spin a little, the faces of the crowd blending into one great colourful mass of taffeta and tuxedos. She could feel Seb's arm gripping her waist tightly as the paparazzi went into action again. Jesus Christ, they were taking pictures of her! Mortified, her face burning with shame and confusion, she attempted to break free of her husband's embrace. Her instincts told her to run, to hitch her dress up and flee from the stage there and then, but her legs felt boneless as they struggled to support her and she was blinded by the flashlights of the unforgiving cameras.

Had Seb deliberately planned this? A sick and twisted attempt to humiliate her in front of hundreds of important guests and the awaiting press? If he had, then it had worked. She had never felt more mortified in her entire life. Imogen squirmed. She would make the news tomorrow for all the wrong reasons; no one would want to hire her now.

Imogen's mind started to go into overdrive as she struggled to make sense of what was happening. How did Seb know that she'd been ruled out of the L'Orelie running anyway? She hadn't heard a word from them since she'd left the States the day after the accident. Had someone called? Had he spoken to them directly?

She told herself that none of it mattered now. The details could wait. All she could focus on was getting herself off the stage and away from the harsh glare of the paparazzi lens.

'Mrs Forbes! Imogen! This way! G'is a smile!' chirped a photographer.

Imogen turned to face the camera, briefly meeting her husband's gaze. And he was smiling, a grim, malevolent smile that spoke volumes.

CHAPTER 20

Calvary Rothschild stepped into her private marble en-suite wet room and allowed the hot water from the enormous chrome showerhead to cascade down her face and body. She looked down at herself as water fizzed onto her small neat breasts, beads forming on her stomach and thighs. Soaping herself with Le Couvent des Minimes Lavender and Acacia Soothing Shower Gel she surveyed the thin folds of sagging flesh on her stomach, pinching the excess skin between her thumb and forefinger with mild self-loathing.

Though she hated herself for thinking it, there was a small part of her that wondered if she had only rid herself of any physical imperfections much earlier, Douglas might never have done what he did with the young and nubile Tamara, and, she suspected, was continuing to do with her.

She dismissed the thought almost instantly. Who was she kidding? Douglas had been searching for his jollies elsewhere for bloody years, long before the boys came along, long before motherhood and the years had inevitably taken their toll on her once perfect size 8 figure.

She took the pouf from the shower rack and rubbed it angrily between her legs.

She had to stop dwelling in the past and think of a way to prevent her son from marrying Tamara Du Bois. *Du Bois*. Calvary grimaced. Even the name sounded common and cheap. She was new money. First generation. Little more than a chav, really. Her father had bought his way into society and consequentially built an in-road for his tramp of a daughter. A road that had had regrettably led directly to her darling son.

The worse part of all of it was that Calvary knew Henry loved Tamara, really loved her, dirty little trollop that she was. He wanted to marry her. To have and to hold her, in sickness and in health, *forsaking all others*. All others seemingly not including her own father-in-law to be.

Tamara had become a far bigger problem than Calvary had anticipated, however.

Their recent meeting with the wedding planner, one which Douglas had emotionally blackmailed her about, had displayed this to her in all its vulgar clarity.

'I'm thinking plain white Egyptian linen with edible crystal favours scattered across all the tables,' Tamara had announced to the overly-attentive wedding planner. 'And for the centrepieces, I've decided upon giant topiary infused with dozens of white roses or perhaps gardenias, I can't make up my mind.' The wedding planner had nodded enthusiastically as she busily scribbled in her Smythson notebook. She relished this type of bride-to-be, the ones with grand ideas and even grander budgets. They were almost impossible to please however, being the spoilt divas they invariably were, but who cared when they were spending this much money?

'My Temperley gown is going to have a detachable lace fitted overlay with thousands of tiny Swarovski crystals hand-sewn onto it, so I want to check that the edible crystals match, OK?'

'Uh-huh,' the wedding planner continued to nod vehemently, hanging on her every word.

'And of course, you'll need to get a lighting team in there too. Blenheim Palace has some awesome chandeliers but there just aren't enough. I want one hung over every table and I want dimmer switches, so that they can be turned up or down. What do you think, Cal?'

Calvary, who had tuned out of the conversation some moments ago, visibly blanched. How dare she address her so informally, like a friend! After everything she had done to her and her family!

'Sorry?'

'Lighting!' she said. 'Dimmer switches on the chandeliers. I want to be able to change the mood in the room if I want to.'

'Tacky,' Calvary had replied tartly.

Tamara glared at her and the wedding planner, sensing discord between the two women, tactfully withdrew from the room.

'We could at least try to be friends,' she had smiled through gritted teeth once the wedding planner was out of earshot. 'For Henry's sake, if nobody else's.'

'Henry's sake?' Calvary had shot back facetiously. 'For Henry's sake it might've been a good idea *not* to have slept with his father, you know, *my* husband.'

Tamara rolled her eyes.

'Listen, Calvary,' she said, her smile fading fast, 'that was a mistake. A mistake I would like to put behind me. If I'm ever allowed to.'

Calvary had stared at the young woman in front of her with a curious mix of disbelief and admiration. How alike she and Douglas were. Cut from the same piece of cloth. As far as Tamara and Douglas were concerned their little indiscretion was something to be brushed aside, forgotten about, put out with yesterday's rubbish. Why all the fuss? It didn't seem to matter to her one jot that she had betrayed her fiancé in the worst way imaginable.

'You had sex with your own father-in-law,' Calvary reminded her.

'*Prospective* father-in-law. Let's not get ahead of ourselves,' Tamara shot back. 'Look,' she said after a momentary pause, her tone softening slightly, 'can't we start over again? Put it all behind us. I've always liked you, Calvary. Admired you. I feel I could learn a lot from you.'

Calvary snorted in derision.

'There's nothing I could teach *you*, Tamara Du Bois. Save for how to keep your knickers on.'

Tamara smirked. She had not wanted to go down this route but this belligerent old woman was refusing to play ball. The reticent, 'let's be friends' approach was getting her nowhere. It was time to change tack.

'You can't stop this wedding from taking place,' Tamara hissed defiantly. 'You know Douglas will disown you if you tell Hen about us. And let's face it; money and status are what's always mattered most to you, aren't they, Calvary?'

Shaking with anger, Calvary had raised her hand and brought it down across Tamara's smug, pretty face.

'How dare you, you poisonous little slut!' she screamed, incensed. Calvary was shocked at herself. She couldn't remember the last time she had struck another person. What's more, she knew Tamara had a point and it had hurt.

Tamara rubbed her stinging cheek. Secretly she was pleased. She would tell Douglas about this. Cry on his shoulder, sob up a kidney if she had to. Douglas would be sympathetic; he would comfort her, hold her quivering body in his arms. And then he would look at her and she would fix him with her stare, the one she had given him before they had ended up in bed together . . .

Incidentally, Tamara did love Henry in her own way. He was a thoroughly decent guy, very attractive with a hefty trust fund and inheritance in due course, but Tamara wasn't prepared to wait that long for a life of unadulterated luxury. She wanted it all now. She wanted Douglas Rothschild – at least, she wanted his money. After all, why settle for gold when you could have platinum? Henry was way too loyal. Douglas, however, was an altogether different animal; exciting, forbidden and more than a match for her both in and outside the bedroom.

She knew Calvary could never let slip what she had seen between them lest Douglas threw her out on the street and strip her of everything. Tamara smiled slyly to herself. She had the Rothschilds all sewn up.

'Feel better?' Tamara asked, her face still smarting from the sharp slap.

'Not really,' Calvary retorted.

'Shame,' she had smirked. 'Because that's the last time I'll ever allow you to do that to me and get away with it.'

'Look at you,' Calvary snarled, feeling a sudden wave of sadness that she could feel so much hatred towards someone so young. By rights she should be bonding with this girl, losing a son yet gaining a daughter, isn't that what they said?

'If you think I'm going to stand back and let you destroy my son's life then you can think again, Tamara Du Bois. I've seen off your type time and time again,' she had said, swatting her away like a fly. 'If you've a shred of decency in that swinging brick you call a heart you'll call this whole goddamn wedding charade off while you still can. It'll destroy Hen but I'd rather see it happen now than in five years' time.'

'Oh, I'm not going anywhere,' Tamara spat back, her nerves rattling behind her bravado. 'I *will* marry your son. Try and come between us and I will see that he cuts you from his life, *indefinitely.*' She smirked. 'Think about it, Calvary. Estranged from your husband *and* son; cut off from your family both financially and emotionally while I become lady of the house.' Tamara smiled broadly then, a self-satisfied, wicked smile. As her words resonated in the air between them, she watched with a deep sense of satisfaction as Calvary desperately tried to hide the look of defeat on her face. She was right: Henry adored her.

'So then,' Tamara said after a few moments of silence had passed between them, an arched eyebrow raised in triumph. 'Which is it to be, the gardenias or the roses?'

*

Calvary rubbed her head with a handful of Kérastase shampoo, hoping that she might wash away all this mess in the process. For the first time in her life she really did not know what to do and what was worse, she had no one to turn to. At least, no one she was *willing* to turn to. She could not bring herself even to tell Imogen the truth about her husband's latest infidelity she was so ashamed.

Calvary had always seen herself as the strong one. She was the backbone of the Chelsea set. She had cast herself in this matriarchal advisory role many years ago and was reluctant to start deviating from it now. Besides, Imogen had her own set of problems, what with that husband of hers making a laughing stock of her at the ball like that. Sebastian Forbes had certainly given Douglas a run for his money in the 'whose husband is the biggest bastard?' stakes.

Calvary turned the heat up in the shower to the point of unbearable in a bid to wash away her thoughts. She simply had to find a way to prove to Henry that Tamara was up to no good with his own father.

Sighing heavily, she glanced up at the bathroom clock on the wall, its black face staring back at her, almost watching her. And then she was struck by an idea.

Calvary began to smile and as she did, the stranger she had met outside the Saachi Gallery popped into her mind.

He had made the solution to her predicament sound so easy, so straightforward.

'*You could always leave. What have you got to be afraid of? The biggest fear we face is fear itself.*'

She wondered if she might bump into him again and the thought gave her a guilty rush of excitement. She pictured him in her mind. His floppy dark hair and disarming demeanour; his slightly dishevelled but oddly appealing appearance. Now she thought of it, hadn't he mentioned something about being a personal trainer?

Calvary looked back down at herself in the shower and pinched the loose skin on her stomach again, tightly this time, until it hurt. Yes, she thought to herself, her mood lifting ever so slightly, perhaps it was time to get fit again.

CHAPTER 21

Imogen couldn't decide between the Heidi Klein red Corsica Bandeau or the navy Monaco bikini. Damn it, she'd take both with her, she thought throwing them haphazardly into the open Louis Vuitton trunk on her bed. She was packing early for the forthcoming trip to Lake Como that Calvary had organised. As far as she was concerned, the sooner she was out of here and on that plane, the better.

Though Calvary had advised against it, the morning after the ball, Imogen had forced herself to look through the press coverage over breakfast at The Wolseley. She had needed to know how bad it really was. Now she wished she hadn't.

'Forget the papers, darling,' Calvary had said, snatching a copy of *The Times* from her hands as she cut into her Eggs Benedict, turning the plate a sunshine yellow.

'Everyone knows they all print a pack of lies anyway,' Yasmin said, flicking her platinum hair back from her tanned face. 'I mean, half the time they can't even spell your name right.'

Try as she had to remain emotionally detached, Yasmin could not help but feel desperately sorry for Imogen. That husband of hers had well and truly stitched her up on the night of the ball. She wondered why Sebastian Forbes would want to do such a thing to his wife? A woman, who, by all accounts, was as decent and kind as she was beautiful, at least from what Yasmin could tell.

'He'd lock her up in a cage if he could,' Calvary had confessed to her in private. 'The man's a complete control freak; he's obsessed with her. He's even jealous of the daughter.'

Men: they were all the same – bastards – Yasmin thought bitterly. They were only happy when they were domineering or destroying. Well, she would have her day of reckoning make no mistake.

'Yasmin's right,' Calvary had continued. 'I mean, look at what they've been writing about *her* over these past few months. There's been mud of all sorts slung in your direction, hasn't there, darling? "Disingenuous Gold-Digger" being a personal favourite,' Calvary teased.

'And those were just the *nice* headlines,' Yasmin laughed, allowing Calvary's dig to pass over her just this once.

'You just have to ride it out,' Calvary instructed. 'You know these things blow over quicker than one of Madonna's relationships.'

Imogen had managed a small smile but she was not convinced. She had seen the look people had given her as she had made her way through the restaurant that morning. The pitiful stares and the low whispers.

The *Daily Mail* had devoted the whole of their society column to the ball's events, waxing lyrical about the Bluebird Diamond and Seb's profitable acquisition, but even that had been overshadowed by her husband's 'romantic ode to his wife, former model, Imogen Forbes, who, at thirty-six, has recently lost out on a lucrative new cosmetic contract on account of her being too old – ouch,' the journalist had written.

It was a similar story in the *Evening Standard* (though

they had gone one step further and suggested that she had lost out to a much younger model *du jour* called Agnes). The whole thing had sparked a huge media debate on ageism in the beauty industry with various prominent female journalists collectively voicing their objections on why it was that once a woman reached 'the ripe old age of thirty-five' she was ruthlessly dumped onto the reject pile. Imogen's phone had rung off the hook with hacks desperate for a quote.

God, how Imogen wished Cressida were here now. She would know what to do. Clear up the whole horrible mess in a heartbeat and make sure that she came out smelling of Chanel No. 5 while she was at it.

Imogen shuddered as she gathered her collection of sun protection lotions and sprays and absentmindedly threw them all into a Chanel cosmetics case, her mind wandering back to the immediate aftermath of the ball, of the excruciating car journey home with Seb.

*

'Why did you do it, Seb?' she had asked, her lips quivering with anger and hurt, tears stinging the backs of her eyes. She was determined he would not see her cry.

'What are you talking about, darling?' he'd replied, feigning ignorance.

'Why did you have to announce to everyone that I didn't get the contract? And more to the point, how did you *know*?'

Sebastian had turned to her, a Machiavellian grin on his face.

'I have no idea what you're talking about, Imogen,' he'd snapped. 'You've clearly had too much champagne.'

'Don't patronise me!' Imogen had shot back, overcome with humiliation and fury.

'I thought I was paying you the ultimate compliment, announcing how much I love you to our guests. I thought you would be *pleased*. Really, you're blowing this up out of all proportion.' He'd turned away from her then, not wanting her to see the small smirk that was threatening to expand across his face. 'Anyway, I genuinely thought you knew you hadn't won the contract. After all, they called and left a message some days ago now. I just assumed . . . well, I didn't mention it to you because I wanted my speech to be a surprise. In fact, I hadn't planned to bring the damned thing up at all. It was a spur of the moment thing.'

She didn't know what to make of it all. She'd not wanted to believe that her husband was capable of such cruelty towards her but she did not trust him either, not one bit. Seb was a born liar; a master manipulator, and she couldn't help but feel that it had all been some kind of sick plan to make her a figure of pity and ridicule.

'Don't be such a drama queen, Imogen,' he had chided her. 'They all loved it. I'm sure none of them even focussed on *you* anyway. You're flattering yourself. The Bluebird was the story. *Is* the story. It'll be all over the papers tomorrow, mark my words. You probably won't even get a look in.'

But Sebastian had been wrong. It might've been all over the papers the next morning, but much to his chagrin, the big furore was all about his wife and that blasted contract, the Bluebird getting little more than a cursory mention. As far as Sebastian was concerned, his plan had backfired. Yes, he had succeeded in humiliating his wife, but in doing so had inadvertently put her firmly in the spotlight in the process. Something he had definitely not intended. And he was livid.

*

Imogen threw the last of her holiday items into the trunk and locked it. Soon she would be on a plane, sipping a vodka tonic, doing her best to numb herself. Just the thought of it helped her to relax.

Imogen thought nothing of hearing the phone ring as she passed Seb's private office, it was only when it clicked onto answerphone that her attention was caught.

'Hello, yes, is this the voicemail of Duncan Phillips? This is Lorraine Harlech here, CEO of L'Orelie. I wonder, could you give me a call back as a matter of extreme urgency? My number is 00 . . .' Imogen flew into Seb's office and snatched up the phone.

'Lorraine . . . Lorraine Harlech?'

'Yes . . . oh, you've picked up.'

'This is Imogen. Imogen Forbes.'

Lorraine was a little taken aback. She had not expected to speak with Imogen directly.

'Imogen,' Lorraine's voice was measured. 'I'm sorry to have to make this call but I need to know what the hell's going on down there . . . all this business in the papers.'

Imogen winced.

'Believe me, Lorraine, if you think you're embarrassed about it, imagine where I'm coming from,' she laughed, attempting to hide her discomfort.

Lorraine bristled.

'I'm more than a little embarrassed, Imogen. I'm fucking mortified! We are on the brink of launching a new product here, one that we've ploughed a huge amount of time, not to mention cost into, and it looks as though one glib remark is about to blow the whole thing apart.'

Imogen bit her lip.

'What can I say, Lorraine?' she said apologetically. 'I had no idea that Seb was going to announce the fact that I hadn't got the job to all and sundry. It was as big a shock to me as it is to you, believe me.'

Lorraine was incredulous. She should've spoken to her directly in the first place, told her in no uncertain terms that her photos just weren't right for what she'd been looking for and wished her all the best, then none of this mess would've happened.

'If it makes you feel any better, I'm prepared to go on record and exonerate you, tell them all it was a big misunderstanding,' Imogen offered.

Lorraine sighed heavily. It was good of her to suggest it and she knew it.

'Listen, Imogen,' she said, her tone audibly softening. 'I'm sorry. This really isn't your fault. Your pictures, they just weren't right for this. You know, it had nothing to do with your age and everything to do with the shots. Honestly. I had you pegged down for this campaign from the beginning. Handpicked you myself. No one was more disappointed with those shots than me.'

Imogen felt crestfallen. They might not have been the best pictures she had ever taken in her life but they were still pretty damned good as far as test shots went. The whole crew had testified as much.

'I understand,' Imogen said quietly. 'Though I kind of thought they fitted the brief.'

Lorraine felt uncomfortable. 'Look,' she said gently. 'I'll e-mail them over to you right now if you like, see them for yourself. You're a beautiful woman, Imogen, but those pictures . . . well . . .'

'Yes, please, do that,' Imogen interjected. 'I'd like to see them again.'

'I'll get Leona onto it right away. Oh and Imogen, really. It's all my own fault for not calling you direct. I should never have given the news to Duncan Phillips when he called.'

'Duncan Phillips?'

'Your PA,' Lorraine explained. 'He called up on your behalf

to find out about the test. I assume he told you? Jesus, he *did* tell you, didn't he?' Lorraine felt her heart miss a beat.

'Er, yes . . . yes, of course he did,' Imogen quickly lied, her mind galloping as adrenalin began to pour through her body like hot lava. 'Anyway, I meant what I said about being prepared to go on record.'

'That's real good of you, Imogen,' Lorraine said, the genuine appreciation audible in her LA drawl. 'And you know . . . well, perhaps we might work together sometime in the future.'

Hanging up, Imogen switched on Sebastian's computer in front of her and stared blankly at the screen, her heart beating a tattoo in her chest. So Sebastian had called L'Orelie claiming to be her PA? But why?

After a few moments, she logged onto her e-mail and true to her word, Lorraine Harlech had sent her shots through right away.

She read the accompanying email message: 'The pictures as promised. No hard feelings? Lorraine.'

With shaking hands, Imogen downloaded the PDF images onto the desktop and, opening them up, stared at the screen, eyes wide.

After a long moment, she calmly saved them onto a USB stick and shut the computer down. So now she knew.

Blinking back tears of rage, Imogen felt a torrent of hatred for her husband crash through her system like a tsunami of poison. With her heart hardening with each passing second, she thought of all the years she had spent kowtowing to Seb's impossible demands. Of all the years she had been worn down by his dominance, too weak to challenge the mighty Sebastian Forbes, even allowing him to deny her the chance to be a proper mother. Well, those days were over. From this moment on, she vowed that she would reclaim the life he had stolen from her, and she would have her revenge while she was at it.

Feeling instantly better at the thought, Imogen held her head high and took a long defiant look at her reflection in the computer screen. She thought of the diamond then, of that magnificent Bluebird that Sebastian had been at such pains to secure, and smiled secretly. 'Duncan Phillips' had better prepare himself. Because Imogen Forbes was going to teach him a lesson he would never forget.

CHAPTER 22

Tamara Du Bois wondered if she had not missed her vocation in life. As performances went, this one was worthy of a standing ovation.

'And then, right in front of the wedding planner, she hit me. Struck me in my face! Oh Douglas, I almost fell to the floor in pain and shock. I mean, the humiliation! She was screaming obscenities at me, calling me every name under the sun; filthy, horrible names, and I was begging her to stop all this, to forgive me and that I was sorry, so, so sorry . . .' Tamara sobbed, her head in her hands as she sat opposite Douglas Rothschild in the large, expensive leather chair inside his office. She liked Douglas's office. Everything about it screamed money and chic from the Philippe Starck lamps and chairs to the Conran desk and sofa.

Douglas took a tissue from a box on his desk and handed it to her, trying not to notice her bare, tanned legs stretched endlessly out in front of her, and the roundness of her ample cleavage visible in her flimsy pale blue wrap dress. Noticing his eyes upon her, Tamara felt a flush of satisfaction and continued.

'The thing is, I'm just so terrified that she'll tell Hen

about . . . well, you know – us.' She glanced up at him and immediately lowered her eyes coquettishly. 'I don't think I could bear it, Douglas, really I don't.' She caught her breath then, her sobs causing her large chest to heave up and down. She really did have the most fantastic rack on her. The best he'd ever seen on a woman bar none. And they were real to boot.

In all fairness, Douglas had tried to keep his distance from Tamara since their mad moment of unadulterated lust. A philanderer he may be but he wasn't totally without conscience. After all, she was his son's intended.

'Calm yourself now, Tamara,' Douglas said soothingly. 'I told you I can handle Calvary.'

Although he could see the girl was laying it on thicker than her make-up, he knew she was in part telling the truth. Calvary was capable of becoming quite vicious when provoked, and she was certainly out to cause trouble.

Calvary had overlooked his many affairs time and time again over the course of their marriage. He knew it was a big ask but why couldn't she just maintain the status quo? He was worried. Especially after the tip-off from Mystern's office. If Calvary was planning to divorce him then the truth would be out. And there was no way Douglas was ever going to allow that to happen. A womaniser he might be, but a womaniser who has betrayed his son? Now that would be bad for business.

Tamara continued to cry.

'She's out to destroy me, Douglas. To blacken my name. She says I'm a slut, a whore who's not good enough to bear her a grandchild. Oh Douglas, what should I do? I just don't know what to do . . .'

The girl was almost hysterical now and reluctantly Douglas came round from behind his desk and went to her.

'Why don't you sit down on the sofa. Relax. I'll have Arabella bring us some coffee.' He buzzed his PA.

Tamara raised a smile as he handed her another tissue which she gratefully took, making sure her hand made contact with his as she did. Her little girl lost routine was not working out quite as she had hoped. Douglas was making all the right sympathetic noises but he wasn't being quite as tactile as she had bargained for. She had half expected her dress to be on the floor by now.

He duly sat down next to her, fixing her with a stare that belied his lustful intentions. 'Tell me it's going to be OK,' she begged softly, her rasping sobs now a low, dulcet purr. 'I want to marry Hen so much . . . Mummy and Daddy will die if Calvary, well . . . if things are said. They'll disown me . . . Oh please, Douglas, tell me that you can make it right . . .' She leaned into him then, resting her head onto his shoulder.

Douglas could smell Tamara's freshly washed, floral-scented hair as it brushed against his cheek, feel the outline of her breast as it pressed against his side. She had brought one leg up onto the sofa now, her knee a little bent, exposing almost all of her soft, smooth thigh. God, she was gorgeous. Gorgeous and young. He had loved screwing her, the feel of her soft, supple skin, a stranger's body underneath his own. That was half the thrill of it for Douglas. A stranger's body, a *young* stranger's body was like a new and complex toy that you couldn't wait to play with, to explore and understand.

'Don't cry, Tamara.' Douglas tried hard not to look down at her cleavage as it strained to free itself from her dress. She was really crying now, tears falling from her face and onto her chest and lap, staining her light blue dress a deep navy. He imagined her nipple in his mouth, tough as a clothes peg, standing to attention as he nibbled away at it.

'Oh, Douglas,' she said, pushing her chest further into him, pulling her legs up underneath her now, the front of her dress opening slightly, exposing her Agent Provocateur finest. It was enough to send him over the edge and she knew it.

In one deft move he released her breasts from the straining fabric and marvelled at them for a moment before unzipping his trousers.

'Let's get you out of those wet clothes,' he smirked, as he tore her underwear to the side. She gasped, arching her back as she let out a long, satisfactory groan.

'Oh, Douglas,' she whispered again, throwing her head back and opening her legs wider to receive him, noting the time on the desk clock opposite them as she did. She had an appointment with her wedding florist in half an hour's time and she couldn't afford to be late.

'Tamara Du Bois,' he whispered hotly in her ear as he plunged himself deep inside her. 'You really are a very naughty girl. A *very* naughty girl indeed.'

CHAPTER 23

Throwing her shopping bags onto a table in the Chelsea Brasserie, Yasmin took a seat opposite Sammie Grainger and announced, 'I've got ten minutes. I'm having a Hollywood wax at Lockonego in ten minutes and then I have a plane to catch, so let's make this quick, shall we?'

'Well, it's really good of you to show up at all, Lady Belmont,' Sammie said, without a hint of irony. Ten minutes was plenty enough time, at least it was for what she had to say. 'I took the liberty of ordering you a fresh pineapple juice. Hope you don't mind.'

'Perfect,' Yasmin nodded, wishing she'd had the foresight to throw a vodka in there too.

The wax appointment was a bare-faced lie and the plane she was due to catch to take her to Como was not for hours yet, but Grainger wasn't to know that. Yasmin just wanted to get this thing over and done with as soon as possible. Sammie had been persistent, having left at least six messages on her voicemail asking her to make good on that lunch she'd agreed to when they had ran into each other at Forbes's ball.

'My editor – you remember, the letch – well, he is very keen for me to do a follow-up piece on you and Lord

Belmont. He was hoping we might be able to do something with you in situ, at home, together. Sort of *Hello!*-style but with a high-end fashion twist. Initial thoughts?' Sammie stirred her juice with a straw, and looked up at Yasmin tentatively.

Yasmin's *initial thought* was to get up and leave, but she figured this girl wasn't about to take no for an answer.

'I don't *hate* the idea – and I'd have to talk to Jeremy first, of course.'

'Of course!' Sammie nodded. 'We can do the in-depth interview then when we've got more time. You know, it seems the fashionable London set has developed a bit of a crush on you, Lady B. Everyone wants to know all about you; your life story, how you came to be where you are today.'

Yasmin felt sick. *In-depth interview*. Jesus, this bitch was going to be harder to get rid of than a case of herpes in a knocking shop.

'Why all the sudden interest anyway?' Yasmin shrugged with as much modesty as her ego would allow. 'Like I said, there really isn't much to tell. I'm from a middle class farming family near Wales. My parents died in a car crash a few years ago, after which I moved to London – Chelsea to be exact – to see if I couldn't find myself a little job somewhere, you know, something to keep me occupied and out of Raffles until the early hours. And then I met Jeremy and the rest is history.'

Sammie noticed that Yasmin's hand was shaking as she held her juice glass and suddenly felt an overwhelming sense of empathy for her.

'You and I both know there's a *lot* more to know about your life than that.' She allowed the comment to hang heavy in the air above them before continuing. 'We thought we'd provide the readers with some background on you; you know, a little about your childhood, what you were like when you were a teenager . . . I assume you have photos? Would you be happy for us to print them, fashion faux pas and all?'

Suddenly Yasmin saw all the months of preparation she'd done in order to have got this far going to waste; all the sacrifices she'd made, the nights she'd had to stomach having that disgusting lump clamouring on top of her, puffing and panting, slipping away before her eyes and felt her panic reach flood alert. She needed to find out the truth about her sister's death as soon as possible.

She would have to get rid of this leech and somehow locate this elusive videotape or whatever it was that useless skank June Larkin had alluded to.

'Actually, you know what, Sammie? It is Sammie, isn't it?' Yasmin said knowing full well that it was. 'I think I've changed my mind. I don't think this is a good idea after all.'

'Oh, really?' Sammie stared at her, crestfallen. 'But why? I mean, it'll all be tastefully done, if that's what you're worried about. You'll have the full works; stylists, make-up and hair, even airbrushing if you want it – not that you need it,' she added diplomatically. 'We'll get some big names on board for you too; Cavalli, Balenciaga, Chanel – whoever you choose.'

Yasmin shook her head.

'Now I've had a little time to think about it, I can't think of anything I'd like *less* than to have my life splashed all over the pages of a *free* supplement.' She stood to leave, throwing her oversized Chloe python bag over her shoulder in one deft move.

Sammie was crestfallen. She had not wanted to play her ace card so soon. She had wanted to choose a much quieter, more private moment in which to unveil her findings, but Yasmin had left her little choice.

'I understand,' she said. 'I mean, I don't suppose I would

want someone to start digging around into my childhood either if I was hiding a secret like yours, *eh, Stacey*?'

Yasmin's heart leapt into her throat. She froze to the spot.

'I have to say, it was quite clever of you,' Sammie continued, 'keeping your own surname like that, integrating it into your new one. After all, how many Joneses are there in the UK? Hundreds of thousands? Millions perhaps. Not an easy name to trace.'

Yasmin swallowed dryly. Grainger knew her name. Her *real* name. But how?

'You don't remember me?' Sammie continued, clutching her chest, a mock wounded expression on her face. 'OK then, I'll remind you. The youth club in Coulsdon? You were slightly older than me, and very pretty. Your hair was brown then, and you had a pair of glittery heart deely boppers that you were rarely seen without. You were fostered by Kerry and Daniel Merton in Croydon, not far from where you grew up on the Perry Estate.'

Yasmin blinked at her, incredulous. How on earth did she know this stuff?

'Look, Stacey,' Sammie said, her voice softening. 'I know about your sister. I know about *everything*.'

A waiter approached their table.

'I'll have a vodka tonic. Large,' Yasmin barked before he'd had a chance to open his mouth.

Although she knew she shouldn't, Sammie was really enjoying this moment. Not because she wanted to hurt Stacey Jones – she'd had more than her fair share of pain in her life by anyone's standards and Sammie had no desire to add to it – but because for the first time in her career she felt like a real journalist. One that investigated and unearthed truths.

There was a pause while Yasmin gathered her thoughts.

'I think . . . I think you must have me confused with

someone else,' she said with as much conviction as she could muster. 'I really have no idea what you're talking about.'

'I'm quite hurt that you don't remember me,' Sammie blithely continued. 'I mean, I remember *you*. I've even got a photograph of the two of us together.' She took the dog-eared picture her flatmate had found out of her handbag and slid it across the table.

Yasmin stared at it for a few moments, paralysed. Seeing herself so young, her life already blighted by so much tragedy, made her want to break down and cry on the spot. She had been all alone in the world and yet she was still smiling for the camera, a glimmer of hope in her eyes.

'Where did you get this?' Yasmin pushed the picture away, fighting back tears.

The waiter appeared with her drink and she snatched it from the tray, downing it in one hit.

Sammie smiled.

'I'm right, aren't I? That is you in the picture. You are Stacey Jones, aren't you?'

Yasmin did not answer. She would listen to what Grainger had to say, and then she would do whatever she had to do to make the problem go away. She'd offer her money – a lot of it if she had to, to buy her silence. If that didn't work, she'd put the frighteners on her. Have her followed, see if there wasn't any dirt of her own she could dig up. And if that failed, well, then she would just have to think again.

'Look. Yasmin. Shall I call you Yasmin or Stacey?'

'"*Lady* Belmont" is fine,' she said flatly.

'Yes, of course,' Sammie said, realising she had over-stepped the mark. 'I take it Lord Belmont and your newfound friends know nothing about your true provenance, then?'

Yasmin slammed her hand down hard onto the table,

narrowly missing Sammie's fingers and causing her to gasp in shock.

'Now you listen to me, you filthy, no-mark hack,' she smiled at her though it belied her fear. 'Whatever you think you know about me, you don't know the half of it.' Yasmin was in a blind state of panic now, her mind awash with fractured thoughts of how she could resolve this mess without her true motives coming to light too soon. *Help me, Chloe*, she said a silent prayer in her mind. *Don't desert me now.*

'I want you to stay out of my business, Grainger. Come near me again and I'll get an injunction slapped on you so hard you'll feel the sting into old age, am I making myself clear?'

Sammie was terrified. Terrified and elated at the same time. This was as good as an admission of truth! She really *was* onto something.

'Oh, but I think you must have misunderstood me,' she said, her voice thick with adrenalin. 'I don't want to *hurt* you, Stacey. I want to *help* you.'

'Oh yeah?' Yasmin smirked, her lip curling into a snarl. 'Supposing I even wanted it, how could *you* help *me*?'

Sammie looked up into Yasmin's impossibly blue eyes and saw a desperate sadness behind her cold, icy stare.

'I could start by telling you where you might find that tape.'

CHAPTER 24

Nothing in life, thought Imogen, was ever quite how you expected it to be. And the inside of the vault at Forbes Bank was no exception. Cold and clinical with a grey slate floor, it was hardly the plush, relaxing carpeted space she had envisaged in her mind.

Imogen pulled a face and looked up as a squeaky, oscillating fan churned the fetid air above them, adding to the chilly ambience. It felt like what it was: a cold, dark basement full of steel boxes. Only these weren't just any old boxes; Imogen knew that inside them lay a thousand secrets, not to mention millions in cash and jewels. She noted the security cameras in each corner, tiny red dots following her every move.

Catching her expression, Sebastian raised an eyebrow.

'Not what you were expecting?'

'No. I suppose it isn't.'

'Well, this is a secure room, Imogen, not a health spa. This is where people come to deposit their valuables. They don't hang around discussing the latest cosmetic surgery procedures.' His tone was the usual mix of condescension and sarcasm and she turned away from him. She could not afford an atmosphere between them at the moment. Imogen knew that if the plan that had been formulating inside her mind these last few days had a cat in hell's chance of reaching any kind of fruition, then she would need to embark upon a charm offensive of epic proportions and get that bastard of a husband of hers onside. Painful though this thought was, buttering him up would be a necessary evil.

'And I'd appreciate it if you could hurry it along a bit.' Seb checked his Cartier watch impatiently. 'I've got a lunch meeting with the Chancellor of the Exchequer in a couple of hours and I've a list of calls as long as your arm to return before then.'

'It's number 1168,' she said, scanning the boxes.

Under the strict, detailed instructions of Cressida's solicitor, Imogen had been asked to go down into the vaults and open Cressida's strong box in person, giving her the perfect excuse to have a dig around. It made her smile to think that even from the grave, her old friend had come to her rescue in her hour of need.

Sebastian tapped his fingers against the metal and a sharp echo cut through the eerie silence of the room.

'It's one of the smaller ones, as I expected,' he sniffed, feigning a lack of interest. Truth was, he was just as intrigued as Imogen was to find out what was inside Cressida's strong box.

Sebastian had never much liked coming down into 'the bowels' of the bank, as he described it, which was why he made the trip for VIP clients only and left the 'hoi polloi' to his most trusted member of Forbes Security, Derrell 'Dickie' Richards.

'I've found it!' Imogen squealed excitedly as she placed the key in the small lock and began to jiggle it.

'Well, come on then – open the damn thing!'

Imogen twiddled the key and wondered if her husband had always been this acerbic or if he had got worse just lately. Truth was, she honestly didn't know. She had been so entrenched in heartache back then that she couldn't really remember.

Imogen was hard pushed to recall any 'firsts' with Seb; their first proper conversation, making love to him for the first time, not even their first argument. All she could remember was the grief she had felt about losing *him,* the perennial knot in her gut that had simply refused to budge. That ache had taken months to soften, and when it finally had, she had found that she missed it. In the end, the pain was all she'd had left.

Imogen would never forget the look of despair on *his* face as he heard the news about Aimee. It would haunt her to her grave.

It was supposed to have been their first proper holiday together. They had flown into Ibiza late at night, arriving at the stunning hilltop villa in the northern part of the island – their own perfect hacienda that Cressida had arranged, 'a little break, darling, before the chaos of London Fashion Week' – and fallen into bed, exhausted. The following morning, Imogen, always an early riser, had beaten him to the small private beach. She had left him gently snoring, allowing him extra time to restore his energies for the days ahead.

As far as they had both been concerned, the next five days signalled the start of the rest of their lives together and they had not wanted to waste a single moment. They had planned to hang out with the beautiful people on Playa d'en Bossa beach and Las Salinas, buy beads and leather goods down at the infamous hippie market in Es Cana and go crazy together at Pacha, dancing until sunrise with all the energy and exuberance that only the young and desperately in love can truly possess.

'Hey, sleepyhead, look what I found!' Imogen had held the conch shell up above her head proudly like a trophy as she walked through the gentle waves towards him. 'Come on in, the water's like a bath,' she'd encouraged. He had walked towards her and their bodies had met, knee deep in the sea. His mouth pressed against hers and she felt the goose bumps on her flesh as he wrapped himself around her, her nipples as hard as diamonds, brushing against his chest as he pulled her closer.

It would be the first time they had made love since he'd been free – properly free – and it had felt like the first time all over again.

She had cast her eyes down towards his impressive hardness. 'I could get used to this as a wake-up call,' she had teased him, raising an eyebrow.

Afterwards, they had lain together on the sand, their bodies warmed with passion and the sun, neither wanting to break the physical bond between them.

'I could stay like this forever,' she remembered him saying as he had traced his finger lightly over her sandy breast.

'Me too,' she had replied, squinting up at the sky. 'Only it might be a bit tricky, you know, taking a bath, using the toilet, that sort of thing,' she'd giggled and he'd squeezed her ribs playfully.

'Stop!' she'd squirmed, laughing.

'Imp,' he'd said.

She pushed him off her playfully, his hotness trickling down her thigh as she had stood.

'Last one to the house has to wash up!' she'd squealed, adopting a runner's stance.

He had shook his head wearily and then suddenly shot past her, laughing as he sprinted off.

'Oooh, you . . . you cheat!' she'd yelled as she hotfooted after him, mimicking his deep footprints, kicking sand behind her as she ran.

Imogen almost laughed out loud as she relived those precious moments they had shared. But her smile soon waned when she thought of what had followed.

After showering, she had gone to look for him in the vast villa.

'There you are,' she had said mock crossly as she had padded outside to the balcony, looking out towards the spectacular view. 'For a moment I thought you were hiding from me.'

The look on his face had told her instantly that something was wrong. Very wrong.

'There's been an accident,' he'd said, his voice low and husky. 'It's Aimee. She's fallen down some stairs . . .'

It transpired that in a desperate and foolish bid to win his affection back, a drunken Aimee had thrown herself down a flight of stairs. In her damaged young mind, her plan was to have a little accident, something that was just serious enough to bring him home to her, jolt him into realising that he still loved her. Only the consequences were far more tragic than she could ever have anticipated. Aimee had severed her spinal column in the fall. At just twenty-five years old, she was paralysed from the waist down and would never walk again.

Imogen closed her eyes as she remembered the expression on his face as he had turned to look at her, so sad and desperate that it had taken the breath from her. And he had not needed to speak; in that moment, she knew she had lost him.

They had made love for the final time on the beach before he left later that morning. Even to this day, she still thought of his lips, soft and trembling against her own, resisting the inevitability of their parting.

That day, a beautiful summer's day in Ibiza with the sun high above her, Imogen Lennard had watched the only man she had ever loved walk away from her into the distance, leaving only his footprints in the sand behind.

In the weeks that had followed, Imogen had thrown herself into her modelling work, and the party scene that invariably accompanied it, in a bid to help her forget the ache inside her chest that had refused to budge. And that's when she had met Sebastian Forbes. Introduced by a mutual acquaintance, his attentions had been a welcome distraction for her, at least at first.

The truth was Sebastian had been keeping a close eye on his object of affection for some months, waiting in the wings for his moment to strike with a carefully orchestrated charm offensive. Eventually, his patience paid off.

As unfair as it was in hindsight, Imogen had initially thought of Seb as little more than a 'band-aid' boyfriend. But before long, she had found herself sucked into the vortex of the much older and manipulative Sebastian's seductive world.

Within weeks, he had whisked her off to Necker Island for the holiday of a lifetime and, little more than a month later, he asked for her hand in marriage. Only what Sebastian had failed to realise at the time was that Imogen's heart belonged to someone else . . .

Sebastian looked at his wife then and wondered if now was a good time to tell her that Bryony had called the house that morning and told him that she would be coming home for the summer term, just in time to help her father celebrate his birthday! He had wanted to feel happy about this, but he simply couldn't bring himself to. As far as Imogen was concerned, the moment Bryony came into the picture, he became as good as invisible.

Imogen's subjugation was seemingly working like a dream. Ever since the night of the ball she appeared to have abandoned any notion of a career resurrection. It was as if, at last, she had seen sense and accepted her place in their marriage. Last night, for the first time in months, they had made love. There had even been talk of them spending more time together as a couple; a holiday, perhaps. But now with Bryony coming home, as far as Sebastian was concerned, it would all be spoiled.

'Look, are you opening the damn thing or not?' he barked at her impatiently, his thoughts beginning to irritate him. 'I'm pushed for time here.'

'I'm sorry, Seb. It's stuck, I . . . oh, here we go.' The tiny wheels made a high-pitched squeak along the runners of the drawer, setting her teeth on edge as she tentatively opened it.

Peering inside Imogen was disappointed to see that it was empty. Cressida had obviously cleaned it out, which only added to her paranoia that the conversation she had overheard between the two women at Cressida's funeral about her being bankrupt were probably true.

'What a bloody anticlimax,' Sebastian remarked and on this occasion Imogen was inclined to agree with him.

'Yes,' she said, a little melancholy, 'I was rather hoping, knowing Cress as I do – as I did – that it might be full to the brim with diamonds.'

'Diamonds? Ha!' Sebastian threw his head back. 'If it's diamonds you want to see,' he scoffed, 'then I'll show you a diamond.'

She looked up at him then, her eyes shining like the jewels themselves.

'The Bluebird, you mean?'

He raised an eyebrow, aroused by her sudden interest.

'But I thought you had things to do,' she said, calling his bluff. 'The Chancellor . . .'

'Do you want to see it or not?' he snapped.

'Well, I'd love to, of course, but I don't want to put you to any trouble. I know how busy you are.'

Sebastian grinned. Grateful suited her.

'Wait until you see her up close, and whatever you do, do *not* touch anything. The room we are about to enter is heat censored as well as sound and touch sensitive. Get too close and the whole goddamn alarm system will go off.'

'Really? And what would happen then?' Imogen asked, wide-eyed with the thought of such impending drama.

'A swat team would be on the scene within seconds. And Prince Saud would have my head on a stick! The bloody fool thinks this diamond is in possession of his dead mother's spirit or some such ridiculousness – he doesn't want to have her upset.'

Imogen raised an eyebrow.

'I see. Best we go careful then.'

She watched as Sebastian began to run his hand alongside the far facing wall.

'Ah ha!' he said, pressing a small button.

Imogen gasped as the seamless wall suddenly opened up in the middle like a set of electric gates, exposing another set of steel doors behind it. Sebastian stood in front of the door and pulled down a large metal flap.

'A secret room!' Imogen breathed.

Sebastian nodded, pleased with himself.

'And what's that?' she asked, looking up at the wall.

'It's a state of the art sensor lock,' he said excitedly, keeping his head still as what looked like a small camera came into view. 'This machine here is scanning my face. It's actually reading my skin like a fingerprint! The contours of my nose, the colour of my eyes, that tiny scar on my lip . . . every pore, every wrinkle unique to me.' He turned to her and grinned. 'Effectively, I am the key!' Seb laughed again then, a horrible startling laugh that could cause a horse to rear.

'It's the most sophisticated piece of security in the world,' he boasted, 'and the most expensive. It's been ten years in project and another ten in production it's a sublime piece of equipment,' he said, gazing at it admiringly. 'There's not another system like it on the planet.'

Imogen watched and listened with a curious mixture of wonder and discomfiture. The whole thing was quite surreal, like something from a James Bond film, with her husband cast as the baddie.

With a low sinister hiss, the steel doors parted. The room was small and everything inside it was perfectly white, from the pristine, plush soft carpet to the flocked-fabric padded walls. It was like the inside of a giant jewellery box, with the Bluebird, in all its stunning, magnificent glory, situated on a cushioned plinth in the middle.

Imogen stared at it for the longest moment, its intense colours pulling her in and holding her there. It was far more beautiful up close than she had remembered. The size of a man's fist, it looked almost alive somehow, like a pulsing entity as its thousand facets sent light and colour dancing all around the clinical room. Somehow the idea that it possessed the spirit of the prince's dead mother did not seem nearly as ludicrous as it had first sounded.

'Do you want to touch her?' Sebastian shot her a sideways glance. Imogen's heart was beating a song in her chest.

'Can I?'

His grin widened.

She stepped forwards and slowly placed the tips of her fingers onto the gem.

'*Jeeesus Christ*!' She leapt back in shock, her face contorting as a sharp pain shot up through her hand and into her arm.

Sebastian gave a high-pitched laugh.

'You bastard,' she said, her voice shaking almost as violently as her hand. 'It's protected by electricity.'

'*Invisible* electricity. Just another little added security measure. Not that anyone would ever get this far, mind you.'

Imogen rubbed her arm.

'That *really* hurt, Seb.'

'It's supposed to,' he chuckled. 'That was 15 amps – enough to kill a rabbit!' He placed his hand onto a pad positioned on the wall and she watched as his palm made an imprint into the soft, pliable substance, deactivating the electric sensor.

She grimaced at him.

'Aw, come on, Imogen. It was just a joke. I turned it down to the lowest voltage. If it had been on full it would have killed you!'

'My hero,' she deadpanned, her heart thudding loudly against her ribs, her arm still warm and buzzing. It was a shitty trick but she would swallow it down. The pain she felt now would be nothing compared to what he would experience when she outsmarted him – and his team of American security experts. She had made some mental notes, enough to search for potential flaws in his 'perfect' system. Somehow Imogen would have to find a way of getting down here again, this time without Seb in tow. She hadn't the first clue how she was going to go about it but one thing was for sure; she would find a way – or die trying.

'I want to go now,' she said, turning to him and clutching her throbbing arm, her mouth bone-dry. 'I think I've seen enough.'

CHAPTER 25

It was busy in Yves Saint Laurent for a Wednesday afternoon, busier than Calvary had expected, causing her to wonder if there wasn't some important event happening that she hadn't heard about – or worse, been invited to. It was paranoia, of course. Calvary knew every important date in the society calendar as well as she knew her own children's birthdays.

As she perused the rails of delicate dresses and chiffon separates – last minute purchases for her girlie getaway to the lakes – Calvary thought about Josia. She was in two minds whether or not to go looking for him. She had sensed a frisson between them something she hadn't felt in years – but what was it they said about curiosity and cats?

'Calvary? Calvary Rothschild . . . is that you? Good God, it's been an age!'

The shrill voice sliced through Calvary's thoughts with all the subtlety of a meat cleaver. She spun round.

'Countess Ledbury! Verite! Goodness me. How very lovely to see you,' Calvary lied, stepping forward and air-kissing the woman on both cheeks.

'Art for Africa, yes, the charity auction at Annabel's – the last time I saw you. Gosh, how long was it now? Two, no, three years?'

Calvary did the maths. 'Three. Almost.'

'Goodness, where does all the time disappear to? It only feels like yesterday I bought that Hockney. Still, all for a good cause, eh, darling? Anyway, I see you're buying . . . off somewhere nice?' She began to inspect the selection of dresses Calvary had in her hand.

The Earl of Ledbury's wife was a Parisian by birth and Grade A bitch by nature. Although they were around the same age, a lifetime of Gitanes and St Tropez sun had added ten years to the Countess's features.

'The Italian Riviera, actually. The Ivanov's place,' Calvary replied breezily. 'Anyway, I haven't seen you on the circuit in a while. You weren't at Cannes last year or the Regatta in June. Come to mention it, I didn't see you at the Markhams' do at Chatsworth House either. Fabulous event. We were on the same table as Charles and Camilla this year. And then of course there was Forbes' bash . . . the most spectacular yet. Shame you couldn't make it.'

Calvary was boasting and felt a small pang of satisfaction as she watched the Countess's lips purse.

'Oh, I haven't had time for all of that.' Verite waved a bejewelled hand dismissively. 'We're having a villa built in St Barts, which hasn't left a lot of time for the *smaller* social events this year. But we've managed to squeeze a few in here and there; skiing with Nicolas and Carla Sarkozy in Val D'Isere and a little jolly to Necker Island with Sting and Trudi back in May. It's not all been work, work, work, darling. Anyway, tell me, how are you and Douglas? Is he still an incorrigible flirt?'

Calvary felt her hackles rise but decided to swallow her tongue.

'Douglas is marvellous, thank you. I'll let him know that you were asking after him.'

'Please do,' said the Countess, raising an eyebrow.

'And the Earl?'

'In fine form,' Verite remarked, 'keeps pestering me to renew our wedding vows, the silly old sod that he is. Personally, I think it's all just an excuse to have an enormous big bun fight. He fancies Sudbury Castle, but then again, who doesn't?' She laughed, a horrible self-satisfied cackle.

Calvary grimaced.

'Well, it's been marvellous to see you, Verite. I'm sure we'll run into each other again soon.' She refrained from adding, 'more's the pity.'

Calvary leaned in and air-kissed the Countess's overly made-up cheeks.

'You too. Don't forget to give my best to Douglas, will you. I do so enjoy hearing about all his latest *adventures* through the grapevine.'

Desperate to escape, Calvary made her way over to the assistant and plonked the large pile of dresses onto the counter.

'Thank you, Mrs Rothschild.' Yvette, the sales assistant, with whom she was on first-name terms, beamed up at her. Calvary didn't even flinch as she handed over her credit card.

'Make it quick, will you, Yvette? I'm in a bit of a hurry.'

Yvette gave an understanding nod and disappeared into a small room to complete the purchases. Moments later, she reappeared looking flustered.

'I'm sorry, Mrs Rothschild. There seems to be a problem with this card. Do you have another?'

'Of course!' Calvary replied, a little miffed as she reached into her Mulberry wallet.

Moments later Yvette reappeared again, her face red.

'I'm really sorry, Mrs Rothschild. There appears to be a problem with this card also.'

Calvary frowned, the first flushes of embarrassment warming her skin.

'But that can't be.' She looked at the card. 'There must be a problem with your machine. Here, try the Amex,' she snapped, beginning to feel a little annoyed.

The assistant nodded apologetically. 'I am so sorry about this.'

Calvary smiled through her indignation.

But moments later the assistant returned and nervously shook her head.

Calvary felt her heart miss a beat. Just what the hell was all this about?

'I can hold on to the items for you,' Yvette suggested nervously. 'You can always arrange to make payment over the telephone and we'll have them sent over as soon as it's been authorised. I am so very sorry, Mrs Rothschild.'

Calvary was mortified. Her cards being declined in Yves Saint Laurent. She would never be able to come here again.

'Is there a problem?' asked Countess Ledbury, sensing a little discrepancy as she stood behind Calvary watching the whole episode unfurl with barely concealed glee.

Calvary felt her face burn with humiliation. This would be the talk of society by morning.

'There's no problem,' Calvary replied quickly.

'Here, put it on my card, darling. You can always send me a cheque in the post,' the Countess smirked.

Calvary did not reply. Hot with humiliation, she was already halfway out the door.

*

'There had better be a bloody good explanation for this, Douglas,' Calvary's voice was shaking with raw emotion as she flew into his office, unannounced, her face almost as red as the tomato Giambattista Valli shift dress she was wearing.

Douglas gave a wry smile. He had been expecting her.

'Oh, do come in, Calvary, please. Make yourself at home.' He buzzed the intercom. 'Arabella, hold all my calls for five minutes, yes?'

'Of course, sir,' she replied, her voice low and breathy.

Calvary raised an eyebrow. 'Arabella? I haven't heard of this one before. Is she new?'

'As a matter of fact she is, yes.'

Calvary let out a trademark throaty laugh.

'You get through secretaries like I get through hosiery, Douglas. Screwed her yet, have you?'

Douglas sighed and shook his head.

'I'll treat that question with the contempt it deserves.'

'That's a yes, then.'

'No, Calvary. It's a no, I haven't *screwed* her, as you so delicately put it.'

Calvary smirked.

'What's the matter, Douglas, losing your touch?'

Douglas bristled. 'What do you want, Calvary? I'm busy.'

'I want to know what you're playing at,' she said, throwing her credit cards down onto his desk. Her voice was low and measured and he smiled as he heard the rage simmering away underneath. He'd known she would be furious, which of course was the whole point.

'Ah, yes. Well, you can't say I didn't warn you. I told you not to upset the apple cart, as it were. But you just couldn't help yourself, could you? Couldn't keep that forked tongue of yours inside your head, where it would be better off ninety-nine percent of the time.' Douglas fixed her with a cool stare. 'Tamara told me all about your little altercation at the wedding planner's. The threats and the violence . . .'

'Violence!' Calvary was pacing the room, too enraged to

sit down. She'd show him violence. Right now she wanted to tear his office apart. Smash those Annie Leibovitz prints he loved so much, rip the blinds down and throw his beloved Philippe Starck chair through the window.

'It was just a little slap, for crying out loud. Long overdue if you ask me.'

'The girl was hysterical, for God's sake. Came to me in an awful state.'

Calvary glanced at him. 'She came to *you*?'

'Well, who else was she going to turn to, Calvary? She can hardly tell Henry why her future mother-in-law assaulted her at the wedding planner's, now could she?'

'You said it, Douglas,' she retorted. 'And not only do you expect me to forget that it ever happened and allow the treacherous little slapper to marry our son, but you see fit to punish me further by humiliating me – in Yves Saint Laurent, of all places! And,' Calvary drew breath. She was ranting now, 'you'll not guess who witnessed this humiliation first-hand. Only that supercilious bitch, the Countess Verite bloody Ledbury. It'll be the talk of the town by now. She even offered to pay for my purchases.' Calvary placed her head in her hands, reliving the shame. 'I'll not forgive you for this, Douglas,' she said, her voice cracking like glass. 'Not ever.'

'We'll add it to the burgeoning list then, shall we?' Douglas shot back, suddenly feeling a touch guilty. He had never seen her so upset.

'You're a bastard, do you know that?' Calvary said, her voice filled with contempt. 'You think you can just cut me off like that, humiliate me in front of all those people?'

'Yes, Calvary, that's exactly what I think.' He looked up at her with a cold stare, his earlier guilt dissipating as he began to lose patience. 'I warned you that if you refused to toe the line with Tamara then I would act – and I have.

Now, I've had the cards reactivated. They should be fine to use while you're up at the lakes, but I mean it, Calvary. If I hear of any more nonsense then next time it'll be for good.'

Calvary looked at her husband with so much hatred that it was all she could do to stop herself from grabbing his letter knife and slitting his throat. For a second, she imagined the look of terror on his face as he realised what she'd done, as he began to bleed out all over his Conran desk, his miserable life slowly ebbing away all over his Gucci suit. It made her feel fleetingly better.

'You know, I had you down as many things, Douglas, but never the spiteful, malicious sort. Oh, she's done a good number on you, our dear Tamara. Has you wrapped right round her pointed little talons, doesn't she?'

'Are you still here?' Douglas murmured.

Calvary snatched up her oversized Miu Miu day clutch and, fixing her husband with a contemptuous glare, prepared to leave. As she was about to flounce from the room, she noticed a post-it note message on Douglas's desk diary with the words: 'Forbes Vault. 2:00 p.m.' written on it. Suddenly the thought struck her like a blow to the chest.

Of course! Stupid, *stupid* woman! Douglas must be stashing his cash down in the vaults at Forbes Bank! She had clean forgotten about the strong box that had been in his family for generations. It's where the Rothschilds kept all their family gems and secrets. Lord knew, Douglas alone had enough of them to keep Forbes in business until time immemorial.

As she turned on her heels, Calvary glanced at the desk clock and into the spy camera she had planted there and felt a small rush of satisfaction. With a bit of luck it would have recorded every word of their conversation. Douglas may have won the battle yet again, but Calvary was quietly adamant that she would win the war. Flicking her auburn hair from her face in an exaggerated movement, Calvary smiled in the camera's direction and hoped that whatever else, it was getting her best side.

CHAPTER 26

Standing on the marble patio of Villa Bellafonte, Yasmin peered over her enormous Dior shades and stared up at the imposing nineteenth century palazzine in all its neoclassical glory.

'Now this is what I call a house!' she said, signalling to a member of staff that her champagne flute needed refilling.

'If Jeremy has a spare £260 million, darling, it could be yours,' Calvary said, blowing cigarette smoke into the warm air. 'I believe it's up for sale.'

'Really?' Yasmin's interest was aroused.

'It used to belong to the Versaces. They've all been here; Madonna, Elton John, Sting. I think Jennifer Lopez even had her honeymoon here. Well, one of them at least.'

'It would make a wonderful first wedding anniversary gift, wouldn't it?' Yasmin sighed. 'I mean, the bathrooms! I almost had a heart attack when I saw that life-sized marble statue of that Greek god, Adonie.'

'Adon*is*,' Calvary corrected her.

Yasmin blanched. It was slip-ups such as these that might eventually lead to blowing her cover if she wasn't careful. After all, she was supposed to have had a very expensive, private education behind her.

'That's what I said.' She took a large gulp of Krug. 'Well anyway, if he was supposedly the god of love, then *God* help us all. I mean, his cup hardly overfloweth in the, you know, trouser department.' She raised a sardonic eyebrow.

Calvary chuckled. She was glad she had invited Yasmin on their little trip. Truth was she had grown quite fond of the girl in recent months. Imogen had warmed to her too, particularly after her show of support at Cressida's funeral. Between them they were forging quite a formidable little threesome.

Calvary clasped her hands together. 'Well, ladies. I hope you enjoy dinner; I flew the chef in from one of the top restaurants in Milan, and tomorrow I've organised a little surprise for us . . . something to cheer us up after these past few hellish weeks,' she smiled broadly. 'I've chartered a jet to fly us over to Milan for an afternoon's shopping! Douglas will have a coronary when he sees the bill, with a bit of luck anyway,' she deadpanned.

'Oooh, fabulous,' Yasmin squealed her approval. She had never been to Milan, not that she was about to let on as much to the others of course.

'How does that sound to you, Ims?'

Imogen looked up.

'What? Oh, sorry,' she apologised. 'I was miles away.'

Ever since her little trip down to the vaults, Imogen's mind had been preoccupied with Seb and the diamond. In truth, she had thought of little else.

Securing that diamond had been the coup of her husband's entire career and as a result his ego had reached new and dizzying heights. Sebastian Forbes thought he was untouchable. Well, she'd soon put paid to that! Tonight, over dinner, she had decided to divulge her little plan, and she couldn't wait to see the look on her friends' faces when she did.

'Can I get you some more champagne, madam?' the hot

young Italian waiter asked, noting Yasmin's empty glass yet again.

'Fill me up!' she purred, admiring his dark, Mediterranean looks.

'Well, really,' Calvary teased, once he was out of earshot. 'What would the old pot and pan think, darling?'

'Don't be ridiculous,' Yasmin dismissed her. 'Just being friendly, that's all.'

In true form the waiter had glanced back at Yasmin over his shoulder. She had known he wouldn't be able to resist, not with her looking so resplendent in a short, nude-coloured body-con Herve Leger bandage dress that was so tight it was like liquid skin. The thought of rounding off the night with a bit of Italian Stallion between her legs almost made Yasmin lose sight of what her real objective was this evening: to steer the conversation onto her husband. Try once again to get Calvary Rothschild to spill the beans on what she knew about *that* night.

'Marriage, you have to work at it you know,' Calvary continued, directing her tutorial at Yasmin. Lord knew she'd worked at her own over the years, for all the good it had done her.

Yasmin rolled her eyes.

'A girl can still look at the menu, even if she's not planning to order from it, no?'

'Ah, and that's the difference,' Calvary sighed, attempting to hide the bitterness in her voice with a modicum of humour. 'Women *look* but men *touch*.' She bristled, adjusting the slim belt on her silk Alberta Ferretti summer dress. 'They all stray at the end of the day. It's in their DNA.'

'Oh, Calvary, don't be so cynical. Not all men do the dirty on their wives,' Imogen chipped in light-heartedly, wondering if now was a good time to make her announcement. She could hardly contain herself.

Calvary snorted and threw back her glass of champagne. It was going down well tonight. Too well in fact. Now that she had an inkling of where Douglas may have stashed his cash she felt able to relax and enjoy herself a little more. Her biggest concern now was how she would go about getting her hands on the damn stuff. To her bitter disappointment, Calvary had learned that any access to her husband's vault had first to be requested in writing, with signatures checked and verified before coming in person to make any deposits or withdrawals.

She cocked her head to one side and looked at her friend in mock sympathy.

'Oh, darling, it's what I love most about you, your naivety. Listen, I was in the dark for years about Douglas screwing half of London behind my back. It was only until I caught him red-handed . . . or should I say butt-naked, that I was forced to face the ugly truth.'

'Speak for yourself, Calvary Rothschild,' Yasmin piped up, keen to keep up with her pretence. 'Just because you've a husband who can't keep it in his trousers for longer than a lunch at Langan's, doesn't mean to say the rest of us have. Jeremy would *never* cheat on me. After all, why would he need to go out for burgers when he has filet mignon at home?'

Calvary shook her head in consternation.

'That's never the point. Look at all these fabulous movie stars, A-listers, politicians, sportsmen, married to some of the world's most beautiful women, yet plenty of them choose to find their jollies elsewhere with some little piece of trailer park trash. Take Tiger Woods for instance, or Hugh Grant.' Calvary raised her hand, animated. 'Now there's a perfect example for you. Stepping out with my good friend, the *divine* Liz Hurley . . .'

'*Divine* being the operative word,' Yasmin giggled.

'Men don't choose to cheat because they no longer find

their wives unattractive. Or even because they've stopped loving them. They do it because they *can,*' Calvary said, matter-of-fact. 'It's really as simple as that.'

Yasmin let out a little whinny of disbelief.

'Really, Calvary, next you'll be saying that actually, money *can* buy you happiness and love.'

Calvary turned to her and smiled evenly.

'Oh but, darling, you of *all* people should know that it can and it *does*.'

The two women glared at each other, their eyes locked in a stand-off. What had started out as playful banter had quickly descended into confrontation.

'Cal,' Imogen interjected gently, 'leave the poor girl alone . . . she's only been married for five minutes.'

Calvary felt the first flutters of remorse settle on her stomach. Imogen was right; she was being a hypocrite.

The three women sat silently around the table for a few seconds, though it felt like much longer, staring out at the beautiful tranquil setting overlooking the lake before them. The sun was gradually disappearing behind the pink and purple pastel-coloured clouds, signifying the end of the day and bringing with it the hopeful promise of another.

Imogen opened her mouth to speak but Yasmin beat her to it.

'So, you're more or less saying that while I'm here, Jeremy is probably at home screwing the hired help?' It would've been an appropriate time to change the subject but if she could just keep the conversation about her husband going . . .

'I'm saying that it's *possible,* that's all,' Calvary reiterated, her tone softer this time. 'After all, sweetie, you don't get a nickname like "Lecherous Lord Belmont" for nothing.'

Yasmin's thoughts turned to the recent conversation she'd had with Sammie Grainger and felt her heartbeat accelerate in her chest.

According to Grainger and her 'reliable' sources, Jeremy had stashed the tape down in the vaults at Forbes Bank some years ago, where it had remained, untouched, ever since.

'He kept it for collateral. In case anyone ever tried to blackmail him – or so the story goes,' Grainger had said. 'The police knew of it but, well, your husband is a rich man, *Lady* Belmont, and everyone has a price . . .'

Yasmin looked up from her plate and met Calvary's line of vision.

'So what if he has a past? You don't get to his age – or yours for that matter – and not have racked up a few notches on your bedpost. Anyway, it's fine by me – let's just say I reap the benefit of all that experience.'

'Oh *please*,' Calvary grimaced, 'spare us the details, darling. The main course is about to arrive.'

As if on cue, a flurry of models-cum-waiters brought a selection of sizzling meats and fish to the table. Yasmin smiled provocatively as her waiter carefully spooned herb encrusted rack of lamb and rosemary jus onto her warmed plate, leaning forward to afford him a better view of her own impressive rack.

'Mmm. Delish,' she said, licking her lips, as she stared up at him. 'Anyway, I mean, it's hardly a crime; it's just *sex* at the end of the day.' She put an emphasis on the word 'sex', briefly making eye contact with the waiter. 'It's not like he's murdered anyone, is it?' She had chosen her words carefully and deliberately.

Calvary glanced quickly at Imogen but Yasmin caught the exchange.

'What?' she asked. 'What's the look for?'

'Nothing,' Imogen said, busying herself with her knife and fork. 'It's nothing.'

'Oh for God's sake, she has a right to know,' Calvary spluttered. 'It's hardly a secret anyway.'

'Know what?' Yasmin's heart began to pound like a jackhammer against her ribs.

'Don't, Cal,' Imogen gently implored, 'don't spoil the evening.'

'Look, is one of you going to tell me what you're on about?'

Calvary looked up at Yasmin's overly made-up, pretty face, the more capricious side of her nature spurred on by alcohol.

'Well actually, darling, rumour has it that in fact he *did* murder someone.' She squeezed a wedge of lemon onto her sardines. 'Polenta anyone? Asparagus?'

Yasmin switched to full-on acting mode.

'Don't be ridiculous,' she snorted dismissively. 'Jeremy, a murderer? I don't think so.'

'It was never proved anyway,' Imogen quickly interjected. 'It was all just a horrible rumour. No one really knows what happened.' She swung her legs underneath the large handcrafted wooden table hoping that the tip of her Lanvin wedge might make contact with Calvary's shin.

'Jeremy has never mentioned anything of this.'

'Well, it's hardly pillow talk, is it, darling?' Calvary snorted, between mouthfuls of fish. 'Oh, by the way, sweetheart, I was once accused of murder . . .'

'I don't believe you!' Yasmin cried, ecstatic that her plan was working. 'So who in God's name is he supposed to have murdered?'

'Well,' Calvary settled into her seat, enjoying the undivided attention of the two women opposite her, 'he was somewhat of a playboy in his prime, was your husband. Liked to throw these terribly debauched parties; sex and drug orgies and all that. Never went to any myself, more's the pity. Was far too young. But they were legendary in their day.'

'And?' Yasmin was shaking now, willing her to cut to the chase.

'And on one occasion a poor little prostitute ended up face down in the pool.'

Yasmin bit her tongue until it hurt. *Prostitute!*

'Rumour had it some sex game went awry and when she threatened to go to the police she was drowned in the pool. Terrible business, sent shockwaves through society.' Calvary shook her head. 'Poor thing was only nineteen.'

Eighteen, she was only eighteen! Yasmin screamed so loudly inside her head she felt sure the others had heard her.

'Are you saying *Jeremy* killed her?' Her voice was shaking almost uncontrollably now as she struggled to keep her emotions in check.

Calvary shrugged.

'No one really knows, there were so many rumours flying round at the time. The police got involved – eventually – but nothing was ever proved. Jeremy's always protested his innocence. But then again, who wouldn't? Anyway, mud sticks, darling. Apparently there's a videotape of it all floating around somewhere. Supposedly, Jeremy paid a handsome sum to keep it out of circulation.'

'It's rubbish,' Yasmin spat. 'I don't believe a word of it. Jeremy would've told me all this himself if it were true.'

'It really was a rather spectacular scandal at the time,' Calvary continued. 'Everybody knew about it. Ludmilla stood by him, of course, silly mare that she was. Look where it got her . . .'

'Really, Yasmin, don't listen to her.' Imogen squinted at Calvary menacingly. 'It was all just malicious gossip and rumour.'

Yasmin sat back into her seat, her mind shooting off into all directions like a lit match in a box of fireworks.

'Look, you've upset her now,' Imogen said.

'Don't shoot the messenger.' Calvary raised her palms. 'He should've told you all of this himself. I'm only telling you because I think you have a right to know. Hearsay or otherwise, it's better it comes from us than from some smug, dirt-digging hack, don't you think?'

'It was all a long time ago.' Imogen turned to Yasmin, trying to reassure her. 'Long forgotten about.' She pushed her plate of food away from her. All this talk of murder was putting her off her fish. It was time to change the subject.

Inhaling deeply, Imogen reached into her enormous Bottega Veneta envelope clutch and pulled out a set of photographs, dramatically throwing them down onto the dinner table like a pack of cards.

'While we're on the subject of revelations . . .'

'What's this?' Calvary asked, reaching for one of the pictures.

'Is this you?' Yasmin moved in for closer inspection. 'From the LA shoot?'

Imogen nodded.

'In a manner of speaking.'

'Hang on, something's different,' Calvary said, bringing one of the shots closer towards the enormous candelabra for a better look. Imogen's small, neat, upturned nose looked somehow rounder and flatter in the picture. The lighting around her eyes had given them a puffy appearance and her trademark full lips looked much thinner and downturned. The effects were subtle and clever, perhaps even undetectable to someone unfamiliar with the intricacies of Imogen's face.

'Good God! These have been tampered with!' Calvary's shrill voice rang out across the open lake like an alarm. She looked to Imogen for an explanation. 'But who would want to . . . oh, hang on a minute. You don't mean . . . surely not . . . Seb!'

Imogen nodded slowly.

'The pictures were the final proof,' she said, throwing

the last of the offending photos down onto the table, unable to look at them a moment longer. 'My darling husband set me up.'

'Set you up?' Yasmin's heart was still galloping in her chest from their earlier conversation.

Imogen drew breath as she began to explain; Seb's uncharacteristic easy-going attitude towards the LA test shoot; Mylo's odd behaviour in the studio; the 'mysterious' Duncan Phillips and her subsequent conversation with Lorraine Harlech.

Dumbstruck, Calvary lit an emergency Sobranie cocktail cigarette.

'Oh, darling, how could he? And I thought *I* was the one married to the biggest shit of all time.'

'But I don't understand. Why would he do that?' Yasmin asked. 'That speech he gave . . . about how much he loved you . . .'

Calvary snorted derisively, blowing smoke into the warm night air. 'See what I mean,' she nodded, 'naive.'

Imogen reached for Calvary's packet of cigarettes. She rarely smoked but right now she needed something, anything, to take the edge off her frazzled nerves. She took a deep drag.

'I can't believe he would do something so cruel,' Yasmin sympathised. But in truth she could believe it. Every word. She had seen firsthand how abysmally human beings could treat one another. How they hurt and destroyed even those they claimed to love.

'Sebastian Forbes has taken everything from me over the years,' Imogen said coldly. 'My career, my daughter, and now my dignity . . . I should have left him years ago.' She looked wistfully out onto the beautiful low sunset, reds and purples all melting into a rich degrade pattern as the sun disappeared behind the clouds. 'I always knew his ego was out of control but I didn't realise just what he was capable of.'

'Why don't you just divorce him?' Yasmin suggested. 'You'd certainly have grounds for unreasonable behaviour. Take these prints to any half decent solicitor and then take the bastard to the cleaners.'

Yasmin felt genuinely, if reluctantly, sorry for Imogen. She had more heart and soul than most, and, trapped inside her own private hell, they had more in common than Yasmin cared to admit. Imogen's cage might be a gilded one, but it was still a cage nonetheless.

'Divorce? He'd see me dead first.' Imogen shook her head. 'Besides, I couldn't risk having him take my daughter away from me permanently. Seb's a well-connected man; he's in bed with QCs, politicians, people high up in the police force . . . there's no one he can't buy. Anyway,' she suddenly smiled a wicked smile, 'I have something far better in mind for him than divorce.'

Calvary's eyes lit up in anticipation.

'Oh?'

'Sebastian thinks I'm stupid,' Imogen said. 'He's always underestimated me. I sussed him out about that diamond from the off.'

'The Bluebird?' asked Yasmin. 'What's that got to do with it?'

'Everything,' she replied cryptically. 'Which is why I'm going to take it right from under his nose.'

'You're going to *steal* the Bluebird?' Yasmin gasped, unable to disguise her excitement. The Bluebird was kept down in the vaults, which was just the place she needed access to if she was to get her hands on this videotape that she was by now utterly convinced existed.

'Not steal it, exactly,' Imogen corrected, her voice low with gravitas. 'I want to show that bastard just who the smart one is in our sham of a marriage.' She smiled slyly.

Calvary felt her pulse race.

'You're not serious are you, darling?' she asked, though

the look on Imogen's face already gave her the answer. 'But how on earth would you get down into the vault? Everybody knows that security system he's got down there is unrivalled.'

Imogen's wicked grin expanded.

'It's not going to be easy, and yes, it's a bit of a risk, but –' she paused for effect, 'I think I might have come up with an idea.'

'Well, out with it!' Calvary shrieked. If Imogen had found a way of getting inside that vault undetected then she damn well wanted in on it!

As Imogen began to reveal her plan, her voice low and conspiratorial, Yasmin twitched in her seat. The line of coke she'd snorted earlier, combined with the thought that she might somehow manage to get her hands on that tape was causing a fresh wave of adrenalin to pump furiously through her body.

'So, what do you think?' Imogen sat back, her speech over, her face alight with possibility. There was a long pause as the two women took in her words.

'Hell hath no fury, eh?' Calvary raised an impressed eyebrow. 'I think it sounds difficult, dangerous, potentially disastrous . . . and absolutely bloody ingenious!' she exclaimed, clasping her hands together in excitement. 'But you can't possibly do it alone.' She shook her head. 'Something of this magnitude needs more than one pair of hands. I'll *have* to help you.'

'Me too,' Yasmin chipped in quickly. 'I mean, I'm game if she is,' she nodded at Calvary nonchalantly, not wanting to make her ulterior motives obvious. 'Like you said, we won't actually be *stealing* anything . . . it'll be more of a . . . a practical joke.'

Imogen shook her head.

'No! I couldn't possibly expect you to do that, either of you!' She was surprised and touched by her friends' show of support. 'Seb's my husband. He's my problem . . .'

'Nonsense, darling,' Calvary cut her off. 'That man needs to be brought down a peg or two. And if your friends can't help you, then who can? Besides, it'll be a victory for us all, outsmarting the great Sebastian Forbes.'

'Absolutely!' Yasmin was quick to agree.

Imogen had not been expecting this. The fact that Calvary and Yasmin were willing to put their necks on the line for her caused tears to prick the backs of her eyes, though it crossed her mind that perhaps they might have their own motives for wanting to help. Something was going on between Cal and Douglas, something her friend wasn't telling her. Imogen had seen the look of pain on Cal's face the day of the *ESL* shoot and had been uncharacteristically reticent when gently probed. Her friend was all too vociferous when it came to Douglas's misdemeanours, so she knew that this time it must be serious. As for Lady Belmont, well, she and Calvary had both agreed that there was more to that one than met the eye. Much more . . .

'Seriously, you'd do that for me?' she said, blinking the tears back. 'You'd help me get back at Seb, for everything he's done?'

'The bastard deserves it if you ask me,' Yasmin said. 'Call it retribution for womankind!'

'Here's to friends with plans,' Calvary said, raising her champagne flute high into the air. The three women chinked glasses, high on adrenalin and Krug.

'To revenge,' Imogen said, watching her friends' reactions closely.

'Revenge,' Yasmin allowed the familiar word to roll off her tongue. 'What is it they say? A dish best served cold?'

'No, darling,' Calvary interjected, 'that's gazpacho!'

And the three of them began to laugh.

CHAPTER 27

Langthorpe's Gym was busy, even for a Thursday evening. Looking around her, Calvary noted the rows of similarly well-dressed women pounding the treadmills, beads of sweat forming on their perfectly shaped brows. She quickly glanced at herself in the mirror; Stella McCartney work-out gear. Check. iPod. Check. Bottle of Buxton. Check. She was good to go.

Having had a little refresher session with 'Tony' a perma-tannned young man with a set of buttocks you could crack a nut between, Calvary tentatively made her way over to the running machines. Smiling graciously at the woman next to her, who briefly smiled back, she began with a steady-paced walk and, settling into a natural rhythm, allowed her mind to wander.

Ever since Lake Como and Imogen's plan revelation, Calvary had thought of little else other than getting down into the vaults at Forbes Bank and relieving Douglas of his tidy stash. She fantasised about the look of horror on his handsome face when he discovered she'd made off with his money. Just thinking about it made her pick up speed.

Calvary looked into the mirrored wall at the other women in the gym. Douglas had probably screwed half of them, faithless bastard that he was, that man had slept with so many women throughout their marriage it was surely an act of God that his dick hadn't turned black and fallen off. Yet still, after everything, after all the cheating and lies and rejection, she had still been unable to walk away. Why had her marriage meant so much to her? These days, getting a divorce couldn't be any easier; a burger and chips sometimes took longer to arrive than a *decree nisi*. But Calvary was old-fashioned at heart. You stuck at it; ironed out the lumps and bumps; you moved on, you *forgave*.

Calvary began to sprint, as if her troubles were right behind her, chasing her.

'Well, looks like someone's had a good workout?' a vaguely familiar voice said from behind her. 'It's lovely to see you again, Calvary,' Josia said, smiling up at her warmly.

'Oh!' she replied, feigning her surprise. 'I had no idea you worked here.' This was a blatant lie and Calvary knew it. The truth was she had wanted to find the young man she had met outside the Saachi Gallery again. She had not been able to stop thinking about their encounter; the quickening of her heartbeat, her coy self-consciousness, how their conversation had disarmed her.

He took her hand and helped her from the treadmill.

'Only on Thursdays and at the weekend. The rest of the week it's all personal clients.' He allowed his eyes to wander the length of her body. 'Who is looking after you?'

'Tony, at least I think that's what he said his name was,' Calvary said nonchalantly in a bid to show that she wasn't the least bit interested in the young man with muscles.

'Ah, you're in safe hands. He's good. Though not as good as me!' Josia grinned. You could say that again, Calvary thought, taking him in properly for the first time. He was taller than she had remembered, and broader too, with a strong, lithe body that looked exceedingly well cared for. He wasn't all 'ripped' or whatever they called it, but his arms and legs were well defined, strong and shapely. In fact, he appeared a whole lot more attractive in the daylight, dressed only in shorts and a Nike t-shirt, than she had thought on the night outside the gallery. He seemed older too; she noticed a few fine lines around his eyes and mouth, giving his youthful face a certain distinguished appearance, and a smattering of grey throughout his dark brown hair. For the first time in years, Calvary felt a jolt of electricity run the length of her body and settle between her legs, where it remained, pulsing and twitching.

'So, you're going to be a regular here now?' Josia enquired, wondering why he felt such a strong attraction to this woman. She was attractive, certainly, but that wasn't it. It was like he could see straight through her offhand veneer to the sensitive, soft woman he sensed was inside, a woman whose sexuality had been lying dormant for far too long, one who needed reminding that she was still worthy of being cherished. He was quite overcome by the desire to kiss her there and then.

'I'm still thinking about it,' Calvary replied, noncommittal. 'Truth be known, I've never been a big fan of the gym.' She wrinkled her nose. 'I always seem to lose momentum.' She shifted her position then, suddenly uncomfortable with herself as she rested her body weight against the metal bar of the machine. He was looking directly at her and it was a little disconcerting. 'I prefer the odd run,' she was babbling now. 'Keeps me in shape. Well, sort of,' she said, patting her belly and laughing nervously. She cursed herself for having drawn attention to the part of her body she liked least.

'It's the best fat-burning exercise there is,' he nodded, tactfully adding, 'Though I can think of one that's more fun.' He smiled at her mischievously and she did her best not to blush. 'Maybe we could run together one morning,' he said tentatively. He knew she was spiky; any suggestion of anything improper and he would be given short sharp shrift, of that he was in no doubt.

Calvary's heart was pounding in her chest. Good God, woman, get a grip, she told herself sternly.

'Yes. Perhaps,' she nodded politely.

'Well, which is it? Yes or perhaps?'

Calvary smiled wryly and paused for a moment.

'Yes,' she said eventually. 'I would like that.'

'Great!' Josia smiled, displaying his perfectly white neat teeth. 'How about Monday, say 6:30 a.m?'

Calvary pretended not to look horrified.

'The earlier the better,' she smiled.

After showering, Calvary left the gym feeling better than she had done in ages. She wasn't sure what it was; the endorphins from the treadmill or the fact that she knew she would be seeing Josia again. Whatever the reason, for the first time since she could remember, Calvary Rothschild felt that anything was possible.

CHAPTER 28

Imogen's getaway to the lakes had been an emotional turning point for her and in the weeks that had followed, meeting regularly with her friends to plot her retribution had given her a renewed strength and confidence. What had started out as little more than an idealistic fantasy was now fast becoming a very possible reality. One that was keeping her going.

Now that their plan was really starting to take shape, she felt the cumbersome weight begin to lift from her shoulders, but it did not entirely erase the sharp sting of betrayal she felt whenever she thought of her husband's cold-hearted deception.

Sweeping her hair from her face and tying it into a loose chignon, Imogen took some cotton pads from her dressing table and began to remove her make-up with some Shu Uemura oil. She would play things carefully over the next few weeks, actually go out of her way to be *nice* to Seb, get him onside, as much as you could get someone like Seb onside, anyway. She would lie low, blend into the background, convince him that his twisted plan had worked.

Imogen watched as Seb exited the en-suite, dressed only in his silk boxer shorts. She couldn't help noticing that he was carrying a little extra weight around his middle these days, no doubt as a result of all those self-congratulatory lunches he'd been to and that his once-thick, dark thatch of hair was beginning to thin out.

'Prince Saud's invited us both on board his yacht for a long weekend in St Barts next month,' he announced, wrapping himself in a cashmere Versace robe. 'If you've got anything else planned, I suggest you cancel it.'

She watched as he began to comb his hair behind her in the mirror.

'No problem,' she replied breezily. 'I'll clear my diary. I mean, I'm sure there's nothing I can't rearrange.'

'Good.' Seb smiled at her in the mirror and she forced one in return. 'It's one hell of a boat by all accounts. Private cinema, gym, platinum-tiled swimming pools, the lot. He's planning on throwing a huge cocktail party and inviting half of the Hollywood aristocracy. I could hardly have said no to that, could I?'

'Of course not. It sounds wonderful. But you do realise this means one thing?'

'That being?' he asked ominously.

'I'll have to go shopping for a few cruise essentials.'

'Any excuse, eh, darling?' Seb smirked, albeit good-humouredly.

'Well, you know me,' Imogen sang. 'Anyway, you wouldn't want your wife to be outshone by all those oligarchs and Saudi princesses now would you?'

'I suppose not.'

'I'll pick up a few things for you too, if you like. Save you having to worry about it all last minute.'

Sebastian glanced over at her.

'Thanks.' He was pleased. They were getting along unexpectedly well at the moment. Even their sex life had improved; something that was as surprising as it was welcome.

'It'll do us good to have a little break away together,' he said. 'It's been a while since we had a proper holiday. I realise I've been overdoing it on the work front and neglecting you a little. So I've made a decision to take a bit more time out for myself – and for us. After all, all work and no play makes Sebastian a dull boy.'

Imogen hid a wry smile and resisted the urge to fire off a facetious retort.

'Good idea. It's about time you sat back a bit, let someone else take the reins for a while.'

'Leave it with me,' he said, watching her as she rubbed the cream into her smooth, tanned skin. Imogen caught his stare and felt her heart sink in her chest. He had that amorous look in his eye again. She knew she was going to have to soft soap him for a while, but she had hoped her recent bedroom efforts might've kept him quiet for a little while longer at least. If anything though, it seemed to have had the opposite effect. Still, she thought as she stood, opening her Carine Gilson silk kimono robe and allowing it to slide down her newly moisturized body, it was all for a good cause. She would put in a performance worthy of an Oscar if the end result meant watching that bastard she was married to squirm.

CHAPTER 29

'Can we stop now, just for a moment?' Calvary struggled to catch her breath. She was bleary-eyed, having got up with dawn's chorus, and now she was jarring her spine by running all the way to Hyde Park, for goodness' sakes – and all on an empty stomach! What had she been thinking? Cute as Josia was, she wasn't sure anyone was worth this much discomfort.

Calvary bent over, placing her hands on her knees and panting heavily.

'You're doing great,' Josia said encouragingly. 'We're almost at my apartment, which means we're over a quarter of the way there already.'

'A quarter? Whoopee,' Calvary groaned sarcastically and didn't care that he'd heard her. 'I'll never make it,' she said, her chest heaving between breaths.

Josia frowned. 'C'mon,' he implored. 'I never had you down as a quitter.'

'Oh, there's plenty you don't know about me,' Calvary snorted.

'For instance?'

'For instance, I lied. I'm no runner. I haven't been to the gym in over two years, unless it's been to have a spa treatment, and my idea of keeping fit is taking the stairs in Harvey Nichols instead of the lift. There, will that do you?'

Josia laughed.

'You must have inherited some great genes to have kept a body like that without any effort at all.'

Calvary felt herself blush and was glad of the fact that her cheeks were already red from running. She wasn't used to compliments, wasn't sure how to handle them.

'Can't we just walk for a bit?' she asked, still panting heavily. 'I feel a little light-headed.'

'Are you sure you're OK?' Josia asked, concern etched onto his smooth-skinned face.

He looked just as handsome today as he had when she had seen him at the gym, she thought, even at this ungodly hour of the morning. She felt worn out just looking at him.

'Let's face it, I'm just not as fit as I once was. If I *ever* was.'

'I think you're pretty fit,' he remarked, tongue in cheek.

'Stop teasing,' she nudged him. 'I mean, I really do need to work out more. After all, I'm not getting any younger.'

'I think age is a beautiful thing,' Josia shrugged. 'Why fight it? I love to see a woman age gracefully. That *is* beauty to me.'

Calvary tried not to be touched by his sentiment, but thought better of mentioning all the little syringes full of help she'd had to stave off the years.

'Well, that's easy for you to say; you're young. And you're a man. It's different for women.'

'Only because you *make* it different. You put all that pressure to be thin and young looking on yourselves.'

'Oh please, spare me the lecture.' Calvary rolled her eyes. 'You sound just like my husband.'

Josia looked momentarily hurt. 'And how *is* your husband?'

Calvary lowered her eyes.

'I'd rather not talk about him if you don't mind.'

'Suit yourself. I just wondered if you'd come to any kind of decision about what you plan to do about your son's wedding . . .'

Calvary admired the man's brazenness. He certainly didn't dance around a subject.

'Did you think about what I said, about fear being the biggest fear itself?'

Calvary stopped walking and turned to face him.

'I appreciate your concern about the state of my marriage, Josia,' she said curtly. 'But I'd rather you didn't bring it up again. It is my business and no concern of yours. So if you don't mind, I . . .'

He lunged forward and kissed her then, his soft, thick lips pressing their warmth against hers, parting slightly as they made impact.

Stunned, Calvary pulled away from him, quickly scanning the street to see if anyone had seen them.

'How dare you!' she said in a tone that was far more horrified than she actually was. 'What the hell do you think you're doing?'

'I live here,' he grinned, pointing up towards a stucco-fronted row of apartments.

'Good for you,' Calvary shot back, steadying herself against the wall. The kiss had left her giddy with endorphins.

She turned on her heels, ready to walk away from him, but he was way too quick for her, and, grabbing her by the upper arm, spun her round and pulled her into his arms.

'Not so fast,' he whispered in her ear, his breath warm against her neck. 'I want to make love to you, Calvary. Let me make love to you.'

She could feel his hardness through his shorts as he stood close and she felt her own desire begin to throb until it hurt. The truth was, as excited as she was by his proposition, she was bloody terrified. She had made love to the same man for over a quarter of a century and had long ago forgotten what burning lust and desire felt like. Now that she was experiencing it again, Calvary was almost blinded by panic and crippling insecurity. Would she be a good lover? Would her aging, naked body turn him off? Would he turn to look at her afterwards and realise what a huge mistake he had made? Anyway, she had never cheated on Douglas throughout their entire marriage. Not once. Not even with a kiss, for all the bloody good it had done her.

Josia took her in his arms again, pulling her body into his. He placed his lips firmly on hers, his warm tongue finding its way into her mouth. The old Calvary Rothschild would've slapped his face, indignant by such advances. But this was the new Calvary Rothschild. The improved version.

Oh, to hell with it, she thought, her body softening as his embrace tightened. It was about time she had some fun.

CHAPTER 30

Smoothing her hands down her asymmetric Preen dress and opening the belt on her Burberry Prorsum trench coat, Yasmin Belmont-Jones thrust her Juicy Couture red patent clutch bag underneath her arm, rubbed her glossy lips together and, taking a deep breath, knocked firmly on the door marked 37.

'It's open,' a small voice sang out.

Entering the hotel room, she was met by the sight of Sammie Grainger. Her face, newly scrubbed and free of make-up, looked dewy and fresh and she was dressed casually in a pair of baggy boyfriend jeans and a Breton top. She looked like any other young, twenty-something lounging around on a Sunday morning and her ease made Yasmin feel suddenly over-dressed and conspicuous.

'I'm so glad you decided to come, thank you for giving me a second chance,' Sammie smiled at her in earnest. 'Please, come in, I've ordered us fresh coffee and croissants. I hope you like pain au chocolat.'

Yasmin held her hand up.

'I won't be staying,' she said tightly.

Sammie closed the door behind her and watched as Yasmin stalked into the middle of the suite, her countenance steely.

Sammie could've kicked herself for having played her ace card so soon – and so publicly too. She had since had to beg Yasmin via numerous text messages to meet her today. This time she planned to go as carefully as possible; she wasn't about to make the same mistake twice.

'I only came here to tell you that if I hear from you anymore, if you call me, text me, turn up at my house, in fact, if I so much as accidentally bump into you on the street, I will take out a restraining order against you.' Yasmin's voice was hard as flint, making it perfectly obvious that this was not a friendly visit. 'Whatever this ridiculous, slanderous story is that you've concocted, I will take it straight to a judge and have him slap a ban on you and your publication from printing a goddamn word of it. Am I making myself clear?'

Sammie stared at Yasmin for a long moment. As unnerved as she was by her menacing tone, she had to admit that she looked beautiful standing there, defiant in all her finery, even if she was a little overstated for a lazy Sunday afternoon.

'Crystal,' Sammie nodded. 'So, was that all you came to tell me?'

Yasmin glanced at her, suspiciously. She had hoped to have seen a little more fear in Sammie's eyes but seemed she'd be left wanting. That was the thing with South London girls, they didn't scare easy.

'Yes. That's all.'

In truth however, Yasmin had secretly wanted to see Sammie Grainger again. She needed her help. As well as needing to know more about this tape, she wanted her to do something for her.

Only trouble was, she didn't want to have to admit that Grainger had been right about her true identity all along. It was a catch-22 and she would have to strike the balance right if she was to get what she wanted *and* protect her alias.

The two women stared at each other for a moment, face to face, unblinking. The brittle tension between them almost at breaking point.

Sammie waited a few seconds before speaking.

'Are you sure you won't stay for champagne?' she asked, glancing in the direction of the chilled bottle of Laurent Perrier on ice. 'Seems a shame to waste it, though it's probably just tap water to the likes of you now. Oh, how things change, eh?'

Yasmin turned on her.

'Don't try and fuck with me, Grainger,' she spat, ramping it up a gear. It worked as Sammie looked up, startled. 'This is a warning from me to you. Just remember what I've said.' Yasmin turned to leave. It was an orchestrated move, deliberately designed for Sammie to try and stop her.

'Don't you want to know more about the tape?' Sammie said quickly. 'The one your husband keeps down in Forbes Bank . . .'

Yasmin gave a small, secret smile before swinging round to face her.

'Tape? Ah yes, the one that the police never found but you seem to know all about. Another figment of your wild imagination, I fear.' She was playing devil's advocate, trying to flush out information.

Sammie shook her head.

'Look, *Yasmin*. I know you don't believe me, but I really *do* want to help you, and I can only do that if you'll talk to me. I know about your childhood, about your mother's addiction and subsequent death; I know about Chloe, about the circumstances of how she died – I know *everything*.'

'MURDERED!' Yasmin screamed, the veins in her neck protruding, her face reddening with the injustice of her whole life. 'She was *murdered*!'

Sammie felt herself visibly relax. This little outburst was

tantamount to an admission and she seized the opportunity to continue the thread of the conversation.

'Is that why you married Belmont? Are you out to get your revenge because you think he killed your sister?' The words fell from her mouth before she could stop them.

'Oh, hang on a minute,' Yasmin slapped her smooth forehead with her hand, recognising her own stupidity. 'You're wearing a wire, aren't you?' She glanced at Sammie accusingly. 'Jesus, Grainger, you really must have me down as a mug,' she sneered, marching round the table towards her, 'pissing in my ear and telling me it's raining. Come on then,' she spat, lunging at her, starting to pat her down, 'where is it? Where's the fucking wire, you slippery bitch?'

'What the hell do you think you're doing?' Sammie attempted to smack her probing hands away. 'Stop it . . . stop it . . . I'm not wearing a bloody wire, I swear.'

'Prove it.'

Sammie backed away, holding her hands up in surrender. 'Look, there's no wire. I promise!'

'Strip, or else I walk right now. Prove to me you're not wearing a wire and we'll talk.'

Sammie stared at her, incredulous. The woman was a nut-job.

'You're not serious?'

Yasmin fixed her with a stare that told her otherwise.

'Jesus Christ,' Sammie sighed, reluctantly beginning to undo the buttons on her jeans. Yasmin watched as they fell to the floor, exposing her slim, athletic legs. 'This is ridiculous.' She pulled her Breton top above her head, static crackling in the air as she discarded it onto the sofa. Finally, she stood in only her underwear, a soft white cotton bra and shorts from Marks and Spencer. Having seen one black sock too many, they were a little on the grey side, but at least they were matching. She was grateful for that much.

'There.'

Yasmin found herself staring. Sammie's body was much more aesthetically pleasing than she had thought it would be, hidden under all that baggy denim; her legs, toned and shapely, were long and her hips slim. She had a full bust too, and long, slender arms like a ballerina's. It was her skin, however, that was undoubtedly her best asset. It was a natural light toffee colour and looked as soft as cashmere. Suddenly, Yasmin was overcome with the desire to reach out and touch her, to see if it was really as smooth as it looked.

'Satisfied?' Sammie asked. Although she felt beyond mortified standing there half naked, she recognised it as a step in the right direction towards winning Yasmin's trust.

'I suppose.'

The tension in the air was finally beginning to lift and good as her word, Yasmin took a tentative seat on the chaise longue.

'Not bad,' she said, surveying the Victorian splendour of the hotel room, looking up at the huge 15-arm chandelier hanging regally from the ceiling, the heavy brocade drapes bringing an austere charm to the place. 'They're obviously paying you too much if you can afford to stay in Marie Antoinette's bloody boudoir.'

Sammie found herself laughing.

'*They* are the ones paying for it, actually,' she said, doing the last of her buttons up. With her embarrassment fading, she felt surprisingly comfortable standing there in just her bra and jeans. Too comfortable in fact. Perhaps it was because she was half-naked in a hotel room, but Sammie felt the first flutters of sexual excitement. She brushed the feeling away, a little embarrassed.

'So you *are* here to do a story on me, then?' Yasmin sneered. 'Well, listen up, lady. There *is* no story.'

Sammie quickly pulled her head through her t-shirt, blindsided.

'I think we both know that's not true,' she replied, cocking her head to one side.

'Look.' Sammie was keen to keep the tone soft and friendly. 'I know that you adored your sister and that she was all you had left. I know that when she died – when she was *murdered* – that you went into care and I *know* that you suffered. What I don't know is why you're where you are today. Why you married Belmont. Do you blame him for her death? Are you planning to fritter away all his money to avenge her, is that it?'

Yasmin felt her body stiffen. Suffered? She had no idea. Sometimes, when she was alone in her bed at night, she still heard the ominous creak of the dormitory door, the soft footsteps approaching her bed in the darkness and the feeling of dread in the pit of her stomach as the rough, unforgiving hands covered her mouth, stifling her screams.

She had spent years trapped in that hell from which there was no escape, no one to hear her cries or wipe her tears, tell her that everything would be alright. All the memories of that pain and anguish had, over the years, manifested itself into a hatred and resentment so potent and fierce that it had become her only friend in the end. And now it was payback time. Someone had to be held accountable for the terrible atrocities she had suffered as a young orphan girl. And that someone, Yasmin had decided, was Jeremy Belmont.

'You ask a lot of questions, Grainger,' Yasmin said, maintaining her composure with such effortlessness that for a moment Sammie wondered if indeed she had got it all completely wrong.

'So you don't deny it, then?' Sammie sat upright now, her eyes wide. 'I want to know what you're planning. Whatever it is, I'll help you with it.'

Yasmin took a cigarette from her clutch bag and lit it,

watching as blue smoke curled slowly up into the air above her like a serpent from a basket.

'If you really want to help me, then there's something you can do for me.'

Sammie's skin prickled with apprehension.

'Name it,' she said.

Yasmin paused for a moment, eyeing Sammie carefully, weighing her up with every blink of her false lashes. She began to pace the room.

'First though, I need to know I can trust you – can I trust you, Grainger?'

Sammie glanced up at her.

'The question is, can you afford *not* to?'

Yasmin threw her head back and laughed.

'I like you, Grainger. You've got balls. And right now, balls are what I need.' She paused for a moment. 'You've heard the name Sebastian Forbes?'

'Of course. I was at the ball this year, remember?'

Yasmin gave a rueful smile. *How could she forget*?

'I want you to request an interview with him. A profile piece for the magazine. Tell him that you're keen to hear all about his *fascinating* life, his meteoric rise up through the banking ranks, his family history, that sort of shtick. The key is to make it sound big and exciting, an offer he can't refuse – not that he will anyway, not with an ego the size of a small continent.'

Sammie smirked. She'd got that right at least.

'This is the important bit.' Yasmin reached inside her bag and pulled out a small shiny chrome Dictaphone, placing it down onto the glass coffee table.

'It's brand new. State of the art technology from Japan,' she said, pre-empting Sammie's next question. 'This little baby could pick up the sound of a sparrow farting in the next room clear as crystal. It's worth a small fortune – and it's yours.'

Sammie leaned forward to pick it up.

'Nice,' she said, giving it the once over. 'It's a pretty decent piece of kit.'

'It's very important that you get him to say his name clearly into it – no background noise, no interruptions. His full name: *Seb-as-ti-an Forbes*. Loud and clear. Think you can get him to do that?'

'Of course,' she shrugged, puzzled.

'Good.' Yasmin smiled then, her expression softening slightly.

Sammie's mind started to go into overdrive. What did Stacey Jones want with the likes of Forbes?

'Why do you want to set Forbes up?'

'Who says I want to set him up? Look, ask no questions and I'll tell you no lies.'

'So, what's in all this for me? Sebastian Forbes is an important man. The kind of man you don't want to upset. He could ruin my career if he catches me out.'

'That won't happen.'

'And how can you be so sure?'

'Because I'm going to grant your wish, Sammie Grainger. I get the tape – you get the story.'

'Story?'

'*The* story – *my* story, stupid. The one you've been bugging me about ever since we met, you idiot.'

Sammie's heart leapt into her throat. At last, Yasmin was finally admitting that there was a story to tell. She felt her spirits soar.

'. . . but I want to get one thing straight, Grainger,' Yasmin's voice cut through Sammie's euphoria like an axe. 'If I'm going to spill my guts to you, make you a name in journalism, then *I* call the shots. It's *my* story and I want to tell it *my* way, understand?'

Sammie fought back the urge to run to her and plant a huge kiss on her lips.

‘Of course, of course,’ she nodded emphatically. *Just wait ’till old Sasquatch found out about this one – he’d shit glass.*

‘But there are things that need to be done first. In the meantime, you must set this interview up – as soon as possible. I’ll be back to collect the tape once your mission is complete.’ Yasmin extinguished her cigarette in an antique vase on the side table. ‘So, Grainger, do we have a deal or not?’

Sammie stood up from the sofa and faced Yasmin, her mind burning with a thousand unanswered questions.

‘A full exclusive, right?’ Sammie said, lowering her eyes and fixing her with an earnest stare.

‘*Lock, stock and front page exclusive*,’ Yasmin said, accentuating the words slowly and deliberately.

‘In that case, Stacey Jones,’ Sammie smiled, holding her hand out, ‘you’ve just got yourself a deal.’

CHAPTER 31

Calvary switched her wiper blades to maximum as the rain pelted down onto the windscreen of her Range Rover, distorting her vision. The country lane was dark and narrow and with such poor visibility, Calvary wondered if she might in fact make it home at all.

It had been a spur of the moment decision to take a weekend sabbatical up at her old friend's gorgeous Georgian bolt-hole in Bath, but it was a much needed one. She needed time to think, to get her head around what had happened with Josia. Calvary bit her lip. She had committed the ultimate sin: she had let him make love to her.

'Josia, look . . . I don't think this a good idea . . . I . . . I've never done this kind of thing before.' Calvary could barely speak her throat had been so tight with desire. Her head was fighting against it with all the ferocity of a tiger but the truth was her body had already surrendered, her legs having wrapped themselves around his back almost subconsciously. It had been so long, she thought, since she had felt such strong sexual desire for a man that every nerve ending in her body had fizzed and crackled with electricity, and he had hardly even touched her yet.

But it was wrong. God, it was so wrong. She had a

husband, albeit a rotten, faithless one. And in Calvary's mind, sleeping with another man would make her no better than him.

'Really? There's been no affair?' Josia asked, covering Calvary's neck with small scattergun kisses.

'Really,' she replied, lowering her eyes. 'You are the first . . .'

Josia was as thrilled as he was surprised. He had stopped for a moment to look at her, his floppy fringe framing his glossy chocolate eyes. And he had smiled at her modestly, a little part of him falling in love with her there and then. She was such a paradox; haughty and stand-offish on the surface, yet soft as melted butter underneath. He was fascinated.

With her eyes closed Calvary had been able to pretend that what was happening to her was just a dream, a lovely indulgent fantasy, but when he spoke, his distinctive, clipped tones whispering in her ear, it forced her to remember that she was actually lying on a stranger's bed, with a stranger's body on top of hers. And it felt so goddamn good that she wanted to cry out.

'Beautiful,' he breathed hotly into her ear, causing her to moan with pleasure. He had wanted to make love to her slowly, carefully, to take his time with her, but he struggled to stop himself from losing control, from thrusting himself deep into her too soon.

Wet with desire, Calvary had almost bit right through her lip trying to prevent herself from crying out. But in the end it had been too much for her and she had let it go, moaning as pleasure ripped through her body, every inch of her skin prickling with the intensity of her orgasm.

Afterwards, they had lain together in silence, with just the sound of low breathing and the warmth of each other for comfort.

'Why don't you just leave him?' Josia had quietly said

after a few moments. He was stroking her shoulder with his hand. Enjoying the softness of her.

Calvary had sighed, a deep sigh of resignation.

'It's not as easy as you think.'

'It's about money, right? You said he would cut you off financially.'

Calvary wished they didn't have to have this conversation right now. She wanted to savour the feeling a moment longer before the blackness of reality seeped into the present like a poisonous fog.

'It's not just about the money,' she answered brusquely, unconvincingly. 'You make me sound like I'm shallow and materialistic. There's more to it than that.'

'Really?'

'Yes, really,' she answered, irritation apparent in her voice now. She pulled herself away from him abruptly, covering her nakedness with the bed sheet.

'You have to understand,' she said, wishing she had a cigarette to hand, 'I come from wealth. I married wealth. My whole life has been about money and status. I mix with society and aristocracy. My children were privately educated, I holiday at least four times a year and fly via private jet, or first class at the very least. Some of the dinner parties I've thrown have cost more than an average person's annual salary. And do you know what, Josia? I have worked for all of it. Every diamond, every piece of art, I have sweated, toiled and sacrificed for. So you see, I can't just give it all up tomorrow.'

Josia raised himself up on his elbow and watched her, her auburn hair a little mussed up from their passion, her smooth ivory shoulders drooping as if they carried too much weight upon them. She was over ten years older than him, he knew, yet sat there, her face a picture of indignation, she looked for all the world like a little girl lost.

'You think money buys you freedom, Calvary. But you're

wrong,' Josia had said, his accent sounding stronger with the weight of his words. 'Money is your ball and chain; you are shackled by it.'

'So you call this freedom, do you, Josia?' she gestured around the tiny room. 'Living in a box painting pictures that no one wants to buy?'

Josia shrugged. If he'd been hurt by the comment he hadn't shown it. 'I have all I need to make me happy.'

'All?' she asked sheepishly, regretting her words. Douglas was right; she had a nasty tongue on her sometimes.

He smiled at her then, a rueful, half smile. 'Almost.'

*

'Shit!' Calvary swerved as a set of oncoming headlights appeared from nowhere, forcing her onto the grass verge and her mind back to the here and now with unwelcome abruptness. Her BlackBerry slid from her lap into the foot well with the force of her braking.

'*Shiiit,*' she hissed again, pulling over for a moment, her heart galloping like a racehorse in her chest. Calvary exhaled loudly and let her head rest against the seat, momentarily enjoying the soft warmth of the leather against her skin. Leaning over she flipped open the glove compartment and sighed with relief as she located an emergency packet of Vogue cigarettes.

'Oh, thank God.'

Calvary regretted how things had been left between her and Josia. She had dressed in haste and stormed out of his apartment like a stroppy teenager. Worse, he had not even tried to stop her.

As tricky as the encounter had ended between her and Josia, the experience had left her with a renewed sense of vigour; she would sort out the mess her life had become, stop this ridiculous charade of a wedding taking place and leave that husband of hers high and dry – and, thanks to the lifeline given to her by her dearest friend, she would make sure she wouldn't lose a penny in the process. Calvary flicked her cigarette out of the window and blew the last of her smoke in its wake. Smiling, she started the engine and listened as it began to purr. It was time to make tracks.

CHAPTER 32

Sebastian Forbes looked at the young woman sat opposite him and briefly wondered for the life of him what she saw in that ghastly old lump Lord Belmont. No doubt it was what they all saw: money. This one, overly made-up in her Graff diamond chandelier earrings, her skin-tight designer dress and vertiginous heels, looked as if she liked to bathe in tubs of the stuff. Still, he was always happy to oblige a friend, help them offload a little of that cumbersome wealth. He liked to think he was thoroughly decent like that.

'The thing is, Sebastian, may I call you that?' Yasmin purred, her glossy red lips quivering lightly as she spoke.

'Please do.'

'Thing is, *Sebastian*, if it's all the same to you,' she leaned forward a little, giving him a glimpse of her generous cleavage, 'I would really rather Jeremy not know anything of our little meeting today.' She looked into his dark eyes and gave him a knowing smile, exposing £25,000 worth of porcelain veneers. 'I'm sure you'll agree that even in the most solid of marriages there are things that are best kept secret.' She raised a provocative eyebrow, leaning back into her seat. 'If you know what I mean?'

'Of course, of course,' he nodded sagely, wishing she

would keep the suggestive looks to herself. Young and pretty she may be but she wasn't his type. Too much like a Barbie doll, all that bleached-blonde hair and sparkly eye make-up. He could tell she had a feisty streak in her too and that was enough to dampen his ardour at the best of times. Natural and subdued, that's how he liked his women. How he liked *all* women.

Yasmin crossed her legs in a slow, deliberate movement and smiled sweetly. It was the first time she had been up close and personal with Sebastian Forbes and now she saw for herself those dark, lifeless eyes that seemed to look straight through her. There was something so cold and aloof about him that it sent a chill down her spine and for the briefest of seconds, Yasmin found herself feeling almost grateful that she was married to Jeremy Belmont and not the man sitting opposite her.

Quick to cotton on to the fact that her charms were falling flat, she swiftly changed tack.

'I was at the ball this year. My first time,' she gushed, coquettishly resting her hands lightly on a tanned thigh. 'I have to congratulate you; it was such a spectacular affair. I mean, the food! The entertainment! And that champagne fountain! I have to say though, my highlight of the entire evening was the speech you gave.'

Sebastian's eyes flickered with interest. 'Really?'

'Oh, yes. It was wonderful,' she said, watching him preen. 'So touching, what you said about your wife, about Imogen.' She placed her hand on her heart in earnest. 'I was almost in tears, I tell you. Do you do much public speaking?'

Always keen to discuss his favourite subject – himself – Sebastian smiled with a heavy dose of false modesty.

'Well, not really, though there was this one time . . .'

'Well, you should!' Yasmin was quick to interject. 'I mean it, you were fabulous, and believe me, I know a good speech from a bad one. I've had to attend so many functions with Jeremy where I've practically fallen asleep at the table.'

'Thank you, Lady Belmont. It's very good of you to say so,' Sebastian replied, feeling himself grow a little taller. 'Tell me, how is Jeremy?' The question was one of polite obligation as opposed to interest. 'Haven't seen the old boy properly in ages.' And he intended it to stay that way. He found the man's company unbearable; an overweight show off, that's what Belmont was. Always had been.

'Oh, he's wonderful, thank you, just wonderful,' she cooed.

'Well, do send him my regards, won't you? Though that might be a little tricky if you're wanting to keep our meeting quiet.' He raised his eyebrows at her, though in truth he couldn't have cared less what she had to hide from that insufferable windbag she was married to. In fact, he secretly hoped the woman was fleecing him on a grand scale. It would serve the old braggart right.

Yasmin shifted in her seat, the leather creaking underneath her.

'Better still, you could tell him yourself when you come to dinner! I know Jeremy would love that.' On the contrary, she knew for a fact Jeremy would hate it. He loathed Forbes. 'A pious and supercilious old fart', as he often referred to him. 'I'll arrange it with Imogen.'

'Ah yes, of course, you're friendly with the old trouble and strife these days, aren't you?' Sebastian was smiling but still the question sounded more like an accusation.

'Wonderful woman,' Yasmin said, opening her palms out towards him. 'You're the perfect couple!'

Sebastian smiled thinly. The girl was laying it on a bit heavy, even for his liking.

'You do realise that it's not usual procedure to do things this way,' he said, bringing the conversation back to the matter in hand, relishing his position of authority once more. 'Usually you would need to come recommended by at least two existing clients; you are aware that there is in fact a considerable waiting list for vault space . . .'

Yasmin fixed him with a dazzling smile. One she had spent long and hard perfecting.

'Flattery will get you *everywhere* with Seb,' Imogen had explained when they had come up with the idea last week over lunch. 'Play it just right and his ego won't be able to resist.'

'I can't possibly tell you just how grateful I am to you,' she said graciously. 'You really would be doing me an *enormous* service.'

Sebastian nodded, unsmiling. He was growing a little tired of her grovelling now and she felt the weight of his scrutiny as he stared at her for a long moment, deciding whether or not to grant her wish.

'Well,' he eventually sighed, 'I suppose I could see to it that you're first on the list, seeing as you *are* a friend of my wife's.'

Yasmin disguised her relief with a gentle smile. It was imperative she pull this little operation off without a glitch. It would be beneficial to her, but there was also a part of her that wanted to show Imogen that she could be trusted to get things done. That she was a team player.

'There will be paperwork to fill out and a fifty percent annual deposit of £50,000, which will need to be paid up front, today, if possible. I trust that won't be an issue?' Sebastian remarked coldly.

'Of course not.' Yasmin shook her head.

'My secretary will send over your contract plus all our terms and conditions. You'll need to sign both copies, retaining one for yourself. Please feel free to have your solicitor look over everything but I assure you it's all pretty standard stuff. All you need to do is decide which type of box you would prefer, a key or a code lock.'

'Oh.' A look of confusion clouded over her pretty face. 'I didn't realise I would have a choice. What's the difference?'

Sebastian brazenly checked his diamond Cartier watch. He had a lunch appointment with his old pal Roger Blandford at San Lorenzo's in half an hour and would be late at this rate. Christ, he'd only agreed to see her at such short notice because Imogen had practically begged him and he hadn't wanted to upset the newfound equilibrium between them.

'It's quite simple,' he said, careful to keep his tone as light as possible. 'One is opened using a key, the other using a PIN code.'

'I see.' Yasmin paused, thinking how she would enjoy screwing this man over almost as much as Imogen would. He really was a condescending bastard. 'Wouldn't a key present more of a safety hazard? I mean, what if I were to lose it?'

Sebastian laughed then, amused by such ignorance. They were all the same, his wife's friends, thick as bricks, the lot of them.

'You really mustn't worry, Lady Belmont,' he said slowly, his tone patronising. 'Everyone who owns a box has to be formally identified and their signature verified as a matter of protocol each time they wish to make a deposit or withdrawal. It would be impossible, I say *impossible*, for anyone else to gain access to it, key or no key. Besides, I make it my personal business to know all my clients by sight.'

'I see,' Yasmin nodded, seemingly satisfied with this answer. 'But I really think I would like to see them for myself before I make such an important decision.'

Sebastian stood then, his patience starting to fray. He didn't have time for this.

'As you wish,' he said, as affably as his irritation would allow. 'I can have Janet arrange for you to visit the vault and take a look for yourself, if you think it will help you make up your mind.'

'Oh yes, I'd like that, thank you, Sebastian.'

'Not at all, *Lady Belmont*,' he gritted his teeth, wishing the silly bint would bugger off so that he could get along to his lunch date. He was looking forward to washing down a nice crab ravioli with a decent glass of Beaujolais and boasting to his old colleague, Blandford, about how business was booming.

'Shall we go then?' she said, making to stand. 'I have a little window right now before my lunch appointment.'

Sebastian blinked at her, amazed. The nerve of the woman, assuming he would just drop everything the moment she clicked her false nails! She was really beginning to test him now.

'I'm very *sorry*, Lady Belmont . . .'

'Please, call me Yasmin. Lady Belmont sounds so formal.'

'I'm very sorry, *Yasmin*, but I'm afraid that's just not possible,' he shook his head, hiding his rising temper. 'I have an important business lunch meeting that I simply cannot cancel. But do check my diary with Janet on your way out. She will see to it that you're given an appointment at the first available opportunity.' That told her. Lady or no, he wasn't about to start dancing to her tune – or anyone else's for that matter.

'Oh, that's a shame,' Yasmin replied, crestfallen, 'I really would have rather wrapped it all up today.' She straightened herself out. 'Not to worry. I'll arrange it with your secretary.'

'Yes, please do,' Sebastian replied. He was moving towards the door now, almost ushering her from the room.

Taking the hint, Yasmin picked up her white leather Jimmy Choo day clutch and strutted towards him.

'Off anywhere nice for lunch?' she enquired breezily, still on the charm offensive. Forbes had been a much tougher nut to crack than she had imagined. He had been completely immune to her feminine charms – something Yasmin was not used to – and had been dismissive to the point of rudeness. She even wondered, briefly, if he might in fact be a closet homosexual. It would certainly explain his lack of interest in her. Still, she needed to pull something out of the bag fast if she was to come away from this meeting victorious.

'San Lorenzo's, actually,' Sebastian replied, his reservoir of polite conversation rapidly running dry.

'Ah yes, fabulous choice,' Yasmin said breathlessly. 'I'm afraid I'm roughing it at The Ivy today. I'm meeting a journalist from *ESL* magazine – her choice, not mine, I might add.' She rolled her eyes in an exasperated fashion. 'The Ivy,' she pulled a face. 'So full of show offs and luvvies.'

Sebastian forced a smile, willing it to be his last. Good God, did the woman ever shut up?

She turned to him on her way out.

'Actually, now I think of it, she mentioned you.'

He hesitated.

'Who did?'

'The journalist. Yes. She brought you up in conversation when we last met.'

'Really?' He was taken aback. 'And why would she do that?'

Yasmin had his full attention now.

'She knew of my connection I suppose, my friendship with your wife. She wondered if I might have some sway with you.'

'Sway?'

'Yes.' She smoothed her dress down and placed her clutch tightly underneath her armpit. 'She mentioned something about wanting to interview you.'

Sebastian's heart flipped in his chest. An interview! With *ESL* magazine. He couldn't think of anything he would like more.

'I told her you were the kind of man who fiercely guards his privacy. I mean, she was talking about doing a real in-depth profile piece. You know, "Who is the *Real* Sebastian Forbes?" Your life story, that kind of thing. I said I doubted you would be interested.' She wrinkled her nose at him, dismissive of the idea.

Sebastian felt like wrapping his hands around her scrawny neck. This was exactly what he'd been waiting for! A chance to tell his life story, to get his name out there. Become the face of Forbes! He had known they would come running the moment he had secured the Bluebird and given that stellar speech at the ball. Exposure on this kind of scale would invariably lead to bigger things, a publishing deal for his autobiography, maybe even his own *The Apprentice*-style TV show! Now she had probably scuppered his chances of securing his first rung on the ladder, the stupid bitch.

'Oh, well, I don't know,' he shrugged coolly. 'These things, when done properly of course, can occasionally be quite good for business,' he added sagely. 'I value my privacy more than anything else, but if they could guarantee copy approval . . . Shall we discuss it while we take a little trip down into the vault?' he suggested.

A small smile crept across Yasmin's lips.

'Oh, well, if you're sure. But what about your lunch date?' she feigned concern.

Sebastian held his hand up and buzzed his secretary.

'Janet, call Roger Blandford at Blandford-Hatch and tell him I'm awfully sorry but I will have to cancel our lunch meeting today. Something's come up,' he said, looking directly at Yasmin and smiling broadly. 'Something that can't wait.'

CHAPTER 33

The Jacuzzi at the Amida Spa in the exclusive Chelsea Harbour Club felt warm and inviting as the three women gradually lowered themselves in.

'An inspired idea of yours, Ims,' Calvary groaned, allowing the hot bubbles to fizz up to her neck, 'hiring this place for the day.'

Yasmin closed her eyes and smiled her agreement.

'I think I might go for a swim before I treat myself to a facial, and a mani-pedi while I'm at it.' She stuck her perfectly painted toes up in the air and pulled a face. 'It's been over a week since my last one.'

'Well, we've got the use of the whole place to ourselves and as many treatments as we like, so knock yourselves out, ladies. I thought we could all do with a treat.' Imogen let her head flop back against the edge of the Jacuzzi pool. 'I know I could.'

It had been a testing week for Imogen. She had learned, from one of the housekeepers, that Bryony was due to fly back to the UK in time for her father's birthday.

'When were you actually planning to tell me that our daughter was coming home?' Imogen had asked Seb that evening, struggling to keep a civil tongue in her head. 'I had to learn about it from Jalena.'

'It slipped my mind,' he had fired back. 'Besides, it's not for a few weeks yet.'

'That's hardly the point,' Imogen had replied airily, through a forced smile.

'Well, I knew you wouldn't shut up about it. Besides, I thought it might've made a nice surprise for you if she just turned up unexpectedly.'

Imogen had held her breath and inwardly counted to ten. She'd texted Bryony only the day before; they'd exchanged a little banter and signed off with their usual love and kisses. No doubt she had been left wondering why her mother hadn't mentioned anything about her impending visit. Maybe even felt hurt by it. God, how she hated Seb then. Loathed the very bones of him.

'Anyway, she'll be back in time for my *big day*,' he'd said, without a hint of irony, 'so here's hoping you've got a little more planned than the anticlimax that was last year's debacle.'

Imogen gave a knowing smile. 'Don't worry,' she reassured him. 'I've got something *much* more exciting planned this year.' Sebastian's interest sparked.

'Have you really?' He was intrigued.

'Oh, yes,' she had nodded profusely. 'And you're going to *love* it.'

Sebastian had given a little harumf. Last year Imogen had presented him with a distinctly underwhelming Breitling diamond encrusted watch at the ghastly dinner party she had thrown for him. He'd had to sit next to the Lamberts all evening, listening to Damien drone on. It had been one of the worst birthdays ever.

'So, are you going to give me a clue?' Sebastian had enquired, adding, 'you know I'm not big on surprises, but I hope you've put a little more thought into my gift this time.'

Ignoring his breathtaking lack of gratitude, Imogen had inwardly smiled.

'You've heard of the sculptress, Amandine Lamarque?'
Sebastian nodded.

'Of course. Hasn't everyone? French woman; top of her game. I was reading in *The Times* supplement just the other day how the PM recently commissioned her to make a life-size bronze of his newborn baby. Why?' Sebastian paused. 'Oh, hang on,' he had turned to face her then, his eyes suddenly alight. 'You haven't . . . have you?'

Imogen grinned, watching his reaction carefully, enjoying it.

'You'll be sitting for her next week! And before you ask, I've already booked it in the diary with Janet.'

Sebastian looked at her. For once he was impressed. Now this was much more like it.

'A statue? Of me?'

'Who else, darling?' she had responded. She had known he would be thrilled. It was the perfect gift for an egomaniac like him. And it was all part of the plan . . .

*

'Anyone for fizz?' Imogen asked, reaching down by the side of the Jacuzzi and producing a magnum of vintage Laurent-Perrier and three chilled glasses. 'I don't know about you, but all these bubbles have suddenly put me in a good mood.'

'Be rude not to, darling,' Calvary surmised, readily accepting a glass. She could do with a little pick me up herself. It had been an emotionally exhausting few days, one way or another.

Calvary had heard nothing from Josia since their intimate encounter and, reluctant as she was to admit the fact, she was disappointed. Calvary was sure something special had happened between them that morning. Now however, she was beginning to wonder if it hadn't all just been in that stupid head of hers. Perhaps he'd just wanted sex after all

– sex she had given him far too readily, now she thought about it. Calvary cursed herself. Christ, she didn't know how Douglas did it. One stolen moment between the sheets with another man and she was a paranoid emotional wreck.

'I'd like to make a toast to Lady Yasmin Belmont-Jones,' Imogen said, adopting a mock formal tone. 'Here's to managing to pull the wool over my husband's dark and soulless eyes.' She raised her glass.

'Ah, yes, I heard you managed to get yourself down into the vaults!' Calvary tapped her glass in salutation and smiled as it made a satisfactory 'ding'.

Over one of their weekly lunchtime get-togethers, which had now been largely overtaken with plotting their impending plans, Yasmin had suggested that she set up a meeting with Sebastian to try and convince him to give her a tour of the vaults.

'I'll tell him I want to buy a strong box, get him to take me down there for a nose around. I can make some mental notes, get a feel of the place properly, look for potential flaws in the system,' she'd suggested. They had all agreed that it was an inspired idea.

'I'm sure Lady Belmont can be *very* persuasive when the mood takes her,' Calvary had remarked to Imogen during a telephone conversation after learning of Yasmin's triumph, adding, 'not that I'm suggesting anything improper occurred!'

'It's OK,' Imogen had laughed. 'Quite frankly, I wouldn't hold it against her if it *had*.'

In fact, Imogen had been rather impressed by Yasmin's tenacity.

'I have to say, he's one chilly customer, that husband of yours,' Yasmin remarked to Imogen.

'That's one way of putting it,' Imogen deadpanned.

'Well, come on then,' Calvary snapped. 'What's the deal? Did you get the code?'

Yasmin snorted, indignant.

'Jesus, Calvary, if it was as easy as leaning over his shoulder for a quick glance then the place would've been done over a million times before now.'

'But I thought the whole idea of you going down there was to see if you couldn't get a glimpse of –'

'Look,' Yasmin abruptly cut her off. 'The code is the least of our worries in my opinion. That place is alarmed to the hilt. There are heat sensors everywhere and enough sequence codes to keep Carol Vorderman busy for a decade and that's just to get to the boxes!'

Yasmin struggled to conceal her bitter disappointment. She had hoped her little trip down into the vaults would bring them one step closer to completing her mission. Instead, it had left her feeling utterly defeated. For the first time in her life, Yasmin had started to feel as if she was part of something; a team, a unit. Though it had all been under false pretences, she had forged unlikely friendships with the two women sitting opposite her, friendships that had gradually begun to mean something to her, to tug gently on the coattails of her conscience, and it worried her.

In her darker moments, Yasmin imagined the look of horror and betrayal on the faces of her friends were they ever to discover the truth about who she really was and her motives for marrying Belmont. She wondered if they would immediately turn their backs on her; cut her from their lives like a malignant tumour, maybe even go to the police. Jesus, she could kick herself. Emotional attachment; it complicated everything.

'I might not have got the codes,' Yasmin bristled. 'But I *have* found a way round the voice activated locking system.'

Calvary shrugged, palms open in expectation. 'And?'

Yasmin thought of the little deal she had done with Sammie Grainger, though she wasn't about to let on as much to the others. They would freak out if they thought she'd involved a journalist in their plan. Even though Grainger knew nothing, it was still risky. But then as far as Yasmin was concerned that was half the fun.

' – And,' she smiled smugly, 'let's just say I'm working on it.'

CHAPTER 34

Upon hearing the sound of the doorbell, the infamous sculptress, Amandine Lamarque made the journey from the third floor studio in her superb Belgravia home down to the ground floor. She made a habit of always answering her own front door, deeming it terribly bourgeois to do otherwise.

As it turned out, she was rather looking forward to meeting her new client, Sebastian Forbes of the Forbes Banking empire. Although she always did her best not to pre-judge someone due to sit for her, Amandine knew instinctively that she would dislike Forbes.

'I do hope he won't be terribly late and hold up your day. He does run to a tight schedule but things often overrun . . .' Imogen Forbes had apologised for her husband in advance over the phone.

'It's really quite alright, Mrs Forbes,' Amandine had reassured her. She did not often take on private clients, unless of course they were ridiculously famous, but Mrs Forbes had been disarmingly persuasive, making it difficult for her to refuse. Besides, the woman had offered to pay double her usual fee – and she certainly didn't come cheap. 'I will clear my afternoon in expectation of his arrival.'

Amandine would have to work round the clock to ensure the sculpture she had been commissioned to do be finished in time for the 'great birthday unveiling' that Mrs Forbes had told her she had planned.

'And I feel I must warn you, Sebastian can be a little, well, difficult at times.'

Amandine had given a sardonic laugh.

A highly acclaimed special effects artist and unrivalled sculptor, Amandine had worked on some serious Hollywood box office smashes, including *Alien Intervention 1* and *2*, and the mythical epic, *Journey's End*, where she had won an Oscar for her superbly lifelike latex animatronics. She was well versed in dealing with the odd hissy fit.

'Mr Forbes, I presume,' she said, her French accent suddenly apparent as she opened the door, dipping her head in greeting. '*Accueillir chez moi!*'

*

As Calvary ran in the direction of Hyde Park, she bit her lip and tried to convince herself that she had done the right thing.

That morning, following a frosty atmosphere over breakfast, Calvary, armed with little more than a sixth sense, had decided to covertly follow her husband into work. Having caught a few furtive glances between her husband and Tamara, she wondered if now might be the time to collect that little insurance premium of hers.

Concealing her brand new Range Rover Evoque behind some road works, Calvary had sat, surreptitiously staring up at Douglas's office window, unsure of what it was she expected to find. She didn't know why she seemed so surprised to see Tamara slip unnoticed into the building some half an hour later. It brought Calvary no joy whatsoever to discover that her suspicions had been correct.

Douglas and Tamara were having an affair, plain and simple. After all, what else had the little slut popped in for? A quick game of Scrabble? As she sat there, her hands shaking behind the wheel, fury and hatred simmering away inside her like a pressure cooker, Calvary contemplated her next move. But before she had time to consider her options, she caught sight of Douglas making his way from the building, deep in conversation with a male colleague and seemingly on his way to a meeting.

Once the coast was clear, Calvary made her way up to Douglas's office.

'Good morning, Lynn,' she'd smiled at one of Douglas's secretaries. The only one she could be sure he hadn't slept with due to the fact she was practically an old aged pensioner, but then again, she wouldn't have put it past him.

'Mrs Rothschild. How lovely to see you!' Arabella smiled disingenuously at Calvary.

'Is Douglas in?' she snapped, knowing full well that he wasn't.

'I'm afraid not. He's gone to an early lunch meeting with the Hendersons. Should be back in an hour or so though. Can I let him know you were here?'

Calvary paused for a moment.

'I'll wait in his office. It's terribly important I see him,' she announced, giving Arabella no option but to nod her agreement.

'You might have a bit of a wait, Mrs Rothschild,' Arabella replied nervously, wondering if she was going to get into trouble for any of this.

'No problem.' Calvary wrinkled her nose, waving the latest copy of *Tatler* in her hand. 'And I'd *love* a coffee. Soya latte, no sugar.'

Closing the door behind her, Calvary cast her eye around the room. It was indisputably the office of an alpha male stuck in a time warp – all leather and chrome and sharp, sleek lines. Douglas was a child of the 80s. He had positively thrived under Thatcher's rule; accruing money and power and women at a rate of knots.

She sat down at his desk, absentmindedly opening the top drawer. The shiny peach and black lace knickers looked incongruous next to the pile of random administration. Sighing, she held them up, suddenly realising to her horror that they were still warm. Grimacing, she slammed the drawer shut, causing the desk to shudder with the force.

As Calvary's mind filled with the unwelcome images of what Douglas and Tamara might have got up to together in that very room, perhaps even on the chair she now sat on, she jumped up and snatched the small clock that contained the spy camera from the desk, throwing it into her Hermès Kelly tote.

Collecting her thoughts and composing herself, she took a deep breath.

'Your latte, Mrs Rothschild.' The perma-smiley Arabella had poked her head around the door.

'You have it,' Calvary said dismissively, snatching up her Hermès bag. 'I've just realised there's something important I need to do.'

*

The Counter Spy shop was busier than Calvary had expected, leaving her to wonder if in fact the whole of London was secretly up to no good.

'So, can you just explain to me one more time, in laymen's English,' she had asked the exasperated, bespectacled young man behind the counter for the third time.

'Look, it's pretty simple, lady.' The young man had rolled his eyes, not even bothering to hide his impatience. He'd met a million Calvarys, technophobic women who'd discovered they had been under surveillance, usually by their husbands. In the eighteen months he'd worked there, he'd literally seen it all.

'The camera and receiver are both powered from PP3 batteries or a mains adapter that simply connect to your TV or video, and by tuning it into the camera's frequency, it will transmit images, you get me?'

Calvary stared at him blankly, and he gave a weary sigh.

'You plug it in to your telly, lady. A five-year-old could do it.'

*

Sitting in front of the TV, her heartbeat rapid and her breathing shallow, Calvary had watched with an air of detachment as the grainy images of her husband and Tamara appeared on the screen. After a few moments of watching Tamara's backside graphically bobbing up and down on Douglas's erection, their loud grunts and groans audible above the low hiss of the recording, Calvary knew what she had to do.

The knock at the door, though expected, still startled her.

'Ah, Henry, my darling,' she had smiled sadly, her heart as heavy as lead as she stood to greet her eldest son. 'I'm so glad you could come; there's something I think you should see.'

CHAPTER 35

The sound of the doorbell caused Amandine Lamarque to curse under her breath.

'*Merde!*'

She had just settled down with a decent glass of Beaujolais and a packet of Gitanes to watch *Female on the Beach*, one of her all-time favourite films. This was the first time she had had a moment to herself since taking on the Forbes commission and now her evening of respite looked set to be scuppered.

'Can I help you?' Amandine said as she answered the door to a very attractive-looking female stranger.

'I'm so sorry to just turn up on your doorstep like this,' Imogen said, clutching a bottle of Château Lafite 1996. 'I'm Imogen Forbes. Sebastian's wife. Would it be convenient if I came in?' She held the bottle out and Amandine raised an eyebrow as she took it.

Imogen smiled her gratitude and followed Amandine inside.

'Would you care to join me in a glass? I was just about to imbibe . . .'

'That would be lovely,' Imogen said, watching as Amandine poured them both a generous glass of the deep mahogany liquid and lit a Gitane with an exaggerated gesture. She was every bit the eccentric artist. 'And again, I am so sorry to impose on you unannounced like this.'

Amandine took a slow sip of her wine.

'It is quite alright,' she nodded, intrigued by the woman's presence. 'What can I do for you?'

Imogen glanced around the studio, surveying the hundreds of sculptures, pieces of art and rows of special effects, including a rather ghoulish selection of monsters and various animatronics. The place was creepy, like an unfinished museum.

'I was just passing your house when I was completely overcome by the desire to meet you. I'm a *huge* fan of your work,' she gushed.

Amandine smiled.

'That is very kind of you to say so, Mrs Forbes.' Though she didn't believe a word of it.

Her sharp, creative intuition told her that she was no more here to wax lyrical about her love of Amandine's creations than she was selling Chamois leathers and clothes pegs. So what did she *really* want?

'I hope you don't mind me asking,' Imogen broached the subject tentatively, 'but I was wondering how everything was coming along with Seb's statue. I would really love to see it. If you don't mind, of course.'

Amandine sighed. Some clients were so impatient. Did they not realise that art could not be rushed?

'As a matter of fact, Mrs Forbes, I *do* mind,' she said, her voice gentle but firm. 'If you look at the work now, it would be like playing you a half-finished song, you understand, no?'

Imogen smiled and nodded.

'Of course. I understand. But can I ask how it is taking shape at least? Will it be finished in time for his birthday?'

Amandine took a large swig of her wine and savoured

the warm sweet cherry top notes as they slid down her throat.

She shrugged. 'It is finished when it is finished.'

Imogen nodded apologetically, and began to look around the unusual apartment.

'I've always loved sculpture, even as a child,' she admitted. 'My parents had a small cast of Rodin's *The Kiss*. I was fascinated by it. The man and the woman, forever intertwined. It's terribly romantic when you think about it, isn't it?'

Amandine, delighted by such a candid display of memory, returned the smile with one of her own.

'Charming,' she said, eyeing Imogen once more.

A long moment passed between them.

'Sebastian said you made a cast of him, just like the ones in your films, the stuff you use for special effects,' she said.

'That's right,' Amandine replied. 'It helps me with my work. This way someone only has to sit for me once, twice at the most. So, officially, there is now two of him, no?' She laughed, a Gitane balanced precariously between her lips. 'Now that I *can* show you, if you like – come.'

Imogen followed Amandine to the other side of the studio and let out an involuntary gasp as she looked up. Inside the large cupboard hung dozens and dozens of latex masks, like a rubber human abattoir.

'Les marionettes!' Amandine announced, bowing theatrically.

'It's so . . . creepy,' Imogen felt herself shudder.

Amandine laughed, pleased that her guest was showing so much interest in her craft.

'I use only the most advanced substances for this. It allows me to capture every detail, every crevice of a person's face.'

'Like a fingerprint?'

Amandine nodded. '*Oui* – the same.'

'They really are quite something,' Imogen breathed as Amandine handed her the eerily accurate cast of her husband's face. She stared at it with a mix of awe and revulsion.

'Would you show me how you do it?' Imogen asked, animated. 'How you make the casts?'

Amandine glanced sideways at her guest to see if the question was genuine or had been born of politeness. 'I'd be fascinated to see.'

Amandine scrutinised Imogen for a long moment before sighing heavily.

'*Qu'est-ce que ça peut bien faire!*' she said, shaking her hands up above her like a manic preacher.

Looks like she wasn't going to get to watch that film tonight after all.

CHAPTER 36

Calvary rolled over onto her side and released a long sigh of pleasure.

'Tell me, how can something that's supposedly so wrong feel so unbelievably right?' she found herself saying aloud.

Josia shuffled in closer to her and linking her hand in his own, gently kissed it.

'The answer is in the question,' he murmured, enjoying his hazy post-orgasm warmth. 'Forbidden fruit. It's always the sweetest, no?'

'I wouldn't know – until now,' she giggled, her exhilaration making her feel a little girlish and lightheaded. She let her head flop lazily back onto the pillow. 'You know, I really thought I would never be here again, in your apartment, in your bed . . .'

He propped himself up on his elbow, a wide-eyed look of surprise on his boyish face.

'Really? Even after that first afternoon we spent together?' He released a little whinny of disbelief. 'You must be crazy, Calvary Rothschild, if you thought I would stay away after that!'

She laughed, feeling happier than she'd done in years.

'May I remind you that it was *you* who walked out on

me. Not so much as a backwards glance, let alone a phone number,' he chided her playfully. 'And then when you weren't at the gym, or down by the gallery walking the dogs, I had to as good as stalk you to find you again.'

Calvary was chuffed. The idea that he had been looking for her was as thrilling as it was new. In Calvary's scant romantic repertoire, it had always been she who had done all the running. And this was certainly true of her marriage.

'You have to forgive me,' she bit her lip. 'I said some horrible things to you the last time I was here. I'm afraid I was a little overwhelmed. You see, it's been a long time since I've had to deal with, well . . . you know, I'm not very practised at this sort of thing.'

'What sort of thing?' He smiled, his eyes narrowing playfully.

'Oh, you know, *this* sort of thing . . . stop teasing!'

'An affair, you mean?'

Calvary wrapped her hair up on top of her head and let it fall loose again, an act that she was aware made her appear girlish and sexy – at least she hoped so.

'Is that what this is then?' she purred.

'You tell me.'

She smiled wryly.

'Well, whatever you want to call it, I'm not used to it – at least, not this way round anyway.'

Detecting a hint of bitterness in the last part of the statement, Josia reached out and lightly touched her face with his hand. He really must get round to painting her – when he wasn't making love to her, that is. She really was quite beautiful; her soft auburn hair and her alabaster skin, like porcelain and virtually line-free, gave her an ethereal quality.

A comfortable moment of silence passed between them before she slowly looked up at him, her green eyes a little glassy.

'Henry knows,' she said. 'He knows about Tamara and Douglas.'

Josia listened quietly. He was aware of her fragility and already knew better than to comment. Right now it was best to let her just talk.

He pulled her close to him then, held her tightly in his arms as she began to cry. In a funny way he was relieved; finally she was beginning to open up to him. The ice had begun to thaw.

'It's OK,' he said, his voice low and soothing. 'Just let it go . . .'

Calvary caught a sob in her throat. His kindness had undone her.

'Forgive me,' she said, wiping her eyes and attempting a small smile. 'These tears are not for *Douglas*, they're for Henry. They're for my son.'

Calvary looked into her young lover's eyes then and felt that exhilaration, that initial rush of first falling in love. It was an odd feeling, simultaneously being at your most happiest and bereft.

'It's all just so bloody hopeless,' she said, wiping mascara from underneath her eyes, suddenly aware of how ghastly she must look.

'Nothing is hopeless, Calvary,' he replied softly. 'There is always hope. In my country, no one believed apartheid would end, but it did.'

Calvary wrapped herself in a section of the bed sheet and, drying her eyes properly, composed herself.

'Listen to me,' she laughed at herself. 'You must think I'm the most self-absorbed, selfish woman you've ever met!'

He smiled. 'It's what first attracted me to you.'

She playfully dug him in the ribs and he was pleased to see her smiling again.

'Tell me about it,' she said. 'Tell me about your country and your life there.'

He glanced sideways at her, his floppy, messy fringe hanging over his eyes, alive and glassy from their love-making.

'You really want to know?'

'Yes! Yes, I do. I want to know what you were like as a child, where you went to school, the house you grew up in. I want to know it all!'

Calvary settled her head onto his smooth chest, at once reassured by the methodical thud of his heartbeat and she listened as he began to talk, his soft voice lulling her into a conscious slumber, making her feel safe and comfortable.

As she listened, she allowed herself to fantasise about what life might've been like if she'd met Josia ten years ago. If she had left Douglas and started a new life in Cape Town. Just thinking about it filled her with regret. She wondered if she would have been so concerned with money and status living in such sunny climes with a man who loved and respected her.

'I could make a habit of this,' she smiled as he ran the tips of his fingers along the contours of her soft, naked curves. 'Making love in the afternoon.'

'I hope so,' he replied, feeling himself growing hard again. 'Because I'm not letting you walk out on me this time.'

'Oh, I'm not going anywhere,' she cooed as he rolled her onto her back. 'I plan to stick around, now I know what I've let myself in for.' He took her nipple gently in his mouth and she arched her back in pleasure. 'And then afterwards, I plan to stick around some more because . . .'

'You talk too much, Calvary Rothschild,' he said, pushing her legs apart with his knee. He was already hard again and she gasped as he gently slid himself into her.

'I do?' she breathed, feeling herself yield to him once more. And she had to admit, he did have a point.

CHAPTER 37

'Ah, Grainger, come in, sit down.'

Sasquatch beckoned Sammie to a small, plastic chair that looked as though it had been designed for a place where comfort was actively discouraged, like an airport or a police station.

Sammie duly sat, her knees tightly pressed together, hoping he would just get on with whatever it was that he wanted as quickly as possible. She had deadlines to meet. The fallout from fashion week was taking up a lot of her time at the moment, as was trying to find the perfect military coat about which to write 500 exhilarating words. None of that fashion stuff was important to her now. If she was honest with herself, it never really had been. What *was* important, however, was Stacey Jones – and her story. She'd honoured her side of the bargain. Now it was Stacey's turn.

Pugh fiddled with the top button on his expensive designer shirt, which he somehow managed to make look cheap, eventually opening it. Sammie stared in barely concealed disgust at the thick black thatch of curly hair that protruded from his collar like a comedy chest wig.

'Thing is, Grainger,' Pugh cleared his throat, 'I'll cut straight to it . . . we're letting you go.'

He paused and glanced at her in a bid to gauge her initial reaction. Was she going to cry? He really hated the criers. You had to pretend to be nice to them, offer them tissues and words of comfort, something he had never had much truck with. If you were sacked it simply meant you hadn't made the grade. Only in this case it was nothing of the sort. Grainger had made the grade alright. And he knew it. She was a natural little hack, good nose for a story, diligent, tenacious. No; the problem was, no matter how hard he had tried, he just couldn't get the girl to suck his dick. And that alone was reason enough to let her go.

'You're sacking me?' Sammie said quietly. 'May I ask *why*?' Her voice was laced with indignation from which he gleaned a tiny slither of satisfaction.

'You must understand, Grain . . . – Sammie,' his voice was duplicitous now and his expression one of over-exaggerated earnest. 'It's nothing personal. Times are tricky at the moment. My budgets are getting smaller and competition is fierce. You have to understand, it's not really *me* who wants this to happen. It's the powers that be.' He looked up to the ceiling as if to a higher being.

Sammie watched him with a mix of disbelief and contempt. He really was an odious little prick. He must've thought she'd been born yesterday. Feeling her heartbeat begin to accelerate inside her ribcage, Sammie took a deep breath.

'This is all because I won't drop my knickers and lay on my back for you, isn't it?'

Pugh dropped his pen lid and stared at her open-mouthed in shock. She was, of course, bang on the money, but he had never in a month of Sundays expected the girl to come right out and say it! Saying it aloud sounded too much like an accusation. And an accusation was something to be worried about.

Pugh laughed then, an incredulous chuckle that was

supposed to convey the fact that she must be joking. Only it didn't. It made him sound nervous and exposed.

'Don't flatter yourself, Grainger. That's got nothing to do with it.' As the words left his dry, cracked lips, he realised himself how much they had sounded like an admission of guilt. *Fucking hell.* Pugh felt his irritation rise, making his ears hot.

'What I mean is,' he continued, flustered, 'I haven't been trying to sleep with you. Whatever gave you *that* impression? You think too much of yourself, young lady. You're really nowhere near as irresistible as you think you are.' He winced at himself. The more he spoke, the less convincing he sounded.

'Whatever gave me that idea? Hmm, now let me think.' Grainger's voice dripped with sarcasm as she tapped her lip with her finger. 'Forbes' Annual Ball. Yes, you leering at me all evening, making lewd comments about my breasts – something about "more than a handful being a waste" – then proceeding to try and convince me that, *gasp*, "conveniently" there was only one room left in the hotel, which would mean us sharing a bed . . .' Sammie paused for effect, 'but no, Mr Pugh, sir, I really have *no* idea where I might've got that idea from.' She blinked at him innocently, mocking him with every bat of her lashes. 'Though we could always go to HR, ask them to give us a second opinion, what do you think?' She cocked her head to one side and flashed him a sardonic smile.

Pugh jumped up from his chair. It was all he could do to stop himself from giving the girl a short sharp crack around her insolent bloody face. The working class ones, they were always the worst. Bloody great chips on their shoulders. And this one had one the size of the Watford Gap.

'Now you listen to me, Grainger,' he was at his full height now, all 5 foot 8 inches of him. 'I gave you a fucking fantastic chance here and you blew it, you blew it big time.'

'Perhaps if I had "blown it" we might not be having this conversation at all,' she smirked.

'Very good, very good,' Pugh nodded, though could think of nothing to better it.

'But the fact remains, you're out. It's nothing personal. It's just the way the cookie crumbles. You'll receive a month's salary and I'll see to it that you get a half-decent reference when the time comes. Can't say fairer than that.'

'Can't say fairer than that . . . ?' The injustice of it almost choked her.

Pugh watched the expression on Sammie's face cloud over as the realisation slowly began to dawn upon her; she was out of work, living in London, with rent and bills to pay, and instantly he felt a little better.

'You see, I just don't think your heart and soul is in it, Grainger,' he continued, suddenly enjoying himself. 'To be top of this game, you need to be prepared to do whatever it takes. And I mean, *whatever* it takes, to get on.'

Sammie began to laugh then. A shrill, high-pitched sound that made him want to cover his ears with his hands.

'You're something else, do you know that, Pugh?' She stood up to him now, her 5 foot, 10 inch frame dwarfing his. 'Prepared to do *whatever* it takes? What, like jump into the sack with a dirty old has-been like you, you mean?'

Has-been? *Has-been*? Pugh looked genuinely affronted. Since when had people started referring to him as a has-been?

'Well, if that's what it takes to get on in this game then you're right, this isn't the world for me. I'd rather lose a limb than prostitute myself to the likes of you with your massive ego and tiny,' she squeezed her thumb and forefinger together, '*tiny* cock.'

He pulled his head into his chin, his mouth forming an 'O' shape.

'Oh yeah, don't look so surprised. Girls talk you know, *Mr* Pugh,' she spat his name from her lips. 'We've all had a bloody good laugh at your, how shall I say, *short*comings?' She gave a short, sharp laugh, throwing him a look of contempt. 'I'm onto something so hot right now – you'll kick your shins bloody when you find out what it is. But hey, I'm not your concern anymore. I'm out of here . . .'

'Hang on a moment.' Pugh held his arm out, preventing her from moving any further towards the door. She brusquely pushed his hand aside.

'What do you mean, "onto something hot"?'

She faced him then, her smile triumphant. 'I mean *super* hot. The hottest story this paper's seen in a decade, maybe more.' Sammie knew she shouldn't even be mentioning it, but she just couldn't help herself.

Pugh felt himself wobble. Suddenly he was intrigued.

'Well, look, Grainger,' he said, his tone suddenly switching to amenable. 'We can always talk about this. Why don't you sit back down and tell me what you're onto and I'll see if I can't have a chat with the powers that be . . .' He rolled his eyes to the ceiling again, to the invisible God above.

Sammie snorted derisively as she picked up her bag and slung it over her shoulder in one deft movement. Fuck Pugh. Fuck all of them. She didn't need anyone, apart from Stacey Jones and her story.

'I would say you can kiss my ass for it,' Sammie said, suddenly feeling as if a strange weight had been lifted from her shoulders. 'Only a pervert like you might take that too literally. So I'll say this: Go screw yourself, Pugh. One day, very soon, you'll regret this moment with every miserable breath in your pathetic body.'

He watched as she stalked from his office in a cloud of

Ted Baker body spray and attitude, her dark cropped hair unmoving as she flounced. And though he hated to admit it, Ralph Pugh had a sickening feeling that in all probability, the girl was right.

CHAPTER 38

Standing in front of the mirror, Calvary took a long, hard look at herself. Rubbing a generous dollop of Crème de la Mer into her skin and slathering her body in bronzer, she wondered if she looked different somehow. If people might actually be able to tell that she was having an affair. And not just any old affair either. *An affair with a younger man.* She was officially what *Grazia* magazine referred to as a 'Cougar' and despite herself, the very idea made her want to laugh out loud.

Pouring herself into an unforgiving, figure-hugging, cream Roland Mouret dress that she worried was too young for her, Calvary inspected herself from all angles. Those Spanx she had invested in certainly hid a multitude of sins, she thought pleasingly as she slipped on a pair of vertiginous Chanel heels. Maybe, just maybe, she would get away with it, she thought, spritzing herself liberally with her signature No. 5 and checking her reflection once more.

Douglas waltzed into the bathroom then, paying scant regard for her privacy and, turning to look at her, raised an eyebrow.

'You've scrubbed up well tonight, Calvary,' he said. 'Looking quite lovely, I must say.'

Calvary, who was now applying eyeliner in the mirror, stopped what she was doing and stared at her husband, open-mouthed.

'Sorry, I didn't quite catch that. Would you mind repeating it?' she retorted.

'I said you look rather nice . . . lovely, in fact,' he nodded his approval, the corners of his mouth turned outwards. 'Not bad at all.'

Calvary was speechless. It had been years since Douglas had paid her a genuine compliment. She narrowed her eyes at him suspiciously.

'What have you done, Douglas?'

'Done? I've *done* nothing,' he shot back. 'Why should I have done anything? Can't I pay my wife a bloody compliment these days without there being an ulterior motive?' He tugged at his tie, a little indignant, loosening it before discarding it onto the floor.

Calvary raised an eyebrow. 'Well, let's face it, Douglas, it wouldn't be true to form, would it? You paying me a compliment for no other reason than the sake of paying me a compliment.'

Douglas sighed. 'Why don't you just shut up, woman, and accept it?' he snapped. 'That's always been your trouble, Calvary. You really do talk too much.'

She smiled then, remembering what Josia had said to her, right before they had had crazy, passionate and meaningful sex – *for the second time* that afternoon. She felt the heat in her loins just thinking about it.

'What's so funny?' Douglas stared at her.

'Oh, nothing,' she said dismissively, opening the compact and dabbing her face with powder in a bid to disguise her hot flush. 'It's just something someone said to me recently, that's all.'

Douglas wasn't sure he liked the sound of that. He above all people knew that 'someone' often meant 'a lover'. He continued to watch her in the mirror, surreptitiously, as she applied powder to her skin. He wasn't quite sure what was different; her hair perhaps, her style of dress or her make-up, but s*omething* had changed. Maybe it was in the way she carried herself. Like she had discovered a new air of confidence. It had made him think about her again. After all, she may be getting on a bit but she was still an attractive woman.

'Another charity function, is it?' Douglas asked, tactfully changing the subject. 'What is it this week: Save The Hoodies, Hug a Leper . . . ?'

Calvary had to laugh despite herself.

'Fashion Against Fur, actually, darling.'

Douglas snorted derisively. 'But you *love* fur, Calvary – you know you've always been partial to a nice bit of mink,' he chuckled, amused by what seemed to be her hypocrisy.

'I could say the same of you,' she shot back. 'Anyway, I used to be partial, darling. *Used* to being the operative word. But then again, I *used* to be partial to a lot of things I no longer care for,' she cast him a loaded look, adding, 'I've finally seen the error of my ways.'

'Oh, really?' Douglas smiled wryly, amused, as he took off his cufflinks and opened his shirt, exposing his toned torso. Walking over to where she was standing in front of the mirror, he stood behind her, naked from the waist up. Undeniably, his body looked good for a man of his age, but it wasn't a patch on Josia's six-pack, she thought. She could see time beginning to show on his face now too. His chin, once sharp and angular, had softened slightly and the skin on his cheeks had finally begun to give in to gravity. Calvary looked at her husband and saw him for what he was, an aging old playboy long past his sell-by date. The longing she had once had for him, so strong and powerful that it had kept her prisoner all her life, had seemingly evaporated into the ether, almost overnight, and now, looking at him in the mirror behind her, Calvary felt something she never thought she would as far as her husband was concerned: indifference.

'You know you don't half talk a lot of rubbish sometimes, *Cally Rothschild*,' his breath was hot in her ear as he moved his body up close behind her. He hadn't called her that in years. He began pulling at her dress, trying to slide it up over her thighs and she could feel his erection digging into the small of her back as he pressed himself into her.

'Come on, old girl, what do you say, eh?' He was nuzzling her neck now, enjoying the powdery scent of her No. 5, his hard-on straining to free itself from his bespoke Paul Smith trousers. 'It's been eons since we last got silly . . . for old time's sake . . .'

Only a matter of weeks ago, Calvary would've welcomed such a surprise proposition from Douglas with more than just open arms. She had spent years trying to make him want her, but things had changed. It was all far too little, far too late.

She turned round to face him, pressing her lips against his. Unshaven, his stubble scratched her skin and his breath tasted unfamiliar and a little sour. Overwhelmed by a sense of desperate sadness, she let him kiss her. It was a purely sexual kiss, his tongue, sharp and hot, darting in and out of her mouth like a knife. There was nothing tender about it. Not like how Josia kissed her with his soft lips caressing hers, his tongue smooth and soft inside her mouth.

'That's right,' Douglas breathed into her ear, 'let me show you what you've been missing all this time, *Mrs* Rothschild.'

Douglas was surprised by how turned on he was. Admittedly, Calvary looked pretty decent tonight, but it was the idea that his wife might be having sex with someone else that seemed to have lit a fire under him. The thought of it both riled and excited him in equal measures. Calvary was like a favourite old toy; Douglas might not have played with her for years but he was hardly about to give her away for someone else to have their five minutes of fun. He decided he would have to start keeping more of an eye on her.

Calvary winced. *Mrs* Rothschild. Was he saying it as if to remind her that they were married? Well, she didn't need reminding. She knew only too well who she was married to and what a lying, cheating scumbag he was.

Douglas undid his belt and let his trousers and boxers fall to his ankles, his erection springing forwards, almost comically.

Typical Douglas, Calvary thought. They hadn't had sex in a little over a year and yet instead of making their re-introduction a romantic, tender encounter, he wanted some sixty second knee trembler up against the sink in the en-suite. He really was a bastard.

'I don't think so, *Mr* Rothschild.' Calvary slapped his hand away from her breast, hard, surprising herself.

'Jesus, Calvary,' he yelped, shaking it out, his face one of wounded pride and shock.

She turned to look at him, smoothing her dress down with her hands and readjusting her hair. He stood before her, naked, his trousers and pants around his ankles, his shiny Italian leather shoes still on his feet, projecting his own ridiculous, warped reflection back up at him. Looking him up and down, her face a mix of amusement and disgust, she said: 'I think I'll pass if it's all the same to you.'

Douglas glared at her, dumbfounded. Was he hearing this right? Was his wife turning him down? His own *wife*. He thought the stupid mare would be *grateful* that he was showing her a little interest after all this time. Suddenly Douglas felt angry. Angry and humiliated. And it was not a nice feeling.

'Suit yourself, Calvary,' he hissed nastily. 'Only I won't be asking twice.'

'I think I can live with that,' she retorted, spritzing herself with a little more Chanel No. 5 in a bid to mask his scent on her. She picked up her Alexander McQueen snakeskin clutch from the side of the dressing table and smacked her lips in the mirror once more.

'Goodbye, darling,' she smiled at him convivially as though nothing had transpired, making her way out of the bathroom, leaving him standing there, his erection rapidly diminishing.

'I could always ask Tamara to pop up if you like,' she poked her head around the door as an afterthought, looking down at his decreasing member with a mournful expression. 'After all, be a shame to waste it,' she said before slamming it shut behind her.

CHAPTER 39

The Fashion Against Fur party at The Kensington Roof Gardens was in full swing.

A selection of *au courant* models, designers and their muses mingled with celebrities and faces from music and politics as waiting staff in traditional Moroccan dress served an exquisite selection of vegetarian entrees from tagines and delicious free-flowing strawberry mojitos in sugar-frosted glasses.

The three women, seated on enormous Moorish floor cushions in a makeshift Bedouin tent, lit by a smattering of hanging lanterns and heated by real wood-burning chimineas, were deep in conversation.

'Well, ladies,' Imogen smiled, sipping her strawberry mojito, 'in just under three weeks' time Seb is due to fly to Rio de Janeiro for a business conference. At around 7:00 p.m. on Friday the 31st July he'll leave his office to catch a 10:00 p.m. flight from Gatwick.' She paused for a moment, a small smile creeping across her lips. 'By the time he boards that plane we'll have been in and out of the vault and he won't have suspected a thing.'

'I'll drink to that,' Calvary said, raising her cocktail glass, still on a high from her earlier encounter with Douglas in the bathroom. For the first time in their marriage, she had rejected him, and it felt so empowering she wanted to celebrate. But she knew she couldn't quite relax until she had got her hands on the contents of Douglas's strong box. It would be her and Henry's escape money; Lord knows he owed them both.

As the three women raised their glasses, Carine Herrison, head designer at Parisian fashion label, Clarice, poked her head inside the tent. A tour de force on the fashion scene, she was young, talented, impossibly beautiful and in possession of that indiscernible effortless French chic that women the world over were forever trying to mimic. She was the kind of infuriating woman who could get dressed in the dark and still look better than everyone else in the room. She gave Calvary a cursory wave.

'Carine, how lovely to see you,' Calvary gushed, making her way over to her and air-kissing both her cheeks. 'And looking *magnifique* as ever. One of yours I take it?' she said rhetorically, standing back to admire the petite designer's tiny outfit as it glittered and shone like a magpie's dream.

Carine nodded with an air of *sang-froid*. 'Of course, of course.' She smiled politely. She had been on the look out for the fashion editor of *POP* magazine but had instead run head first into Calvary Rothschild and Co. Still, she supposed it wasn't all bad, wasn't that Lady Yasmin Belmont-Jones with her? The one all the gossip and fashion mags were raving about?

Yasmin acknowledged Carine by holding her glass in the air. Great, she thought sardonically, just what the world needs: another stuck-up, skinny French bitch.

'*Enchanté*, Lady B.' Carine placed herself delicately down on a cushion next to Yasmin. She was intrigued by what she'd seen and heard of her in the glossies and had secretly been thinking she would be *parfait* to model for her next collection, one she had already given the working title of '*La Princesse Chav*.'

As Carine attempted to engage a reluctant Yasmin in conversation, Calvary turned to Imogen.

'You know, the only flaw in our plan is that blasted code. You know it's practically a non-starter unless we somehow get our hands on it.'

Imogen raised an arched eyebrow.

'Oh ye of little faith,' Imogen said, detecting the doubt in her friend's voice. 'You've got to trust me on this.'

She waved over at a familiar high-profile PR by the name of Susie Flankman, who waved back enthusiastically.

'We're going to make history, Cal,' Imogen said from the side of her mouth, squeezing her friend's arm in a bid to reassure her, 'and the best part is that no one will suspect us in a million years!'

Yasmin was only half listening to the silly French bint sitting next to her, chirping into her ear some inane bollocks about wanting her as a muse, whatever *that* meant.

It was laughable, really. Carine Herrison, *the* Carine Herrison of the almighty international fashion house that was Clarice was asking *her* to model her clothes on the runway. She wondered if she would be quite so keen to see her sashay up the catwalk if she knew she was really just Stacey Jones from Croydon.

'So you see, I would adore it if you came to my studio in Paris. At a convenient time for you, of course. Maybe we can have lunch at B4, some wine perhaps . . . discuss my ideas a little further?'

'Hmm?' Yasmin had stopped listening to her now, her attention fully focussed on the devastatingly attractive, young male model who had just entered the tent. She took one look at his dark brooding eyes and tanned torso just visible beneath his plain white t-shirt and instantly felt the evening improve tenfold.

'Excuse me, Carine,' she said, pulling on her Isabel Marant boots. 'I need to use the bathroom.' Yasmin turned to Imogen apologetically. 'Something's come up,' she said, hastily grabbing her quilted Chanel bag.

'But you can't leave yet, darling,' Calvary called out, 'we're celebrating, remember?'

'I'll call you,' Yasmin sang out behind her, already strutting purposefully across the room in the direction of the model, a tigress stalking her prey.

CHAPTER 40

Yasmin Belmont-Jones sat on the uncomfortable futon sofa that served a dual purpose in Sammie Grainger's poky Earls Court apartment, tentatively sipping a skinny soya latte she had picked up at Starbucks on her way over.

Wrapping her slim, finely manicured fingers around the cardboard receptacle, one DVB denim-clad leg slung casually over the other, she looked up.

'Well,' she waved the small Dictaphone in her hand and casting her eye around the depressingly shabby studio, 'you did good, Grainger.' Yasmin pressed the play button.

'. . . yes, well, it's a pleasure . . .' Sebastian Forbes' unmistakable braying tones filled the room. 'Shall I speak directly into the tape? Good, oh yes, right.' Sebastian cleared his throat. 'For the benefit of the tape,' he announced authoritatively, 'my name is Sebastian Forbes. Is that clear enough? *Seb-as-tian For-bes.*'

Sammie, dressed casually in a fake Juicy Couture tracksuit and Ugg Boots, gave a wan smile.

'For all the good it's done me,' she remarked, bitterly. 'You know that bastard Pugh sacked me last week? All because I wouldn't get down on my knees and suck his tiny cock.'

Yasmin raised an amused eyebrow. Secretly though, she admired Sammie for refusing to compromise herself. She only wished she could've had some of her resolve herself. Like at that ridiculous Roof Gardens fashion party where she had blown that male model in the men's toilets without even bothering to ask his name.

Usually, Yasmin gleaned a sense of power in these meaningless, transient sexual encounters. At least, that's what she convinced herself. On this occasion, however, she had been left empty and filled with self-loathing. She wondered, when all this was over, if she would ever be able to love another person properly, or if she was damaged beyond repair, incapable of loving or being loved.

'What a drag,' Yasmin remarked glibly. In reality though, she felt genuinely sorry for Sammie. Once again, a woman's bright future had been dimmed at the hands of a man.

'You could always sell this,' she suggested, shaking the Dictaphone in her direction once more.

'You're too kind,' Sammie replied sarcastically, reaching for it. As their hands touched both women felt a small jolt of electricity pass between them, though both pretended that neither had felt it. 'Though I was rather hoping that I wouldn't have to.'

'Meaning?'

'Meaning, I was wondering when you might start delivering on *your* side of the bargain. That is why you're here – isn't it?'

Yasmin smirked in a bid to hide her disappointment. Sammie Grainger was just the same as everyone else at the end of the day, out for herself and what she could get. Fleetingly, she had believed that Grainger had genuinely wanted to help her. And now she cursed herself for having let down her guard.

Sammie pressed the button on the Dictaphone. '. . . so you see that was in the early 1800s when my grandfather's grandfather's father . . .' Sebastian Forbes' self-important voice rang out through the airless room like a public announcement.

'The man thought he was James bloody Bond. "The name's Forbes . . . Sebastian Forbes",' she said in a low mimic of Sean Connery. Yasmin laughed despite herself. 'Jesus, that man could talk a glass eye to sleep. There's three hours' worth of conversation – largely one-sided I might add. So, I reckon I've earned at least the same amount of time from you, interview-wise that is,' she added.

'Oh, you do, huh?' Yasmin shot back, her voice a little chilly. 'Well, like I said, all in good time, Sam, all in good time.'

Sammie glanced at her.

'What?'

'Nothing. It's just that only my mum ever calls me Sam.'

'Why the long face? Is she dead or something?'

'Dead? Jesus, I hope not! No. She's well and truly alive – and no doubt kicking some arse as we speak.'

'Like mother, like daughter, eh?' Yasmin deadpanned.

Sammie smiled. 'Something like that. Anyway, she's living in Deptford, telling anyone who'll listen how fucking great I am, that I've got this amazing job.' Sammie rolled her eyes and sighed. 'Only I'm not really, am I?' She shrugged, gesturing around her damp, poky studio apartment. 'She's not seen this shithole yet – probably thinks it's some bijou little crash pad all done out in Laura Ashley – and she's not likely to either if I don't pay the rent I owe within a week.' Sammie's voice trailed off and she shook her head ruefully. 'Anyway, I can't bring myself to tell her that I've lost my job.'

Yasmin nodded as if she understood where the conversation was leading.

'So, how much do you want?' she said, reaching for her Miu Miu day clutch. 'I've got about a thousand in cash right now or I can write you a personal cheque . . .'

Sammie blinked at her, a look of horror clouding over her pretty face.

'No. No!' she shook her head, 'you got me all wrong. I wasn't . . . I didn't mean . . . look, I don't want your money!'

Yasmin raised an eyebrow in disbelief.

'Of course you don't,' she said sardonically. 'Anyway it's not *my* money, is it? I'll quite happily hand some of it over to you if needs be. Say two grand, that do you?'

Sammie had the grace to look offended.

'I don't want your money,' she repeated. 'Or your husband's money, or anyone else's for that matter.'

Yasmin lit a cigarette and blew the smoke from her lips with some force. 'Oh come on, Sam, pull the other one,' she snorted derisively, 'it plays a fucking tune.'

Sammie felt her hackles rise.

'Jesus, you're a bitch, do you know that?' she said.

Yasmin shrugged, flicking her platinum mane behind her.

'Didn't anyone ever tell you, Grainger? Nice guys finish last.'

Sammie raised an eyebrow. 'Ain't that the truth.' She glared at Yasmin on the sofa and wondered just what it was about this woman she found so beguiling. It went way beyond her physical appearance. Way beyond anything she had ever felt before. As spiky and caustic as she was, Sammie could not stop herself from wanting to reach out to her with the hand of friendship, even if she was more likely to rip it off than she was to shake it.

'Do you ever take off your armour?' she asked, looking into Yasmin's eyes that seemed to change from an icy blue to green right before her. 'Do you ever let anyone in there?' She bent down and tapped Yasmin's chest, the sound of her fingers hollow against bone. 'You know you might find that you'll be happier if you open up to someone, talk about it.'

Yasmin snorted.

'When I need a shrink, *Doctor* Grainger, I'll buy one, thanks. In the meantime, if you'll just let me smoke this cigarette in peace and finish my coffee, I'll bid you good day.' She made to place the Dictaphone back in her tote but Sammie grabbed her hand, preventing her.

'Easy, tiger,' she said, her friendly tone taking on a harder edge all of a sudden. 'Before I let you walk out of here with that tape, I need some kind of reassurance from you that I'll see your face again. I mean, we have a deal here, don't we? I give you the tape, you give me your story. Unless of course, you have no intention of coming good on your side of the bargain.'

A rush of adrenalin coursed through Yasmin's body, exploding in her stomach. She looked at Sammie's hand upon hers for a long moment before saying in a small low voice: 'Are you going to move your hand or am I?'

Sammie pulled a face, suddenly furious at the thought that Yasmin might be about to retract on the deal.

'You'll have to cut it off before I let you walk out of here with that tape and no guarantees.'

Yasmin laughed, a silly, high-pitched piss-take of a laugh.

'You couldn't cut your own fringe, Grainger,' Yasmin barked, switching to South London default setting and tearing Sammie's hand from her own. She wasn't going to give up that Dictaphone without a fight. Both women stood then, squaring up to each other, Sammie's 5 foot 10 inch frame towering over Yasmin's much shorter 5 foot 4 inch. Wisely however, Sammie did not underestimate her. Tiny she might be but she guessed that Yasmin had the strength and determination of an ox and all the viciousness of a pit bull when provoked. For all Sammie's height and build advantage, she was no fighter. But she was angry now. They both were.

The two women began to tussle for the Dictaphone.

'Give it back to me,' Sammie screeched. 'I worked for that tape and I'm not giving it up until you give me some kind of guarantee that you won't double-cross me.'

'What part of: it's *my* Dictaphone and *my* tape, don't you understand, Grainger? And there I was thinking you had a few brain cells up top.' Yasmin, her heart thudding like a caged animal, tapped Sammie's temple with a sharp manicured fingernail. Sammie exploded.

'You fucking bitch,' she screamed, and pulling her clenched fist back, landed a punch straight in Yasmin's face, the force of the impact almost knocking her on her backside.

Momentarily stunned, Yasmin felt the warm trickle of blood as it began to ooze from her nose. Only a few seconds could've passed before she set upon her; striking Sammie with her small but hard fists in retaliation. And then all hell broke loose. The two women began to fight, tearing at each other's hair and clothes, screaming and slapping, swearing that they would kill each other. The blood from Yasmin's nose was smeared across her face now, making her injuries look worse than they really were, and Sammie could feel the beginnings of a swollen eye.

'You double-crossing bitch, Stacey Jones. I'll go to that husband of yours and I'll show him what I've got on you . . .'

'I'll blow your fucking brains out first . . . if I can find them, that is,' Yasmin quipped as they circled each other around the coffee table. 'You've got nothing on me darlin'. . . just hearsay and speculation. Jeremy will laugh you all the way to court. Now just give me that goddamn tape and let me the fuck out of this shithole.' She went for the Dictaphone in Sammie's hand again but Sammie was too quick and held it high above her head, out of reach.

Yasmin began to jump up in a bid to snatch it from her grasp. Grunting and straining, the two women suddenly made eye contact and, as the sheer ridiculousness of the situation began to dawn upon them, started to laugh. Soon they were in stitches, with Yasmin on her knees, almost crying with laughter, and Sammie, snorting and gasping for breath as tears rolled down her cheeks.

'Stop,' Sammie gasped after a few moments. 'I can't breathe.'

Yasmin was on her back now with her knees up against her chest, her whole body shuddering. She wasn't even sure what was so funny, only that whatever it was, it was making her feel better. Much better. She hadn't laughed with such abandon in years.

Sammie shuffled over towards her, laughter spurting from her mouth like gunfire. She looked down at Yasmin's pretty face and immediately stopped laughing when she saw the blood.

'Oh, God.' She put her hand to her mouth in horror. 'What have I done? Jesus, I'm sorry, let me get you a cloth or something.'

Yasmin sat up, her sides tender. She wiped her nose and looked down at the blood.

'It's alright,' she shrugged. 'Just a lucky shot, that's all.'

Sammie came towards her with a clean towel from the bathroom.

'Here, let me,' she said, moving in close, dabbing at Yasmin's face.

'Leave it out.' Yasmin shooed her away, her voice suddenly sounding more cockney than ever. 'Don't make a fuss.' For a split second their eyes locked and suddenly they were kissing, their faces pressed against each other's in urgency, their mouths open and hungry for the other.

Sammie tasted the blood on Yasmin's mouth, a strange tinny taste, as it mixed with the sweetness of her saliva, her lips full and wet, her tongue warm and gentle as it explored her own.

Yasmin felt the passion rise within her like she had never

felt with anyone before. Sammie's kiss, tender and more gentle than any she had ever experienced, had taken her completely by surprise and yet she had allowed herself to dissolve into it, to fall into the softness of her arms as if it were the most natural thing in the world.

'I'm sorry,' Sammie whispered to Yasmin as she gently wiped the claret blood stains from her nose. 'I'm so, so, sorry.'

CHAPTER 41

'For God's sake, woman, will you just relax? It's only a bit of turbulence. Have a drink why don't you? You're making me nervous, all that bloody twitching.' Sebastian snapped at his wife, irritated.

'I can't help it, Seb,' Imogen replied tremulously, digging her fingernails into the butterscotch leather seat, panic etched on her face like a mask. 'All this wobbling about, it's scaring me.'

Ever since the plane crash that had claimed Cressida's life, Imogen had become a nervous flier and consequently had spent the most part of the plane journey to St Barts in a heightened state of awareness. For most people such apprehension would be understandable, given the circumstances, but Sebastian was not most people.

'Fix me a martini, would you, Pierre?' Imogen smiled nervously at the attendant, thinking that perhaps, for once, her husband might be right. 'And please, make it a strong one, would you?'

'Of course, madam. Coming right up. And you, sir?' He turned to Sebastian.

'Oh, to hell with it! Bring me a large scotch on the rocks!' he said, adding, 'I am on holiday after all.'

Sebastian reclined his seat and grinned broadly, oblivious to his wife's distress once more. He was in a good mood today. An exceedingly good mood, in fact. They were on their way to St Barts as guests of honour of his new friend and business associate, Prince Saud. For the next three days, they would be staying on his magnificent yacht, *Carpe Diem*, enjoying his generous hospitality while rubbing shoulders with some serious Hollywood heavyweights.

The thought of being among such calibre of guests excited Sebastian to no end; this trip would undoubtedly offer him some truly sublime networking opportunities. Though as it was, things weren't looking too shabby in that direction, thanks due, in part, to that airhead friend of his wife's, Yasmin Belmont-Jones, who had just helped him secure an interview with *ESL* magazine. Seems she had been good for something after all.

Sebastian recalled his recent interview with the charming young *ESL* journalist with a deep sense of satisfaction. He had seduced her with his dazzling wit and repartee. The girl had practically hung off his every word and had left his office grinning from ear to ear. His chest swelled with self-importance at the recollection.

Sebastian took a slug of his scotch and let out a satisfied 'ahh' as the smooth amber liquid slid down the back of his throat. In a couple of weeks' time it was his birthday and far from fretting about the passing of another year, he positively welcomed it. In particular he was looking forward to seeing the final sculpture that Amandine Lamarque had come up with.

And while Bryony was due to fly home for a visit, it was to be more brief than she thought. Sebastian had secretly arranged for her to go dry-slope skiing with family friends, the Orsmby-Bowles, in Saas Fee, Switzerland. He felt the slightest twinge of guilt as he thought of it. He was well aware that Imogen would be beyond furious when she found out what he had done, but he was convinced that their daughter's presence would get in the way of this newfound harmony between them, and he just couldn't afford to jeopardise that. Anyway, to assuage his guilt, he would buy her those Dolce and Gabbana salopettes she'd been going on about, kit her out in all the latest high-fashion designer après ski wear so that she could show off to all her friends. Then, he could head off to Rio for The International Banking Association Annual Conference the following week with a clear conscience. Ah, the IBAs. Yet another reason to be cheerful.

This year, Sebastian had been asked to appear as a key guest speaker at the annual industry event. Randolph Walmsley CBE, Chief Executive of the ABB (Association of British Banking) had personally requested he 'do the honours'. Sebastian had been only too happy to oblige. In fact, if his speech at this year's ball was anything to go by, then he was looking at another standing ovation.

The turbulence had begun to settle now and with it Imogen's nerves, thanks, in part, to the martini that she'd thrown back in almost one hit.

'We'll be landing in less than an hour,' Sebastian said, resting his hand lightly just above her knee. She fought down the urge to slap it away. The next few days were going to ask a lot from her. But she knew what she had to do. What she *must* do.

'I've always loved the Caribbean,' Imogen sighed. 'Ever since you took me to Necker Island.'

She placed her hand lightly on top of his. 'Seems like so long ago now, doesn't it?'

'I suppose it does, yes,' he replied, appreciating her unexpected gesture of affection.

'Do you remember it?'

He glanced up at her, pulled a face.

'Necker Island? Of course I remember it, woman!'

Sebastian would never forget it. He had waited what

felt like a lifetime to finally get her into his life – and his bed . . .

'Do you remember the day we flew out?' she asked, her eyes glazing over. 'That morning you sent a car for me. I had no idea where it was taking me. And then the next thing I know I'm on a flight to Necker Island! It was all so thrilling! I was only twenty-one. So young . . . so naive.' Imogen gave a small sigh and snuggled into Sebastian's stiff shoulder, resting her cheek against his arm. His smell was unfamiliar to her. Like a stranger's.

'I don't know about naive, Imogen,' he sniffed sardonically. 'You were quite worldly-wise if I remember rightly.'

She resented the ungallant remark but chose to ignore it.

'I was terribly nervous about flying that day too.'

'Oh really, were you? Why?'

'Don't you remember?' She glanced up at him, feigning mild indignation.

'Remember what?'

'It was Friday the 13th.'

Sebastian pulled his head back into his chin.

'Was it? Can't say that I do, to be honest.'

'Well, *I* remember. I remember everything – all the little details, right down to dates and times.'

Sebastian was as surprised as he was delighted. He couldn't recall the last time Imogen had spoken about Necker Island with such fondness. In fact, he couldn't remember the last time she had spoken about Necker Island at all.

'We made love on the beach that evening.'

'Ah, now that I *do* remember.'

'On the sand, with the sound of the waves in the background. I fell in love with you then.'

He turned to her, stunned. What was all this about? Was she drunk? He'd never heard her speak with such tenderness before.

Imogen fixed him with a penetrating stare and slowly raised an eyebrow, placing her tongue provocatively to one side of her mouth, her lips gently parted.

'You know what day it is today, don't you?' she said slowly, her fingers wandering towards the button on his shirt. She began playing with it gently.

'Yes, it's Thursday, 12th July, *why*?' He glanced at her, suspicious.

'What time do we land in St Barts?'

Sebastian looked at his Patek Philippe watch. 'I make it just under one hour's time.'

'So with the four hour time difference, by the time we get there it'll be, what, just gone midnight?'

'About that, yes what are you up to?' He narrowed his eyes at her.

'Well,' she ran her fingers along his, linking them in her own. 'By then it'll be Friday the *13th*. Wouldn't it be nice to recreate that moment again,' she smiled at him mischievously. 'Just the two of us together, alone on the beach?'

Sebastian grinned so broadly that he exercised facial muscles he never knew he had. He leaned forward and kissed her full on the mouth, parting her lips with his hot, probing tongue. She would never know of his crimes against her, must never find out. Not that he was particularly worried that she would. Beautiful she might be, but she was hardly the sharpest knife in the drawer.

Imogen tentatively broke off their kiss by excusing herself to the small but perfectly luxurious bathroom, complete with 22-carat gold taps and lavatory seat. Locking the door, she visibly blanched as she gripped the wash basin with both hands. Tasting his salty saliva on her lips, she began rinsing her mouth with water in a bid to wash it away, her hands shaking as she patted her mouth with a paper napkin.

Imogen stared at herself in the mirror and looked into the face of a stranger. Some time during the next twenty-four hours she knew she would have to make love to her husband like she had never made love to him before – with passion and sincerity, like she really meant it.

Taking a deep breath, Imogen exited the cubicle and rejoined Sebastian. She smiled as she noticed that he had ordered her another martini.

'You read my mind,' she said, genuinely grateful.

'Well, cheers, my darling.' Sebastian raised his tumbler of scotch and tapped the rim of her cocktail glass.

'Here's to Friday the 13th!' Imogen smiled provocatively, raising her eyebrows at him once more as she pressed her lips to the glass. 'To us.'

CHAPTER 42

Clutching a $7,000 bottle of Cristal Brut 1990 and her diamond-encrusted Jimmy Choo shoes in one hand, the other holding up the trailing silk chiffon fabric of her dove grey embellished Marchesa gown, Imogen ran barefoot along the jetty.

'Catch me if you can!' she called out to him, her voice trailing behind her, a silky whisper in the ubiquitous inky blackness.

Sebastian straightened his bow tie uncomfortably and glanced tentatively over his shoulder, looking back at the magnificent yacht in the near distance. The sound of music and laughter punctuated the warm Caribbean night air above him and he felt a little irritated by his wife's sudden outburst of spontaneity. She really knew how to pick her moments.

Unrivalled king of the *bon viveurs*, no expense had been spared for Prince Saud's collection of most prestigious guests. As well as treating them to a gastronomic feast, he had arranged for a real live white tiger act to be flown in from Las Vegas alongside exotic dancers, illusionists, singers, acrobats and comedians, all on hand to thrill and amuse them until the early hours of the morning.

The champagne was flowing freely and a high-brow mix of international royalty, Hollywood heavyweights, politicians, playboys, supermodels and business tycoons mingled and chatted with abandon, revelling in each other's company and marvelling at such an opulent display of wealth and splendour.

Sebastian had not wanted to leave. The party was just beginning to warm up. But Imogen, it seemed, had other ideas.

'What's the matter, Seb, too risky for you?' She stopped halfway along the jetty, goading him, one hand on her hip, the other swinging the $7,000 bottle of vintage Cristal. 'I thought you were a man who liked to take risks . . . live on the edge a little.'

Sebastian watched as the lights from the boat danced like flames on the ocean's surface, illuminating his wife's milky skin, her chest visibly heaving from her sprint along the jetty.

He turned to look behind him once more, torn. 'Oh, to hell with it,' he muttered under his breath, stooping to take off his bespoke Berluti shoes. It would be churlish to look a gift horse in the mouth.

Imogen smiled triumphantly as she watched him approach.

'Come on,' she said, throwing her arms around his neck, 'let's run down to the beach.'

Sebastian shook his head and gave a small laugh of incredulity. She was clearly quite drunk.

'What's got in to you, Imogen?' he asked. 'You've been like a different woman these past few weeks.'

She dropped her arms from his neck and laughed. She was swaying a little, he thought.

'Let's just say I'm tired of all the fighting. Besides, can't a woman desire her own husband anymore?'

'Of course,' he said, immediately aroused by her use of

the word 'desire'. 'But don't you want to appreciate a little more of the entertainment first? There's a rumour that Céline Dion is on board . . .'

'Céline Dion?' Imogen screwed her face up. 'Oh Seb, you always were such a stuffed shirt!'

He laughed then, even if he was a little put out. He'd always been a huge fan of Céline's.

'Come on,' she said, turning on her bare feet. 'I'll race you.'

The sand was cool underfoot as they ran along the shoreline, the sound of the gentle waves methodical and reassuring, threatening to catch their toes.

Imogen braced herself.

'Kiss me, Seb,' she said, suddenly pulling him close to her. Duly obliging, they fell backwards onto the sand, the ruffles of her chiffon gown incongruous against the soft white powder as she sank into it. He wanted her badly now, his early apprehension at having left the party – and all those networking opportunities with it – all but disappeared as he found himself caught up in the moment. He pressed his mouth hard against hers, his breath hot and meaty from all that rich barbequed food he'd eaten.

'I want you, Seb. I want you now,' she whispered into his ear and he responded with a small moan of pleasure. Unzipping his trousers and pulling them down to his knees, he climbed on top of her and, pulling at her couture gown and delicate La Perla underwear, thrust himself deep inside her, pushing through her body's initial resistance, his hands roughly grabbing at her bare breasts exposed in the moonlight. Sebastian felt his orgasm begin to build almost instantly and willed it back, wanting to savour the moment for as long as possible. She felt delicious beneath him, tight yet juicy, her skin soft and smooth as stone.

Sebastian felt powerful in that moment, slamming himself into his wife's delicate flesh. Tonight he was going to show her just who Sebastian Forbes was – her husband, her lover, the only man who had ever really loved her. Yes, Seb thought to himself as he blindly pumped away at her, oblivious to her pleasure – or lack of it – she was his wife. *His* wife.

As Sebastian came, a great crescendo of shudders and cries he could no longer contain, he was oblivious to the hot salty tears that had escaped from the corners of Imogen's eyes and slid silently down her face onto the sand below. Collapsing on top of her, his whole body spent, he let out a long and protracted sigh. He had not had an orgasm as intense as that in years.

'That was amazing,' he panted after a few moments.

Imogen blinked back silent tears. It felt as if something terribly wrong had just happened.

'I do hope no one saw us,' he added, glancing around, suddenly a little paranoid. 'It wouldn't do to be caught having sex on the beach by the Douglas-Zeta Joneses.'

'I don't care if anyone *did* see us,' Imogen forced herself to reply. She had to regain her composure. To see this through.

He sat down next to her, his body still glowing and twitching from his powerful orgasm.

'I feel like I did all those years ago when I was twenty-one,' she said carefully, looking up towards the sky and sighing. 'Look Seb,' she said, pointing to the blackness above them after a long pause. 'I count thirteen stars! Thirteen stars for Friday the 13th! Surely that has to mean something, doesn't it? A good omen for us . . .'

'I suppose so,' he said disinterestedly, already thinking about getting back to the boat. What he really fancied now was a brandy and a cigar – and if they got a wiggle on, they might just make it back in time to catch the end of Céline's set.

'Lucky for some,' she said.

He smiled at her then, enjoying the rare moment of closeness between them.

Caught up in Imogen's new appreciation of him, Sebastian didn't stop to wonder what might have caused such a change of heart in his wife. He liked to think that maybe she had just woken up one morning and realised that she was a lucky woman, a *very* lucky woman indeed, married to someone as important and powerful as he was.

'*Lucky* for us,' he said, taking her hand and kissing it. Imogen smiled an empty smile, one that a real lover would have seen straight through. She squeezed his hand in return.

'Seriously, Imogen,' he said, his eyes full of earnest as they met with her own. 'I know these past few months things have been, well, a little difficult between us . . .'

Months, she thought bitterly, *try years*.

'But I want you to know that I forgive you. It's just so wonderful to see that you've come to your senses.'

Imogen looked at her husband, stared into the black holes of his eyes for the longest moment, and swallowed her tongue. She thought of Bryony then, of the daughter who would soon be back in her arms, and wondered if the secret she had held in her heart for all these years would ever see the light of day.

'Thank you, Seb,' she replied, blinking at him. Once, she had felt a modicum of pity for him; a man who could never love anyone more than he loved himself. But now she felt nothing.

As far as she was concerned, Sebastian Forbes had exactly what was coming to him.

CHAPTER 43

Sebastian had to say this for his wife: she had come up trumps tonight – for once. The canapés and three course meal consisting of pressed foie gras with Madeira jelly, oven-roasted pigeon with fondant potato and date sauce followed by a walnut and pear soufflé with bitter chocolate ice cream, had been an absolute culinary triumph. The guests had loved it – especially that vociferous show-off, celebrity chef, Richard Ramsden and his long-suffering wife, Tomasina – who had had little choice but to positively rave about every mouthful. Imogen had been on top form all evening, playing the perfect hostess, ensuring everyone was having a marvellous time and enjoying themselves at his birthday soirée. She had even laughed at a few of his 'jokes' and shown him rare displays of affection in public, kissing him on the cheek and stroking his arm occasionally, making his chest swell with pride. Even the attendance of her insufferable friends and their equally tedious husbands hadn't given him cause for complaint. In fact, he was quite relishing the opportunity to rub Jeremy Belmont and Douglas Rothschild's noses in his recent good fortune and success.

Even Bryony was behaving herself, not stealing too much of the limelight as he had predicted she might, staying in the background, speaking only when spoken to. Perfect, it was all perfect.

The hum of conversation, chinking of glasses and cigarette smoke wafted up into the warm evening air above them as the group stood outside looking into the orangery, cleared by the staff to make way for the grand unveiling of Amandine's masterpiece.

Sebastian felt the first flutters of apprehension as he looked at the sculpture, covered with tarpaulin, as it stood in the middle of the vast, high-ceilinged room. A small part of him was worried in case that mad French artist might have stitched him up. He hoped the time he had spent sitting for her, allowing her to cover him in all sorts of viscous substances, would have been worth it. Regardless, Amandine Lamarque was a seriously cool name to drop in social circles. No one would want to criticise for fear of looking like a philistine. It was a win-win situation as far as Sebastian was concerned.

Anticipation hung heavy in the air as the conversation lowered to a hushed silence.

'Ladies and gentlemen, our dear friends and family.' Imogen lightly tapped the edge of her crystal champagne flute with a silver knife and glanced at Calvary and Yasmin who were standing together with their respective husbands. 'On behalf of the birthday boy and I . . .' There were claps and cheers of approval from the crowd, 'I would like to thank you all for joining us this evening and for helping my darling husband,' she gestured over at Sebastian who, conscious of all eyes upon him, bowed theatrically, 'to celebrate becoming another year older though debatably wiser.' The crowd tittered good-humouredly and Sebastian forced a loud chuckle.

'This year I wanted to do something special for my husband, something different, to show him my appreciation and above all, my love,' Imogen spoke earnestly and a cacophony of 'ahhhs' emanated up into the balmy evening air.

Sebastian watched his wife with a mix of awe and caution. She was playing the devoted wife part extremely well, almost too well in fact. He still couldn't quite get his head around just how much she had changed over these past few weeks.

'And so it is with my greatest pleasure that I unveil this token of my affection, a tribute to my brilliant husband, everyone, I give you . . . Sebastian Forbes!'

A stunned gasp echoed around the room as Imogen theatrically pulled the tarpaulin from the life-size sculpture, followed by a swift and appreciative round of applause.

Sebastian stared at the statue and resisted the urge to punch the air in triumph. There he stood, all six foot of him in all his brilliant, bronze beauty. He looked handsome, regal even, his posture poised and commanding, his jawline strong and his cheekbones prominent.

In truth, Amandine had been more than sympathetic in her interpretation of her subject. From the true-to-life casts she had taken and used as a guide, she had recreated an image of Sebastian Forbes in his own mind's eye. It was a narcissistic interpretation, though this subtle observation was lost on him completely.

'Well, what can I say?' Sebastian breathed, feeling genuinely emotional as his guests looked to him for a reaction. 'It really is marvellous, truly, *truly* marvellous.'

He put a stiff arm around Imogen, as he stood up to make an 'impromptu' speech, rather than one he had spent days preparing for, one he hoped would yet again showcase what a fine raconteur he was in front his influential guests.

'. . . and so I said to myself that if I loved it enough, I would place it in the grand entrance of Forbes Foyer . . . so first thing Monday I think I'll arrange for *two* cars to pick me up! One for me and one for my friend here.'

Laughter rang out through the evening air as guests clasped their hands in sycophantic appreciation.

As the guests settled back into chatting amongst themselves, Imogen sidled up to Calvary and Yasmin.

'We were just admiring such a fine piece.' Calvary gave a knowing smirk, champagne flute in hand as she and Yasmin glanced up at the bronzed statue. 'Such an inspired idea.'

'And such a pity that something so beautifully created will play such a pivotal role in your husband's downfall,' Yasmin felt compelled to chip in, jovially.

Imogen grinned.

'Tonight might be Seb's night, but tomorrow will be mine.' She turned to her friends. 'Ours.'

'So, we're all systems go for tomorrow then?' Yasmin asked as Calvary continued to stare up at the statue.

'Ready as we'll ever be, right, Ims?'

Imogen, transfixed in morbid curiosity at the bronze, took a deep slug of her vintage Dom Perignon.

'Absolutely,' she said with conviction. 'There's just one thing left to do. Excuse me, ladies.'

Slipping away from her guests, Imogen made her way up the winding staircase towards her husband's office, catching a glimpse of her daughter on the way.

Bryony was chatting proficiently to various guests, an amenable smile on her young face, her expression wide-eyed and earnest. She looked so young and beautiful standing there in her mother's dress, in the first flushes of womanhood, dazzling like a ruby in the dust among all the jaded figures around her.

Imogen recalled the conversation she had had with her daughter while dressing for the party earlier, of the sadness she had seen in her own child's eyes as she had begged her mother not to send her back to Switzerland, and she felt a blackness descend upon her heart once more.

Locking the office door behind her, she sat in Sebastian's leather swivel chair and, booting up his computer, began to compile an e-mail to one Derrell 'Dickie' Richards. Her hands hovered nervously above the keyboard as she wrote the words in the subject matter: 'Tomorrow night.'

CHAPTER 44

As he made his way into his office on the morning of Friday July 31st, Sebastian Forbes had never felt better. For the first time in as long as he could remember, life was treating him just how he felt he deserved to be treated. Everything had fallen into place and he couldn't help but feel a deep sense of contentment. His business was going from strength to strength, thanks in part to his recent association with a certain Prince Saud, and his plan to break into the media was beginning to take shape too, what with all the distinguished contacts he'd made in St Barts, not to mention his new hotshot agent who was promising him the earth. But above all else, the thing that had brought about this true feeling of satisfaction was Imogen. The new amenable, obliging Imogen. For the first time in his married life, his wife wanted him, *really* wanted him. And it felt good.

Sebastian was suddenly struck by an idea: he wondered if now might be the perfect time to ask Imogen to renew their marriage vows! He knew full well that when she had stood next to him on that beautiful sunny afternoon in August almost fourteen years ago, she had not meant a single word of them. But as he'd said his own vows that day, Sebastian had silently added another to himself; he had vowed that one day she would mean those words she had spoken on her wedding day, that he would make sure of it. It had been a long time coming, but now it seemed as if finally that day had arrived. And Sebastian wanted to celebrate it. Yes, the more he thought about it, the more the idea appealed. A wedding! On Necker Island. He'd get on to his pal Richard Branson about it right away. He'd arrange it for the 13th, whisk her off to the beautiful Caribbean island and surprise her with a wedding ceremony on the beach. Then he'd fly out 500 special guests, hire in world-class caterers and entertainment for a truly lavish party that society would still be talking about in a decade's time.

'Morning, Janet,' Sebastian said convivially, as he breezed past his PA into his office.

'Good morning, Mr Forbes,' she said as she looked up, a little surprised. Usually he skulked by of a morning without so much as a grunt of acknowledgement her way.

'If you could come into my office in five minutes, I've a few instructions for you,' he said.

'Of course, Mr Forbes,' Janet smiled obligingly as always, picking up a pen and pad to the ready. 'Can I bring you your usual morning espresso and pistachio biscotti?'

'Why not, Janet?' he smiled rhetorically. 'Why not? And might I say how lovely your hair looks this morning. Are you wearing a new style?'

Janet could barely disguise her pleasure.

'Well, yes, Mr Forbes' she said, preening her hair self-consciously, blushing slightly as she lowered her eyes coquettishly. 'How good of you to notice.'

Switching on his computer and absent-mindedly opening his mail, Sebastian went about his morning rituals with more purpose than usual. He had a list of calls as long as his arm to make before he jetted off to Rio this evening and was knee deep in paperwork that needed reading and signing but even that wasn't going to cloud his mood today.

He was still thinking about Imogen and Necker Island as he reset the vault's security code for the forthcoming week. 'Lucky for some,' he said aloud to himself, smiling broadly.

CHAPTER 45

Up on the nineteenth floor of the imposing Forbes building in his vast, penthouse suite office, Sebastian Forbes gathered together the paperwork he needed for the conference that weekend and threw it all into his Gucci leather briefcase.

His driver, Raoul, had just called to say that he was already waiting outside ready to take him to the airport. It was 6 p.m. and he was a good hour earlier than expected, but according to Raoul, the traffic was particularly thick in London that evening and therefore had advised they set off as early as possible to avoid getting stuck, or worse, miss the flight altogether. This suited Sebastian fine. The idea of grabbing a glass or two of champagne and a dozen oysters in the first class lounge before take-off appealed to him enormously, especially since that old bastard Walmsley would be footing the bill.

Suddenly feeling the urge for a scotch to kick-start the weekend, Sebastian walked the length of his office to his well-stocked drinks cabinet and poured himself a generous measure of single malt in a crystal tumbler, making an appreciative sound as he took a small sip of the smooth liquid. He picked up the phone and buzzed down to reception.

'Come up to my office and collect my luggage, will you?' he barked. 'I've decided to head off early this evening.' He put the phone down without waiting for a response.

Admiring his reflection in the large office window, Sebastian smirked and gave himself a little congratulatory pat on the stomach. In less than twenty-four hours he would be taking to the stage in front of hundreds of extremely important businessmen, fellow bankers and contemporaries who had flown in from all over the world, all listening intently to what *he* had to say. He imagined them hanging off his every word, their eyes shining brightly with admiration as his well-rehearsed speech brought the house down.

Pouring himself another scotch and downing it instantly, he grinned. Oh yes, he told himself unequivocally, the world had better be on its guard: Sebastian Forbes's moment had finally arrived.

*

Paulo Martinez, one half of the front desk night security team, took his boss's small overnight bag and followed him out towards the chauffeur-driven Aston Martin.

'Good idea to set off early, sir,' he said, tremulously. He always felt nervous in his boss's presence, though he wasn't entirely sure why. 'I heard on the radio that the traffic report is bad tonight. Something about an accident on the A2 . . .'

'Yes, thank you, er . . . Martinez,' Sebastian said vaguely, glancing at the boy's name on his security badge.

'Have a safe flight, sir,' Paulo gushed with sincerity, watching his boss's formidable figure as it settled back into the soft leather seat. Sebastian acknowledged his well wishes with a small nod before slamming the door shut.

As the car disappeared into the London traffic, Paulo

felt pleased with himself. It was the closest he'd come to having a conversation with his employer in the whole year that he'd been working at Forbes Bank. As far as he was concerned this was definitely progress.

Making his way back to the imposing reception desk, Paulo settled down to covertly read his copy of the *Daily Star* – newspapers were forbidden from front reception at all times – that he had hidden under the desk and attempted to distract himself from thoughts of his girlfriend, who was almost two weeks overdue to give birth to their first baby.

'Hey, Dickie.' Paulo stood and greeted his senior colleague, watching him as he finally walked through the revolving doors. 'For a moment there, my friend, I thought you were going to be late,' he teased.

'As if,' the fastidiously punctual Dickie shot back good-naturedly, but he checked his watch all the same. 'Traffic was particularly congested this evening,' he grimaced. 'No news on the baby yet I take it?' he asked, changing the subject, his young colleague's presence providing him with the answer.

'I'm telling you, man, the missus is going spare.' Paulo slumped back down into his swivel chair, shaking his hands towards the sky like a possessed preacher. 'She can't walk, can't sleep, snaps at everything I say . . . this little guy . . .'

'Or girl,' Dickie interjected.

'Or girl,' Paulo added, 'man, they had better hurry up and make an entrance or I reckon I'm in for it over the next few days, big time.'

Dickie smiled knowingly. He liked his young Spanish colleague. Many men of his tender years would've considered the prospect of parenthood terrifying, trading in all that partying and freedom for sleepless nights, dirty nappies and the constant worry that a small baby brings – yet from the moment Paulo had discovered that his girlfriend, Elisia, was in the family way, he had taken his forthcoming parental duties seriously and with a maturity far greater than his twenty-two years.

Glancing at Paulo, a mix of fear and excitement etched on his boyish face, Dickie saw something of himself forty-one years ago just before Patrice, his eldest had been born: a knot of nervous anticipation, overwhelmed by the thought of becoming someone who meant something: a father.

'How many days is she overdue now?'

'Coming up for ten,' Paulo replied miserably. 'We've tried everything, man. Hot curries, long walks, pineapple for breakfast . . .'

'Pineapple?'

Paulo shrugged. 'Something about enzymes, apparently.'

Dickie raised his eyes incredulously as he sat down next to his colleague behind the large reception desk. 'Just let nature do its thing. The little one will come when they're ready.' He paused thoughtfully, rubbing his eyebrow with his finger. 'Now I think of it, our Patrice was a little overdue. You know, I'm sure things got going after a little bit of what got Dolly in that condition in the first place, if you catch my drift . . .' He flashed Paulo a wink and watched as the weary look on the boy's olive-skinned face was replaced with a cheeky grin.

'Yeah, man, maybe we can try that tonight! If she's still awake by the time I get home that is.'

Dickie smiled warmly.

'Alright,' he sighed with resignation, 'you can head off early tonight if you like.' Well, he reasoned generously, it wasn't every day your girlfriend was overdue with your first baby, was it?

Paulo punched the air triumphantly.

'If the little kid's a fella, we'll name him Ricardo, after you.'

'Yeah, yeah,' Dickie laughed, shooing him away. 'Never mind all that. Why don't you give her a ring while you're on your way to Starbucks to grab me one of those fancy coffees you've got me onto, eh? See how things are at home.'

'Cappuccino, yeah? Plenty of froth, no sugar, right?' Paulo called out. He was already halfway to the door.

Dickie nodded and gave the thumbs up.

'Right.'

He chuckled to himself as he settled back into his chair, flipping open the visitors' book to check out who had been into the bank that day, a little ritual he enjoyed far more than he cared to let on.

'Evening, sir,' Dickie called out across the vast reception area as he saw his boss walk through the revolving doors accompanied by two men in navy blue boiler suits with matching peaked caps. The two men were carrying what looked like workmen's cases and he surmised that they had to be the two maintenance men from Ballentyne Security. The ones Mr Forbes had mentioned in his important e-mail to him the previous evening. It had struck Dickie as a little odd that Mr Forbes had left it so late to inform him of Ballentyne's impending visit. Mr Forbes was an absolute stickler for anything to do with security and, up until last night, had not previously mentioned the need for any urgent maintenance down in the vaults. Still, he had signed off his important e-mail with an amenable, 'best regards, Sebastian,' which had made Dickie feel ridiculously chuffed. Never before in his whole career had his boss addressed himself so informally and Dickie had taken this as a great compliment.

Dickie watched as the group hurriedly made their way towards the lift doors.

'I will call the lift for you, sir.' He made to stand but Sebastian held his hand up in silent objection and together with the two men, stepped into the open lift.

Dickie was a little surprised; it was protocol that he always called the lift for his employer whenever he was in the building.

He watched from a distance as the doors closed behind the group with a soft hiss, and wondered just what it was that was making him feel so peculiar. Was something amiss? He instantly dismissed the thought. He was getting old, he thought ruefully, as he settled back down in his seat and continued to study the visitors' book.

Imogen breathed a sigh of relief as the lift doors clamped shut. 'Seb must've decided to leave early,' she said. They had been watching the comings and goings from the 'getaway' car parked around the corner and had seen both Sebastian leave and Dickie arrive to take over from his colleague, who had left the bank shortly afterwards – or at least so they thought.

'All the more time for us, darling.' Calvary had flashed her a reassuring smile. 'Do you think Dickie suspected anything?' Imogen enquired, her hushed voice fraught with nerves.

'He looks a bit doddery to me,' Yasmin nodded confidently. 'Probably wouldn't recognise his own mother if she walked in.'

Imogen placed a small piece of cloth over the tiny CCTV camera in the corner of the lift. Her heart was pounding against her ribcage so hard that it almost hurt. 'I guess if he'd suspected anything we wouldn't have even made it this far.' Awash with adrenalin and giggling, the three women glanced at each other, suddenly aware of how absurd they looked.

'Stop staring, Cal, you're putting me off,' Imogen said, catching sight of her reflection in the mirror.

'I can't help it, darling,' she replied. 'It's just so bizarre to see you looking . . . like that. You really could pass as the real thing.'

Imogen stifled a laugh.

'Let's hope so,' she remarked as the lift juddered to a halt.

As Yasmin handed her the tiny Dictaphone, Imogen made her way towards the Voice Activated Locking system that would allow them through the access hall and to the vault itself. It was a make or break moment and the three of them knew it. If the system rejected the recording of Sebastian's voice then it would be instant abort mission.

'Shit or bust,' Yasmin shrugged, forgetting herself for a moment.

Imogen held the Dictaphone up towards the Voice Activated Locking system and with a visibly shaking finger, slowly pressed the button.

CHAPTER 46

Outside the vault, Imogen glanced down at her Cartier watch. It was 20:53. If she had calculated correctly, and she was sure that she had, they were just seconds away from making history. She could barely believe it. The Voice Activated Lock had opened without a hitch. They were in, and now the three of them were as high as kites on adrenalin and nerves.

Crouched down, a tremulous, gloved hand hovered over the stainless steel keypad, her heart pounding furiously inside her chest, she hoped and prayed that she had done enough. This was the pay-off. This moment was the biggest gamble of all. Imogen had no way of knowing the code for sure – only Seb knew that – but she hoped with every fibre of her being that her calculated guess would be a good one. And if it was, then she had outsmarted that husband of hers. Well and truly.

Slowly, with considered movements, the gloved hand that felt as though it didn't quite belong to her anymore, hovered over the keypad. She could hear only the soft, shallow sound of her own breath and the rhythmic thud of her heartbeat in her ears as she glanced up at the two expectant faces standing obediently behind her, motionless as wax work dummies.

Not wanting to prolong the agony any longer she pressed the four digits in succession: 1313. For a nanosecond nothing happened. The room's eerie silence became so thick with tension it was almost tangible, then at once broken by rhythmic, mellifluous clicks that echoed around the steel walls like a joyful hymn. Slowly, flooded with a sense of euphoria and relief, she turned to her accomplices She did not need to say a word. Her eyes had said it all.

As Imogen made her way over towards the diamond room, Calvary hung back a little alongside Yasmin. Both women stared at each other as if willing the other to follow Imogen but it seemed neither would budge. Both had their reasons for wanting to stay near the strong boxes.

'Remember we have to look as if we're carrying out a maintenance task.' Calvary began removing tools from her workman's bag. It was a ruse that meant she could legitimately start hacking away at Douglas's box without raising too much suspicion from Yasmin.

Yasmin, mirroring Calvary's exact thoughts, wasted no time getting to work as Imogen began disarming the electric wall around the mighty Bluebird Diamond. Pressing the cast of her husband's hand into the soft pliable substance, she thought of the electric shock Seb had allowed her to endure upon their first visit. It had hurt at the time; but it would be nowhere near as potent as the shock she was about to give him in return. Triumphantly snatching the diamond up in her gloved hand, Imogen glanced back at her friends who were busy pretending – although she had a distinct feeling that some *real* snooping was going on – to work on the strong boxes. It was almost over.

Making her way back up from the vaults, her heartbeat rapid beneath her mask, Imogen held her breath as she exited the elevator. She would need to walk the length of the reception area, past Dickie, towards the opposite elevator that would take her up to the nineteenth floor. Acknowledging who he thought was his boss from his seat behind the imposing desk, Dickie raised his hand for the second time that evening, momentarily wondering if not having called the lift quickly enough for him earlier would be regarded as an oversight on his behalf. He hoped not.

Glancing at his security monitors, Dickie noted that the two boiler-suited men who had accompanied Mr Forbes, were both still in the strong room, doing what, at a glance, appeared to be maintenance to some of the security deposit boxes. It was unusual, he thought, that Mr Forbes had seen fit to leave the pair unaccompanied inside the vault. Leaving unauthorised personnel alone was considered a breach of security, a subject he knew his boss to be fastidious about to the point of obsession, but he wasn't overly concerned, given that he had just witnessed Mr Forbes make his way back up towards his office. He assumed his boss must have forgotten something and would be down to rejoin the maintenance men shortly.

Up on the nineteenth floor of Forbes Bank, Imogen, light-footed with adrenalin and perspiring beneath the sticky latex mask, swiftly made her way into Sebastian's office. Closing the door behind her gently, her heart violently jumping in her chest, she reached into the inside pocket of her husband's expertly altered Savile Row suit she was wearing and produced the enormous diamond that it contained. Staring at it for longer than she would've liked, hypnotised by its sheer brilliance and beauty, with a sticky, shaking hand she finally placed it in the middle of his desk and stood back to afford herself a better view of her efforts.

Turning to take one last look as she made her leave,

Imogen smiled, a smile that seemed to come from the very bottom of her soul and light up the room.

'From me to you, Sebastian, darling,' she said, blowing a kiss into the air before closing the door softly behind her.

CHAPTER 47

One thing that Dickie had learned in all his twenty-two years' service at Forbes Bank was that people were creatures of habit. Over the years he had seen the same faces come and go as regular as clockwork. The last Friday in the month saw the likes of the exotic-looking Miss Milena Pleshkova and the lovely English rose, Ms Alice Dawling. Old Earl Bamberger usually dropped by with his son in-law, Henry Hudson-Brown, and then of course there was the stalwart regular, Dame Margaret Montifiore. Dame Montifiore had been a lifelong Forbes client. Highly respected, she was almost part of the furniture, 'one of the family' as Mr Forbes always told her with a saccharine smile. She'd been coming to the bank regularly since time immemorial.

Despite what many would consider to be a lack of respect and recognition for his loyal and lengthy service, Dickie had always been proud to work for Forbes Bank. Drenched in history, Forbes' humble beginnings dated back to 1691 when a young Englishman, John Forbes, set up business as a goldsmith-banker in Aldwych. Having been granted royal patronage in 1705, today, it was the only place privileged peers and the super rich deemed befitting enough to house their wealth.

As a young man, Dickie had dreamed of being part of such a world, but now that he was practically in his dotage, had long ago accepted that would never be. Still, he was happy to be on the peripheries; the old boys he socialised with down at the Dog and Whistle in Sydenham were impressed at the mere mention of the Forbes name.

Dragging Dickie from his thoughts was the reappearance of his young colleague, Paulo. With a look of sheer panic etched on his young face, he almost fell through the revolving doors, holding the two Starbucks cups tremulously in his hands.

'Her waters have broke, Dickie!' he said breathlessly, his eyes so wide with a mix of shock and excitement that they seemed to have taken over his entire face. 'She just called me to say she was in the middle of watching *Coronation Street* when suddenly, pop! And now the contractions are coming . . . screaming the place down she is, the ambulance is on its way.'

Dickie rushed towards the young lad concernedly, relieving him of the scalding cups of coffee and placing them precariously onto the pristine glass desk.

'Well, that's just wonderful,' he said, impassioned. 'See, I told you the little one would come when it was ready and not a moment before.' Paulo nodded, his breathing audible as he absentmindedly wiped the spilt coffee from his arm with his sleeve.

'Well, what are you waiting for, lad?' he cried, ushering him back towards the doors. 'Go to her! You're no use to me here. That girl needs you by her side. If you hurry, you might make it in time to see your son or daughter come into the world.'

Paulo nodded enthusiastically, his face suddenly growing a little pale as the gravity of the situation began to dawn upon him.

'I'm going to be a father, Dickie,' he said, gripping his

colleague's arm, his voice full of emotion. 'It's really happening.'

'Yes! Yes, it is!' Dickie laughed, overwhelmed on the boy's behalf. 'Now get yourself in a cab and get down that hospital, sharpish. Don't worry about anything here. I'll be right as rain.'

Paulo nodded, visibly trying to compose himself. 'I hope I make it in time. The traffic . . . Mr Forbes had to set off for the airport early because it was so bad and . . .'

'More speed, less haste, boy!' Dickie commanded, taking him in hand. 'Look, there's a taxi with its light on – what are you waiting for?' he bellowed with fatherly concern, shooing him from the building, 'the child will be in long trousers if you don't get a move on!'

Shaking his head, Dickie sat down in his chair behind the desk once more and thought what a funny old world it was. A baby born. Chuckling jovially to himself, secretly chuffed to pieces for the young colleague he had grown so fond of, he suddenly remembered what Paulo had said about Mr Forbes having left early for the airport. He had to have got that wrong, he thought as he glanced at the security monitors. Because if Paulo was right and Mr Forbes *had* left for the airport some time ago, then who the hell was that up on the nineteenth floor and who were the two shadowy figures down in the vault?

CHAPTER 48

The vault at Forbes Bank was not so much a strong room as an impenetrable one. Situated in the basement of the building, the entire bank had been built around its solid steel and concrete foundations, and for good reason. Dickie was well aware that it housed the prized possessions (and scandalous secrets) of the world's wealthiest; it was little more than a giant trinket box brimming with priceless pieces and incriminating evidence that would have any blackmailer or tabloid editor salivating.

'Hiroshima could happen all over again, Richards, and that vault would still be in perfect tact,' Mr Forbes had once boasted to him. 'It's indestructible. Completely and utterly impenetrable to man or beast.'

Forbes's vault was a felon's nightmare and it was for these very reasons that Dickie didn't give too much credence to his initial sense of unease.

He was just being paranoid, that was all. He had seen Mr Forbes go down into the vault and come back up again himself, with his own eyes. There was nothing to worry about. In his panic, Paulo must have been mistaken, got his timings mixed up. He settled back into his seat, only somewhere in the back of his mind, an alarm was sounding.

Dickie had known Sebastian Forbes for almost all of the man's life. He had seen him grow from a boy to a man, take over the reins from his father before him. Though he might not have known his favourite restaurant, city or film, time had ensured that Dickie was highly familiar with every inch of his boss's physical appearance, including the small idiosyncrasies that were peculiar to him. Something in his gait, the way that he had carried himself, had been different tonight – and it troubled him. It troubled him a great deal.

Paralysed in front of the small CCTV screen and unable to ignore his increasing sixth sense any longer, Dickie felt a violent surge of adrenalin hit his stomach and explode like a mushroom cloud. During his whole twenty-two year career at Forbes's he had never had to deal with any real major breaches of security. Signing people in and out, fire drills, walking people through the metal detector on their way in – that was about the extent of it.

The sudden reappearance of Mr Forbes dragged Dickie away from his thoughts and he watched with a deep sense of relief as his boss exited the elevator and marched off back down towards the vault. Watching the security monitors closely, he saw the three men greet each other and moments later make their way back up towards the reception area. He shook his head wearily. His old mind working overtime, that was all.

'Goodnight, Mr Forbes,' Dickie called out to him from his seat behind the desk. 'Have a safe flight to Rio.'

'Goodnight,' came the faint response as his boss disappeared through the revolving doors. Dickie stood, suddenly paralysed to the spot. The voice. Mr Forbes's voice. There was something unusual about it. Dickie suddenly felt compelled to activate the alarm and alert the authorities. But of what? He would have to go down to the vault and take a look at things.

Dickie had been down inside the vault many times during

his service at Forbes. As head of night security and with his unblemished long-serving record, he was one of a carefully selected group of security staff entrusted to assist Mr Forbes and clients in depositing or retrieving their valuables. Dickie checked his watch again. It was 20.42. The door to the vault would deactivate at 21.00 hours – he had better get a wiggle on.

As he purposefully stepped inside the lift, having pressed the red button for the basement, Dickie suddenly experienced something he hadn't felt in a long time: fear. Real, gut-wrenching, chest-crushing fear.

Making his way from the lifts towards the first set of security doors, Dickie entered his unique PIN code access and spoke into the voice-activated lock.

'Derrell Richards,' he said as authoritatively as he could. The doors opened with a satisfying hiss and he tentatively walked through them towards the vast iron entrance to the vault lobby. Dickie shuddered. Pull yourself together, man, he told himself sharply, inhaling deeply as he spoke into the microphone on the wall.

'Derrell Richards,' he said again, his voice tremulous this time, the loud clicks of the numerous locks opening echoing sinisterly around the steel walls. Leaning on the lobby door, which was slow to open given its substantial weight, Dickie immediately noticed something wasn't right. The door to the vault was ajar. *Jesus Christ; it was open.*

Surreal as the moment was, initially he found himself more confused than scared, his mind struggling furiously to make sense of the scene before him. Always a glass half full kind of a man, he tried to rationalise the situation, telling himself it must've been an oversight on Mr Forbes's part.

Shaking, he tentatively made steps towards the open doors, the sound of his own heartbeat pulsing an elaborate pattern loudly in his ears. It was only when he got within spitting distance that Dickie realised that something was wrong. Horribly, diabolically wrong.

The diamond, usually cradled by the cushioned plinth that stood regally in the small white room, was missing. It had *gone.*

Blinking furiously, as if he did not trust his own, ageing eyes, his hand instinctively clutching his chest, Dickie made to move towards the empty plinth, only the room had begun to spin now and the movement made him feel a little light-headed. Suddenly, all too aware of his solitude, his heart racing so furiously that it had begun to hurt, Dickie made to press the panic button – a big red beacon of a switch that was positioned on the other side of the room. But as he went to move, he stumbled, struggling to put one foot in front of the other, as if the bones in his legs had been removed.

As a younger man, Dickie had fantasised about what he might do faced with a robbery situation. Not because he wanted it to actually happen, more that he enjoyed the idea of reaching his full potential as a security guard. Now, faced with the reality, Dickie was not quite the sharp-thinking hero he had always imagined himself to be. He tried to gather his thoughts, to compose himself, but his heart was beating so loudly inside his chest that he found it almost impossible to concentrate.

As he fell to the floor, clutching his chest, Dickie realised the ugly, rasping gurgle he could hear was coming from him. He did not think about his wife or his children as his head made contact with the cold, hard stone beneath him, of never holding his grandchildren in his arms, kissing their tiny fingers and toes. Instead he thought how Mr Forbes would undoubtedly sack him after this little scenario came to light. Shame really, he thought as he began to lose consciousness. He knew at his age that he'd never find another job that carried as much kudos *and* gave you £5.75 a day for sustenance.

CHAPTER 49

'Three cheers for the Forbes Three! Hip Hip!' Imogen pushed the cork from the bottle of 1990 Vintage Tattinger and squealed as it exploded with a gaseous bang, spraying the contents over an elated Calvary and Yasmin, shrieking and flinching as they joined in with the celebrations.

'Hooray!' the three women sang in unison, the sound of their crystal glasses making contact sending a melodious, triumphant ring throughout Calvary's perfectly designed, if a little austere, drawing room.

'I can't believe we did it!' Imogen bit her lip as she squealed. 'We *actually* bloody well did it!' she laughed as she threw herself down onto the antique chesterfield, kicking her legs up in the air with girlish abandon. 'I can't wait to see Seb's face come Monday morning,' she giggled, clearly thrilled by the prospect. 'Watch that smug look disappear . . .'

Calvary laughed along with her.

'Darling, it was genius. *We* were genius.' She was buzzing with adrenalin and excitement; she didn't even care about the champagne spray all over her soft furnishings.

'And no one suspected a thing,' Yasmin chipped in. She was flying high on endorphins, and it was even better than a champagne and coke buzz. 'I mean, that security guard, he didn't have a clue! "Goodnight, Mr. Forbes!"' she mimicked Dickie's low, masculine voice. She tossed her platinum hair over her shoulder victoriously, pulling her silky pyjama-clad legs up to her chest. 'We made it look like a walk in the park. I tell you, wasted talent, that's what we are. We could make a killing if we turned pro.'

As per the plan, with Douglas away 'on business', or so he had said, the three women had returned to Calvary's house to dispose of their disguises and change into something more comfortable. Calvary had ensured there would be plenty of vintage bubbly on ice and a selection of delicious canapés waiting for them upon their victorious homecoming, and Yasmin was taking full advantage of her host's generosity. As far as she was concerned, tonight had been one of the greatest nights of her life so far. Now that she had that tape in her clutches, there would be no stopping her. She was on a home run.

Snatching a glance at Calvary, Yasmin briefly wondered if that all-seeing eye of hers had caught her rifling through Jeremy's possessions while they had been down in the vault together. Knowing Calvary, as she had come to over the months, Yasmin assumed she would have mentioned it by now if she had. After all, she was hardly the reticent type.

Calvary, pulling the peaked workman's cap from her head, allowing her silky auburn hair to tumble to her shoulders, threw it onto the open fire and listened satisfactorily as it crackled.

Although the evening had not entirely panned out as she had expected, it was still a roaring success as far as she was concerned. Her heart had initially plummeted through the floor when she had opened Douglas's strong box only to find it empty – or so she had thought. Upon closer inspection, however, she had found something she now, with hindsight, deemed even better than the cold, hard bundles of cash she had hoped to find: details of a Swiss bank account and information of a transfer of funds written in her husband's instantly recognisable, elaborate scrawl.

As far as Calvary was concerned, and no doubt any courtroom would be too, this small scrap of paper was existing proof that Douglas had deliberately liquidated his assets and hidden them in a secret bank account for the sole purpose of hiding it from her. The devious bastard would be begging to give her half of everything by the time Nikolas Mystern was finished with him.

Calvary glanced over at Yasmin, watching as she and Imogen laughed and chatted animatedly together. It was odd but she was sure she had seen Yasmin rummaging purposefully around Jeremy's strong box herself while they had been in the vaults. She had got the distinct impression that Yasmin had been looking for something, something specific. Calvary dared not ask any questions, however, just in case Yasmin started making enquiries of her own. If Calvary had seen her, then it was just as likely that she herself had been seen.

'I could never have done any of this without you both, you do realise this, don't you?' Imogen looked over at Calvary and then back at Yasmin, her eyes glassy with emotion. 'I mean it,' she said, her voice dropping an octave. 'I owe you both, so much.'

'Oh stop it, darling, you'll set me off,' Calvary said, tears pricking the backs of her eyes. 'And you owe us nothing,' she scolded her like a child, her conscience not allowing Imogen to dwell on her gratitude for too long.

'When you were about to punch the code in – *Jesus*,' Yasmin rolled her eyes and bit her lip, reliving the excruciating moment over again, 'I could barely breathe I was so nervous!' She clutched her chest in an over-dramatic rendition. 'When I heard those clicks, let me tell you, I have *never* felt such a sense of relief in all my life!' Yasmin sat back on the chaise longue. 'I'll say this for you, Imogen Forbes,' she turned to face her, wishing in that moment that it was *she* who could thank *her*, thank her for providing her the tape, 'you're certainly more than just a pretty face!'

'Why, thank you,' Imogen replied graciously. 'But you know what they say, where there's a will, there's always a way.' She got up and walked over towards the enormous bay window and looked out onto the pretty London square, lit up by street lamps.

The whole situation felt unreal, *surreal*, but by God, she had done it! She had outsmarted the mighty Sebastian Forbes and his unrivalled Interface Locking Security system! Soon, everything he believed in would come crashing down around his ears and Imogen could barely contain her sense of vindication.

'I don't know about you, but all this excitement has given me an appetite, I'm starving. Where's Lucia with those canapés I asked for?' Calvary enquired crossly. 'Honestly, that girl is about as much use as an ashtray on a speedboat – ah!'

As if on cue, Lucia entered the drawing room, carrying a large platter of amuse-bouche.

'Perfect timing.' Calvary smiled at the girl. Nothing was going to dampen her spirits this evening.

Lucia nodded, placing the tray onto the low antique day table. It struck her as a little odd that Mrs Rothschild had the fire going, it being the middle of summer after all.

'Mrs Bridges in the kitchen says you might want to switch on the TV, Mrs Rothschild,' Lucia announced nervously, her heart pounding in her chest at having to speak so openly to her new employer. 'She says you should take a look at BBC News 24, that there's something that might interest you and Mrs Forbes.'

'Thank you, Lucia,' Calvary nodded, the lightest flutter

of fear settling upon her euphoric mood. She glanced at Imogen who shrugged.

Switching on the TV screen, Imogen instantly recognised the front of Forbes Bank, even flanked, as it was, by police cars and sealed off with tape. Sitting bolt upright and staring at the screen, her heart fighting to free itself from her ribcage, Imogen felt her euphoria come crashing to the ground and violently explode in a cloud of debris and ash.

'A night security man, known to colleagues simply as "Dickie", was rushed to the Chelsea and Westminster Hospital just moments ago with a suspected heart attack. It seems, Sandra,' the BBC female reporter spoke earnestly to the studio presenter, 'that Mr Richards may in fact have stumbled upon a robbery and collapsed at the scene, at least that's what the police are currently suggesting . . .'

'Is there any news as to the diamond, Vasha? What's happened to the Bluebird?' Sandra asked, her heavily made-up eyes intense as she looked directly into the camera. There was a delay in the live link before Vasha replied, 'Not as yet, no. We can't confirm whether it is missing or not at this stage.'

Calvary's champagne flute slid from her grasp and exploded onto the polished wooden floor.

'Jesus Fucking H Christ,' Yasmin said in a thick cockney accent.

Blinking at the screen, Imogen, stunned into silence, suddenly became aware of the latex mask of her husband's face lying next to her on the chesterfield where she had discarded it. Even now, it appeared to be smirking at her.

Snatching it up, she half screamed as she threw it on the fire, watching, her chest heaving, as it began to bubble and melt, the features twisting and contorting until there was nothing left of it at all.

CHAPTER 50

As the plane touched down in Rio de Janeiro, Sebastian Forbes contentedly threw back the dregs of his scotch and popped a stuffed pimento olive into his mouth.

It had been a long, albeit comfortable flight, and he was looking forward to making it to the hotel suite in the Copacabana for a nice hot shower and room service. Hell, he might even push the boat out and get himself a chilled bottle of Krug to wash it all down with while he was at it.

Alighting the Boeing 747, Sebastian jauntily skipped down the aircraft steps and breathed in the warm, tropical evening air, sweet and fragrant. The smell of success, he thought as he handed his Vuitton flight bag to an obliging minion.

'Meester Fords? Copacabana Palace, *si*?' the young man nodded enthusiastically.

'Yes. The Royal Penthouse Suite,' Sebastian muttered, handing over his luggage. 'And it's *Forbes*.'

'You have good flight, sir, from England, yes?' the boy asked, his broad, bright grin displaying perfectly white teeth.

'Yes, yes,' Sebastian replied irritably. 'And a long one. So I'd appreciate a little peace and quiet if you don't mind.'

He put his hand patronisingly to his lips, as if the man might not have fully understood him. 'No talking on the way there, *si*?'

'*Si*,' the boy nodded, wondering why he always seemed to get stuck with the assholes. His colleague, Davi, always got the *chicas caliente* and he got the assholes. Life was a load of *kahunas colhoes* sometimes.

Settling into the backseat of the Mercedes C-Class saloon, Sebastian allowed his head to rest against the warm leather seat.

'You here on business, sir? For the conference, yes?' he asked, watching his passenger from his interior mirror. 'I tell by the suit you are wearing. Rio, today, it is filled with suits!'

'What?' Sebastian muttered, distracted. 'Yes, yes, here for the conference.'

'You have time for a leetle holiday while you are here, sir?' the boy continued, seemingly oblivious to his passenger's earlier request for silence. 'The weather is good. Always good here in Brazil,' he chuckled, his hands barely making contact with the steering wheel as he gesticulated wildly. 'Not like in England, no?' He had heard that the weather in England was dire. No wonder these businessmen that flew in all looked so miserable.

Sebastian ignored him, and closing his eyes, willed him to shut up and drive. Thankfully, the boy's mobile phone rang and Sebastian tuned out as he spoke into it in lightning fast Portuguese.

'Sir, it is for you,' he said after a moment, passing the phone back to Sebastian. 'It is someone from the Copacabana. They say it is *very* important they speak with you.'

'For me?' Sebastian pulled his face into his neck, surprised. What the hell was all this about then, he wondered, taking the handset from him. There had better not have been a mix-up with his room, he thought, already on the offensive. Walmsley had guaranteed him the Royal Suite and he would be making damn well sure he got it. He was their key speaker after all.

As Sebastian listened to the voice on the other end of the phone, the young driver watched inquisitively from his interior mirror as his offhanded passenger's eyes widened and his skin turned a deathly shade of white. Whatever the news was, he had a feeling it was not especially good. Straining to understand the conversation thanks to his limited English, he almost crashed the car in shock when the man in the back seat suddenly bellowed:

'Stop the car! Goddamn it, man, I said STOP THE CAR!'

CHAPTER 51

The sound of the curtain rings sliding against the pole was somehow ominous as Yasmin drew the heavy drapes in the study, blocking out all daylight.

Her heart was galloping inside her chest so fast that it almost hurt as she settled down onto the cream leather sofa and pressed the play button on the VHS recorder. This was it; her moment of truth, and the gravity of it was not lost on her. She felt sick to her stomach as the grainy images began to come into focus on the huge flat-screen TV that suddenly seemed to take up half of the wall space.

It was a party, that much was obvious; men and women were dancing with abandon, cocktail drinks in hand and Robert Palmer's 'Addicted to Love' was playing in the background. She could tell the rudimentary footage had been shot in the 80s by the hairstyles alone – women in too much make-up sporting cropped wedges and huge, crimped bouffants held stiff in place with hairspray, and the men with their mullets and flicked fringes reminiscent of George Michael milled around, gesticulating wildly. Their glamorous attire, tuxedos and loafers, the women, all spray-on minidresses and giant shoulder pads, white stilettos and enormous earrings, were straight out of a scene from *Dynasty*.

'Jezza! Get that damned thing out of my face, won't you?' a man's voice rang out. His face came into view, young and tanned and handsome, though she did not recognise it. A woman openly snorting cocaine from a glass coffee table attempted to disguise herself by holding a puffed sleeve denim jacket over her head as the person behind the camera zoomed in on her.

'Naughty naughty, Eliza,' the male voice said. 'Save a line for me.' This time she recognised the voice: It was her husband's. Jeremy was the man behind the camera.

The screen started to flicker then, distorting the images, and Yasmin felt her heartbeat accelerate in anticipation.

'. . . and this is Lady Rosemary Keane, Keane by name and *very* keen by nature. Don't let the title of "Lady" mislead you!' Jeremy was giving a running commentary of his guests as he weaved through the room and . . . June Larkin! Yasmin sprung forward from her seat. There she was, in amongst the crowd, talking to a group of men, her short peroxide cropped hair, fag in hand and a sneer on her pinched face, dressed in a garish coral pink dress that looked as if someone had poured her into it and forgotten to say 'when'.

'Oh God,' Yasmin whispered aloud, the intensity of the moment making her feel a little giddy.

People were littered throughout the whole house, couples draped over each other on arm chairs and bodies losing themselves in one another on sofas. The footage cut out for a second, causing Yasmin to hold her breath once more, before suddenly resuming. She could tell that some time had occurred between filming as the guests suddenly seemed much more worse for wear; people had stripped off now; a young, androgynous looking woman with tiny tits was dancing, naked, up on a table while Jeremy zoomed the camera into her crotch, laughing lasciviously as she twirled around and shook her hips to the sound of 'Wham Rap'.

Yasmin searched the crowds for her sister's face but she was nowhere to be seen. Why had that bitch June Larkin left her all on her own? The film resumed once more with Jeremy walking precariously up a flight of stairs and tremulously opening a door.

'Well, look what we have here!' he exclaimed as he focused on the bodies of the men on the bed. There were three of them at least, though it was difficult to tell in the darkness of the room, and they were all in various states of undress. The sound was inaudible, muffled, as they all seemed to speak at once. And then she saw her.

'Chloe,' Yasmin yelped, touching the screen as her sister's face came briefly into view, 'Chloe . . .'

Chloe was on the bed, her nakedness illuminated in the dim light, her beautiful young face, small and pale, though otherwise just how she had always remembered it. She was silent as one of the men pushed her back down onto the bed and mounted her, the others jeering in the background. Yasmin saw the camera momentarily zoom in on her sister's young face, her eyes tightly shut, her mouth a grimace as the faceless body pumped away on top of her.

'Come and have a go, Jez,' she heard a low voice say and then someone else had the camera and suddenly Jeremy came into view. He looked younger, much younger, dressed in a cream tuxedo suit, his shirt untucked, visible beneath his jacket. He looked like a different man, though there was no mistaking it was him.

With her heart in her mouth, Yasmin blinked as her husband began to tear his clothes off to the chants of the others and dived onto the bed. She noticed that he had kept his socks on. The footage ended there and Yasmin blinked at the screen, her heartbeat audible in her ears, tears streaking her face and falling into her lap.

She had felt her sister's fear; could almost reach out and touch it on screen as though it were tangible. She had looked so young, so scared and vulnerable that it was too much for Yasmin to bear and she began to sob. But her tears were closely followed by rage, by a hatred so fierce that it claimed every cell in her body.

There was a low hum emanating from the video recorder and Yasmin stooped to turn it off, but suddenly the footage resumed again, startling her.

This time the camera zoomed in on an indoor swimming pool. The blue water still and calm, the light reflecting from the surface into the lens of the camera. There was something in the pool. A naked body floating on top of the water, face down, arms and legs outstretched in a starfish shape, long hair fanning out like a beautiful mermaid's as it gently swayed with the momentum of the water. Yasmin instinctively knew it was Chloe, the familiarity of her sister's form was unmistakable to her. Her hand instinctively covered her mouth in shock and horror.

'Jesus Christ!' the voice behind the camera said, a woman's this time.

'Turn the camera off!' Jeremy said, his voice low in the background, his panic audible. 'I said turn the damn thing off!'

And then the screen went black.

*

Jeremy Belmont looked around the restaurant. It was coming up for lunchtime and La Mirage was full to bursting with well-heeled women, chatting animatedly amongst themselves, piles of designer shopping bags from a hard day's spending collected around them like trophies as they sipped on their Cristal and eyed each other competitively.

The place had gone downhill since he was last here, admittedly some years ago now. Shame, Jeremy thought, it had been a favourite haunt of his back in the 80s and early 90s, superb hunting ground for a bit of genuine aristocratic totty. Now it was full of euro-trash and wannabe wags. Gold-diggers, the lot of them, Jeremy thought derisively. Reeking of their husband's money, they didn't have a shred of class between them. Not like his Yasmin, he thought, smiling to himself, his chest visibly swelling. She knocked the spots off all of them. And despite the damn press forever insisting to the contrary, she had never been after his money. After all, she was rich in her own right, what with the substantial inheritance her parents had left her after their tragic death. In fact, it had been she who had insisted upon signing a pre-nuptial agreement before their lavish wedding had taken place. You'd think such a gesture would've silenced all the naysayers but still they continued to insist she must have an ulterior motive – money being the obvious one – to have even considered sharing her life with a man old enough to be her grandfather.

As far as Jeremy was concerned, they were all just jealous. Well, they could scoff all they wanted, he thought, indignant, he knew the truth and that's all that mattered. He sighed as he caught sight of his reflection in his butter knife. If only he had met Yasmin thirty years ago, when he had been in his prime. He had been so handsome back then. Women had adored him, worshipped his dark, brooding good looks and strong, masculine physique. At least that's how he liked to remember it.

Those were the days, eh? A soft chuckle escaped from his lips. All those wonderful women and all those fabulously debauched parties – Good God, they had been something else. If there was one thing Jeremy Belmont knew how to do exceptionally well it was throw a decent bash. He'd been the host with the most back in the day. If only that unfortunate incident with the young girl in the pool had never taken place then perhaps the press would not still be seeing fit to come down so hard on him, as they had done ever since.

It had been a long while since Jeremy had thought of the whole unpleasant episode with the young prostitute and it bothered him that it had entered his consciousness after all this time. It had been a dreadful affair, one which had taken him years to successfully put behind him. The last thing he wanted to do was rake it all up again. If there was ever a memory to put him on an instant downer it was that one.

Jeremy checked his Cartier watch, the first feelings of impatience beginning to settle on his nerves. Where was Yasmin? He ordered a bottle of Château Margaux and some bread sticks from a passing waiter and tapped his fingers on the table. And then he saw her walking towards him through the crowded restaurant, a vision in a short white one-shoulder DKNY dress, her matching white-blonde hair piled high up on her head in a slick chignon, a lightweight silk cardigan draped over her shoulders as she teetered over in his direction in the highest of Alexander McQueen snakeskin platforms.

She threw her matching snakeskin clutch down onto the table, leaning in to kiss him lightly on one of his full cheeks. It took every ounce of emotional strength she had left in her.

'Sorry I'm late, darling,' she said breezily, 'I had something to attend to this morning, something that couldn't wait – and the traffic was horrendous, as always. Joseph had to take a detour down the back streets.' He noticed that her hands were shaking as she took a sip from a glass of San Pellegrino.

'I took the liberty of ordering us a dozen oysters to start,' Jeremy smiled affably, his earlier irritation gradually dissolving once he had seen how much of an effort she had made with her appearance. She looked positively stunning and, proudly, he was aware of all eyes on her as she took a seat.

'So, what was so important that it kept you from your adoring husband?' he enquired, flashing her an uneasy smile. She looked at him for a moment, wondering how he could've visually changed so much from the man she had just watched on film. She remembered her mother had once made the comment that 'people eventually got the face they deserved in life' and as far as she could see Jeremy was living proof of it.

'I had to watch a film,' she said cryptically. 'One I've been waiting to see for a long, long time.'

Jeremy shrugged.

'A film?'

'Call it research,' she smiled tremulously, her heartbeat accelerating due to the line of cocaine she had snorted in the back of the car on the way over. She hadn't slept in over twenty-four hours, her nerves were in shreds and she had needed something to help steady them. All this business with the security guard having a heart attack had put an instant kibosh on their celebrations, that was for sure. It was only a matter of time before the police started asking questions.

'Well anyway, you're here now. Shall we order?'

Yasmin nodded. Nothing came between Jeremy Belmont and his stomach she thought, barely able to conceal her contempt.

'I was thinking,' she said as she pretended to scan the vast menu, her eyes unable to focus.

'Hmm,' Jeremy murmured, his mind already firmly on the Châteaubriand.

'I think we should get away for a few days. Charter a yacht somewhere, the French Riviera perhaps . . . do a little snorkelling and sunbathing . . . maybe even some baby making,' she added poignantly.

Jeremy's eyes lit up.

'What a splendid idea, darling,' he said, thrilled at the suggestion. 'I'll make a phone call, have my PA onto it right away. When were you thinking of going?'

'Today,' Yasmin replied casually.

'Today?' he shot back.

'Well, why not?' she said. 'Oh come on, darling, let's be spontaneous. We're rich, we're in love – we can do whatever we want to!'

Jeremy laughed at her exuberance.

'Anyway, I need a holiday,' she pouted. 'I've a whole suitcase full of bikinis dying for an airing. What do you say we just throw a few things in a trunk and jet off this afternoon?'

It was a half truth. Yasmin did need to get away from all this ghastly business with Forbes Bank. She'd got what she needed; evidence she had spent years searching for, and now she had to finish this business with Jeremy once and for all before the cops came sniffing around.

'But I'm supposed to be having a meeting with Duncan Reynolds about that property I was looking at in the Hamptons,' Jeremy objected.

'Oh darling, whatever happened to spontaneity?' Yasmin purred, embarking on her charm offensive. 'Surely there are some things in life that are more important than business, hmm?' She rubbed his meaty thigh underneath the table, causing him to twitch inside his trousers.

Jeremy smiled, displaying bits of breadstick between his teeth.

'Well, I suppose it *could* wait for a few days,' he sighed, relenting. 'I can always give Reynolds a call, arrange something for when I'm back.'

'Oh darling, that's wonderful.' Yasmin clapped her hands together loudly, causing the diners on the adjacent table to look over at them. 'I'll make it worth your while,' she sang, raising an eyebrow provocatively. 'You can deal with it all well rested and with a clear head on our return,' she beamed, though inside she had already made her mind up. As far as Jeremy Belmont was concerned, this would be a one-way trip.

CHAPTER 52

Imogen attempted to apply her lip gloss in the mirror, only her hand was shaking so violently that she was making a right hash of it and eventually threw it down onto the dressing table in defeat.

Jalena had just called up to her room to say that Sebastian and a policeman were waiting for her downstairs in the library and that the policeman wanted to 'ask her a few questions.' Subsequently gripped by panic and paranoia, Imogen's mind had spun into overdrive. Why would they want to speak to *her*? Did they know something? Was she about to be handcuffed and frogmarched out of her own front door? She bit her lip as she imagined the worst. She hadn't had the chance to speak with Sebastian since he had made a U-turn back from Rio but a small part of her sought solace in the knowledge that had he known, or even suspected anything, she felt sure he would've flown up the stairs to her the minute he had walked through the front door.

Imogen's heart was knocking so hard against her ribs that it was making her feel light-headed. She had to get a grip; stay calm, just like Cal had said. But she had never been a very convincing liar. Now she would have to stand before a figure of authority, as well as Seb's watchful eye, and lie like her life depended on it.

Unsteady on her feet, her chest tight with anxiety, Imogen cautiously made her way down the winding staircase towards the library, her silky, cream Yves Saint Laurent jumpsuit gently clinging to her curves with the momentum of her footsteps. Stopping for a brief moment, Imogen stared at herself in the mirror and forced a smile.

You had better make this good, she told herself sharply as she hovered outside the door to the library, the muffled voices within unsettling her instantly. Looking up at the ceiling, Imogen took a long, deep breath, said a silent prayer to a god she had never believed in and turned the handle.

'I do apologise for taking so long, I was sle–'

She cut herself off as he turned round to face her.

Imogen stood, halfway in the doorway, paralysed by confusion, a torrent of adrenalin rushing so furiously through her system that she thought she might pass out. Holding on to the door frame for support, she did not hear the sound of shattering crystal as his glass slid from his fingers.

Her eyes told her it was *him*, though she could not believe them; the soft, dark hair was still the same, albeit a little shorter, a little tidier than it had been all those years ago; his face had retained that slight boyish prettiness to it, a prettiness he had always been at pains to hide with a five o'clock shadow. But it was the eyes that convinced her, those deep teal green eyes, now surrounded by the faintest lines of time, somehow indicative only of him.

Her first thought was that he had somehow found her, tracked her down after all these years, and her heart involuntarily soared. Had he spent the past fourteen years searching for her, just as she had searched for him inside her mind every day that had passed since they had parted? Questions shot through Imogen's brain like a spray of bullets. Was he here to rescue her from this unholy mess she had found herself in?

Suddenly, Sebastian's presence seemed very real and frightening as he stood, stony-faced next to a man she truly believed that she would never see again, shouting for Jalena to come and clear the broken glass.

'Imogen!' Seb's voice cut through the fog of her thoughts with all the subtlety of an axe felling an oak. 'Imogen, are you alright? You look terribly pale.' Sebastian feigned concern, desperate to give the somewhat clumsy DI a good impression of himself.

'Yes . . . yes I'm fine,' she lied, paralysed to the spot, her heart beating so loudly inside her ribcage that she was sure both men could hear it.

'This is DI Mitch McLaren. DI McLaren, this is my wife, Imogen Forbes.'

Mitch McLaren? Surely he meant Michael, though she dared not question him. She could not allow Sebastian to suspect that they were familiar with one another, that Mitch McLaren was in fact *Mickey. Her* Mickey. The silent ghost who had been the third person in their marriage throughout all of these years. Suddenly she felt grateful for the fact that Seb and Mickey had never met – until now. She knew her husband only too well; he never forgot a face.

Tentatively Imogen made her way into the room, putting her hand to her chest in a bid to calm the thud within. She felt Mickey's eyes on her and, conscious of her every move, made her way towards him, holding her hand out. As he took it, shook her hand lightly, she felt she might collapse. The sensation of his skin against hers made her want to close her eyes and moan softly. Did he recognise her? she wondered, searching his face for clues.

Rooted to the spot, his eyes met with hers. She looked the same yet somehow different. Her face had only slightly changed in that indefinable way that a person's does with age and time. She was still beautiful, perhaps even more so, he felt as his eyes drank her in. Her dark hair, still shiny and glossy, was longer, much longer now, and it suited her. And those lips he had kissed almost as many times in his dreams as he had during the short time he had spent with her were still full and fleshy, the same rosebud shape as before. Her cheekbones had remained prominent, accentuated as the fullness of youth had gradually slipped away. And her eyes, oh God, those dark, almond-shaped eyes . . .

It *was* her. Imogen Lennard. His Imp. She was here. In front of him. And suddenly Mitch McLaren was that young man in the British Library again. Painfully self-conscious and confused. Standing next to her husband in the professional capacity of policeman and investigator. And right now, more than anything, he needed to get a grip.

'Pleased to meet you, Mrs Forbes,' he added softly, his teal green eyes meeting hers for a fleeting moment. 'I must apologise for the mess.' He gestured to the shards of crystal glinting against the dark oak floor like diamonds.

Imogen shook her head graciously and wondered if he was thinking the same as she was: that it would be wholly inappropriate to make their recognition known. After all, what would they tell Sebastian? 'Well, darling, would you ever believe it, but DI McLaren and I were once lovers . . .'

'Likewise,' she replied, her voice a low, husky whisper as she struggled to regain her composure.

'DI McLaren would like to have a few words with you, if that's alright. Nothing to be worried about, darling,' Sebastian reassured her. 'So I would like you to do whatever you can to help, yes?'

Imogen was listening with only half an ear. 'Yes?' Sebastian repeated himself firmly.

'Sorry, yes, of course,' Imogen said, distractedly. 'Though I could use a drink,' she added, glancing at the decanter of brandy on the sideboard. Frankly, it was the understatement of the year. Sebastian looked surprised. Imogen rarely drank alcohol this time of the day, not even in a social capacity. Still, he supposed these were extenuating circumstances.

'My wife and I haven't had a chance to talk since my return from Rio,' he explained to Mitch. 'So I'm afraid we will have to fill her in on everything.'

Imogen suddenly remembered herself.

'I'm so sorry, Seb,' she said, turning to her husband who had begun to fix her a brandy. 'It's terrible news about the break-in at the bank. You must be devastated,' she said tremulously.

*

Mitch watched her closely, enjoying the sound of her voice, absorbing every word. It was strange, he thought, how despite not having seen her for so long, she could remain so familiar to him.

Imogen lightly touched Seb's arm as he handed her the drink, a gesture that seemed somehow contrived to Mitch's watchful eye, and it bothered him. Years of studying other people's body language told him that they were not close, that the laboured and stiff exchanges between them were not indicative of a close, happy marriage, and he felt ashamed of himself that this observation gave him a small slither of satisfaction.

'If it's OK with you, Mr Forbes, I would like to speak to your wife alone,' Mitch said after a few moments. 'Like I said, it's simply routine.'

'Do what you can to help the inspector, darling,' Sebastian instructed her, switching to his bullish default setting. 'We'll talk later. I'll be making calls in my office if you need me.' He rose from the chesterfield and shook Mitch's hand.

'I'll be in touch, Mr Forbes,' Mitch said. 'In the meantime, if there's anything you can think of, anything that springs to mind, however insignificant you think it might be, then please, call me direct.' He handed Sebastian a card with his details. 'And try not to worry – get some sleep.'

Sebastian smiled coldly.

'I'll expect a daily update. In the meantime, please understand that my wife has had a dreadful shock – we all have. So if you could keep it brief . . .'

Mitch nodded and watched as Sebastian stormed purposefully from the room, the door making an ominous thud as it closed behind him.

And suddenly they were alone.

CHAPTER 53

Imogen spoke first.

'It really is you,' she said, as if saying it aloud might somehow convince her of the fact. She looked up at him, her soft, doleful dark eyes causing his heart to stand still in his chest. 'I thought perhaps you were dead,' she said, though she didn't know why she had said this, never once had she thought such a thing.

Mitch stood opposite her, watching as she surreptitiously brushed a tear from her face. His need to go to her then, to embrace her, was so strong that he had to hold on to the side of the chesterfield to prevent himself from doing so.

'I'm sorry,' he apologised. 'This is all such a shock . . . I didn't believe it when I saw you.' His voice sounded a little gruff and he cleared his throat. 'When I saw the name on the crime sheet, I didn't think for a moment that Imogen Forbes was you, the wo . . .' He stopped himself, unsure of what to say.

Over the years Mitch had thought of a thousand things he had wanted to say to her should he ever get the chance to. There had been so many moments in time he had wished she could've been there to share with him; funny incidents, the day-to-day inanities of life that he would have given anything to appreciate with her by his side. Only now that this day had arrived, all conversation seemed to have abandoned him.

'Anyway, you . . . you look well,' he eventually said, cursing himself underneath his breath. She had always had the ability to make him feel tongue-tied. Mitch attempted to compose himself; he was here to do a job, for God's sake. And she was married now, had probably forgotten all about him and their affair long ago.

Imogen smiled softly.

'You too, Mickey,' she said. Just being able to say his name aloud gave her a sense of joy. 'Or should that be Mitch?' She looked up at him then, her eyes, lightly smudged by mascara, a little playful.

He smiled apologetically.

'I became Mitch when I joined the force,' he explained, 'too many Michaels.'

She resisted the urge to reply, 'But only ever one for me.'

'Mitch,' she said aloud, as if trying it out for size. 'I suppose you must want to ask me some questions – about the bank, I mean,' she added for clarity. 'I was sorry to hear about the security guard. They do think he'll be OK, don't they?' she enquired, careful to keep the panic she felt from betraying her in her voice.

'He suffered a massive coronary by all accounts,' Mitch replied. 'Probably down to the shock of finding the diamond missing, though we can only be sure of the details when he comes round. *If* he comes round.'

'If?' she enquired nervously.

Mitch wondered if all the questions were a diversion, a means of avoiding having to talk about the obvious. There were so many things he wanted to ask her, so many questions.

'There's hope,' he smiled softly.

Consumed by guilt, Imogen dropped her head and nodded. Hope. She had spent the last fourteen years of her life secretly hoping; hoping that one day she would see him again, that he had not forgotten her. And yet now that her faith in hope had been rewarded, her conscience could not allow her to enjoy it.

'Look, Imogen, I– '

'It's OK,' she said, interrupting him suddenly. 'I realise you couldn't possibly have known that you would see me here today, that you're just here to do your job. It's just that it's been a bit of a shocker all round.' Mickey nodded. There was a moment's pause.

'Tell me,' she said eventually, mustering up a smile from a place she never knew existed inside of her. 'How's Aimee?'

Imogen watched his expression cloud over.

'She died, a little over eighteen months ago now,' he replied quietly, almost instantly. He turned away from her, making his way over towards the large sash window, the grey London sky peeping from between the shutters offering him little comfort. He didn't want her to see his face as he spoke, lest she see straight through him like she had always been able to. 'Pulmonary embolism. There was nothing that could be done.'

Imogen shook her head and covered her face with her hands.

'Oh Mickey, I'm sorry,' she said genuinely. 'I'm so sorry.'

The softness of her voice made him smile and for a fleeting moment he felt his spirits lift. He turned to face her then, moving in a little closer to her, but not too close. He didn't trust himself.

'Don't be,' he replied. 'In a way, it was for the best.' Mitch shocked himself with the honesty of the statement. 'I came back from New Zealand a little over a year ago now. Transferred to the Met.'

'You were in New Zealand?' she said, almost relieved

by this admission. So her fantasies of bumping into him had been way off the mark. He had emigrated to the other side of the world!

'I've heard it's very green, lots of greenery,' she said, suddenly feeling painfully self-conscious.

'Yes,' he replied, 'it is. There's lots of open space and . . . greenery.'

They both laughed a little awkwardly and Imogen thought that even though he had hardly changed in over a decade, everything else around them had. She felt the sadness and regret of all the time that had been lost between them. However much she had wished it could've been different, they were strangers now, strangers who had once been intimate lovers and she didn't know how to behave; how to rectify the two together.

'So here we are again, in a library,' he said, pointing out the irony.

'Yes,' she smiled. Life, it seemed, had somehow come full circle.

'I'm pleased to see you've done so well for yourself,' he said, careful to keep the tone of the conversation light. He looked up at the ornate ceiling, as if to admire it. 'And that you're married and happy.' He had chosen his words carefully, keen to observe her reaction.

Imogen turned away from him and closed her eyes. The words 'happy' and 'married' had never sat well together in the same sentence as far as she and Seb were concerned.

'None of it's mine,' she said. 'Not really. It all belongs to my *wonderful* husband.' It was a sarcastic remark and she recognised it immediately as a foolish one. Imogen realised that how she felt about her marriage was probably something she should be keeping from Mitch. He belonged to his job now. She could not allow herself to trust him.

'I gave up modelling when I had my daughter,' she said, quickly changing the subject.

'Your daughter?' Mitch felt a stab of anguish. She had a child. A family. He did not know why he felt so aggrieved by this news. After all, he could hardly have expected her life to have stood still the day he had walked from it.

'Yes. Her name is Bryony. She's at school in Switzerland. In fact, you just missed her. She was here visiting for her fath . . . for Seb's birthday.'

'How old is she?' Mitch enquired curiously, his hands absentmindedly fiddling with his notebook and pen.

'She's thirteen, fourteen in April. She's a wonderful girl, Mickey,' she gushed, her eyes lighting up at the mention of her daughter's name. 'You would be so prou . . .' Imogen stopped herself and Mitch stared at her, his heart racing inside his chest. They paused for the longest moment, neither one able to look directly at the other.

Mitch finally spoke.

'Please forgive me for asking this, Imogen,' he said. 'But I need to know where you were yesterday evening. It's just a formality, but I have to ask.'

'Really, it's OK,' she replied softly. 'I understand. You're just doing your job.' Though she had to admit that it felt strange, him questioning her like she was a stranger. 'I was with friends at Calvary Rothschild's house. Calvary's an old – and very good friend. I have her address if you need it.' She smiled and paused for a moment. 'We had a little cocktail party, you know, a sort of girls' night in.' The rehearsed words spilled quickly from her mouth like lemmings. 'There were just the three of us. Myself, Calvary Rothschild and Lady Yasmin Belmont-Jones.'

Mitch nodded, making notes as she spoke. 'Well, anyway. I must have got to Cal's around eight-ish, didn't leave until the early hours of this morning. Hence my little lie-in,' she smiled again, though he noted that it did not reach her eyes.

'And you drove home?'

'Yes, about 4:00 a.m. this morning.'

'After all those cocktails?' he raised an eyebrow.

Imogen smiled but it belied her panic.

'Well, I'd only had a few. It's just round the corner and I . . .'

'It's OK,' Mitch laughed then, breaking a little of the tension that was mounting between them. 'I'm not about to cuff you and drag you off down the station.'

The idea conjured up an image that caused them both to turn away from each other in mild embarrassment and he wished he had not said it.

'It's purely procedure to need to corroborate this,' he added quickly. 'We think that this was probably an inside job, committed by persons who knew your husband well, had access to personal information only he could have known.'

The word 'crime' resonated inside Imogen's head, throbbed like a migraine. God, it was never meant to have been like this. Any of it.

'I see,' Imogen said, her voice small. She felt his eyes on her then, even when she had turned away from him, and she wondered if he knew something. He had always been so good at being able to read her.

Mitch's sharp instincts were telling him that Imogen was holding something back. That she knew far more about all of this than she was letting on. He would need to watch her closely, he thought, as he made the motions to leave.

'Wow, Mickey, a policeman,' Imogen said, shaking her head in a subconscious bid to stall him. She had waited so long to see his face again, and now he was getting ready to leave. 'And you always hated the idea of a uniform. Said that it tried to "instil intangible values and institutionalised the wearer".'

Mitch chuckled softly, touched that she had remembered such a conversation verbatim.

'I said that?' He wondered when he might be able to find another excuse to see her, to talk to her alone. 'Well, the truth is, I can't believe it either. I fell into it, I suppose. After law school no longer became an option . . .' he paused, thinking it wise not to revisit any old, painful memories. 'Well, let's just say I was lucky to find something else that I could learn to be good at,' he said instead. 'As they say, life's full of surprises.'

'Isn't it just?' Imogen replied, watching as he made his way towards the door, leaving a lifetime of unspoken words hanging heavy in the air between them.

CHAPTER 54

'We're going to have to stop making a habit of this,' Sammie Grainger said as she stood at her front door, a bathrobe wrapped around her wet skin. 'People will talk.'

'Can I come in?' Yasmin asked tremulously. She looked pale and drawn and Sammie noticed the visible bags underneath her eyes that not even her usual thick undercoat of foundation could disguise.

'What's happened?' Sammie asked, her smile fading fast as she stood back from the door.

After what had happened between them during their last meeting, she had half expected never to see her again.

The kiss had taken Sammie as much by surprise as she was sure it had Yasmin. And although Yasmin had run away immediately afterwards, practically sprinting from the room, Sammie had sensed that she had felt it too, the tiny bolts of electricity that had passed between them as their lips had touched, the comfort they had felt in each other's arms. Was that such a terrible thing?

Yasmin pushed past Sammie through into the small studio apartment.

'There's something I need you to do for me.'

Sammie smiled, raising an eyebrow.

'Isn't there always?' she deadpanned.

'This is no joke, Sam,' Yasmin said and Sammie saw from the look on her face that she meant it.

'I need you to promise me that you'll keep something safe for me.'

Sammie absentmindedly rubbed her wet hair with an old chewing gum-white towel.

'Keep what safe?'

'This.' Yasmin pulled the VHS cassette from her Marni shopper and handed it to her. 'If anything should happen to me, I want you to promise me that this tape will see the light of day, do you understand? More importantly,' she continued, not giving Sammie the chance to respond, 'you have to promise me that you won't watch it. At least, not yet, not until I'm back.'

'Well, you know, that's a lot of promises.'

Yasmin looked at her with pleading eyes.

'Hang on a minute,' Sammie said, throwing her towel over the chair. 'Is this what I think it is? Is this *the* tape? The tape of your sis– '

'Just promise me that you'll take good care of it and that *please*,' Yasmin interrupted her, 'make a copy of it; make a dozen copies! If anything should happen to me, take one to the police, and the others to the papers '

'OK. OK,' Sammie said softly, concerned. 'Look, why don't you sit down . . .'

Yasmin shook her head fiercely.

'I don't have time. I'm flying out to the Cote D'Azur this afternoon with my husband and I don't know when I'll be back – but I *will* be back. And when I am, rest assured you'll have your story, like I promised.'

Sammie watched as Yasmin held the tape out to her with a shaking hand. She paused for a moment, suddenly reaching for a copy of the *Evening Star London* on the coffee table, her mind switching into journalistic overdrive.

'You've seen the papers today?' Sammie asked, picking it up and tossing it in her direction.

Yasmin shook her head, casting her eye over the headline: 'BUNGLED BANK JOB SEES SECURITY GUARD FIGHTING FOR LIFE.'

'Can't say that I have,' she replied, feigning ignorance as her heartbeat quickened in her chest.

'So, you know nothing about a break-in at Forbes Bank then?'

Yasmin shrugged. 'No. I don't. And I can't say I'm all that interested either.' She glanced sideways at her. There was a loaded pause.

'Where did you get the tape?' Sammie asked, her tone a little accusatory.

'What does it matter?' Yasmin snapped back a response. 'All that matters is now I have it, I can finish this goddamn thing once and for all. Look,' she said, her tone softening slightly. 'Lord knows why but you're the only person in the world who I can trust to take care of this for me. I need you to promise me that you'll keep this tape safe. Promise me!'

Sammie felt the first flutters of fear inside her belly. It had not taken her long to put two and two together; she had told Yasmin that the evidence she'd been searching for was down in that vault and then, oh God, then there was the interview that *she* herself had conducted with Forbes . . .

'What have you *done*, Yasmin?' Sammie asked gravely, tentatively taking the cassette from her grasp, her eyes narrowing with suspicion and fear. 'Tell me, what in God's name have you done?'

Yasmin laughed then. A malevolent low cackle that sent a shiver the length of Sammie's spine.

'Oh, it's not what I *have* done that you need to be worried about,' she said, fixing her with an icy stare that was cold enough to chill the entire room. 'It's what I'm *about* to do.'

CHAPTER 55

Imogen sank back into the antique Victorian claw-foot bath and immersed her body in the warm, fragrant water. Adding some more Jo Malone Lime, Basil and Mandarin bath oil to the tub, she took a deep breath.

Seeing Mickey again so suddenly, so unexpectedly, had left her in a state of total shock, rendering her incapable of concentrating on anything else, least of all deciding how best to deal with the situation at hand. A situation that seemed to have spiralled way out of her control.

Earlier that day Imogen had taken a frenetic call from Calvary. She'd had an unannounced visit from the police. From Mickey.

'They know something, Ims, I'm telling you, they *know*,' she had hissed down the line, panic all too evident in her voice. 'An Inspector McLaren something or other; he was asking *a lot* of questions.'

Imogen watched the steam as it rose up from the water, disappearing into the atmosphere above her like smoke. She had decided against telling Calvary about who Mickey was, for now at least. She needed to give herself time to get her head round the situation first. It wouldn't be long before the police started to pick holes in her story, start to take apart her alibi and probe further and deeper into her marriage.

If only she had come clean from the off. Explained it away as a silly prank, a practical joke that had got out of hand. Now she would probably go to prison, especially if Dickie didn't pull through, and certainly if Seb had anything to do with it. Even with such a dark threat looming over her, Imogen couldn't dwell on the thought for too long, not now that Mickey was back in her life again. He was all she could think of.

Imogen re-enacted the moment she had walked into the library and seen him standing there over and over again. Like a broken record, she replayed everything in her mind, reliving every word he had spoken, every detail, to ensure she had not missed a thing. He had told her that Aimee was dead and to her ever-burgeoning shame, she had felt a guilty slither of elation at this news. The look on Mickey's face had somehow told her that Aimee's death had been his emancipation. And in that moment Imogen felt sure of it; fate had brought them together again.

Pouring some matching Jo Malone body wash onto a pouf and working it up into a zesty fragrant lather, Imogen began soaping herself, covering her skin in tiny bubbles, allowing her hands to explore her own breasts, imagining for a moment that they were Mickey's hands. She let out a low, soft sigh of pleasure as she closed her eyes and thought about the time they had been together on the beach, the very last time they had made love, with the sound of the sea behind them and the scent of the sand and pine trees in the air. She could almost smell his skin as it touched her own, that familiar scent of lemon soap and cigarettes that had never left her after all these years. The smell of *him*. But a voice whispered to her, penetrating her intimate thoughts, and it told her that she must tread carefully because Mickey McLaren was now *Mitch* McLaren. *Detective Inspector* Mitch McLaren.

Sitting up abruptly, causing the water to almost slosh over the sides of the large Victorian tub with the momentum, Imogen was struck by a vicious clarity. She needed to get a hold of herself. Stop all this silly daydreaming about the past and forge a way out of the present mess she was in without detection; she owed it to her daughter, to the friends that had risked so much to help her – and above all, she owed it to herself. Only she knew that with Mickey, it would be tough. She had never been able to lie to those she loved. And the fact was, though time had made them strangers, she did still love him. Truth was, she had never really stopped.

CHAPTER 56

It would be fair to say that the weather in Nice was nothing short of spectacular. The sun shone high and fierce in the sky, causing the heat to rise up from the roads and the air to ripple. A little later in coming than was usual for the time of year, the French were already calling it '*une été Indien*' and flocking to the coast on their boats; the wealthy and beautiful all there to see and be seen.

'It's perfect driving weather,' Yasmin remarked as she attempted to put the Porsche Cayman in gear, the loud crunch causing both her and Jeremy to wince.

'You need to put your foot right down on the clutch, Yasmin,' Jeremy instructed, a little apprehensively. It was the first time he had been a passenger in a car with his wife driving and he was a tad nervous to say the least.

'Are you sure this is a good idea?' Jeremy asked, wishing they could've just stayed at the hotel and watched the La Perla fashion show that was taking place this afternoon instead. It appealed far more than traipsing all the way up some mountain just to have a look at a few crumbling old villages, that was for sure. 'It's a hell of a climb and it looks as though the air con's playing up.' He fiddled with a few buttons impatiently. 'We'll expire in this heat.'

'Oh come on, darling,' Yasmin prodded his chubby leg playfully, leaving an indentation mark on his white skin. 'Where's your sense of adventure? I had the chef at The Château prepare us the most divine picnic lunch – fois gras and sashimi – two of your favourites, and we've a few bottles of ice cold Veuve Clicquot to enjoy.' She glanced sideways at her husband who appeared to be sulking.

'Anyway, I thought we could find a secluded little spot somewhere for our lunch. You know, where no one will see us.' She ran her hand along his hairy, meaty thigh and up towards his crotch.

'Well, I suppose it could be fun,' Jeremy conceded grumpily, his double chin juddering with the uphill momentum of the car. 'Though I still think we might've hired ourselves a driver for the afternoon. I mean, have you seen just how steep those cliffs are?' He looked up towards the imposing Var Valley. 'They've got to be at least five hundred metres high.'

'Seven hundred to be exact,' Yasmin replied breezily. Jeremy turned to her, surprised. 'I read it in the tour guide back at The Château,' she explained.

'And there was me thinking you only ever read *Vogue*,' he teased her.

Yasmin laughed.

'Oh, there's *a lot* you don't know about me, Jeremy,' she smiled wickedly.

That morning Yasmin had woken her husband especially early so that they could get a good start ahead of the weather. 'We don't want to be driving in the midday heat,' she had remarked, shaking him awake. 'And don't forget to pack a camera.' Jeremy had groaned as he dragged his overweight, unfit body into the en-suite wet room and gasped as a cool blast of water from the shower hit his milky white skin, forcing him from his sleep-induced coma. He had never seen her so determined.

Yasmin had watched with barely concealed disgust as a naked Jeremy had walked from the bedroom, his hairy pink backside wobbling like a blancmange behind him, back fat hanging in fleshy rolls from his large frame.

Everything Yasmin had done, every sacrifice she had made, had culminated in this day. Today was going to be beautiful, perfect even. Today, Stacey Jones would finally, after what had felt like a lifetime, avenge her sister's death.

'This seat is terribly uncomfortable,' Jeremy whinged, attempting to adjust himself, his knees lodged uncomfortably up towards his chest, his imposing bulk seeming to take up half the entire car space. 'I say, they certainly didn't build these things with comfort in mind, did they?'

Yasmin grinned and said breezily, 'Not long now, darling. We're almost at the top!'

Jeremy rolled his eyes and said a secret prayer to himself. He wished he'd just organised a chopper to fly them up to the bloody mountaintop. They'd be there and back again in a quarter of the time. As it was, the way things were going, it would be a miracle if they made it to the top in one piece.

'Easy on the accelerator, darling,' Jeremy said, panic seeping through his affable tone. 'We really are terribly high up.'

'What's the matter, don't you trust me?' She cast him a mocking glance.

'Of course I trust you,' came the riposte. 'But we're on a bloody knife's edge here, and your driving is a little erratic to say the least. Slow down a bit, there's a good girl.'

'Of course, darling, if that's what you want,' Yasmin laughed manically, pressing down on the accelerator a touch harder. 'How about a little music? Get us in the mood, eh?'

'Why not,' Jeremy sighed, acquiescing. He felt sick. There was little point in suggesting they turn back now despite his instincts telling him everything to the contrary. Besides, they couldn't even if they wanted to. The road was far too narrow. Attempting a U-turn would be suicidal. The only way back down, so it seemed, was to make it to the top.

Jeremy glanced nervously out of the window at the vertical drop below and felt a chill run the length of his spine.

'Perhaps I'll drive on the way back,' he suggested, watching in barely concealed horror as she haphazardly turned the wheel, teetering dangerously close to the road's edge. 'Give you a break.'

'If you like, darling.' Yasmin continued to chuckle with abandon as that morning's coke binge held her tightly in its manic grip. She was thoroughly enjoying watching her husband squirm, and was in half a mind to confess to him that she had snorted half a gram of the finest powder his money could buy before getting behind the wheel that morning, that would really shut the murdering old fucker up.

Yasmin glanced sideways at her husband and pushed a CD into the stereo.

'Don't tell me,' Jeremy remarked dryly, 'Chris Rea's *Road to Hell.*'

'Oh, darling, you *are* funny,' Yasmin replied, collapsing into false laughter.

Stupid old bastard, she thought to herself as she threw her head back. He had no idea just how close to the truth he really was.

CHAPTER 57

'Just a little further,' Calvary said, barely able to contain her excitement as she covered Josia's eyes with her hands and led him out of the elevator and to the vast doors of apartment 166.

'Seriously, Calvary, can I look now?' Josia said a little tremulously. 'You know I'm not big on surprises.'

'We're almost there,' she sang. 'Watch your step! And keep your eyes closed until I say so,' she said bossily as she swung the doors open. 'No peeking!'

Josia shook his head and sighed. 'You're making me nervous.'

'You can look now,' Calvary said triumphantly, dropping her hands from his face and watching as he fluttered his watery blue eyes open.

'Ta-da!' She clasped her hands together and raised her eyebrows. 'What do you think?'

Josia stood inside the living room of the enormous penthouse, the panoramic view of the London skyline staring back at him from the floor to ceiling sliding glass doors, and looked around in a visible state of perplexity.

'Don't you just adore the view?' she trilled. 'The light is absolutely *perfect* for painting – and I chose all the soft furnishings myself.' She sighed. 'And just wait until you see the bedroom! It's wall to wall Ralph Lauren! I didn't go overboard on the artwork though, I wanted you to have some input of your own, after all you'll be living here too, and . . . well, come on then, say something!'

Josia was, quite literally, lost for words.

'You have got to be kidding me?' he finally said.

'Don't you like it?' she said, reading his expression and suddenly feeling a little crestfallen by his obvious lack of enthusiasm. She had gone to great lengths to find an apartment for them and this was not the reaction she had expected. 'It's the colour, isn't it? The French Grey. It's too dark, isn't it? Too austere. I must admit I had reservations myself but . . .'

Josia shook his head. 'No, Calvary. It's not the paint. The paint's fine.'

'Then what is it?' she pouted. 'Oh, darling, I thought you'd be pleased. A place of our own! Somewhere we can be together properly like we discussed. I couldn't bear that poky little apartment of yours any longer. This way we can see each other whenever we want to, for as long as we want to, in pure unadulterated luxury.' Calvary twirled around the room in an over-dramatic effect, her silk Chloe dress making a circle as she spun. She had wanted to make this moment special for them both and had even arranged for a superb three course lunch with champagne to be served on the heated terrace as an extra surprise.

Josia stared at her for the longest moment and thought how beautiful she looked, her megawatt smile bringing sunshine into the room, the swell of her chest from underneath the soft silky fabric of her dress, and her hair, scraped back from her face, loose tendrils framing her prominent cheekbones. He wondered just how someone quite as beautiful and smart as she was could get it all so terribly wrong.

'You bought this place? For us?'

'Yes!' Calvary squealed. 'Well, not bought it exactly. I've negotiated a fixed six month rental with a view to buy at the end of it. Aren't I clever? There's a Jacuzzi and a steam room, an en-suite in the bedroom, all mod cons in the kitchen – the appliances are all Bodum and Alessi. Go ahead, look!' she said, clapping her hands together twice, causing the lighting in the open plan kitchen to dim. 'It's magic!'

Josia walked over towards the gigantic glass wall that overlooked the bustling streets of Mayfair and looked out onto the view, his heart heavy.

'It's got twenty-four hour porterage – and – here's the best bit – room service!' Calvary continued, animated. 'It's like a hotel but isn't a hotel. A *hometel* if you like.'

Pleased with herself, she let out a small squeal of delight.

'It's lovely, Calvary. Really,' he said flatly.

'I knew you'd like it!' she gushed, overcome with a sense of relief. It had been a bloody awful week, what with the security guard still in hospital and the police beginning to sniff around. She had needed this to lift her mood.

'But there's no way on God's green earth I'm moving in here.'

Calvary felt her euphoria pop like a bubble.

'What do you mean?' she said, her excitement halted in its tracks. 'But this is everything we had planned! A place of our own, to be together, that's what you wanted, wasn't it?'

Josia turned to her, a strange solemn expression on his boyish face, one she hadn't seen before. One that made her nervous.

'It *is* what I want, Calvary, believe me. I want nothing more than for us to be together. To have a home of our own. But not like this.' He stood opposite her, his brow furrowed, accentuating those little wrinkles across his nose that she enjoyed so much. 'Besides, renting a place like this must cost a small fortune.'

'Two thousand a week, actually,' she replied sheepishly.

'That's ten thousand a month!' he shrieked. 'You know I could never afford it.'

'Nonsense, darling,' Calvary waved his words away. 'I'm paying the rent. You can settle the room service bill each month if it makes you feel better.'

'For God's sake, Calvary!' Josia shouted. He had never shouted at her before and it shocked her into a stunned silence. 'I'm not a child! I thought we agreed that when the time was right we would look for a place *together*. Choose somewhere we *both* wanted to live.' Josia shook his head again, the frustration in him rising. 'You knew I would never agree to living here, and that's why you decided against telling me about it. I mean, look at it! It's not a home, it's a hotel! Did you honestly expect that I would give up my place, poky though it may be, and live here, like a kept man, for you to drop by and visit whenever you can fit me in around your busy schedule? Let's face it, Calvary, it's not *you* who'll be paying the rent on this place, it's *him*. Douglas. And eventually Douglas will want to come and take a look at his investment. And what will happen then? Will I have to hide in the wardrobe with my toothbrush?' Her stunned expression caused him to feel a momentary flutter of regret, but he was just so angry.

'Look,' he said, his voice softening a little. 'When I said I loved you, Calvary Rothschild, I meant it.'

'Loved? You're talking in the past tense already,' Calvary said, her voice cracking like the embers of a bonfire.

'And when I said I wanted us to be together, I meant – I *mean* – that too. But not like this,' he shook his head, 'definitely not like this.'

Calvary fought back the urge to burst into tears. She had been almost deranged with excitement about unveiling the apartment. She had expected him to be a little surprised, yes, but not this.

'But . . . but I thought you'd be happy. I thought if anything you would *thank* me,' she croaked, her words choking her. This was supposed to be a new start, the beginning of the rest of her life with a man she really loved. Now it felt as if she had made the biggest mistake of her life.

'But you said . . .'

'I know what I said!' Josia snapped. 'But you don't listen, Calvary. You make all the right noises and nod in all the right places but you just don't listen!' He was so cross with her now that it was beginning to scare her. She had never seen him so upset. 'I can no more live here than you can live in my *poky* little studio.'

Calvary snorted, suddenly feeling an attack of anger herself. 'A rat would turn his nose up living in that place. This is everything we ever wanted – at least, I thought it was.'

Josia glared at her. 'No, Calvary, it's all *you* ever wanted,' he said firmly. 'My feelings don't come into it. I wanted us to start off on an equal footing. I'm not this season's handbag that you can just put in one of your walk-in closets and bring out every now and again. I'm a human being!'

Calvary pulled her head into her chin. 'You make it sound as if I'm trying to buy you! Does it really matter which one of us has the money, for God's sake? I mean, if it was *you* who held the purse strings then we wouldn't even be having this conversation. A *real* man wouldn't feel threatened by the fact that the woman he supposedly loved had money,' Calvary said, unable to stop herself. 'A *real* man would see that this makes perfect sense and wouldn't be so bloody minded about everything. Besides, it won't be long before people start snapping up your paintings and you'll probably have more money than– '

'As much money as you and Douglas, eh?' Josia flicked his mop of dark unruly curls from his brow, his usually soft expression hardening.

'I didn't mean it like that, I – '

'I know what you meant, Calvary,' he said without looking at her.

They were silent for a moment and Calvary made her way over to the window where Josia stood looking over Mayfair.

'Look, I'm sorry,' she said, placing her hand on his arm and gently moving him away from the window. 'I know I should've consulted you, but really, I did it all with the best intentions. I got ahead of myself, that's all. Please don't be so cross with me. I want what you want at the end of the day.'

Josia looked up at her and into her bright green eyes, wondering why he loved her more than he'd ever loved anyone else before. They were so very different. Chalk and cheese. Calvary's first love was money and he had been quite arrogant to think that he would ever be able to change that. He glanced around the apartment, at the plush soft furnishings she had lovingly hand chosen for them, that had probably cost the equivalent of a lottery win and he knew that it would never work.

'But that's just it,' he said sadly. 'We don't want the same things, do we? You want . . . you want this – and me, well, I just want you. I don't care about any of it. The fancy lighting and the Jacuzzis, the en-suites and the underfloor heating.' He gestured around the apartment accusingly, as if somehow the fixtures and fittings had personally slighted him.

'Please don't say that,' she replied quietly.

'It won't work,' Josia said, taking hold of her hand. 'I love you but it won't work. It's best we say goodbye now. Before we cause each other more pain. You are you – and

I love you because of who you are. To try and change you would be wrong. Our worlds are just too different.'

'You don't mean that,' she found herself saying in panic. 'Don't give up on me now. I need you. For God's sake, I love you!' She hated herself for begging.

Josia felt his chest constrict. He had never wanted this to happen and he cursed himself for ever having allowed it to.

'It's the age thing, isn't it?' she suddenly said, fighting back tears with a ferocity that frightened her. She was damned if she was going to cry in front of him.

'Don't be ridiculous, it's got nothing to do with it,' he replied, offended at the suggestion.

'All this business about money and changing me. You're just worried that you'll be stuck with an incontinent old woman while you'll still be in your prime!'

'Well, since you put it like that,' he smiled at her then, realising instantly from her expression that his attempt at humour had fallen woefully flat.

She turned away from him them, embarrassed, ashamed of herself and who she was. At having been foolish enough to believe that a younger man would love her unconditionally, immaterial of age, of status and wealth. Once again, Calvary Rothschild had made a complete fool of herself.

'Just go!' she said shortly. 'I mean it, Josia; please leave,' she said stoically.

'Calvary,' he implored. 'Not like this, please. I don't want to hurt you.'

'Hurt me? Don't be ridiculous,' she lied, her pride getting the better of her. 'It was fun while it lasted but you're right.' She turned from him then, lest he saw the despair on her face. 'We're too different; worlds apart. It was quite naive of me to think that I could turn an impoverished artist into a man of society. It would never have worked.'

Josia sighed. He knew she was saying these things to hide her pain.

'I hope we can still be friends, Calvary,' he said. 'Whatever you think, I still want to be here for you. I know your son's wedding is coming up and . . .'

'Sorry, darling,' Calvary said, taking herself in hand and swinging round to face him. She smiled affably, though it did not reach her eyes. 'But I've got enough friends. Now if you don't mind, I've got a spa appointment at three and don't want to be late.' She began to collect her things from the untouched cream sofa, the sofa she had half hoped they might've made love on that afternoon.

Josia looked at the floor, at the imprint his shoes had made on the soft Axminster carpet. 'Have it your way,' he said with a resolute sadness that caused her to inwardly wince. 'Goodbye, Calvary,' he said softly.

'Yes, goodbye,' she said, turning her back to him once more.

It was only when she heard the door close behind him that she allowed the tears to come.

CHAPTER 58

Le Caprice was filling up with lunchtime trade and Mitch congratulated himself for having had the foresight to book in advance. He looked around the restaurant, admiring the homage to monochrome, the matt black floor tiles and black leather chairs offset against the crisp white table linen. It was all terribly chic and sophisticated, though he figured Imogen was probably used to dining in such style.

He watched her from across the table, her silky dark hair cascading down her shoulders, occasionally licking her full lips as she perused the menu enthusiastically. She looked beautiful and understated in a pretty summer dress with the tiniest flowery print all over it that lightly skimmed her slim curves, exposing a little of the creamy flesh of her shoulder, and it was all he could do to stop himself from reaching out and touching her.

'I think I'm going to go for the grilled asparagus and the lemon sole,' she said, 'no, the Thai sea bass . . . oh, I don't know, what do you think?'

'They both sound delicious,' he said, wondering if it would appear a little safe of him to order Bannockburn ribeye and pommes allumettes – steak and chips.

'Why don't we order both?' he suggested. 'That way we can share.'

'Great idea,' she said, snapping the menu shut. She couldn't quite get her head round the fact that Mickey was actually sitting opposite her, dressed in a smart crisp white shirt and dark blue fitted trousers, his deep teal eyes offsetting his lightly tanned skin. She had dreamt of this moment for years, and now that it was actually here, she was conscious of enjoying every moment.

'Did you know this was one of my favourite restaurants?' she asked, looking around her and smiling.

'Really? I had no idea,' he lied. Mitch had read, in the dossier that a member of his team had compiled on her, that Le Caprice was a regular haunt of hers. 'I chose well then,' he smiled, scanning the wine menu, worrying whether it was *de rigueur* to order in French or not.

'We'll have the Château des Gravières 2005, *s'il vous plaît*,' Mitch nodded at the waiter who dipped his head in approval.

'*Très bien, monsieur.*'

'That OK with you?' He glanced over at Imogen. 'I'm not a big lunchtime drinker myself,' he said, cross with himself for being so nervous. 'Especially when I'm on duty.'

'Aren't policemen *always* on duty?' Imogen questioned him playfully, their eyes briefly locking.

Mitch had gladly taken his superior on his word to 'keep an eye' on Imogen but given his suspicions, he felt compromised. He knew he had orchestrated today's lunch partly to pump her for information. But another part of him was content just to look at her, to talk, enjoy the sound of her voice once more. Mitch felt torn. Instinctively, he had known Imogen had something to do with the break-in at the bank. He had always understood her.

The CCTV footage recovered from the night of the

break-in had thrown up some interesting information. Information he'd rather have not been privy to.

It had taken Maggie Barber three days, and two sleepless nights, repeatedly watching the footage over and over again before she noticed it. Breathless with excitement, she had called her superior in the middle of the night, dragging him from his fretful slumber, requesting he meet her at the station immediately.

'There, gov,' she had pointed animatedly at the screen, 'do you see?'

Mitch had shrugged, rubbing his tired, gritty eyes as he strained to see what had got her worked up into such a lather.

'The Forbes character,' Maggie had explained with a self-satisfied smile. 'I couldn't put my finger on it at first. But now I realise what it is, what's odd about it.'

'And?' Mitch encouraged her. 'Don't keep me in suspense, Maggie.'

'Look at the slight curve in the jacket; at the way his hips move as he walks. That could never be Sebastian Forbes, sir,' Barber had surmised. 'Never in a million years.'

'No shit, Sherlock,' Mitch had replied facetiously.

Maggie had shot her boss a mock wounded look.

'Yes, but do you know how I know that?' she asked, relishing the sense of drama, her moment in the spotlight.

'Tell me, Maggie,' Mitch had smiled, indulging her.

'Because,' she had exclaimed, tapping her fingernail at the freeze-frame figure of Sebastian Forbes on the screen, with a self-congratulatory smile. 'That, gov, is a woman!'

*

'I never thought I would see you again, let alone be taking you out to lunch,' Mitch said, meeting her gaze.

'We were lucky to get a table at such short notice,' Imogen said, casting an eye around the bustling restaurant.

'Usually they're booked up way in advance,' she added, being careful not to allow him to steer the conversation in an intimate direction.

'Policeman's perks,' he smiled at her and she smiled back, watching as he absentmindedly brushed his fringe from his eyes.

'Lovely as this is, you know a sandwich in the park would've done just as nicely,' she said purposely, in a bid to make sure he knew she had not developed any ideas above her station.

'Now she tells me!' he laughed and she joined in, the slight tension between them lifting.

The waiter brought the wine to the table and they watched in silence as he poured two glasses of the deep burgundy liquid.

'To old friends,' he said, touching her glass lightly with his own, the mellifluous sound of glass on glass ringing out through the restaurant.

'Old friends,' she smiled softly, though they both knew they had been much more than that.

'You know I always knew you would do well for yourself,' Mitch said, taking a large gulp of the deep rich fruity wine, resisting the urge to smack his lips. 'Even when I moved to the other side of the world I always expected to see your face staring down at me from a billboard, or a TV screen or something. When did you stop modelling?'

'Who says I ever stopped?' she replied.

'It's just that I read something recently about you resurrecting your career. Some big make-up contract in LA . . .'

Imogen inwardly winced.

'Oh, you mean the L'Orelie thing?'

'Yes, that's the one.'

He felt bad about having to bring it all up, by all accounts her losing out on the contract had caused quite a stir in the media, and no doubt some personal embarrassment, but it was integral. He needed to get her talking about her husband.

'Yes.' Imogen shifted in her chair, feeling the discomfort of her humiliation once more. She could see no point in lying about it, not when it had been so well documented. 'They gave it to someone younger in the end. The press had a bloody field day about it. Ageism in the media and all that. I see you've been doing your homework.' She raised an eyebrow, impressed.

'Just my job,' he replied gently. 'Anyway, they're fools – L'Orelie, I mean.'

Imogen felt herself flush pink.

'It's a young women's game today,' she sighed, glossing over the compliment. 'You've got twelve-year-olds walking the shows now. I'm practically a relic by comparison!' she laughed, but it sounded hollow. 'It was a shame though; I wanted to do that one last campaign, in memory of my agent – and friend – Cressida Lucas. Do you remember her?'

'Small woman, big personality – how could anyone forget her?'

She was pleased he'd remembered.

'She died in that dreadful plane crash, you know the recent London to LA flight a few months back? I was in LA waiting for her to join me when it happened. It was so tragic, all those lives lost . . . poor Cress.'

'I'm sorry to hear that,' he said genuinely. 'She was quite a character if I remember.'

'Yes.' Imogen gave a sad smile. 'She was.'

'So you gave it up then, the modelling?'

'My career was just about to peak when I discovered I was expecting Bryony,' she explained. 'I worked for a little while after she was born but then Seb . . .' Imogen paused for a moment. 'Seb and I agreed it would be better if I concentrated on motherhood.'

'I see,' Mitch said, adding, 'you're lucky.'

'Lucky?'

'To have a daughter, I mean.'

Imogen looked into his teal green eyes and sensed regret in them.

'You and Aimee never . . .'

Mitch shook his head. 'She couldn't. The doctors said it was too dangerous for her, and for an unborn child.'

There was a moment's silence.

Mickey had given up everything to do right by Aimee and Imogen couldn't help but wonder if he would've done the same thing again today. Blessed with perfect hindsight, would he have stood by Aimee now? Something inside her told her that he probably would; he was just so good and decent and right, and it was for all these reasons and more that she had loved him.

Instinctively, Imogen slid her hand across the table, gently covering his with it. As her skin made contact with his own, Mitch took a silent intake of breath. He dared not look at her for fear that she could read his every thought, would see the raw desire for her etched upon his face like a tattoo. He had to get a hold on himself, remain professional.

'Anyway, enough about me,' he said, abruptly changing the subject. He watched her hand as it silently returned to her lap and he stared at his own for a moment, enjoying the tingling sensation the tips of her fingers had left upon his.

'You've certainly come a long way from coffee bars in Camden Town, it has to be said.'

She lightly shrugged.

'It depends on how you measure a long way,' Imogen said.

'Well, I mean, you're Mrs Imogen Forbes of Forbes Bank now. The house, the cars, the clothes . . .' He cast an eye over her outfit – an Isabel Marant tea dress, a butterscotch shrunken leather Balmain jacket casually draped over her chair, a large YSL tote at her feet – it all screamed of wealth and success, though the truth was, she was so naturally beautiful and stylish she could've worn a paper bag with panache.

'I didn't marry for money if that's what you're thinking,' she replied, a little defensively, a little wounded that he would even think such a thing.

Mitch lowered his eyes and smiled. Had he been that obvious?

'So it was true love then, you and Sebastian?'

'Yes,' she said, a little too quickly.

Mitch nodded, unconvinced. He did not want to believe her.

'I'm glad,' he said. 'So tell me, how did you and the infamous Mr Forbes meet then? It must've been pretty soon after we– ' he stopped short of finishing the sentence.

'We fell in love on Necker Island, since you ask,' Imogen replied, playing with an olive by means of a distraction. 'Seb pursued me relentlessly for months . . . and well, you know . . . in the end I gave in.' She swallowed a sip of water in a bid to wash away the bitter taste of her lies.

Imogen's whole body was screaming out to tell Mickey the truth; make him understand that it had been in a fug of heartbreak and had been the single biggest mistake of her entire life. But she bit her tongue. She had to remember that Mickey was no longer *Mickey* and she couldn't afford to give anything away.

'It was a very romantic proposal,' Imogen added for good measure. 'Underneath the palm trees with the sound of the sea in the background.'

He nodded.

'It sounds it.'

Imogen thought she saw a flicker of hurt flash across his

eyes. 'I'm pleased for you,' he added, 'genuinely.' Now it was Mitch's turn to lie. There was a long pause between them before he said, 'Listen, Imogen, I want to talk about what happened all those years ago . . .'

'Please!' she cut him off, abruptly. 'Let's not. I mean, it's all water under the bridge now, isn't it? So many years ago. And we were so young . . .'

He watched her carefully.

'Yes,' he agreed, lowering his eyes, 'I suppose we were.'

'It's never a good idea to rake over the past,' she said with an air of forced nonchalance. 'What's done is done, right? What is it they say; why waste time worrying about the things you cannot change?'

'Something like that.' Their eyes lingered upon each other for a moment longer than either felt comfortable with.

Adrenalin pulsed furiously through Imogen's body, destroying any appetite she had. More than anything she wanted to have that conversation with him. To tell him how much she had missed him, had yearned and ached for him all these years, but it was far too dangerous. She couldn't be sure he wasn't simply trying to trick her into trusting him, into telling the truth.

'So,' he said, pointedly changing the subject, 'tell me about this husband of yours.'

'What do you want to know?' Imogen asked, a little disappointed that he had not pressed the issue of them further.

'Well, what kind of a man is he, for one thing?'

'Sebastian? Well, you've met him; what kind of a man do *you* think he is?' Imogen replied cryptically, sipping her wine. She didn't really want to talk about her husband, least of all to him, but she could tell he had switched into full-on policeman mode now.

'Well, since you ask, I would say he is a powerful man, a dictator, the kind of man who always gets what – and who – he wants, at any cost.'

Imogen gave a wan smile.

'It sounds like you already know him well.'

'Well, I'd wager that whoever did this to your husband certainly wasn't his biggest fan,' Mitch said. 'In fact, I'd go as far as to say they wanted to hurt him pretty bad.'

He glimpsed at her neck to see if she was wearing the necklace, the thin silver chain with the tiny shell pendant he had given her all those years ago on that beautiful beach in Ibiza, but the light summer scarf she was wearing obscured his view and he couldn't quite tell.

'Well, you don't get to the kind of lofty heights my husband has reached without ruffling a few feathers,' Imogen remarked. 'He told me he'd compiled a list of names for the police to have a look at; names of people who might've had reason to want to see him on his uppers.' She imagined it was probably heavier than the phone book. 'Maybe you should start with that.'

Mitch nodded, sagely, pausing for a moment.

'Can I ask you a question?'

'Of course,' she smiled through her nerves.

'Are *you* on that list?'

'Me!' Imogen feigned surprise. 'Why on earth would *I* be on such a list?' she replied, a little too quickly, a little too indignant. He noticed her hands were lightly shaking as she brought her wine glass up to her glossy lips.

'Oh, I don't know,' Mitch shrugged, 'it's not as if you'd be the first wife ever to want to do her husband a disservice.'

'A disservice?' Imogen gave a little whinny. 'Breaking into his workplace would be a little extreme, wouldn't it? Why would I?'

Mitch shrugged. She was lying. He could see it in her eyes, those dark, almond-shaped eyes. Like windows to her soul, they betrayed her.

'Imogen, listen to me,' Mitch said, his voice was low and

grave now, almost a whisper as he leaned in closer to her from across the table. Suddenly she saw Mickey again. 'I need to know the truth. I can't help you unless you tell me the truth.'

Imogen shrugged and gave him her best puzzled look. Her chest was so tight, she could hardly breathe.

'The truth about what? About my marriage? About Seb? I've already told you. I don't know what else to say.' She blinked at him.

Mitch sighed and sat back in his chair.

'The security guard, Dickie. He's still in intensive care, you know,' he said, watching carefully for her reaction.

Imogen looked down at the menu and began to reread it.

'I'm sorry to hear that,' she said quietly, refraining from meeting his eye. 'Do they think he'll recover?'

Imogen felt the heat of his stare upon her.

'Poor chap obviously walked right in on the scene and collapsed there and then,' Mitch said. 'Those heartless bastards must've walked right over his body to make their escape. I mean, the man could've been dead, for God's sake.'

Imogen couldn't help but look up at him.

'How can you be so sure that they were there when he collapsed? They might not have even known what had happened to the poor man until after the event.'

'So, is that how it really happened, then?'

Imogen stared at him, unblinking.

'I . . . I have no idea,' she said, mock incredulous. Her mouth felt bone dry and she took a sip of water. 'I'm just looking at all possible scenarios, that's all.'

Mitch wrestled with his inner conscience. If he could just get her to talk then maybe, just maybe, he could try and help her out of this mess, but he could see that she was frightened, too scared to open up to him because of who he was. His heart wanted to scream at her to run, get the hell out of the country, take her daughter with her and never look back, while his head wanted to stop her, reprimand her for what he knew, deep down, she had done.

Not for the first time in his life, Mitch found himself faced with having to make a difficult choice, and this time, he was determined to make the right one.

As if on cue his phone rang, breaking the tense moment, and he smiled apologetically at her.

'McLaren,' he said, wiping his mouth with his napkin as he answered it.

It was his colleague, Jack Warren.

'There's been a breakthrough, boss,' Warren said, sounding as happy as a tick on a fat dog. 'One I predicted all along. Rothschild's alibi, it's bogus.'

Mitch felt his sphincter muscle contract. 'Go on.'

'Uniform questioned some nosy old nocturnal neighbour of Calvary Rothschild's and it turns out she swears she saw her leaving her house that evening at around 8:00 p.m. and return just after 10:00 p.m. with two other people in tow, one of which she swears was that Imogen Forbes. That means there's a two hour window that's unaccountable for.' Warren paused, waiting for a response. When one didn't come he continued, 'I knew that Rothschild woman was lying. Had it written all over her horsey face, the stuck up bi . . .'

'Yes, yes, alright, Jack,' Mitch interrupted him.

'Mullins wants you to bring Forbes in, but he wants it done quietly. Only trouble is I've already been to the house and no one knows where she is.'

'I see,' he said solemnly, glancing up at Imogen. She smiled at him and it felt like a knife through his ribs.

'You might sound a bit happier about it, gov,' Warren said, aggrieved that his boss wasn't showering him with praise for a job well done.

'I'll need to speak with this neighbour,' Mitch said with quiet resignation.

Jack Warren felt his frustration peak. There was just no pleasing some people.

'I'll be bringing Rothschild in,' Warren said, enthusiastically. 'Though apparently Lady Belmont-Jones is off on a jolly in France.' There was a pause on the line. 'So I'll tell Mullins you'll be bringing Forbes in then, when you find her that is?' he said, filling it.

'Yes, you tell him that,' he replied sharply before snapping his phone shut.

Placing it down on the table, Mitch's eyes glazed over as he desperately tried to think. He could lie to his boss; say he'd never seen her, that when he tried to find her she'd been one step ahead and had already made her escape. Only deep down, he knew that he couldn't. Too many people had seen them together.

'Everything alright?' Imogen enquired, watching his expression cloud over with some concern. Before he could answer her however, the waiter brought their starters to the table, placed the steaming, fragrant plates of delights in front of them.

'Mmm, looks lovely,' she smiled, licking her full, fleshy mouth in anticipation, her appetite returning. 'Well, *bon appétit*,' she smiled, lighting up her face from within.

'*Bon appétit*,' Mitch replied weakly, though he knew, as he tentatively picked up his knife and fork, that he would not be able to eat a thing.

CHAPTER 59

Sebastian Forbes, for once in his life, was reticent as he sat on the powder blue crushed velvet chaise longue inside The Royal Suite at The Lanesborough hotel, watching as Prince Saud paced the magnificent room, his face as dark as thunder.

'Moved? But how? *How*?' The prince shook his fist in frustration, and even his robes, billowing out behind him, looked angry. 'The most secure bank in the world, isn't that what you said? Impenetrable to man and beast!'

Sebastian nodded, his mood sombre.

'Yes, I did, your grace, I did. Somehow, someone discovered a way of breaking into it.' He looked up at the Arab prince with imploring eyes. 'They tricked the bloody system. The man – or rather, men – who did this, were clever and meticulous.'

'Tricked the system? The system you assured me was foolproof? This one-of-a-kind system that could guarantee the Bluebird's safety for, now what was it you said, "a thousand years and then some"?'

'I can assure you that the diamond is safe . . . again,' Sebastian attempted to reassure him, but even he had to admit it sounded a little pathetic. 'I've had it under round the clock security ever since, and I have the best policemen in the United Kingdom, if not the world, working on this,' Sebastian interjected. 'They have promised me that they will get to the bottom of it – whoever did this, they will not get away with it, I can promise you that much.'

The prince grunted.

'Your promises mean nothing to me, Forbes,' he boomed, causing Sebastian to cower a little in his seat. 'You have already proved yourself to be a liar!'

Sebastian made to stand but thought better of it as he watched the prince's two burly bodyguards move in closer, a look of menace in their otherwise dead expressions.

'And they took only the diamond?' the Prince clarified.

Sebastian sighed as he nodded.

'They took it from the vault and moved it up to the nineteenth floor, to my desk.'

Prince Saud glared at Sebastian.

'But why?' he pressed. 'Why would someone want to do this? Is this some kind of message? A warning?' He scratched his long, dark beard in question.

'We should never have announced our coalition, let people know of its whereabouts,' he said, angry at himself almost as much as the sad little man sitting opposite him. He turned sharply towards Sebastian. 'I should never have let you talk me into this! You wanted to publicise our agreement, I knew this would make her a target for thieves the world over.'

'I appreciate that you're upset . . .' Sebastian said tremulously.

'Upset!' the prince shot back, his eyes wide and maniacal, as he paced the exquisite suite. 'You have no idea what this means, Forbes! The Bluebird, she is not simply the most valuable diamond in the world,' he threw his hands up in the air and shook them, 'she is the spirit of my mother, of the Queen of Arabia! She is a living, breathing entity! It is like having my own mother violated.'

Sebastian swallowed dryly. He knew that he had lost the prince's confidence and that any reassurances he gave him now would fall on deaf ears.

'First and foremost, Forbes, I am a prince,' Prince Saud said. 'And second to this I am a businessman. One who has always taken great pride in his sharp instincts and intuition. I had my reservations about you,' he said, pointing a perfectly manicured finger in Sebastian's direction, 'right from the beginning; a feeling here,' he said, thumping his chest with his fist. 'Only I chose to ignore it,' he berated himself. 'I chose to listen to my head and not my heart – and now my heart has been proved right. You have allowed her safety to be compromised, and for that you must pay.' Prince Saud turned to him then, his eyes as dark as onyx.

'But I couldn't possibly have known that this was going to happen,' Sebastian objected. 'Believe me when I say I am as upset as you are about this. After all, it is *my* reputation that is in tatters, *my* good business name all but destroyed.'

The prince laughed again, a booming, incredulous sound that seemed to intoxicate the air all around them.

'You expect me to sympathise with you?' he snorted, mirth thick in his voice.

Disgruntled though he was at having to take insults from a man wearing a dress, Sebastian bit his lip. The pair of human Rottweilers snarling either side of the prince looked as if they hadn't been fed for a few days.

'The police are following up leads as we speak,' Sebastian said with a little less apology than before. He had allowed the Arab fool to castigate him as much as he would ever allow anyone to. 'I *will* find out who did this, Prince Saud. And rest assured I will make sure they pay for your inconvenience.'

Sebastian watched as the prince stood, looking out at

the magnificent view of Buckingham Palace, which probably seemed like a quaint little cottage in comparison to the vulgar and gargantuan palace that was his own dwelling.

'It is the love of, how do you say, the limelight, that has brought about this most unfortunate of circumstances,' he said, mostly to himself, an idea forming in his mind, 'and so it will be this that will help us turn this catastrophe into a success. Yes . . . that's it!'

'I'm sorry,' Sebastian said, confused, 'I don't think I follow.'

The prince turned from the enormous bay window.

'We will call a press conference,' he announced.

Sebastian felt his heart sink into his hand-stitched Italian leather loafers.

'A press conference? Really, Prince Saud, do you think that's a good idea? We've already had the press sniffing around and they . . .'

'I'm not *asking* you, Forbes,' he interrupted him. 'I'm *telling* you. We appeal to the public for information. I will offer a reward – ten million dollars.'

'Ten million dollars!' Sebastian repeated the words out loud. 'Are you mad?'

The prince silenced him with a steely glare.

'Mad? Yes. I am mad. I am, how do you say, hopping mad,' Prince Saud said, the veins in his temple protruding as if on cue.

'But that kind of money will have all sorts of cranks crawling out of the woodwork,' Sebastian protested. 'It'll hamper the police investigation.'

The prince ignored him.

'I will make a direct plea for anyone with information to come forward. If it leads to a conviction, I will reward them handsomely.'

'Now hang on a minute!' Sebastian stood now. Stuff the

bloody bodyguards, he thought defiantly, he'd rather they broke every bone in his body than allow the perpetrators to profit from this catastrophe.

'I'm afraid, your grace,' Sebastian simpered again, 'I simply cannot allow myself to do that.'

'You can, Forbes,' the prince shot back menacingly, 'and you will. In fact, you will get on the phone to your people right now and have them organise the conference for as soon as possible. You can consider our little agreement null and void as from this moment on . . .'

The sound of Sebastian's phone ringing cut the prince off mid-sentence and Sebastian scrabbled around in his suit pocket to retrieve it.

'It's the police,' Sebastian said, relief audible in his voice as he recognised the number flash up on his BlackBerry. 'I should take it,' he said, grateful for the distraction. 'They might have some news.'

Prince Saud turned his back on him and listened to the conversation as he once more drank in the magnificent view that his £15,000 a night suite afforded him.

'She's *what*?' Sebastian shrieked, horror evident in his voice, his eyes widening with shock. 'When? I see. Yes . . . yes, I will be there right away.'

Terminating the call, Sebastian stood up and Prince Saud turned to face him.

'Good news?' he enquired, though he knew by the fact that all the colour had drained from Sebastian's face that it had been the opposite.

'No, not good news at all,' he responded bluntly, with a look of stunned confusion. 'It's my wife.'

'Your wife?' The prince remembered that Forbes was married to a remarkably beautiful and charming woman – far too attractive and personable for the likes of him.

'Yes,' Sebastian looked up, incredulous, his beady eyes slowly darkening to match his soul, 'she's been arrested.'

CHAPTER 60

Imogen sat on the orange plastic chair inside the small, windowless and oppressive room and called upon herself to find the strength she needed to keep calm. She kept telling herself over again that the police knew nothing, that whatever they had on her must be circumstantial. She could not go to prison. She *would* not. Seb would take Bryony away from her, make sure she never saw her beloved daughter again. Imogen knew that should the truth come out he would rather see her languish in prison than ever forgive her.

Imogen glanced at the rudimentary white clock on the wall and panicked. Seb would know where she was by now. He would start putting two and two together, would start asking questions. She had to hold it together, lie like a consummate actress. Remember what Calvary had said: stick to the story. Good God, Calvary! It was fair to assume that if they had Imogen in custody, they would have got to her, and maybe even Yasmin too!

Imogen burned with guilt at the thought of her friends being placed in such a precarious situation. She buried her head in her hands, her legs swinging violently back and forth on the chair as adrenalin pulsed frantically through every muscle in her body.

Mickey had betrayed her. He had tricked her into having lunch with him, then grilled her for information before escorting her to the police station.

'Well, come on then, *Detective Inspector*', she had mocked him through her fear as he had helped her into the car, 'I'm assuming you're going to drive. Do I get sirens and everything, the full works?'

Mitch tried to laugh but the sound that came out sounded forced and hollow.

'Imogen,' he'd seized hold of her shoulders, causing her to look up at him in alarm, 'I want to help you, please, let me help you.' Imogen had stared into his teal green eyes, she wanted to hate him for doing the right thing. For always playing by the rules. Only she couldn't. It was who he was; who he'd always been.

'How can you help me?' she had asked him through glassy tears. 'When I can't even help myself?'

*

The door opened and Mitch walked in.

'The time is 3:47 p.m. on Thursday 19th August . . .' he spoke into the tape recorder, his voice low and resigned. 'This is Inspector Mitch McLaren interviewing Mrs Imogen Forbes in the presence of Mr Archibald Parkinson of– '

'It's Theobald, actually,' Parkinson corrected him.

Mitch corrected himself. 'Forgive me, *Theobald* Parkinson, of Parkinson and Reynolds Legal Representation.' He paused for a moment. 'For the benefit of the tape, Mrs Forbes, may I remind you that you are under caution and that you do not have to say anything, but it may harm your defence if you do not mention, when questioned, something which you may later rely on in court, is that understood?'

Imogen looked up at him with her dark almond eyes and nodded.

'For the tape, please, Mrs Forbes,' he said, his chest tight with emotion.

'Sorry, er, yes,' Imogen said, leaning forward closer to the machine.

'Right, well then, let's start, shall we?' he said gently. He didn't care what his boss had said about 'wringing the truth out of her', he would go easy. This was going to be as painful for him as it was for her.

'Mrs Forbes, where were you the night of Friday 31st July from 8:00 p.m. onwards?' He sat back into the grey plastic chair and Imogen wondered if there was any significance behind the fact that his chair was grey and hers was orange. She hoped, like the evidence they had against her, it was purely circumstantial.

She glanced at her solicitor who gave her a reassuring smile.

'I was at my friend Calvary's house,' she replied evenly.

'That being a Mrs Calvary Rothschild of number 11 Cheyne Walk, Chelsea?'

'That's right,' Imogen said.

'You said in your original statement that you were with Mrs Rothschild and another friend.'

Imogen nodded.

'For the tape, please,' Mitch gently reminded her again.

'Yes. Lady Yasmin Belmont-Jones. We'd gone to Calvary's for a cocktail party, you know, a few cosmopolitans and cucumber mojitos, some canapés, that kind of thing.'

Mitch stared at her intently. She was just so beautiful, even when she was lying.

'And at what time did you leave Mrs Rothschild's residence?'

'Oh, I suppose it must've been rather late,' she said, trying hard to sound as casual as possible. 'These evenings can sometimes go on when us ladies get together.'

'Answer the question, please, Mrs Forbes,' Mitch said,

aware that his bosses were looking on from behind the two-way screen.

'About 3:00 a.m.,' she shrugged. 'It was early dawn, the birds had started to sing.'

'But you didn't check your watch?'

'No.'

'And did anyone see you arrive home? A member of your staff perhaps?'

'I don't think so,' Imogen shrugged. 'I don't know. Have you asked them?'

'I am asking *you*, Mrs Forbes,' he pressed her gently. 'Did a member of your staff see what time you might have arrived home?'

Theobald Parkinson cleared his throat and Mitch wondered if this was a deliberate gesture to ensure he kept himself in check.

'Not that I'm aware of,' Imogen replied. *Keep it going,* she told herself, *you're doing great.*

Bryony's face flashed up in Imogen's mind, young and smooth and full of laughter. She could not go to prison.

Suddenly a woman popped her head round the door.

'Gov, a word,' she said.

Mitch was grateful for the distraction.

'For the benefit of the tape, WPC Maggie Barber has just entered the room.'

'There are a hundred reporters outside already,' Barber whispered to him. 'Someone must've tipped them off again about the Forbes case. Sebastian Forbes is going nuts, demanding to see his wife and threatening all sorts. The Commissioner is on his way, and boy, does he sound pissed off – thought I should warn you.'

Mitch sighed deeply and rubbed his temple roughly with his hand.

'Jesus Christ, Maggie, this really is turning into the day from hell.'

Barber nodded sympathetically.

'Forbes is having a major hissy fit, blathering on about a press conference with the Arab prince or something. Anyway, the snouts are having a field day – we've already had all the majors on the phone demanding to know if we've got Imogen Forbes in custody. Innocent or not,' Maggie said gravely, 'I'd hate to be in that woman's Manolos come tomorrow morning.'

Turning back to Imogen with a heavy heart, Mitch resumed his questioning.

'Mrs Forbes, are you familiar with someone by the name of Amandine Lamarque?'

'Yes. Of course. She's a very famous artist. I recently commissioned her to produce a statue of my husband . . . a birthday present.'

He paused for a long moment. 'Mrs Lamarque confirms that as part of her commission, she made casts of your husband's face and hands. Lifelike casts in a human skin-like substance that could, if required, pass as the real thing, fingerprints and all. She's infamous for using this special material by all accounts, isn't that so?'

'Perhaps,' Imogen responded, carefully. 'I know her only as an artist. I'm not too familiar with the substance you mention.'

'Would you say then, that it was coincidence that after having been paid a visit by you, personally thanking her for her work on your husband's statue, that those casts should go missing?'

'Missing?' Imogen feigned surprise. 'I had no idea they were missing,' she said tightly.

'I think we both know that's not entirely true,' Mitch said, feeling the conflict within himself rise. This all felt so wrong. Horribly wrong. He wanted to be making love to her, not sealing her fate and helping to send her to prison.

'Inspector McLaren, may I remind you that it is protocol

not to intimidate a witness,' Parkinson said in his perfectly clipped tones. 'My client has answered your questions most fully and without prompt. She is here of her own free will to help . . .'

'She is here,' Mitch replied quietly, 'because on the night of July 31st, your client, *Mister* Parkinson, did, alongside two accomplices, break into her husband's bank and move the Bluebird diamond – am I right, Imogen? That is right, isn't it?'

'No!' Imogen retaliated. 'That's absurd! You're wrong.'

'And on said night in question,' Mitch continued, 'a one Mr Derrell Richards did stumble upon you and your accomplices after which he suffered a coronary and collapsed at the scene, is that not also right, Mrs Forbes?'

'No!' Imogen said, louder this time, though less convincingly. A vision of Dickie suddenly flashed up in her mind, lying there in that hospital bed, rigged up to a machine that was keeping him alive.

'No! Nooooo!'

Mitch paused for a moment, a rush of self-loathing threatening to choke him. He took a sip of his water in a bid to disguise his anguish.

'May I ask why, Mrs Forbes, if you claim to have been at Mrs Rothschild's house between the hours of 8:00 p.m. and let's say, for argument's sake, 3:00 a.m. the following morning on the night in question, does Mrs Rothschild's neighbour claim to have seen you leave the premises soon after arriving at 8.30 p.m., only to then return some two or so hours later?'

Imogen lit another cigarette, unable to stop her hand from shaking uncontrollably.

'I don't know,' she replied. 'I was there all night like I told you; we all were.'

'Aside from yourself, Mrs Rothschild and Lady Belmont-Jones, who, might I add, conveniently seems to have left the country, no one can vouch for having seen you come or go anywhere that evening. Neither your own nor Calvary Rothschild's respective and combined fleet of hired help saw or heard what time you came or went. I find that rather funny, don't you?'

'Mrs Rothschild's neighbour must be mistaken,' Imogen said flatly.

Mitch sighed ruefully. Imogen was not going down without a fight and this saddened him more than he knew possible. He had ruined her life once before and now he would be complicit in doing it again.

'A coincidence then: three women whose whereabouts is at best ambiguous and three perpetrators of a crime committed on that very same evening their whereabouts is in question.'

'I'd say that's just it; a coincidence,' Imogen said evenly, her confident tone belying the raw terror she felt inside. She looked up at Mitch, her eyes glassy with the tears that were threatening to spill from them and extinguished her cigarette in the small glass ashtray. 'And anyway, how on earth would I have known the codes?' Imogen met his gaze, watching her reflection in his teal green eyes. 'Even if, as you suggest, I had casts of my husband's face and hands to allow access to the vault, how would I have possibly known the code to get down into the vault? My husband changes the code each week. I am many things, Inspector,' she said, 'but I'm not a mind reader.'

Mitch held her gaze. He loved her in that moment, just as he had done the second his eyes had rested upon her that day in the British Library over a decade ago.

'Perhaps you already knew the code,' he suggested, 'even before your husband did.'

Imogen smiled.

'That would be terribly clever of me, don't you think?' she remarked, unblinking.

Mitch nodded.

'Yes,' he conceded. 'It would.'

A soft, sad snort escaped Imogen's glossy lips.

'Anyway, you're forgetting one thing in all of this, Inspector,' she said, meeting his eyes with her own.

'Oh?' He stared at her, forgetting, momentarily, that there were others in the room, others watching them.

'Motive,' she said eventually. 'What possible motive could I have to want to hurt my own husband?'

CHAPTER 61

Outside of the interview room, Sebastian Forbes paced along the narrow corridor.

'Can I bring you something more to drink, Mr Forbes?' WPC Maggie Barber asked, out of kindness more than duty.

'Yes,' Sebastian snapped back rudely. 'You can bring me some proper coffee. None of this instant muck. Tastes like the bloody Thames,' he complained, nodding at the full plastic cup on the small table.

Maggie Barber held her tongue. She had been considering how to help Sebastian Forbes make an escape from the press who had been congregating outside for the past few hours, spare him the indignity of having to face their questions. Now, however, she was of a mind simply to open the doors and feed him to the lions. 'My wife, for goodness' sake!' Sebastian continued to rant. 'Arrested! You don't have any *real* suspects, so you thought you'd persecute my family instead, eh?' He snorted, incredulous. 'I mean, Imogen, of all people. Beautiful she might be, but a criminal mastermind? It's preposterous. The woman struggles to remember what day of the week it is.' Sebastian continued to vent his anger and frustration on the young WPC. 'Well, once the Commissioner hears about this, he'll have your bloody jobs – all of you.'

'Mr Forbes,' Maggie said tightly, 'I appreciate that you're upset but this is a police station, not Starbuc . . .' Suddenly her attention was caught by a commotion going on at the reception desk.

'Miss, I'm afraid you can't go in there . . . Miss!' the desk sergeant cried as the small figure, ignoring his pleas, waltzed right past him down the corridor towards where Maggie Barber and Sebastian Forbes were standing.

As she grew closer, Maggie Barber watched all colour drain from Sebastian Forbes's face.

'Dear God,' she heard him whimper as he stumbled back into the wall, attempting to grab on to it for support as he slid down, his face contorted in horror and disbelief. Maggie immediately rushed to his aid. 'It can't be . . . *It can't be . . .*'

'Something the matter, Sebastian?' the small woman smirked as she breezed past them, nose in the air. 'You look like you've seen a ghost!'

'Mr Forbes!' Maggie said, alarmed, as she watched Sebastian lose consciousness. 'Mr Forbes, are you OK?'

*

Imogen searched Mickey's face as she stood, attempting to communicate with him through her eyes: *Please, Mickey, if there was once anything between us, anything at all, you will stop this and let me go. Please, just let me go.*

Seeing the fear in her eyes made Mitch McLaren want to scream with frustration.

'Imogen, please, sit down,' Mitch said calmly.

She sat back down on the orange plastic chair and looked at him, the ghost of a man she had once loved; a broken man who had lived by his choices, choices that had robbed him of a lifetime of happiness and love. Mickey was dead. And she would mourn him all over again.

'Do you own a necklace? A small silver necklace?' Mitch asked, his voice was gentle, like a baby's breath and she allowed it to envelop her, to remind her of the sound of his voice in her ear as he had made love to her all those years ago.

Imogen resisted the urge to bring her fingers up to her neck, to gently play with the thin strand of silver hidden underneath her light summer scarf. She had kept her promise; she had rarely taken it off since he had given it to her. It had been around her neck on the night of the heist and it seemed ironic somehow, that it would now help seal her fate. 'I have many necklaces,' she replied, her voice a little croaky. Parkinson handed her a plastic cup of water and she smiled, grateful to him.

'One in particular,' he said lightly. 'A thin silver chain with a tiny shell pendant.'

She looked up at him then, her eyes wide and wet with tears and she smiled, a smile so small and sad that he was forced to turn away from her. She knew she had nowhere left to run, and she was tired of all the lies. It was time to come clean.

'Yes,' she sighed, after a long pause, bringing her hand up to the chain around her neck, 'I do . . .' But just as she made to continue, the door to the interview room swung open and through it breezed a small, exquisitely-dressed woman, closely followed by a harassed looking Maggie Barber.

'I'm sorry, gov,' Maggie spluttered, raising her shoulders apologetically, 'she just – '

'I just barged right in, sorry about that,' the woman said, finishing Barber's sentence for her, as all eyes rested upon her.

Imogen let out a scream as she dropped her plastic cup, a look of sheer terror and confusion etched on her beautiful face as water spilled across the table and cascaded down onto her lap in silver ribbons. She did not even feel it as it soaked through her silk dress and onto her skin.

'It's just that I *had* to come, you see,' the woman announced, her loud voice belying her diminutive size, 'when I saw on the news about Imogen's arrest. I had to come and tell you the truth about where she was that night, about who she is protecting and why. You see, she was with me,' the woman explained, matter-of-fact, 'they all were. And I swore them all to secrecy – oh and poppet,' she said, pulling a handkerchief from her quilted Chanel shopper and handing it to Imogen whose eyes were as wide as saucers. She had stopped screaming now and seemed to have gone into a state of shock, 'you're spilling water all down your Marant.'

'I'm sorry,' Mitch McLaren said, shaking his head perplexed, not to mention a little irritated, by the sudden interruption, 'and you are *who* exactly?'

'Oh come now, Mickey,' the woman turned to face him, looking him up and down, indignant. 'Don't tell me you've forgotten?' She flashed him a wounded look. 'The name's Lucas,' she said, raising one very arched, very dark, and perfectly plucked eyebrow, 'Cressida Lucas.'

CHAPTER 62

'Isn't it just the most spectacular view you've ever seen?' Yasmin stood at the edge of the cliff, looking down upon the magnificent Var Valley below, admiring the miniature hamlets dotted in the distance like doll's houses.

'Yes, I suppose you could say it's rather nice,' Jeremy replied, disinterested, as he peeped over the edge of the rock face and flinched.

'Well, I think it's beautiful,' she breathed in deeply, enjoying the cool air as it rushed into her lungs.

'Perhaps you ought to take a step or two back though, darling,' he suggested, 'we're terribly close to the edge here.' Jeremy's vertigo had been playing havoc with him all afternoon; in fact, it had got so bad it had quite ruined his appetite.

'The picnic lunch was divine,' Yasmin said as she began to delve into the large wicker hamper they had brought with them, pulling out a second bottle of Veuve Clicquot.

'Are you sure you want another, darling?' he asked tremulously. 'Remember, one of us has to drive back down that bloody rock face!'

One of us being the operative word, she thought to herself, her head a little hazy from champagne and adrenalin.

'Oh come on, Jeremy, live a little. We're hardly likely to run into any gendarmerie up here,' she said, popping the cork and filling two Tiffany champagne flutes to the brim. Jeremy sighed, acquiescing. Perhaps she was right; he would feel more relaxed with a drop more fizz inside him, he thought, gulping back almost half the glass in one hit.

'Chin chin, darling,' Yasmin said, raising her glass and eyebrow simultaneously. 'Here's to new beginnings.'

'New beginnings?' he enquired, tapping her flute with his own.

'Yes,' she purred. 'Today I am reborn; today I begin my life all over again.'

'I don't think I quite follow you,' Jeremy said, one eye distractedly glancing down at the gorge below them.

'More sashimi?' she asked, placing some onto a fork and bringing it up towards Jeremy's mouth.

'Mmm, very good,' he said, swallowing it greedily. 'You were saying something about being reborn . . .'

Yasmin smiled a wicked smile. 'I've been reading up on a little Buddhism,' she said. 'It really does make a lot of sense.'

'I've always been an eye for an eye man myself,' Jeremy remarked, with a healthy dose of cynicism. 'Though fate has a way of righting the wrongs in life, in my experience.'

'Is that so?' Yasmin smirked. 'My mother always said that we make our own fate in life . . . or maybe it was luck, I can't quite remember which,' she said, an image of her mother suddenly flashing up in her mind. She had once been so beautiful, before the drugs and the drink had taken hold of her, turning her haggard and old before her time.

Jeremy's interest was ignited. His wife rarely ever mentioned her parents.

'You miss your mother?' Jeremy asked, rolling onto his enormous stomach, resting his chins in his hands.

'Yes, I do,' she said wanly, though she had stopped

grieving for her years ago now. The fact was, she had done most of her mourning while she had still been alive. 'But I think I miss my sister more,' she added.

'Your sister?' Jeremy was surprised. 'I never even knew you had a sister.'

'Oh, yes,' Yasmin nodded. 'Did I not mention her before?'

'Well no, you certainly didn't!'

'Oh,' she shrugged. 'Her name is Chloe.'

'A pretty name,' Jeremy said, guzzling back the remains of his glass.

'She's off travelling the world at the moment, saving children in Africa and that sort of thing.' Yasmin liked the way that sounded and wondered, sadly, if indeed Chloe might have gone on to do such laudable things in life, given the chance.

'She's a VSO?' Jeremy asked, shocked that he was only just learning of her existence now.

'Something like that,' she replied. 'She's terribly beautiful and terribly kind and I love her dearly.' Yasmin felt a lump form in the back of her throat as she peered over the edge of the cliff.

Refocusing on the task ahead she purred, 'No one can see us up here,' and pulled her dress up over her head, revealing the fact that she wasn't wearing any underwear. Jeremy's eyes widened from beneath his Ray-Ban aviators and he let out a little whistle.

'I say darling, you really are a sight for sore eyes,' he said, drinking in her perfect form. Just for a moment, Jeremy forgot all about his vertigo.

'I want us to make love, naked, in front of the sunset.'

Jeremy didn't need telling twice as he struggled to wriggle his fleshy body out of his snug golfing shorts.

Yasmin watched him with a mix of pity and contempt as he lay there, naked and exposed, his white, fleshy body incongruous with the warmth and beauty of such surroundings.

Swigging from the champagne bottle, she straddled her husband for what she decided would be the last time, sliding herself down onto him, gently rocking back and forth until he began to moan with pleasure. As she built up her momentum, grinding her pelvis hard down onto him, her generous breasts bouncing up and down, she found herself thinking about Sammie Grainger. Yasmin wondered if she had been as good as her word and had taken good care of the tape for her. She found herself hoping she would see her again soon, her mind whirring with thoughts of her cashmere soft skin and that kiss.

'That's it,' Yasmin whispered under her breath as she felt Jeremy's orgasm building beneath her, 'that's it, you filthy, murdering bastard.'

'What? What are you saying, you naughty girl?' he asked breathlessly, red and sweaty from a few moments exertion. But before she could answer, Jeremy's face contorted into an orgasmic grimace and he let out an almighty groan. Yasmin swallowed back her nausea. She was so close to the final part of her plan now that she could almost reach out and touch it.

Jeremy lay beneath her, arms and legs outstretched like a starfish, his chest wheezing like an old boiler.

'You are *amaaaaazing*,' he said, blowing air through his lips, tiny beads of oily sweat beginning to form on his chubby face.

She climbed off him and pulled her knees up to her chin, wrapping her arms around them in a bid to comfort herself.

'Let's go for a walk,' she suggested after a moment.

Jeremy stifled a groan. It was the only downfall to being married to a young, fit woman. She had so much energy.

'Come on,' she said, dragging him by the arm. 'Just a short one I promise, old man,' she teased. Jeremy groaned, only this time there was nothing orgasmic about it.

'Alright, alright, if you insist,' he relented. 'But at least let me put some shorts on first '

'No!' she cried, 'I shan't!' Snatching up his pile of clothes, she began to make off with them.

'Yasmin!' he shrieked, 'come back here! What are you doing? Give me my clothes back.'

'Come and get them!' she sang, her laugher ringing out across the landscape.

'Bloody hell,' Jeremy muttered, as he proceeded to follow her. Frankly he was not that amused. He had done everything she had asked him to do today; he had agreed to forego the underwear catwalk show to come on this ridiculous trip, had risked his life allowing her to drive up the rock face and now he was chasing her, naked, running like a madman along the edge of a cliff. What he really wanted to do was return to the Château, take a nice long bath and indulge himself in a little five star butler service, not play silly buggers like this.

'Yasmin, I mean it, I want you to stop!' he called out to her, more firmly now, but she had disappeared from view and suddenly Jeremy was worried.

It was rough and craggy at the top of the cliff, great tufts of mountain grass dotted across the landscape between the dips and dells. She was probably hiding behind one of the trees, Jeremy thought, casting his eyes all around him, grateful that she had not taken his shoes with her.

'Yasmin!' Jeremy called out across the landscape, the echo of his own voice suddenly chilling him. Dear God, he hoped she hadn't come to any harm.

'Over here, Jeremy,' a small voice cried out. 'Please, help me, Jeremy, I'm hurt.'

'Jesus bloody Christ,' he wheezed, seized by panic. They were high up on a godforsaken mountain. It was rocky; full of dips and slopes and uneven surfaces. It was bloody treacherous.

'I'm coming, darling, hold on,' he called out to her, turning in the direction where the voice had come.

'I'm down here,' she called out, thinly. 'Over by the tree.'

Icy fingers of panic gripped Jeremy's throat as he made his way over to the large tree overhanging the rock face. Dear God, had she fallen?

'Yasmin, darling, where are you?' Jeremy's voice was desperate with anguish. 'I can't find you.'

'Come closer to the edge,' her voice rang out, 'I'm down here . . . I've fallen, please help me, Jeremy, help me!'

Jeremy gasped as his naked, overweight body lumbered towards the tree. Reaching it, he heaved an audible sigh of relief as he spied his pile of clothes on the ground.

'Oh, thank God,' he panted, stepping into his golfing shorts. Reluctant to look over the edge, he was terrified of what he might find; his wife, lying there, her arms and legs sticking out in all directions like a broken doll. But he knew he had no choice and so he shuffled a little closer.

'Gotcha!' she yelled as she sprung out from behind some bushes, causing him to stumble backwards in alarm.

'Jesus fucking Christ, woman! What on earth are you playing at?' he barked, properly cross with her for the first time since they had met.

'Oh sorry, darling,' she smirked, her voice dripping with sarcasm. 'Did I frighten you? Were you scared for your life?'

Jeremy heard the bitterness in her voice and frowned, angry and confused and, yes, if he was honest with himself, a little scared.

'We're 700ft up, Yasmin, and I have vertigo if you must know,' he snapped back.

'The heart bleeds,' she retorted, her face a mask of contempt.

Jeremy was baffled by the sudden switch in his wife's

behaviour. She was acting as if she hated him or something. *Really* hated him.

'What's got into you, Yasmin?' he enquired. 'Is this because I said *I* want to drive on the way back?'

There was a pause as she met his eye.

'I lied,' she finally said.

'Lied?' Jeremy shrugged, nonplussed.

'About my sister.'

Sister? She had never even mentioned a bloody sister until today.

'I have no idea what you're talking about,' he barked, making to walk past her, only she stepped forward, blocking his path.

Surprised, Jeremy glanced nervously behind him at the drop below.

'Let me pass, Yasmin,' he commanded. He was tiring of this game now and had half a mind to give her a short, sharp slap across the face, shock her into submission.

'You knew my sister,' Yasmin said. 'Her name was Chloe Jones. Jones – like me. Do you remember the name?'

Jeremy shook his head, blindsided. Chloe Jones . . . Chloe Jones . . . Thinking on it, wasn't that the name of the girl who had gone and bloody well died in his swimming pool all those years ago? He had been accused of murdering the poor thing at one point, although this was soon put right once the police realised there was no evidence against him. But if Chloe Jones was Yasmin's sister then who the hell was Yasmin Jones? Jeremy began to panic.

'I remember a Chloe,' Jeremy eventually said weakly, eyes nervously darting towards the cliff's edge and back to her again. Two steps backwards and he knew he would fall to instant death. 'She died in my swimming pool.'

'You mean you *murdered* her in your swimming pool,' Yasmin corrected him, her voice almost sinister in its sweetness.

'No, no, I didn't.' Jeremy shook his head vehemently.

'You and your friends violated and abused her, and then left her to drown in the pool.' Yasmin's heart was knocking against her ribs so hard that it physically hurt. This was it; this was the moment she had worked so hard and sacrificed for, finally confronting her sister's killer with the truth that she hoped would destroy him. 'And then, as her life was ebbing away, you carried on with your filthy, debauched party as if nothing had happened. Did you know that Chloe was a virgin until that night at your house? Untouched by a man,' she added, picturing her sister's young and innocent face from the video footage as all those men had clamoured on top of her, one by one. 'She was pure and lovely and good – and you destroyed it,' she said, barely able to conceal her hatred. 'You and those animals you called friends destroyed it all . . .'

Jeremy's mouth was so dry he had to think about removing his tongue from the roof of his mouth to speak.

'Look, Yasmin, please,' he begged. 'Let's move away from the edge of the cliff and talk about this properly, shall we?' She watched as great beads of sweat trickled down his ruddy cheeks. She could see he was terrified and felt dismay in the knowledge that this did not please her as much as she had hoped it would.

'Are you frightened, Jeremy? Afraid? Well, I hope so, because now you know what it felt like for my sister. An eighteen-year-old, young and innocent with her whole life ahead of her. A life *you* stole, snuffed out like a candle without a second's thought.' Yasmin paused. 'Did you know, I went into care after her death? No, of course you didn't,' she berated herself. 'Why would you? You couldn't have cared less about whether or not Chloe might have a family, people who loved her, who relied on her, she was just another meaningless hooker as far as you were concerned; a piece of meat. But to me she was *everything*.'

'Yasmin,' Jeremy spluttered, mindful of antagonising her.

She was dreadfully upset and suddenly he wasn't sure of what she was capable of. 'Darling please, we can talk about this. Let's just get in the car and drive back to the Château. We'll talk over dinner, smooth all this mess out . . .'

Yasmin let out an incredulous laugh and Jeremy felt his heart sink.

'And my name is *Stacey*,' Yasmin said, lighting herself a pink Sobranie cocktail cigarette and blowing smoke in his direction. 'Stacey Jones. Yasmin Jones doesn't exist. She is a character that I made up. One that I knew would help me to exact my revenge, revenge for Chloe and for all those years I suffered in care as a result of you taking her away from me.' Jeremy flinched, the gravity of the precarious position he found himself in hit him in all its clarity.

'So you planned all this then,' he said, 'to marry me and then destroy me, because you think I am responsible for destroying your life, for your sister's death? An eye for an eye, is that it?'

'I saw the film,' Yasmin said, blowing perfect smoke rings into the air above her.

Jeremy's mind began to race.

'Film?'

'Yes, Jeremy. Footage from the party. It's all there in colour. You and your friends sticking it to my beautiful young sister, her body floating face down in the pool. I saw it all.'

Jeremy wondered if he could make a run for it, barge right past her, but he knew that although tiny, she was young and strong and he was just so overweight and unfit. She would only need to give him a half-decent shove backwards.

'How did you get it? The film, I mean. It was in the strong rooms at Forbes Bank.'

Yasmin gave a sardonic laugh.

‘Where there’s a will, Jeremy.’ She raised an eyebrow. ‘Another good philosophy in life.’

‘I didn’t kill her, I promise you,’ he protested pathetically, the realisation that his marriage was probably over beginning to hit home. ‘She had been given drugs, told that they were harmless – and she drowned. It was an accident. *A tragic accident.* Believe me. I suffered for years afterwards, Yasmin, years I tell you . . .’

Suddenly Jeremy thought about taking those two steps backwards. He wasn’t sure he wanted to live with the knowledge that his wife was not who he had thought she was, and that she had never loved him. The shame would be too much to bear.

‘I was a young man when it happened,’ he said resignedly. ‘I cared about no one and nothing back then. I may not have killed Chloe with my bare hands,’ Jeremy said, ‘but yes, I used her and discarded her and did not care what happened to her, and for that I will be sorry for all eternity. But I didn’t kill her, *I didn’t kill her* . . .’

He saw the look on Yasmin’s face as she approached him and, forgetting himself, instinctively took a couple of steps backwards, losing his footing in the process. Jeremy screamed as he grasped on to a tuft of mountain grass, the only thing that stood between him and assured death.

Instinctively, Yasmin ran to him, dropping to her knees as she grasped hold of both his thick wrists.

‘Hold on!’ she found herself saying. ‘For God’s sake, hold on!’

Jeremy let out a blood-curdling scream.

‘It’s OK, it’s OK,’ she reassured him. ‘Try and get a footing if you can. I will pull you up.’

Yasmin looked down at Jeremy, his face a pathetic display of terror and despair, and cursed herself for the stab of pity she felt in her guts. By rights she could let him fall to his death. That’s what she had wanted all along, wasn’t it?

She could tell the authorities that he had fallen in an accident and gone on to claim his considerable wealth for herself. But now it came down to it, she just couldn't bring herself to let him come to any harm.

Yasmin hooked one of her legs around a tree for support and slowly began to help her husband heave his heavy bulk back up the cliff face.

'You saved me?' a sobbing Jeremy spluttered as she helped him scrabble to the safety of land. 'Why didn't you just let me fall?'

Yasmin sighed, her chest heaving with exertion and adrenalin.

'You forgot another saying,' she said sadly. 'Two wrongs never make a right.'

CHAPTER 63

Dressed in her uniform of Chanel Boucle skirt suit, her Morello Cherry red hair cut into a neat, shiny bob, Cressida Lucas cleared her throat and looked directly into Camera 2.

'Can I have a little more up-lighting for my close-up, Terence, there's a poppet,' she smiled broadly at the DOP. 'I realise I'm back from the dead but I'd rather not look as if I am if it's all the same to you, darling.'

Cressida knew that the interview she was about to give would be watched by millions of people the world over. It was her moment of glory, and, if she played it just right, she knew she had the potential to become an overnight star.

As a way of saying thank you to Sammie for not having exposed her true identity, Yasmin had asked Imogen to introduce her to the inimitable Cressida in a bid to see if the media maven couldn't put a little work her way. As a result, Cressida had insisted that Sammie Grainger was to conduct her interview and Cressida watched as the sound man adjusted the excited-looking young journalist's microphone, carefully prepping her for her first live TV link.

'Ready to go in five, Sammie,' the director said. 'Cressida, are you ready?' he asked as he began to count down. 'Five, four, three . . .'

'As I'll ever be, darling,' she smiled, taking a deep breath. 'As I'll ever be.'

*

Perched on the edge of the Balinese four poster bed inside the master suite that was his bedroom, Sebastian Forbes agitatedly switched on the flat-screen TV. Watching as Cressida Lucas's face flashed up on screen, larger than life itself, he felt physically sick. There could be no mistake; it really was her.

Sebastian had hoped that somehow it had all been a horrible mistake and that the woman who had burst into the police station just happened – unfortunately for her – to simply *look* like Cressida Lucas.

Sebastian felt his blood chill. That insufferable woman had always been his nemesis, lingering in the background of his life like a nasty smell. Now she was back from the dead, like something from a horror film, even if he was reluctantly a little grateful to her for saving his wife's liberty.

'Hello and welcome to *Live at Five*,' Sammie's dulcet tones rang out across the room. 'Tonight we have an exclusive interview with the woman whose sensational story has sent shock waves around the world. The international press have dubbed her, quite simply, "The Survivor", and Hollywood bigwigs are already clamouring for the film rights to this most shocking tale of courage and survival,' Sammie said, expertly addressing the nation with just the right amount of gravitas and spin.

Sebastian grimaced as the camera panned in on Cressida, looking suitably persecuted, her eyes a little watery and doleful.

'Back in June of this year, when the ill-fated Virgin

Atlantic flight VA02367 from London to LAX suffered engine failure and tragically crashed, killing over 300 passengers, it was believed that there had been no survivors until now,' Sammie spoke earnestly into the camera. 'But yesterday, forty-six-year-old former media agent and model scout, Cressida Lucas . . .'

'Forty-six!' Sebastian snorted. 'Yeah, right! And I'm twenty-one!'

. . . Ms. Lucas, of Mayfair, London, presumed dead, suffered temporary memory loss following the minor brain injuries she sustained from the air crash and claims to have no recollection of events from that fateful night. It is believed, however, that she was eventually picked up by Caribbean pirates in the Atlantic Ocean and taken to Bermuda, where she has since been recovering in a private medical spa.'

*

Sammie turned to her, 'Cressida, thank you for agreeing to be on tonight's show. As you can imagine, the world is in shock to learn about your incredible tale of survival. Please, in your own words, can you tell us what you remember, however little, from that ill-fated night?'

'Well, Sammie,' Cressida began, her earnest expression a little too rehearsed for Sebastian's liking, 'the crash itself is somewhat of a blank. The first thing I remember is waking up in a strange bed, not knowing where I was, or indeed *who* I was . . .'

'Ha!' Sebastian smirked, 'and not for the first time in your life, I'm sure, eh, Cressida?'

Sammie turned to the camera and stared into it, her face a picture of sincerity, building just the right amount of tension in the studio.

'Though she cannot recall the events immediately

afterwards, it is believed that Ms Lucas drifted inside a piece of debris from the wreckage for days before she was picked up by pirates and taken some 5,000 kilometres to the remote island of Bermuda where gradually, her memory has slowly returned.' She turned back to Cressida. 'Cressida, it must've been overwhelming when you discovered that you in fact were the sole survivor from that horrendous plane crash.'

'I don't know if overwhelming is a big enough word, Sammie,' she said, 'living with the guilt has been, well . . .' Cressida turned away from the camera, visibly distraught. 'I'm sorry,' she stammered, holding her hand up in front of her face. 'Can I please have a moment?'

'Of course, of course,' Sammie nodded sympathetically. 'I can only imagine just how difficult this must be for you.'

'*Oh, please*!' Seb sneered, wondering if people were actually buying this stuff. It was the biggest crock of shit he'd heard in his whole life.

The truth was, having checked in late and thanks to a long queue in the duty-free Chanel shop, Cressida Lucas had never even boarded the ill-fated LA flight. It was only when she heard about the crash, and the lack of survivors, that the plan to rid herself of her insurmountable debts had popped into her head. As far as the authorities knew, she too had died alongside her poor fellow passengers that night, and so, her body unrecovered, Cressida had been able to slip away, unnoticed, to begin a new life in Bermuda, where she planned to start her life again, one that was free of financial burden. And things were all going rather nicely until Cressida – whose conscience still burned whenever she thought of the terrible lie she had told Imogen – had read about her old friend's predicament in the newspapers. She'd chartered a flight back to London that very same day.

'Take your time,' Sammie leaned forward and touched Cressida's arm reassuringly, 'take your time. Is it true that you only decided to come forward when you saw on the news that your friend and one-time protégée, Mrs Imogen Forbes, had been taken in for questioning regarding the recent robbery at her husband's bank?' Sebastian felt his heartbeat accelerate so fast inside his chest that he thought he might have a coronary.

'Yes, that's right,' Cressida explained, dabbing at the corners of her eyes with a handkerchief. 'Imogen Forbes is a dear friend of mine. She has been my rock throughout all of this, helping me to plan my announcement, to integrate myself back into society and come to terms with what's happened. We had been meeting in secret and so when I heard on the news that she had been taken in for questioning, I had no choice but to bring my announcement forward, explain to the police that she was with *me* on the night of the alleged robbery . . .'

Sebastian's mind wandered back to the journey home following Imogen's release. Their driver, Raoul, had picked them both up from the police station under a siege of paparazzi flashbulbs, Sebastian angrily pushing their intrusive lenses out of the way before they had sped off, tyres screeching as they went, adding to the high drama.

He was beyond furious with the police. How they could have arrested Imogen like that beggared belief. Now he would have to deal with the paparazzi camping on his doorstep round the clock and Imogen would be in the spotlight once more. It was this that bothered Sebastian more than anything, his wife's face splashed all over the newspapers and magazines. Editors would be sharpening their elbows to the ready, see who could get to her first, bag an exclusive with his beautiful, wronged wife who had simply been protecting a friend. Sebastian flinched. He knew how it worked. First came the papers and then came the job offers, big brands wanting to cash in on his wife's newfound popularity. She would become famous again, overnight, and everything Sebastian had planned, all the hard work and effort he had put into keeping her to himself would all have been in vain. It made him want to explode with rage.

Sebastian cursed loudly as he hit the off button on the remote control before throwing it onto the floor in protest. He had seen quite enough.

CHAPTER 64

'You should have told me,' Sebastian said, as Imogen appeared from the en-suite, clutching a pile of summer dresses in the crook of her arm, her hands full of sandals and straw hats. 'You should have told me about Cressida.'

'How could I?' she replied, throwing them all onto the bed. 'I made a promise to her.'

Sebastian grunted.

'So you thought you would drag your own name – our good name through the mud just to save that old hag's skin? Have the world believe that you were somehow involved in a break-in that took place at your own husband's bank, to spare Cressida Lucas's feelings?'

'It's called loyalty, Seb,' Imogen riposted. 'But I wouldn't expect *you* to understand . . .'

She threw the pile of dresses into the Louis Vuitton trunk that lay open on the bed and began sorting through the toiletries on her dressing table.

Sebastian ignored the caustic remark.'How long had you known that she was alive?'

Imogen gave a casual shrug.

'A few months, I suppose; I had no idea she was just

going to turn up like that though,' she said, aware that he was scrutinising her every move.

'The bloody press will have a field day with this, you realise that, don't you? Mud sticks, Imogen,' Sebastian said, exasperated. 'They'll start digging into our pasts, our private lives, you mark my words.'

Imogen continued with her packing, deliberately refraining from making eye-contact with her husband. 'It was really rather reckless of you to go behind my back with this,' he chided her. 'I'll have to take out injunctions and all sorts now, stop the bloody press intrusion, as if I haven't got enough on my plate.' Imogen could hear that he was talking himself into an angry state and was mindful of saying the wrong thing.

'Stuff what the press say, Seb,' she said, holding up a Missoni maxi dress and matching bikini for inspection before throwing them in the trunk. 'It's over now. Cressida is safe and well, and that's all that matters, isn't it?'

Sebastian gave a nasty laugh.

'And taking a holiday isn't going to help matters much either . . . they'll think you're running away.'

'It's just a short break,' Imogen lightly protested, 'let the dust settle a bit. Besides, the press will get tired soon enough. Cressida's the big story now. By the time I come home, we'll be tomorrow's chip paper, as they say.'

'Well, perhaps you're right,' he sighed. 'A bit of distance might not be a bad thing.'

'I'm right, you'll see,' Imogen said, allowing herself a fleeting glance in his direction.

'Well, at least now the police can stop following a dead end and start getting down to the business of sorting out all this mess,' Sebastian said ruefully, his self-pity returning in spades. 'That McLaren had better pull his finger out or this time next week I'll have his job. I'm telling you, the man's been as much use as a back pocket on a shirt.'

'To be fair, he hasn't exactly had much to go on,' Imogen said, unable to stop herself from leaping to his defence.

Sebastian sighed. 'Well, if you and your bloody friends hadn't steered them off track they might've caught the bastards by now.'

Imogen couldn't help but smile to herself.

'Yes, I know. And I'm sorry,' she said. 'I never thought it would come to this.'

Sebastian watched her place the last of her things into the enormous trunk and struggle to shut the lid.

'That's rather a lot of luggage for a few days in Portofino, isn't it?' he remarked. 'Anyone would think you were off on a round the world cruise.'

Imogen gave a breezy smile.

'Well, you know me; I never travel light.'

Sebastian stood. 'I'll come with you to the airport.'

'There's really no need,' she replied quickly.

'I insist,' he replied. 'I'll ask Raoul to get a car ready immediately.'

'Well, if you're sure,' she said, knowing better than to object.

'I'll have Jalena send someone up for your luggage. Someone *strong*,' he remarked sarcastically, casting an eye over her Louis Vuitton trunk.

As she watched him leave, Imogen took a final look around her magnificent bedroom and smiled wistfully before placing a small white envelope on her husband's pillow, partially obscuring it inside the soft goose eiderdown. Imogen hoped that he would not discover it until he retired to bed that evening, by which time, she would be long gone.

*

Staring out of the car window on her journey to the airport, Imogen felt lighter with the knowledge that in a matter of hours she would be a free woman, far away from Sebastian Forbes and their stifling marriage forever. But it was not until she had her daughter by her side that she knew she would be able to fully relax.

Sighing as she gazed out of the window as the last of the King's Road disappeared from view, her thoughts turned to Cressida and despite herself, she could not help but smile.

It had been such an incredible shock to have seen her old friend standing there larger than life inside that police interview room; so unexpected and so very surreal!

She had been unable to fully digest what Cressida had told the police, having been too paralysed in shock to absorb the words that had come from her lipstick red mouth. But whatever Cressida had said, before she knew what was happening, she was being released.

Later that evening, joined by Calvary, Imogen had waited for Cressida to arrive for a celebratory dinner at Daphne's, Cressida's favourite restaurant.

'Well, I'll say this for the woman, her timing was impeccable,' Calvary had said, tucking into the chilled bottle of Cristal. 'I don't think I could've spent another moment in that awful police station, really I don't.'

'I'm so sorry, Cal.' Imogen had reached for her friend's delicate hand. 'I'm sorry I put you through this – all of it. I should never have . . .'

'Enough, darling,' Calvary had interrupted, her own guilt resurfacing. She had not told Imogen of her own motives from that fateful evening. Some things, she decided, were best left unsaid. 'It's over now. Finished. We can put it all behind us and start getting on with our lives. I for one intend to. Just as soon as this frightful wedding is over.'

Imogen stared into her champagne flute, chewing her bottom lip.

'I need to tell you something, Cal. I won't be there, at the wedding, I mean. I'm sorry.'

Calvary audibly exhaled.

'Well, not to worry, darling,' she sighed. 'Anyway, I'm sure you'll be able to watch it on YouTube – as that's where I'm afraid it will end up.' She was only half-joking.

'I'm leaving, Cal. On a plane. Today.'

'Somewhere hot and fabulous, I hope. Well,' she sighed. 'I can't say that I blame you after everything that's happened. A holiday will do you the power of goo . . .'

'Not a holiday, Cal.' Imogen had leaned in closer to her friend and whispered. 'I'm leaving, for good.'

Calvary had almost dropped her glass in shock.

'Leaving? For good? But where . . . where will you go?' Her stomach fluttered with the onset of panic. Imogen was her greatest friend. The thought of losing her forever was too big a blow for Calvary to contend with.

'I will let you know when I get there,' Imogen said, tears suddenly visible in her eyes. She seized her friend's hand once more. 'You know I love you, you've always been like a big sister to me, Cal.'

'Less of the big,' Calvary had laughed, holding back tears of her own.

The heat was rising on the concourse at the private airfield, making the air above the tarmac rippled and hazy.

'Well, this is me,' Imogen said, turning to Sebastian who was busy admiring the Gulfstream – his pride and joy – from a distance. 'I'll call you when I arrive at the house,' she smiled, squinting at him in the harsh glare of the sun.

She stared at Sebastian, the g-force from the jet engine causing his shirt to stick to his arms and his neat hair to flap in the wind.

'Have a good trip,' he said, suddenly feeling a rare moment of regret and shame for all he had done to her. In spite of everything, he loved her. He always had. He decided that when she was back he would run that idea he'd had of them renewing their marriage vows by her.

Sebastian embraced Imogen, allowing himself to fleetingly enjoy the warmth of her skin against his own. She smelled fresh and clean, like a bouquet of flowers and he was suddenly struck by the terrible thought that he might never see her again. Sebastian released her from his arms abruptly. He was getting all maudlin, quite unlike himself. She was only going away for a few days to their house in Portofino, for goodness' sakes.

The private butler stood, welcoming, at the doorway to the plane and Sebastian watched as his wife gracefully took the stairs, the natural curve of her slim body as she walked a pleasure to the eye. As she reached the top she turned to him, her long dark hair whipping up around her face.

'Goodbye Seb,' she called out to him. 'I wish things could've been different between us – and I'm sorry. It was never meant to end like this.'

Sebastian smiled. She had said something but he couldn't hear her, the noise from the engine was too loud.

'See you in a few days' time,' he called out to her, waving.

*

The inside of the Gulfstream was the height of decadence. Its ultra-luxurious retro chic combined with the latest state of the art technology smacked of a potent combination of sex and danger – it was the ultimate boy's toy. Whenever Imogen had ridden in it, she had half expected a man in a white suit with a fluffy cat under one arm to appear at any given moment.

'Can I fix you something to drink, Mrs Forbes?' the butler asked, bowing obligingly.

'A dirty martini would be absolutely lovely,' she smiled up at him. After all, why shouldn't she celebrate?

'The captain has instructed me to let you know that we will be preparing for take-off in five minutes,' the butler informed her.

'Perfect,' she smiled, 'only I wonder if you could send a message to him, let him know that our destination has changed and that instead of flying out to Genoa we will be landing in Eivissa.'

'Very well, Mrs Forbes,' the butler said, nodding graciously. 'I will inform him right away.'

Imogen watched from the window of the plane, feeling the tension in her body gradually ease as Sebastian returned to the limousine and began to drive from the concourse. She would start over again in a different place, somewhere no one knew who she was.

Imogen appreciated the warming sensation of the alcohol as it hit her belly and softened the edges of her thoughts. Once she had settled in her destination, she would call Calvary and let her know that she was safe. She knew it would be a long time before she saw her friends again and the thought made her curse her husband once more. The source of all her pain could be traced back to him, every time.

Sipping her martini, Imogen's thoughts inevitably turned to Mickey. She saw his face as he had watched her leave the police station, a mask of sadness and regret. Were they cursed, she wondered. Her mother had always told her that 'what is for you won't go past you,' and yet Mickey had, twice. But somehow Imogen could not believe that it was not meant to be. The love she had felt for him had never left her heart; from the day they had met it had pulsed like a vein under her skin.

Imogen let her head flop back against the cool leather seat and raised her glass in the air as she felt the jet begin its ascent.

'Here's to freedom,' she whispered softly to herself, watching as the UK gradually disappeared from view.

'To freedom,' a familiar voice said from behind her.

Startled, Imogen's heartbeat accelerated inside her chest as she swung round.

'Mickey!'

'Well,' he said, his warm smile telling her she had nothing to fear as he took the glass from her hand and brought his lips close to her own, 'you didn't really think I was going to let you go without saying goodbye this time, did you?'

'How . . . how did you know I was leaving?' she stammered in shock as his lips met her own.

'A lucky guess,' he replied, his eyes searching her own.

Imogen smiled. He was the only man ever to have understood her, to know her better than she knew herself. It was as if he had been born this way.

'Freedom,' she said, her voice cracking with emotion as she took her glass and tapped the edge of his.

It made a perfect sound.

CHAPTER 65

Tamara Du Bois admired herself in the ornate full-length mirror of her dressing room and sighed happily. Life would struggle to get any better than this, she thought, twisting and turning her body, enjoying herself from every angle. She couldn't wait for Henry to clap eyes on her as she strutted down the aisle in her wedding dress, an exquisite and expensive Temperley strapless gown, embellished with thousands of tiny beads, uncut diamonds and hand sewn crystals. As she moved, it dazzled and simmered, highlighting her generous curves, her breasts spilling out over the top like a pair of peach cream puffs. She looked every inch the fabulous, rich, society bride-to-be.

'Oh, darling,' Alexis Du Bois, mother of the bride, cooed breathlessly, covering her mouth with a gloved hand and feeling the tears welling up behind her eyes, 'you look . . . you look like an angel.' She dabbed at her eyes with a Hermès handkerchief and stood back to admire her daughter as though she were a rare piece of art.

'Don't I just,' Tamara remarked without a hint of modesty as she continued to preen herself in the mirror, slapping her personal dresser's hand away as she made to straighten an imperfection that wasn't there.

'Where's my bouquet?' She turned to her long-suffering wedding planner, Eliza. 'The flowers should be here by now,' she barked. 'Find out where the hell they have got to.'

'They'll be here,' Eliza nodded her reassurance.

'Now!' Tamara added, without taking her eyes from herself in the mirror.

Eliza Fairbrother gritted her teeth and smiled obligingly. She had come across some serious Bridezillas but Tamara Du Bois trumped the lot of them.

Tamara eagerly rubbed her glossy lips together and took one last look at herself in the mirror. This was her big moment and she was determined to make the entrance of a lifetime. Having already slept with half the male congregation, she wanted to make sure that every single one of them took one look at her and wished that they had 'put a ring on it' when they had had the chance.

Tamara secretly congratulated herself; she had done well to get this far, especially in light of what her soon to be mother-in-law knew had gone on between herself and Douglas. But none of that mattered now. Calvary Rothschild could drop dead for all she cared. She was marrying her precious son and there was nothing she, or anyone else, could do about it. 'Poor Calvary,' Tamara had said to Douglas one afternoon in his office as he pumped away at her from behind. 'She's beside herself about this wedding, you know.'

'Fuck Calvary,' Douglas had chortled, as he flipped her over, pulling her down on top of him. 'Just fuck me!'

Yes, she decided, smiling wickedly to herself, she was going to enjoy married life very much. Very much indeed.

*

It was a beautiful day for a wedding, even Calvary had to admit as much. The sun was high in a cloudless, pastel blue

August sky. The perfect light for photographs, she surmised, her years spent on-location at fashion shoots giving her an eye for such things.

Today, over 250 prominent guests would all congregate together for what the society rags had dubbed the 'Wedding of the Summer'.

Hello! magazine were already setting up shop in a prime location just outside of Blenheim Palace in a bid to secure some superb shots befitting of the six-page spread that Calvary had secured. Little did they know that they would be getting a far juicier exclusive than they had anticipated.

Calvary and Henry for that matter knew that what was about to take place today would be the talk of society for years to come. But they had decided that a little humiliation on their part would be worth it. Today would be *their* day. A day of redemption for both mother and son.

Calvary watched as Douglas began to ingratiate himself among the guests who had begun to congregate outside Blenheim Palace, the sound of laughter and chat filtering through her thoughts. She saw him make a beeline towards a group of young, attractive women – obviously friends of Tamara's by their attire, or lack of it. He would never change, Calvary thought pityingly as she observed him from a distance. He'll be chasing skirt until he takes his last breath.

'Looking divine, Calvary,' Verite, the Countess Ledbury, said snidely, sidling up towards her from behind and interrupting her thoughts.

'Love the Chanel, darling. Very . . . Bianca Jagger circa Studio 54. I've heard it really was *the* era to be seen, is that true?' she smirked.

Calvary slowly turned to face her.

'Well, hellooo, darling,' she said, air-kissing the vile countess.

'Can I get you some champagne and kirsch?' she asked, swiping a couple of glasses from a liveried waiter.

'Bottoms up,' Verite smirked as they chinked glasses. 'Mmmm, Dom Perignon?' She pulled a face. 'I prefer a nice vintage Roederer myself. I find the Perignon leaves rather a bitter aftertaste.'

'Much like an encounter with your good self,' Calvary retorted. 'Do excuse me,' she said, 'there's something I have to do.' She stalked off, leaving the stunned countess open-mouthed in her wake.

Slipping away from the wedding party as it slowly filtered inside the magnificent palace, Calvary spied who she was looking for – a little man ferreting around behind the scenes with the screen projector, loading the various slides of images that Tamara had insisted on having projected onto a huge white backdrop behind them while she and Henry said their vows. Looking around her, she approached him surreptitiously.

'I'm Calvary Rothschild, the groom's mother,' she introduced herself, smiling affably at him from beneath her magnificent cream Philip Treacy floral and feather fascinator. 'I wonder if I could have a quick word . . .'

*

'Calvary,' Nikolas Mystern, took her hand in his and enveloped her in a warm bear hug. 'You look marvellous,' he said, standing back to survey her. 'Your father would be so proud of you – and his grandson – if only he were here today.'

'Oh, if only, Nikolas,' Calvary said, enjoying the fleeting comfort of the older man's embrace. 'So glad you could make it,' she warmly smiled up at him. 'And the family?'

'Ah yes, the wife's here somewhere,' he guffawed, 'no doubt gossiping somewhere. Perfect day for a wedding though, don't you think?' He gave her no time to answer him. 'Tell me, how are you, Calvary? How are you *really*?'

'I'm good, Nikolas, really good – and you?'

Unconvinced, Nikolas nodded.

'Look, I realise now is not the time, Calvary,' he said, his voice suddenly low and conspiratorial, 'but I wanted to have a little word about that thing we discussed the last time we met; the missing money,' he whispered. 'Thing is, thanks to your tip-off, I think I've located it.'

Calvary's spirits rose along with her eyebrows.

'You do?'

Nikolas nodded.

'Come and see me after the wedding. I'll have my PA make time for you whenever. We'll talk then.'

'That's wonderful,' Calvary beamed, suddenly distracted by a familiar face seated right at the back of the congregation. 'Please, Nikolas, do excuse me,' she said as she walked towards it, her heart thumping so loudly in her chest that she was convinced it could be heard above the harpist.

'Josia,' Calvary said, the familiarity of his face lighting up her insides. She realised then, in that moment, that she had never loved anyone in the way that she loved him. 'What are you doing here?' she asked. 'I thought I told you not to come.'

Josia smiled up at her, his handsome features filled with earnest. He was wearing a suit and she could not help but notice how devastatingly attractive he looked. The whiteness of his shirt offsetting his natural olive-skinned tan, his lean muscular body lending itself perfectly to the slim, sharp cut of the three buttoned jacket and tailored trousers.

Calvary wondered if it was designer – and then realised that she didn't care if he'd found it in a bin bag; he looked smart and sophisticated regardless.

'And miss your big day? Never.' He smiled at her, lightly taking her hand in his own. 'You look wonderful, Calvary,' he said. 'Beautiful.'

'So do you,' she shot back a little faster than she would've liked.

'More handsome than Johnny Depp?' he squinted back at her.

'Don't push it,' she replied, smiling.

'I'll be here,' he said, adding, 'if you need me.'

She wanted to tell him that yes!, she did need him. She needed him more than ever right now. But she sensed he knew that already. His presence alone told her as much.

*

As the opening notes to Wagner's 'Here Comes the Bride' began to play, Calvary Rothschild stood between her youngest son and her husband and watched as Tamara Du Bois made her way down the aisle arm in arm with her smug father until she met with a nervous-looking Henry in the middle. The guests gasped as she came into view, just as Tamara had hoped they would, and Calvary turned to her son.

'It's OK, Mums,' Henry had mouthed to her with a wink, sensing her sudden attack of nerves. 'It's going to be just fine.'

'Dearly beloved, we are gathered here in the sight of God . . .'

As the sermon began, Calvary watched on tenterhooks, her breathing shallow, as the tasteful black and white images of Tamara and Henry began to flash up on the giant projector screen behind him, photographs of the two of them together, taken during the duration of their courtship; Tamara, smiling with a group of girlfriends, holding a cocktail glass up towards the camera; a shot of her and Henry kissing at a party, seemingly oblivious to the world around them, their faces covered in a light oily sheen from dancing, their bodies close; one of them on board a yacht, Tamara pulling a pose in her bikini and sarong, a picture of exuberant youth, young and beautiful without a care in the world . . .

'Henry Douglas Rothschild,' the vicar said in his dulcet, soothing tones, 'will you have Tamara Alicia Du Bois to be your wedded wife, to live together after God's ordinance in the holy estate of matrimony . . .'

Another shot of them on a beach, semi-clad, Henry's silky flaxen hair, reminiscent of Calvary's own father, knotted by sand and saltwater and Tamara in a colourful kaftan, her arms linked around his neck, her legs wrapped around his waist . . .

'Will you love her, comfort her, honour her, and keep her in sickness and in health, and forsaking all others, keep yourself only unto her, so long as you both shall live?'

Another shot of Tamara, her face a grotesque grimace of pleasure, naked, her legs open, her private area on display for all to see, and Douglas in the foreground, naked from the waist down on top of her, about to mount her . . .

Calvary heard the first rumblings of unrest among the congregation. 'What's going on?' she heard someone whisper. 'Did you just see that! On the screen – there!'

Another grainy image of Tamara, naked and on all fours, with Douglas knelt behind her, his hands cupping her ample breasts, his face a contorted mask of ecstasy, a champagne bottle . . .

Oblivious to the gasps and shocked screams that had now begun to filter through the air around them, Calvary watched the confused expression on the guests' faces as the grotesque images flashed above them.

Henry turned to look at Tamara. 'No,' he said, his clipped voice projecting clearly throughout the magnificent building as he addressed the congregation. 'I'm afraid I don't. You see, my fiancée, my intended here, has been, how shall I put it without causing too much offence? Forgive me,' he turned to the reverend, 'fucking my own father.'

Tamara glared at Henry and then up at the screen behind

her, and gasped before letting out a blood-curdling scream that echoed around the perfect acoustics.

As the congregation glanced at each other in shock and confusion, some admittedly enjoying the sense of drama, Calvary turned to Douglas; his mouth was slightly open, a look of utter shock frozen on his handsome features as people began to look over at him and point disdainfully.

'What's the matter, Douglas?' Calvary smirked. 'Cat got your tongue?'

The music stopped then and Calvary watched as the hapless reverend made a fruitless attempt at restoring some order.

'Please, if we could all just calm down . . .'

'You bloody bastard, Rothschild!' Calvary heard a voice approaching. Arthur Du Bois was marching towards them, his face as angry and red as a balloon about to burst. 'I'll bloody kill you for this,' he spat, taking a swing at Douglas and catching him square on the jaw, almost knocking him to the floor. Quickly regaining his balance, Douglas made to return the gesture but a male member of the congregation restrained him.

'Don't you think you've already done enough?' he hissed, holding him back.

As Calvary stood back from her husband, disowning him with each step, she saw Tamara coming towards her, her young and pretty face now contorted in blind rage, her couture gown hitched halfway up her thighs as she ran.

'*You*,' Tamara hissed, baring her teeth, her eyes like slits, 'you twisted, evil bloody bitch! You planned all this, to humiliate me!' She lunged at Calvary as the crowd gasped in shock.

'Well, you always said you wanted a day to *remember*, Tamara,' Calvary remarked dryly.

'I'll . . . I'll kill you!' Tamara screamed, launching herself at Calvary with some force. Guests looked on in horror as the two women began to fight.

'You've no one but yourself to blame, you filthy little slut!' Calvary screamed as she slapped Tamara hard across the cheek, pulling her veil clean off her head. The women wrestled on the floor for a few moments, twisting and rolling as onlookers stood, hands over their mouths, unable to look away. It certainly beat the usual boring sermon, that was for sure.

Henry ran towards his mother as various guests began to help her up on her feet. His eyes turned a flint grey as they fixed Tamara with a look of such contempt that some of the onlookers actually gasped.

'How dare you touch my mother!' Henry roared at her.

'More like how dare she touch his father!' a female guest quietly deadpanned to a woman standing next to her. 'Quite,' she replied from the side of her mouth, one eyebrow firmly raised.

'Get out of my sight,' he spat, shaking his head. 'I never want to see you again. My own *father* . . .'

Tamara began to sob uncontrollably.

'Oh please, Hen. *Please.* I'm so sorry. You have to forgive me. I was drunk; he told me he'd stop the wedding from going ahead if I didn't . . . he made me do it . . . he forced himself on me . . .'

Henry looked down at her with a bilious mix of pity and disgust and shook his head. His mother had been right about her all along.

Nursing a swollen eye, Douglas, having heard Tamara's little speech, felt obliged to chip in.

'Forced myself on you? Don't be ridiculous! You couldn't get enough of me, you little slut. Look, Henry,' Douglas turned to his son, with an air of arrogance that was breathtaking, even by his usual standards, 'I'm sure we can sort all this mess out.'

Even now, thought Calvary, as she recovered on a nearby pew, comforted by guests, Douglas seemed unperturbed by the enormity of the situation. He didn't even have the grace to look suitably ashamed in front of all these people. 'Let's step away from the crowd for a minute and have a man-to-man chat, what do you say?' Douglas said. He made to put an arm around his eldest son's shoulder but Henry shoved it away. 'I have nothing to say to you,' he said, his voice calm and even. 'Except that you are no longer my father.'

'Now, Henry, don't be silly . . .' Douglas implored; he was growing a little cross now. 'She's just a little tart, that's all,' he called out to him as Henry turned away, 'it was a few moments of weakness . . . she was offering herself to me on a plate. I mean, what's a man supposed to do? There'll be other women, son. Better women,' Douglas implored. 'Women who won't lie back for their prospective father-in-law . . .'

The last sound Douglas heard before he blacked out was that of his own jaw breaking. And the last thing he saw as his son felled him with one punch was Calvary's smug face smiling triumphantly down at him.

Clearing her throat, Calvary addressed the stunned congregation with her unconscious husband at her feet.

'Do feel free to continue with the celebrations,' she smiled obligingly, as if all this was perfectly normal. 'There's champagne and amuse bouche followed by a wonderful four course wedding breakfast, for which I hope you'll all stay and enjoy.' Guests blinked back at her, stunned into silence. 'Please,' Calvary smiled sagely as she stepped over her husband, head high as she took Josia's outstretched hand, waiting to escort her from the palace, 'knock yourselves out.'

CHAPTER 66

It had been another trying day, Sebastian thought as he brushed his teeth vigorously in the mirror of his private bathroom, examining the deep lines around his eyes that he was sure had not been there this time last week.

The press were proving to be even more intrusive and persistent than he had envisaged, camping outside his front door, demanding to speak to Imogen and hassling him relentlessly for quotes. He knew he would have to speak to them eventually, before the unscrupulous bastards began making things up in the absence of anything tangible, but the truth was, he wasn't entirely sure what to say that would help drag his sullied reputation out of all this mess. He would have to hire the best troubleshooter he could find, see if he couldn't buy his way out of the doldrums with a PR offensive of epic proportions. He would have to hope the lawsuit he planned to file against the Met for wrongful arrest of his wife would help him to recoup the mounting cost of it all.

Still, it would be money well spent if it meant buying his way back into public and professional favour. Then he would talk to the press, give them the full exclusive of how he had been 'set up' by someone intent on destroying his good name and reputation.

Sneering, Sebastian pulled back the goose eiderdown from his bed and slid his body beneath its coolness. The sheets still contained the lightest scent of Imogen's perfume and he breathed deeply, enjoying the residue of her. At least she was out of the way of all this media attention. Even with the pendulum swinging against him, there was still a part of Sebastian that couldn't help but enjoy being the one in the spotlight, even if it was not entirely how he had planned it.

Rolling over onto the pillow, he felt something brush against his skin and, sitting up, noticed a small white envelope next to him. He instantly recognised his wife's familiar handwriting. Aw, she must have left him a note, on his pillow. How terribly sweet, he thought as he tore it open, the smile on his face instantly dissolving as he read.

'Jesus Christ!' he whispered. 'I will kill her,' he said as the note slipped from his grasp. '*I will kill her.*'

*

Detective Chief Superintendent George Mullins sighed wearily and looked over at the sorry-looking man in front of him with heavy eyes. Sebastian Forbes was proving to be an even bigger pain in the rear than he could have envisaged.

'Mr Forbes,' Mullins said, standing, unable to mask the light sarcasm in his tone, 'twice in as many days, I *am* honoured.' He proffered his hand but Sebastian ignored it, preferring instead to slam a piece of paper down onto his desk with such momentum that it caused the pile of paperwork upon it to flutter.

'Don't patronise me, Mullins,' Sebastian barked at him. 'The Commissioner will have your job for this!' he boomed, shaking with rage.

George Mullins rolled his eyes. He had heard it all before. The obnoxious Forbes had been threatening to have him and the entire Metropolitan Police force sacked these past few weeks and quite frankly, he wished he'd shit or get off the pot, as they said.

'Mr Forbes,' Mullins forced an affable smile. 'I can assure you we are doing all we can on this investigation, but as you yourself know, we have come to a bit of a moot point, especially now that your wife . . .'

'Read it,' Sebastian said, jabbing at the note on his desk, casting a disdainful eye over the small piece of lilac paper as if it were his death warrant.

Mullins sighed heavily again and, picking up the piece of paper, read aloud the three-word handwritten scrawl it contained: '*Unlucky for some.*' He paused and shrugged, 'Unlucky for some . . . ?' he repeated, shaking his head, bemused. 'I'm sorry. Is this supposed to mean something?'

Sebastian began to laugh then, a nasty, malevolent chuckle that made Mullins feel uneasy. He leaned in close towards the superintendent, placing his hands on his coffee cup-stained plastic desk and Mullins was surprised to detect the scent of whisky on Forbes's breath. He'd never had him down as a drinker.

'The number thirteen,' Sebastian explained slowly, 'unlucky for some . . . unlucky for me more like, the conniving fucking bitch,' he spat. 'I want her found, Mullins, do you understand? Found!' he roared, 'and if you and your bunch of keystone coppers aren't up to the job then Lord help me, I'll find her myself, and when I do, I will KILL her, do you hear me, Mullins? I will kill the treacherous, vengeful bitch with my own bare hands.' Sebastian was so incensed that even his hair looked angry, standing up on end as it was, his face a blood red, purple veins throbbing in his neck like dark rivers of poison.

'Now, Mr Forbes – Sebastian – if you could just calm down and explain . . . you say, *her*?' Mullins continued to shake his head in weary confusion.

'Yes. *Her.*' Sebastian spat the word from his mouth as though it were poison. 'That bitch I'm married to – *my wife.*'

'Forgive me,' Mullins apologised, unable to help himself from experiencing a slither of satisfaction from Forbes's obvious distress, 'but I'm not sure I quite follow.'

'Do I need to spell it out?' Sebastian bellowed, his eyes straining from their sockets as he poked at the piece of paper once more. 'It's there, man, in black and bloody white, as good as a confession. Thirteen, thirteen – that was the code I used for the vault, I changed the code to "one three, one three"!'

Mullins blinked at him, nonplussed. The man was drunk, or crazy, or both.

'Don't you see?' Sebastian was so incensed he thought he might self-combust. 'The only person who could've possibly known the code I used that night was the perpetrator . . . and do you know *how* they knew?' Sebastian was fitting the jigsaw together, piece by piece in his mind. 'Because *she* was the one who gave it to *me. Lucky for some*, that's what she said to me that morning of the robbery . . . *lucky for some.*' He was ranting now, his eyes bulging manically from their sockets as he marched the length of Mullins' office like a drill sergeant.

'I didn't believe it at first, couldn't believe it . . . Imogen, the mastermind behind such a clever, carefully considered plan?' Sebastian shook his head and gave an absurd laugh. 'But it was her . . . it was her all along,' he snorted, utterly incredulous. 'That bloody bitch outsmarted all of us.'

Mullins emitted a heavy sigh.

'Mr Forbes,' he offered cautiously. 'Your wife has been exonerated from any wrongdoing; she has a watertight alibi for the night in question, remember?

'I realise this must be a difficult time for you,' he said, his voice softening, 'but I really think that perhaps you ought to go home and get some rest . . .'

'Rest?' Sebastian shot back, testily. 'How can I rest when she's out there, taken my daughter with her and absconded.' He caught the look of interest on Mullins' face. 'Oh, did I not mention?' he added, sarcasm dripping from his words, 'my *darling* wife flew out to Genoa yesterday, supposedly to stay in our villa in Portofino for a few days. Only it seems she never actually arrived and, miraculously, the crew that took her there seem to have – poof!' he clapped his hands together, 'disappeared into thin air – the bitch has paid them off to keep silent, with my own money! So – what do you think of that, eh? The actions of an innocent woman?'

Mullins poured a generous shot of whisky into a used glass on his desk and handed it to Forbes who downed it in one, and held it out again for a refill. It was obvious that Forbes's wife had left him, done a bunk with the kid and, frankly, Mullins could hardly blame the woman. Still, he did have a little empathy for the man.

'You know she never loved me,' Sebastian said, his thoughts turning maudlin with the aid of the whisky. 'Right from the day we met, it was never me.'

Mullins cast him a weary look.

'I'm sorry to hear that, Mr Forbes, truly. I hope the pair of you can patch things up. But I do have some good news that might cheer you up; you'll be pleased to know that Derrell Richards – Dickie – has regained consciousness,' Mullins announced cheerfully, steering the conversation in a more positive direction.

Sebastian looked up.

'Well? And?' He blinked expectantly.

'And,' Mullins said, 'he can't remember much at all at the moment . . . but he's going to be alright.'

Sebastian rolled his eyes and smacked his hand on his thigh.

'Well, that's just fantastic!' he deadpanned. 'Bloody

fantastic. My life is in tatters; my wife, my stupid, airhead, ungrateful bitch of a wife who would struggle to break into song, let alone the most secure bank in the world, has fucked me good and proper and our star witness can't remember a damn thing!'

'Give the man a few days at least . . . a chance to recover his faculties.' Mullins was shocked by such a brazen lack of compassion.

'He's no better off to me alive than he would be dead,' Sebastian snapped.

Mullins felt his earlier sympathy evaporate. There was just no helping some people. 'I think it might be time to go home now, Mr Forbes,' he lightly suggested. 'I'll have Maggie organise a car to take you.'

'A car!' Sebastian slurred. 'I don't need a bloody car! I've got a whole fleet of the damn things. What I *need* is for *you* to find Imogen. Find her and bring her back to the UK to face justice.'

Mullins buzzed his intercom and moments later, Maggie Barber appeared.

'You're all fools!' Sebastian slurred as Maggie began ushering him from the room.

'Yes, yes, fools.' Mullins rolled his eyes in Maggie's direction. 'Good evening, Mr Forbes. Get some rest. We'll be in touch.'

Sebastian was still ranting as the door finally closed behind him.

CHAPTER 67

Dawn was breaking in Ibiza as Imogen walked towards the tiny speedboat that was moored on the rocks of the private bay of Salinas beach, and she stood for a moment absorbing the sheer beauty of the spectacular view before her.

The last time she had stood in this very same spot, they had admired it together, just the two of them, young and happy and carefree, neither of them knowing the tragic turn of events that lay around the corner, waiting to tear them apart. And now they were here again. Together at last.

'I never thought I would see this place again, it's just so . . . so beautiful,' she breathed, looking out onto the horizon, at the magnificent, imposing villa in the distance. Cressida had helped arrange it for her to make her escape, just as she had done all those years ago. 'Anywhere in the world you want to go, darling, just name it.'

He pulled her close to him and it was there again, the scent of lemon soap on his lightly tanned skin as he took her in his arms, the feeling of everything being right with the world once more.

Imogen had been shocked to see Mickey on the plane. Shock that was closely followed by panic.

'Are you here to arrest me again?' she had asked tremulously.

Mickey had smiled softly as he took her hand in his.

'You thought I would ever let you leave without saying goodbye?'

Imogen smiled as he took her hand and helped her onto the boat. She had confessed everything on that plane journey; told him all about her sham of a marriage to Seb, of his treachery towards her and her subsequent revenge.

It had been a relief to purge herself. Deep down, Imogen knew that no matter how far, or wherever she might run to in the world, she would never be free of her conscience.

'So, you're not here to cuff me then, take me back to the UK?' she had asked shakily, only half joking.

He had shook his head and smiled softly.

'So why *are* you here, Mickey? Why the sudden change of heart?'

He had looked up at her then, his teal eyes glassy and wet. 'I came to tell you that Dickie Richards will make a full recovery.' He watched as her face broke into a relieved smile. 'Oh, and because I love you, Imogen Lennard,' he said. 'I always have.'

He had kissed her again, deeply this time.

'You know, I only lied to protect my daughter,' she'd said, unable to fight back the tears that were threatening to come, '. . . our daughter.'

He had pulled back from her then and she had watched the expression on his face change as her words sunk in.

'*Our* daughter?'

'Please forgive me,' she had begged him, stroking his face with the back of her hand. She was crying now, hot salty tears streaking her face. 'All those years ago . . . I thought about trying to find you, but you had chosen your life . . .' Her voice trailed off. 'You know, I wasn't sure at first, at least, not until she was born . . .' Instinctively he wiped her tears away. 'Oh Mickey, from the very first moment I held her in my arms, I knew she belonged to you,' Imogen's voice cracked like the embers of a bonfire. 'You have no idea what it's been like to live with such a secret all these years . . . watching her grow, seeing your face staring back at me every time she smiles . . . say you forgive me. . . forgive me.'

'Shhh, it's OK, it's OK.' He had put his arms around her, his warmth and strength at once reassuring her. 'I should never have left you, never. It was the biggest mistake of my life . . . it is *you* who should forgive *me*,' he said, wishing he could erase the pain of the last fifteen years. '*Forgive me*,' he whispered into her neck as he held her tightly, knowing he would not let her go.

*

From the beach, Imogen looked up at the magnificent villa and waved to her daughter, beckoning to her as she came into view from the balcony.

'Don't be nervous.' She turned to him, taking his shaking hand in her own as they watched Bryony skip down the imposing white steps towards them. Dressed in a light floral summer playsuit, her soft dark hair loosely plaited to one side, she was the image of her mother as she had been at her age, only with her father's eyes, those deep, lagoon green eyes that seemed to draw you right into them. She cocked her head coquettishly to the side as she reached them, one coltish leg crossed awkwardly over the other.

'Hello,' she said, smiling nervously, her hand outstretched in greeting. 'I'm Bryony.'

*

In the middle of the night, Bryony, jet-lagged and unable to sleep for the myriad questions fighting for space in her mind, had crept downstairs and out onto the vast balcony, enjoying the cool night breeze on her skin. Subconsciously woken from her shallow slumber, Imogen had followed her daughter out onto the balcony where they stood together in silence.

'Mum, are you going to tell me what's going on?' Bryony had eventually asked in a small voice. 'Why did you take me out of school? Are we running away? And who *is* that man you're here with? He looks oddly familiar.'

Imogen had sighed deeply as she turned to her daughter, gently stroking her soft, smooth face with the back of her hand. It was time.

Watching the two of them together as they carefully embraced each other, father and daughter, strangers yet so alike, Imogen felt the sting of all the years they had lost together like a graze on her heart. Bryony, through her tears, had confessed to having felt guilty at not feeling a strong connection with the man she had grown up calling 'daddy'. That she had always somehow known in her heart that something was missing. And now she knew what that something was. Although naturally shocked and upset by the news, she was not angry with her mother – something that Imogen was grateful for – perhaps now life would start to make more sense.

Mickey stared at the young girl in front of him, marvelling at how beautiful she was. She was his daughter, the child he had always longed for! And he just wanted to look at her, to take in every inch of her as though she had just been born and he was seeing her for the first time. But he was cautious, he didn't want to overwhelm the poor girl any more than she had to be already. They would need to take things gently.

Bryony, smiling nervously, looked back at Imogen who nodded at her reassuringly. The man in front of her was her father, her real father, flesh and blood! And she wasn't sure whether to laugh or cry. She looked up at him shyly, unsure if she should follow her instincts and hug him. Although he was a stranger, paradoxically, he felt somehow familiar and her young mind struggled to digest such a complexity.

'Shall we all go for a walk?' Imogen suggested. 'It's a beautiful morning.'

Hanging back a little, Imogen watched from behind her Ray-Ban aviators as Mickey quietly held his hand out to his daughter, and swallowed back a lump as hard as a diamond as Bryony tentatively took it with a shy smile. Suddenly, for the first time in years, she was met with the feeling that things were going to be OK.

The sun was creeping higher in the sky now and Imogen felt it replenish her strength as it emerged, glorious from beyond the stillness of the ocean. Soon the beach would begin to fill with the first sun worshippers of the day; it would no longer be theirs alone. But that didn't matter, she thought as she caught up with them, sliding her fingers between Mickey's as they walked along the shoreline. It was just the three of them together now. They had all the time in the world.

EPILOGUE

Eleven months later

The traffic on the King's Road was thick and congested and Imogen sighed as she looked out of the tinted window of her Bentley. Nothing changes, she thought wistfully as she checked her watch. She would be late for their first annual girls' get-together and Calvary would be cursing her. She always was such a stickler for good timekeeping.

As she watched the last of the day's shoppers go about their business on the King's Road from the window, the glamorous yummy mummies with their fancy strollers, the smart European tourists with their Harvey Nichols shopping bags hanging from the crooks of their suntanned arms and the young and impossibly beautiful girls in their trendy outfits straight from the pages of *Vogue* magazine, Imogen thought how, in spite of all the unhappy memories, she still loved this place. A piece of her heart would always belong to this small, iconic part of London that she had once called home.

*

'Over here, darling!' Calvary's clipped tones rang out across San Lorenzo's as she waved enthusiastically towards an approaching Imogen. She had ensured they had the best table in the house tonight. After all, this was a celebration.

Embracing warmly, the two women hugged for the longest time.

'You look wonderful, Cal,' Imogen eventually said, thinking how she had never seen her friend look so relaxed and happy. 'South Africa must be doing you the power of good. And, by the looks of things,' she raised an eyebrow as she grabbed the cocktail list and seated herself, 'so is that toy boy of yours. Tell me, how *is* Josia?'

Calvary sighed, her eyes glazing over a little at the mention of his name.

'He's wonderful, darling, truly wonderful.' She clasped her hands together in the way she always did when she was over-excited and Imogen felt a stab of sadness at the familiarity of such a small gesture. It had been almost a year since they had seen one another, the longest time they had ever spent apart, and she had missed her friend so much. 'The Beckhams have just commissioned him to paint them a double portrait. Can you believe it? And Cape Town is everything I hoped it would be; beautiful, warm, full of friendly people. Josia and I go for a run on the beach every morning with the dogs, and in the afternoons I write my *Tatler* column from the patio, overlooking the ocean.'

Calvary had eventually divorced Douglas on the grounds of adultery, citing Tamara Du Bois as the third party, though frankly, the choice of names could've filled a phone book. Nickolas Mystern QC, made history by securing her the biggest divorce settlement of his entire career, and Calvary had caused an even bigger sensation by promptly pledging half of it to a children's charity in South Africa where she now lived on a pretty, albeit more modest, ranch with Josia and her beloved dogs.

'Oh Cal, it all sounds so . . . so idyllic. No one deserves to have found happiness more than you. Especially after everything with Doug . . .' Imogen stopped herself. This was a night for celebration, not recrimination.

Calvary grimaced.

'I only wish I'd divorced the bastard sooner,' she snorted. 'Can you believe he's been sending me flowers and diamonds and all sorts,' she sighed. 'He thinks a rock and rose is all it takes to win me back. Anyway, my spies tell me he's currently in Thailand, licking his wounds with the help of a young girl called Pooloom.' Calvary threw her head back in her trademark throaty laugh. 'He'll never change,' she said, only this time with an air of indifference.

Imogen smiled warmly. She admired her friend. Calvary had been through so much humiliation at the (wandering) hands of her husband, and yet had come back stronger than ever.

'You'll come visit us, won't you? Now that I've let my good friend, Henrietta Percival-Spencer and her team of designers loose in the ranch, I'm dying to show it off.'

'Wild horses wouldn't keep me away,' Imogen laughed, thinking how you could take the girl out of Chelsea . . .

'And bring Yasmin with you? Or is it *Stacey* now?' Calvary raised an eyebrow. 'Anyway, the girl is late.' She looked at her watch. 'Still, what can you expect? No breeding.'

Imogen laughed guiltily. Calvary had been the first to crow 'I told you so!' when Yasmin's true identity had finally been revealed. 'Still, after everything the poor love's been through, I certainly don't begrudge her a generous slice of that bastard's fortune. In fact, if anything I admire her.'

'And the irony is, she's the real deal now,' Imogen said. 'Jeremy gave her half of everything in the divorce, *and* she got to keep the title.'

Yasmin had eventually returned to Chelsea from the

French Riviera with a repentant Lord Belmont in tow. Though he had begged her forgiveness, and another chance to try to save their marriage, she had remained stoic, and, heartbroken, reluctantly he eventually agreed to a divorce.

True to her word, Yasmin had gone on to give Sammie Grainger the exclusive of her journalistic career, firmly planting her name on the media map and helping to secure her a roving reporter slot on *Five Live*. Currently, the two of them were holed up together in Yasmin's newly acquired Hamptons residence with a Dictaphone and a deadline for a sensational, forthcoming tell-all book. Already the talk of the town among the locals who watched them take their stroll along the beach, hand-in-hand each morning, Yasmin had never felt happier. With Sammie's help, she was slowly learning what it was to love for the first time.

'Ah, speak of the devil,' Calvary remarked as she saw Yasmin approaching, heads turning to stare at the perma-tanned, peroxide young blonde in her spray-on Alexander McQueen dress and vertiginous Louboutin cage heels, a trail of sweet Thierry Mulger perfume in her wake. These days, with her scandalous story making headline news, Lady Yasmin Belmont-Jones was practically a household name. Fashion designers and TV producers were crawling all over her, throwing dresses and invitations her way. There was even talk of infamous fashion house, Clarice, naming a bag after her, 'The Yasmin'. She had loved that particular idea. Now that she had nothing to hide, Yasmin was able to revel fully in her newly acquired celebrity status. And it would be fair to say she was making the most of it. In an act of altruism close to her heart, she had set up a children's charity, 'Friends of Chloe' in remembrance of her beloved sister, throwing lavish lunches and celeb-studded parties whilst raising money for underprivileged children in care. Much to Calvary's delight, she had become something of a competent hostess and a bona fide face in the social circuit.

'Ladies!' Yasmin trilled, her arms outstretched in greeting.

'You're late,' Calvary chastised her.

Yasmin rolled her eyes. Still the same old Calvary, she thought, throwing her arms around her. She hoped she would never change.

It had been Yasmin's biggest fear that the women she had come to call her friends over the past eighteen months would turn their backs on her once her story was out, but she needn't have worried. Imogen had been the first to offer her support and Calvary had been a tower of strength.

'Turn our backs on you, darling? After all we've been through together?' Calvary had said, horrified. 'Besides, it would be a little foolhardy of me, wouldn't it?' She sighed, over-dramatically. 'Now you've got that house in the Hamptons . . .'

'I hear congratulations are in order,' Yasmin said, helping herself to the chilled bottle of Cristal. She would allow herself a few glasses tonight, after all, this was a special occasion, but then she was going clean. She was done with drugs and alcohol. It had been time to start seeing the world with clarity.

'Ta-da!' Imogen produced her Decree Absolute document from her McQueen clutch and waved it in the air triumphantly.

'So, how does it feel to be free, finally?' Yasmin asked her.

Imogen made to answer but suddenly stopped herself.

'You know,' she said, after a long moment's pause, 'I thought this day would never come. And now it's here, it feels like . . . like I've been reborn. That I can finally start living the life I should've had, with the man I love and our daughter – just the three of us.' She had tears in her eyes as she spoke.

Despite his suspicions, Sebastian's protests of his wife's guilt had fallen on deaf ears. Not even he could be saved by his millions this time. And so, keen to avoid yet more unflattering press intrusion into his private life, he had bitterly agreed to a quickie divorce on the grounds of irreconcilable differences, refuting Imogen's initial claims of his unreasonable behaviour as 'absurd'.

Part of the stipulation for his cooperation, however, was that neither Imogen nor Bryony receive any part of his estate in the divorce settlement. The moment Sebastian had learnt the truth of Bryony's true parentage was the moment she ceased to be his daughter as far as he was concerned.

Hurt, though not particularly surprised by such a cold-hearted dismissal, Bryony, in the wisdom she possessed beyond her years, had tried to look upon the situation as not so much as losing a father but gaining a dad. Her *real* dad.

Imogen felt her emotions rush to the surface as the realisation dawned upon her. The only time Sebastian Forbes would ever see his ex-wife again would be when he looked up at one of the enormous great bill posters of her face that were currently dotted across the capital.

Learning the truth about Sebastian's skulduggery on the L'Orelie test shoot and feeling personally responsible, Lorraine Harlech had promptly signed Imogen up to star in their next major campaign and she had shot the first commercial in Barbados some weeks earlier. Since then, the offers had come rolling in and Cressida, thrilled by the prospect of Imogen's much-anticipated comeback, had told her it was 'just the start'.

'Stop it, darling, you'll set me off.' Calvary dabbed at her own eyes as she raised her glass of champagne. 'A toast,' she said. 'Well, I think I can speak for all of us when I say it really has been a hell of a year!'

'You can say that again,' Yasmin chipped in.

'But we made it through – together. Of course,' she added, 'with a little help from the indomitable Miss Cressida Lucas!'

'The soon to be *Princess* Cressida Lucas,' Imogen added, adopting a regal tone. 'Can you believe that she's marrying Prince Saud? I can just imagine the look on Sebastian's face when he heard that little piece of news,' Imogen laughed, tickled.

'Did you receive the wedding invitation to Dubai?' Yasmin enquired. 'The gold-embossed one encrusted with real diamonds?' She gave a little whistle.

Calvary pulled a face.

'Terribly gauche, I thought. Can't imagine what she's got in store for the reception. Camels dripping in gold and belly dancers serving the food no doubt.'

They all began to laugh, enjoying the moment, just three women together, forever bonded by the secrets they shared and their love and respect for one another.

'I suppose that'll be the next time we get to see each other again – at Cressida's wedding,' Yasmin remarked, a little wistful.

'We should make this dinner an annual thing. Every year, no matter where we are all living, we come home, back to Chelsea,' Calvary suggested. 'A celebration to remind us of everything we've been through – and how we came through the other end, victorious!'

'I'll drink to that,' Yasmin said, raising her glass once more.

'To friends,' Imogen said.

'To us.'

*

As she looked out from the balcony into the inky blackness of the Ibiza night sky, Imogen reflected on her trip back to London.

It had been a celebration of her emancipation and friendship, but it had also been about moving on.

Feeling the soft silky touch of his hands upon her shoulders as he approached her from behind, Imogen smiled.

'Mickey,' she said lovingly.

'So, how was dinner with the girls?' he asked, wrapping his arms around her waist, looking out towards the sea. Though he could not see it in the darkness, he knew it was there.

Imogen smiled. 'It was wonderful,' she replied, still a little choked up.

He pulled her into him, enjoying the cashmere feel of her hair against his cheek, the scent of her skin as she rested her head against his chest.

'Bryony and I had supper on the terrace,' he said. 'Seafood paella.'

'Mmm, my favourite,' Imogen replied, smiling at the image of them both, father and daughter together. It meant so much to her that they were forging such a strong, loving relationship.

'I'm so glad to be home,' Imogen said. And she meant it.

'Me too,' he said affectionately. 'I've missed you.' He paused for a moment. 'So, now that you're a free woman, there was something I wanted to ask you.'

She turned round to face him then, watching as he flicked the switch on the wall. Instantly, the small bay below them became illuminated in light.

'Look down,' he said smiling, enjoying the look of bemused interest on her face.

Leaning over the balcony, she brought her hand up to her mouth and gasped.

There, in giant letters in the sand, he had written 'Marry me?', decorating the words with stones and shells that Bryony had helped him collect earlier in the day.

Mickey took her shaking hand and she looked down at the modest and simple diamond platinum band as he slipped it onto her finger. It was not the biggest rock, nor the most fancy she had ever seen, but as far as Imogen was concerned it was perfect, perfect because it had come from him.

'Well?' Mickey asked, watching the tears as they slid down her smiling cheeks. 'Is that a yes?'

'It's a yes! Oh God, yes, yes, yes!' she squealed as he scooped her up off the ground, twirling her around the balcony, the sound of their laughter ringing out across the bay.

'I love you, Imp,' he said.

'I love you too, Mickey,' she replied as his soft lips gently touched her own.

'Imogen McLaren,' she said aloud, trying the name out for size. And like the ring on her finger, it fitted perfectly. In fact, she thought as she looked up at the stars, nothing had ever sounded so good.

AN INTERVIEW WITH ANNA-LOU WEATHERLEY

Where does your inspiration come from?

Everywhere and everything! People I meet, conversations I have, places I visit, magazines and books I read, my family and friends. I think I was also blessed with quite a vivid imagination! One of the main inspirations for Chelsea Wives was London – and the women who inhabit it. I used to live near the King's Road and have always been fascinated by the glamour and wealth there. Chelsea Wives is basically a love letter to the city I grew up in and adore.

Have you always wanted to become a writer?

I cannot remember a time when I did not write. As a child I wrote poetry and kept a diary until I was in my early twenties. I was always writing letters to my family and friends too. I knew it would always factor in my life, even if I wasn't lucky enough to be able to make a living from it. Writing is a compulsion for me and I cannot imagine a life without it.

What is a typical working day like for you?

With two young children, my writing schedule tends to be a bit haphazard, but I am very disciplined. I have learnt to snatch any spare time whenever possible! I find the best time for me to write is during the early hours of the morning when everyone is asleep and I have some peace and quiet! Writing Chelsea Wives involved lots of weekends nursing lattes in cafés on the King's Road, lots of late nights in front of my laptop – and lots of red wine! It wasn't always easy but when I finished writing it, I missed it!

Do your characters ever surprise you?

All the time! Like real people, they can act out of character, or take a direction I had not planned for them. They develop a life of their own and I grow to love them all, even the baddies, in fact, especially the baddies! I get to know my characters inside out; what they eat, which side of the bed they sleep on, what they would order in a restaurant, what makes them laugh or cry. I love bringing them to life and am fascinated with developing flawed but ultimately sympathetic characters. For me these are the most interesting and authentic.

Which five people, living or dead, would you invite to a dinner party?

Stephen King; he's such a prolific writer and what an imagination! I'd ask him how he does it. Audrey Hepburn for the glamour and the stories. Derren Brown; if the food was bad he could make the other guests forget. Kenny Everett; he was a comedic pioneer and outrageous for his time; Vivienne Westwood; purely so she could lend me some of her amazing dresses!

If you were stranded on a desert island, which book would you take with you?

A long one! Or anything by Daphne du Maurier.

What's the strangest job you've ever had?

In my first job as a magazine journalist I was asked to become a nun for a day. Seeing a wedding ring on one of the sister's fingers I naively queried, 'but I didn't think nuns could get married?' They were lovely people, but I'm not sure they thought I was nun material!

What can't you live without?

Aside from my family and friends, on a completely shallow level it would be Chanel Rouge Coco lipstick; Champagne; my laptop and internet shopping!

Do you have any secret ambitions?

I've always fancied myself as a Vegas showgirl – I'd love all the camp glamour! I'd also quite like to read the weather too, though geography is not my strongest point!

When you're not writing, what are your favourite things to do?

Spending time with family and friends, shopping and pole fitness! It's an amazing way to keep fit and brilliant for self-confidence. I'm a qualified instructor now and teach classes in London. I love it!

When you were a child, what did you want to be when you grew up?

An actress, dancer or a writer (so I guess one out of three isn't bad!). As a child I appeared in various plays and stage shows in London and did some modelling. I've always been a bit of a performer, though I don't think I would like being famous now. I'd hate to be chased by paparazzi first thing in the morning!

And what can you tell us about your next novel?

It's a sizzling tale of three women who are all linked by one delicious, but dangerous, man. It's packed full of forbidden lust, secrets and revenge as well as larger than life characters, exotic locations, and of course lashings of glamour!

Anna-Lou's Guide to the King's Road

The King's Road. Vibrant, buzzing, and oh-so terribly chic; it's the jewel in Chelsea's sparkling crown and a shopper's heaven. When I die, I want them to erect a blue placard there in my honour: 'she came; she saw; she shopped!' Here are a few highlights:

Fashion – It's a way of life, darling!

Austique: 330 King's Road, SW3 5UR Tel: 0207 376 4555. This stylish high-end boutique is a Chelsea girls' secret and a life-saver if you're looking for that perfect one-off number. Think darling dresses by the likes of Alice & Olivia and Markus Lupfer, plus an assortment of gorgeous jewellery and accessories. It's fabulous for bespoke gifts and a favourite with Grazia girls too.

Anthropologie: 131–141 King's Road, SW3 4PW Tel: 0207 349 3110. There is only one word to describe this US fashion and home ware emporium: divine. It's the building itself that makes Anthro (as those in the know refer to it) such a pleasure to visit. Airy and spacious with wooden floors and colourful tiles that hint at the art deco era; this treasure trove even has its own indoor waterfall and garden complete with trees! Here you can discover an eclectic mix of fashion and interior gorgeousness; from vintage tea dresses, shoes and jewellery to designer denim, artisan glass and bespoke bedding (the Camille range is to die for). Remember to bring your (or your husband's) Platinum Amex, darlings; you'll need it!

Brora: 344 King's Road, SW3 5UR Tel: 020 7352 3697. And on the eighth day God created . . . cashmere. Tactile and soft as a new-born's skin, Brora, the quintessential Scottish cashmere kings, is a must-visit for all your luxury woollen needs. Their selection of scarves, hats, hosiery and blankets is unrivalled.

Beauty & Pampering – because you are so worth it!

Gina Conway Aveda: 199 King's Road, SW3 5ED Tel: 0207 352 3697. The ultimate urban retreat and one of the best places to head for an organic wax (their Hollywood is the best). Perfect for a spot of pampering after a hard day's shopping. Also worth a mention is boutique beauty salon, **Chelsea Day Spa:** 69a King's Road, SW3 4NX Tel: 0207 351 0911. Their New York mani and pedi is totes amaze.

Richard Ward Hair: 82 Duke of York Square, SW3 5UR Tel: 020 7730 1222. The go-to salon for red-carpet worthy hair. Catering for all your coiffure needs, you'll leave this award-winning salon feeling pampered and paparazzi ready. Their blow drys are the stuff of legend. Well, if it's good enough for the Duchess of Cambridge . . .

Harbour Club Gym & Spa: Watermeadow Lane, SW6 2RR Tel: 0207 371 7700. Princess Diana's old stomping ground is absolutely fabulous for bit of celeb-spotting – oh, and keeping fit too. One of the highlights of this iconic health club is the award-winning Amida Spa. Once you've finished your tai chi class or a workout with your personal trainer, head off to one of the nine treatment rooms for some serious self-indulgence. They use Elemis and Sisley products – only the best for the women of Chelsea – or you can shave off a few years with one of Jan Marini's glycolic treatments. Absolute heaven.

Jo Malone: 150 Sloane Street, SW1X 9BX Tel: 0870 192 5121. Can you imagine what Jo's house must smell like? Her flagship store filled with signature candles, bath products and body essentials is a welcome assault on the senses. The perfect place to purchase a gift for a girlfriend, (or one's self) no self-respecting Chelsea home is complete without one of her gorgeous lime, lime basil and mandarin candles.

Rococo Chocolates: 321 King's Road, SW3 5EP Tel: 0207 761 8456. If you adore chocolate (and let's face it, who doesn't?) then paying a visit to Rococo's, arguably the most luxurious bespoke chocolatiers in the world, is an absolute must. Here you can indulge your wildest coco dreams with a selection of their bites of joy, all wrapped up in vintage boxes with purple ribbon. Try the artisan bar containing basil and Persian lime. Better than sex.

Visit

The Saatchi Gallery: Duke of York's HQ, King's Road, SW3 4PY Tel: 0207 811 3082. This beautiful building is a must-see for all contemporary art lovers – and offers the perfect setting for a clandestine date! Fall in love as you browse the exhibits in the high-ceilinged rooms, take a leisurely stroll in the gorgeous grounds of Duke of York Square or stop for an alfresco skinny latte in the café (weather permitting, of course, you wouldn't want to ruin your blow dry!).

Bars & Restaurants – Well, a girl's got to eat something.

The Bluebird Restaurant: 350 King's Road, SW3 5UU Tel: 0207 559 1000. If this King's Road institution were a person it would most definitely be a woman – and a sophisticated one at that! This warehouse style building houses a restaurant, bar, café, shop, bakery and a spa all rolled into one – it even has a wine cellar! Oh, if only a man could be this multi-talented . . . The menu is a mix of classic comfort food and modern European dishes and it serves amazing cocktails – perfect to enjoy al fresco as you watch the perennially fashionable of the KR strut by.

Daphne's: 112 Draycott Avenue, SW3 3AE Tel: 0207 589 4257. Ah, la dolca vita! Ok, so it's a cab ride from the King's Road, but it'll be worth it, promise. A sophisticated Italian restaurant sandwiched between Chelsea and Knightsbridge, Daphne's is effortlessly charming and serves heavenly food, (the beef carpaccio starter is gift from God). In summer the front doors open to give it that al fresco feeling; whilst in winter, open brick fires create a cosy intimacy. Perfect for dinner with the girls or a romantic tête-à-tête.

JuJu: 316–318 King's Road, SW3 5UH Tel: 0207 351 5998. The finest cocktails on the KR bar none. JuJu is the glamourous hang out for all the beautiful people and boasts the most extensive list of champagne and cocktails a girl could wish for. The perfect place to get trashed with your girlfriends on a Friday night; drink Chelsea Iced Tea, Espresso Martinis or one of their many champagnes as the DJ spins an eclectic mix of tunes. Lush.

Beaufort House: 354 King's Road, SW3 5UZ Tel: 0207 352 2828. Like a home from home, BH is a private members club that also opens to the hoi polloi (or at least some of it is, at certain times of day) It's spread over three floors and boasts a bar, restaurant and club room. The champagne penthouse is not to be missed, as are BH's vast array of cocktails shaken and stirred by its oh-so clever mixologists.

Harvey Nichols: 109–125 Knightsbridge, SW1X 7RJ Tel: 0207 235 5000. No guide to Chelsea hang outs would be complete without a mention of the sartorial and beauty mecca that is the iconic HN. Situated a gem's throw from the KR at the end of the inimitable Sloane Street and the beginning of Knightsbridge, a girl can spend hours losing herself among its five floors of fabulousness. You'll find an endless list of the most exclusive brands (think Chloe, YSL, Herve Leger, Jimmy Choo, Mulberry, Louboutin, Gucci, Prada et al). Once you've maxed out your plastic, head to the Fifth Floor for lunch and cocktails, the restaurant for dinner or the pièce de résistance (in my humble opinion) the newly revamped Champagne Bar. Inspired by Emile Galle's iconic 1902 anemone design for the Cuvée Belle Époque Champagne bottle, it's utterly darling; a divine place to quaff vintage fizz (paid for by hubby, of course).

CPSIA information can be obtained
at www.ICGtesting.com
Printed in the USA
BVHW031937050921
615853BV00023B/42